THE
ALIEN
EQUATION

KENNETH TAM

ANDRA URSLA
ADMIRAL, SECOND FLEET

THE ALIEN EQUATION

THE SECOND EQUATIONS NOVEL

KENNETH TAM

ICEBERG

Published in Canada by Iceberg Publishing, Waterloo

Library and Archives Canada Cataloguing in Publication
Tam, Kenneth, 1984-
    The alien equation : the second equations novel / Kenneth Tam.
ISBN 978-0-9865017-2-2
    I. Title.
PS8589.A7676A63 2010   C813'.6   C2010-900084-6

Iceberg Publishing
55 Northfield Drive East, Suite 171
Waterloo ON N2K 3T6
contact@icebergpublishing.com
www.icebergpublishing.com

First trade paperback printing: May 2004
First pocket paperback printing: May 2005
Special international edition: January 2010

Cover Artwork: Wesley Prewer
Cover Design: Kenneth Tam

For Jacqui,

The first reader and the final editor,
the one who makes all this possible,
and the best mother I could ask for.

With my love and thanks.

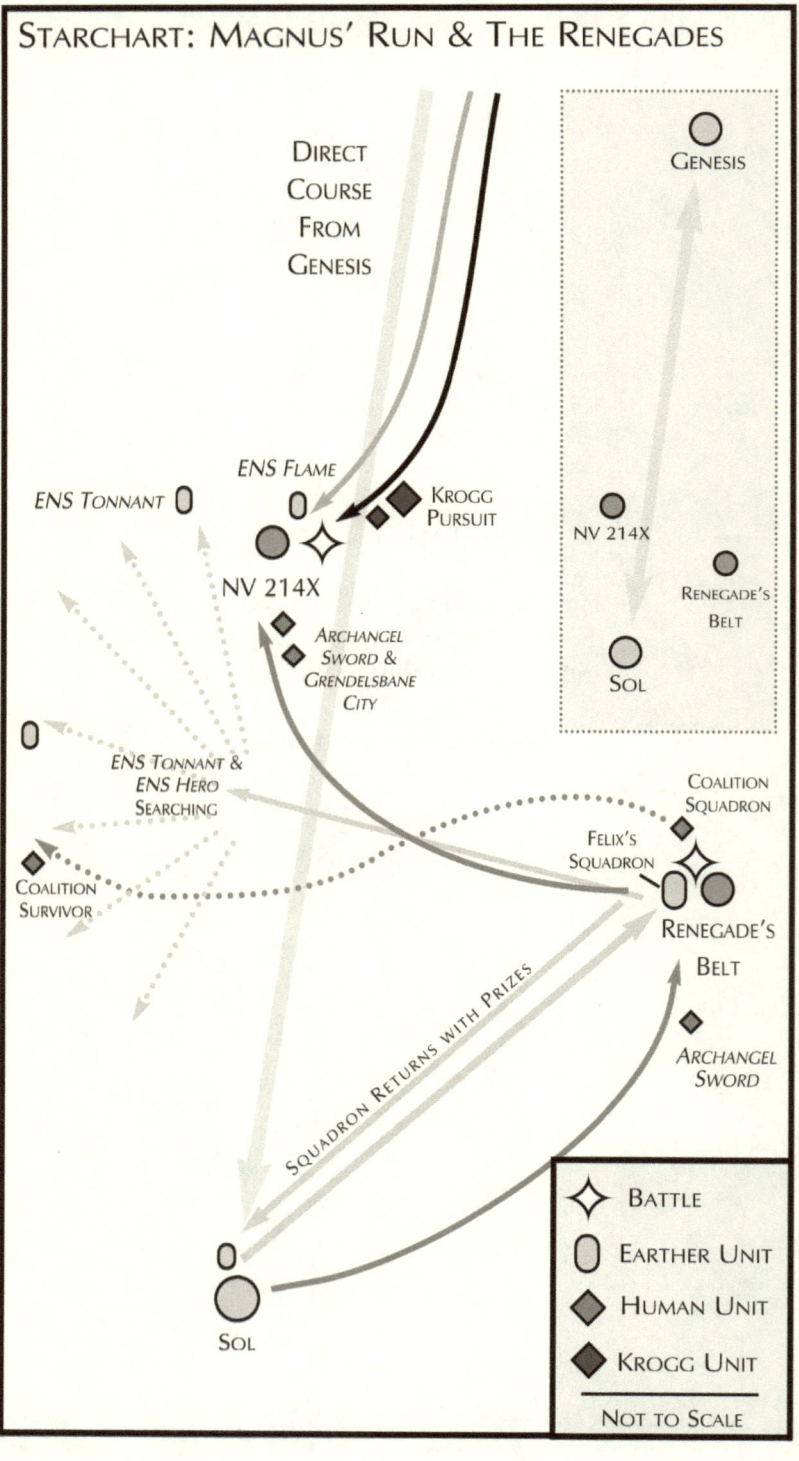

STARCHART: MAGNUS' RUN & THE RENEGADES

DIRECT COURSE FROM GENESIS

GENESIS

ENS FLAME

ENS TONNANT

KROGG PURSUIT

NV 214X

NV 214X

RENEGADE'S BELT

ARCHANGEL SWORD & GRENDELSBANE CITY

SOL

ENS TONNANT & ENS HERO SEARCHING

COALITION SQUADRON

FELIX'S SQUADRON

COALITION SURVIVOR

RENEGADE'S BELT

SQUADRON RETURNS WITH PRIZES

ARCHANGEL SWORD

SOL

BATTLE

EARTHER UNIT

HUMAN UNIT

KROGG UNIT

NOT TO SCALE

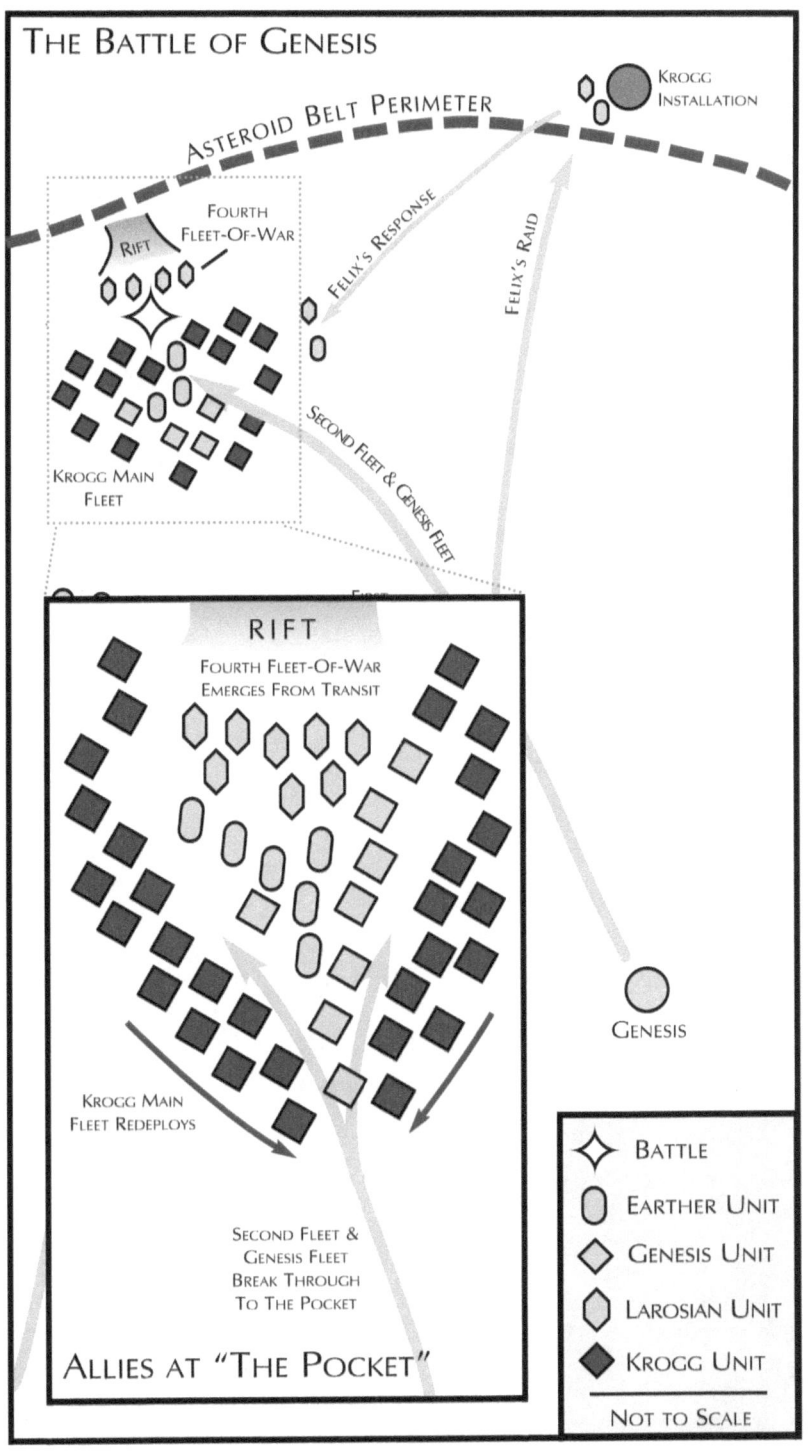

THE BATTLE OF GENESIS

ASTEROID BELT PERIMETER

KROGG
INSTALLATION

FOURTH
FLEET-OF-WAR

RIFT

FELIX'S RESPONSE

FELIX'S RAID

SECOND FLEET & GENESIS FLEET

KROGG MAIN
FLEET

RIFT

FOURTH FLEET-OF-WAR
EMERGES FROM TRANSIT

GENESIS

KROGG MAIN
FLEET REDEPLOYS

SECOND FLEET &
GENESIS FLEET
BREAK THROUGH
TO THE POCKET

ALLIES AT "THE POCKET"

◇ BATTLE

◯ EARTHER UNIT

◇ GENESIS UNIT

⬡ LAROSIAN UNIT

◆ KROGG UNIT

NOT TO SCALE

FOREWORD

I've always been one who chooses his friends carefully. I try to treat everyone with equal measures of respect, but very few individuals grow close enough to me to earn the designation of 'friend'. And if someone isn't my friend, that limits the extremes I'm willing to go for on his or her behalf. I don't think this is an uncommon way of life — I'd guess many people take this approach.

That being the case, the Earthers' actions in this book seem all the more remarkable to me. I was seventeen when I was writing *The Alien Equation*, still fairly idealistic and very enthusiastic about throwing the Earthers out into the universe, where they'd come across some very powerful and not-terribly-friendly alien adversaries. I was also curious to see how the humans would react when the Earthers began to export their worldview — when they lived up to their word, given in *The Human Equation*, and returned to Genesis to help free the Naval class from the grip of the Church.

The Earthers are willing to go to war with a powerful alien race they've never actually met, because they promised their new human friends that they'd help restructure their society.

That's fast friendship.

And that's the Earther way. You follow through on your promises.

I'm compelled to recall what I talked about in the foreword of *The Human Equation*, when I mentioned that I learned a great deal from my dog Atlas. Think about a dog, one of those often-overlooked companions in our ordinary lives. Think of how loyal and how dependable a dog can be, even when the person he or she is teaming with really doesn't deserve it. I speak with some personal authority on that last part.

You can quite easily dismiss a dog's loyalty as a function of the pack mentality, or of inferior intelligence. I don't buy either. As you may have figured from *The Human Equation*, I don't think much of the notion of patent human superiority. I think we have good qualities as a species, but I can't help but feel that our reliance on technology to survive is an indication that we're really inferior in some ways to those beings that can survive and thrive unassisted on their own — and who can do so in spite of everything we do to manipulate their environment to suit our needs.

So I look at a dog like my old friend Atlas, and I wonder how he sees the world. Why does he loyally stick with a person, always try to help, always have faith? We're not related by blood or genetics, and we're often self-absorbed and needlessly complex. Yet many dogs stick with us, as do other creatures. What's their malfunction?

Or is there a malfunction at all? As a species, I think we're often guilty of personifying the worldview of other creatures in a very human way. We assume they see the world as humans do, but who says they have to? In point of fact, doesn't the evidence point to them having a fundamentally *alien* way of life?

Oh yes, that really was the worst groaner of a segue you're likely ever to see. Unless you read Defense Command.

The Alien Equation is ostensibly about the Earthers coming to grips with a bunch of aliens, but as much as anything it's about a race of beings who have a point of view similar to that of our loyal friends, dogs, and who are still trying to come to grips with the very alien attitudes of humans. They just don't understand us, but as far as they're concerned, that's no reason to give up on us, or to abandon their own way of doing things — their seemingly innocent way of life.

Will this backfire on them? Well, the universe they're discovering seems to have a lot more in common with the human worldview than the Earther one, so who knows...

But for the moment, we get to see equal measures of force and acceptance on the part of the wolves, cats and bears of the Earther Navy and Marine Corps. We also get to meet some fan-favorite characters like dapper little Fox Magnus and the much-less-dapper Graham Manchester for the first time. *The Alien Equation* is quite an adventure, and I hope you enjoy it!

Before we begin, of course, there are thanks to be given.

Once again, we start with my old comrade Cody Herauf, the originator of the Kroggs and the Larosians. Here we get a full introduction to Cody's creative brilliance, coming face-to-face with his two warring alien races. Their long and bitter struggle informs this book, and indeed, the entire background of this series. I am most grateful to him for providing them to me for the *Equations*.

Next to Wes Prewer, whose stunning cover art continues to floor me. If you're the sort of person who enjoys the details surrounding ships shooting at each other in space, go ahead and stare at the cover of this book for a moment. That's ENS *Agamemnon*, a 150-gun ship of the line. You can tell because its gunports are individually numbered; those ten stern chasers, you might notice, are numbered from 140 to 150. Wes' attention to detail, and his ongoing determination to get these images right, is a great asset to this series.

His writing contributions are also a great addition. While we don't come across any of his characters in this book, we'll certainly see the Earthers from his spinoff novel *Retaliation* again soon. As ever, many thanks to my friend Wes.

Peter Caron made this book work. That's no small statement to make, but as I mentioned in the foreword to *The Human Equation*, my great friend's contributions to this series have been nothing short of fundamental. You'll soon be reading about a ship called *Archangel Sword*, and a group of human dissenters who have a problem with their leadership. Some of this was previewed in the new novella, *The Quest*, in the special edition of *The Human Equation*. Now we get to see the outcomes of that ill feeling.

And I can safely say none of it would have happened if Peter hadn't come to me with the suggestion that we need to spend more time on it. Peter always seems to see things from angles that I don't, and I am eternally indebted to him for providing me that insight. I have no idea how these books could have gone past *The Alien Equation* if not for his contribution.

With these acknowledgments done, I have just my family left to thank. Jacqui and Peter are my parents and partners in Iceberg Publishing. They are the greatest friends and allies anyone could ask for, and I had the incredible fortune of getting them for parents.

Lastly, again, I'll thank Atlas. His alien perspective on life was really behind the Earthers, and I think we'll get another taste of that in action in this book.

But, like Atlas, I've no taste for lengthy, dull and circular philosophical discussions; better to show a philosophy in action (preferably fun and exciting action) than to prattle on about it. With that in mind, let's see what happens when the Earthers cross paths with the Kroggs and the Larosians.

I'm sure it'll end well...

PROLOGUE

Fifteen-hundred ships representing two planetary Navies cruised at faster-than-light speeds between the star systems known by humans as Sol and Genesis. Aboard the flagship of the larger fleet, one flag officer could not sleep.

Sarah Manchester twisted savagely under the covers of her bed, trying to find comfort in the tangle of plain sheets. Her mind seemed determined to keep her awake. Half kept insisting that she was uncomfortable while it reflected on the current situation... the other half desperately wanted sleep.

"Oh for Gods' sake!" she finally muttered, sitting up in bed and heaving a defeated sigh.

The glowing red chrono next to her bed told her it was 03:12 hours — far too early to be awake. As commander-in-chief of the Genesis Fleet, she could theoretically be called to duty at any hour of the day, but only when the possibility of action or emergency existed. Neither situation was likely to be found in the great black void between the planets Earth and Genesis.

She knew; she'd traveled through it before.

"Bugger this," she continued quietly in her pseudo-British accent. "Nothing I can do about it like this!"

The frustrated young ArcGeneral struggled out of bed with unbecoming grumblings, and marched into the bathroom adjacent to her quarters. The Superdreadnought *Pope Joseph Barron*, Sarah's flagship, provided generous accommodations for the fleet ArcGeneral, so the bathroom was vast... by Naval standards, anyway. The most appreciated item in the room actually owed its existence to the Earther Navy — the Earthers had been kind enough to donate one to her flagship and, incidentally, to every human vessel interested in having one.

No human ships had ever before put to space with fully-functioning, true-water bathtubs, but now the wanton luxury was not only present, it was a favorite of many officers. Especially Sarah.

As she gently turned on the faucet, sending piping hot water into the tub from several neatly-placed tanks, she realized that yet again she was thinking too much.

"Who cares about the bloody thing's history. Damn well better put me to sleep..." she really had no idea why she was muttering, but the vocalization of her musings satisfied her.

If anything could settle her mind and put her to sleep, it had to be a nice hot bath.

The tub filled at a moderate pace, and Sarah leaned against the bathroom counter while she waited. The auto shut-off sensors kicked in when the water reached a level that the ship's AI determined would perfectly cover her once she got in, without spilling over the tub's rim. Owing to her slight form, her potential displacement didn't require too much compensation.

Sarah prided herself on her fitness, and maintained her tall, slim frame as a matter of course. What exercise she did actually tended to be more therapeutic than health-conscious — sparring in the ship's gym helped her remain civil around some of the rather unpleasant people she dealt with.

Sliding into the hot bath, Sarah consciously forced such people out of her thoughts. She rested her head against the tub's padded side, took a centering breath, and closed her eyes. The sloshing of the water on the sides of the tub helped settle her mind, and her thoughts began to drift easily back through the past year, and the past 600 years of human history, two topics that were closely tied.

Six hundred years, she mused, *so much has happened in 600 years...*

Indeed, in the mid twenty-first century CE — 600 years in the past — things had gotten entirely out of hand. The human race had spun into another fit of religious violence, and one of the involved factions had managed to create an 'Omega Virus' — an intelligent, sentient plague genetically developed with a single goal in mind: to kill humans.

Whether by intention or accident, the plague managed to escape into Earth's atmosphere, and humanity was served nothing less than a death sentence. Contemporary science couldn't develop any effective counters because Omega was able to adapt and consciously evade them... and soon, the scientists who could create effective treatments had fallen to the plague. Even Earther scientists and historians were unable to explain the adaptive ability in what had at first been named a 'virus' — whatever Omega's biology, it clearly had been poised to eliminate all human beings in that bygone century.

The United Nations, of course, hadn't stood idly by as humanity was being wiped out. It isolated an elite group of individuals and was able to adapt a new and highly advanced, deep-range space exploration vessel into a colony ship. More than half of these 'colonists of the future' were psychologically conditioned to believe in a new Earth-centric religion. Upon arriving at their destination planet — one creatively dubbed Genesis by the UN planners — the conditioned humans established a Church, and set about fulfilling their 'Quest' to return to Earth.

But the plan, unsurprisingly, was laden with flawed assumptions, not the least of which was the assessment of Omega's capabilities. When the plague had killed all the humans remaining on the planet, it had become acutely aware of its own potential mortality, and quickly sought alternatives. Once the primate animal family was almost completely consumed, Omega was again in danger of losing its food supply, and so began to create its own stable victual source.

Turning to the types of animals known as 'order Carnivora', it began to modify the genetic makeup of select wolves, cats and bears, changing both their physical and mental structures to make them more human. It was a resourceful and clever plan, but Omega never had the chance to take advantage of it, disappearing before it could feast upon its new hosts.

Left without any immediate knowledge of who or what they were, the changed predators had discovered the remains of human civilization. Upright and humanoid, these animals found that their mental capacity was more than a match for the remaining human records, and they quickly learned to understand what had come before them. They determined that humans were irrational and dangerous, and they also found evidence of the Genesis mission. Their intellects demanded they keep a second Omega-style weapon from being released on Earth, as the death brought by the first had simply been catastrophic. Humanity, they decided, had to have its claim on Earth checked and monitored.

So the animals organized into a unified society, adopted the English language that was prevalent in the remaining human records, and labeled themselves 'Earthers'. They not only learned from human science, but very quickly began exceeding its limited concepts of physics and biology. Studying human history, they accepted the likelihood of violence when the humans returned, so they focused their efforts on the construction of a spectacular Navy, built on the tenets of one of human history's best but updated to consider both Earther enlightenment and scientific advances. The Earthers, like their human counterparts, had begun preparing for a prophesized clash.

Lightyears away, humanity's efforts to manufacture that clash had been neither united nor enlightened, as Genesis society was segregated from the colony's outset. The psychologically-conditioned colonists dominated society, while the technicians and pilots of the original colony ship — their minds left untouched for fear of the negative impacts on their skills and abilities — were subjugated and discriminated against. Society had been split into two classes, and the lower class of 'nonbelievers' had quickly been reduced to a state of pseudo-slavery under the Church of Genesis.

The Church had gone farther, though, when human minds proved incapable of dissecting the colony ship for knowledge. In their desperate bid to fulfill prophecy, they forged an alliance with an alien race, the Kroggs, and in so doing, joined a war against the mysterious Larosians. It was as cryptic as it sounded — for the past two centuries, the Kroggs had used Genesis ships and crews to stand against Larosian incursions.

That particular alliance sent a shiver down Sarah's spine, even despite the warmth of her bed. From her perspective, the Kroggs were a dark species.

They'd offered technology to the Church in return for the use of the Genesis Fleet against Larosian patrols that infrequently visited the area, and with the acceptance of the deal, the already marginalized Naval class was nearly slotted for extermination. Krogg Warlords repeatedly demanded that the ArcGeneral Staff send hundreds of Genesis ships against incursions of just twenty-five Larosian 'Warcruisers', only to see five of the invaders destroyed at the cost of hundreds of thousands of human lives. And yet no human had ever so much as *seen* a Larosian — the Kroggs would never allow such an encounter.

Unsurprisingly, the Navy had come to harbor a deep animosity toward the Kroggs. Meanwhile their interest in the Larosians had been piqued as small indications in battle had shown the unknown aliens to be moral beings — they didn't fire on escape pods, they seemed to disable rather than destroy ships whenever possible, and when one of their own ships was wounded, their entire squadron attempted to shield it.

No Larosian had ever been captured, and no human had ever so much as spoken to one, but Sarah, and many of her colleagues, were certainly willing to entertain the belief that they'd be better allies than the Kroggs. It was, of course, a massive leap — to assume that an alien race you'd spent centuries fighting at another race's behest would in any way be interested in letting you switch sides... but Sarah had a mind to investigate the opportunity, if it ever came. Perhaps the precedent set in the befriending of the Earthers was affecting her...

Just under a year ago the Genesis Fleet had boosted to Earth, only to find the Earther Navy waiting for them. After an abbreviated character analysis, the personnel of the Genesis Navy had decided to escape the tyranny of their Church, and had joined the Earthers in protecting the home planet of their ancestors. Abandoning their ships, most of them reached the safety of Earther guns and left the human force in inexperienced — and frankly incompetent — Church hands. When the fleets finally came to broadsides, the Earthers carried the day — rather handily, in fact.

After countering the single Church landing at Antarctica — a bloody battle, but one with as inevitable an outcome as the duel in space — the Earthers helped the Naval humans establish colonies on Earth. Distant and benevolent Earther guidance ensured the humans' good conduct, while in space Earther yards repaired over 900 of the disabled Genesis ships that had been recovered from the Church's assault, and restored them to Naval control.

And now Sarah commanded the Genesis Fleet as it made its way back to its namesake star system. The Earthers had added a fleet to aid her own — 600 ships under Admiral Andra Ursla, a three meter tall kodiak bear who had become Sarah's good friend. It was a two-week trip for the mixed force, each Genesis ship committing its resources to its FTL *Flux* drive, and to shaking out any kinks left after the Earther reconstruction. But the ships were performing better than ever — Earther reconstruction seemed to be better than the original — and with tactical maneuvers impossible at the speeds they were traveling, there was literally nothing for Sarah to do.

Except worry and think too much. There were seven more days of hard travel to Genesis, and the inactivity was killing her. Or at least keeping her awake. But at least thinking about the whole mess had helped her calm down...

The bed had become remarkably comfortable — its warmth seemed to be skin tight and liquidy. Sarah smiled happily and slid further under the sheets, letting the tiredness take over.

Then she remembered she wasn't in bed. She took in a sharp breath of surprise, only to get an unpleasant nose full of water. She sat up jerkily, coughing and splashing the water that had been so carefully measured to avoid spilling.

For Gods' sake, I can't catch a break this week. Too bad Pat's not here...

Sarah Manchester got out of her bath and returned to bed for another duel with insomnia.

CHAPTER 1

Admiral Andra Ursla was bored.

Now, that's the sort of thing the three-meter tall fleet commander couldn't really admit to anyone — she fully believed she should be stoic at the top, a patient and thoughtful leader even if it was unnatural to be anything but bored while in transit. So she was spending a lot of time away from prying eyes, sparring in the gym next to her cabin, and reading and re-reading briefing notes she'd read dozens of times before.

Worse, the constant sparring, when coupled with the stress she was under, was actually making her muscles ache to an abnormal extent.

Sitting back in her cabin's desk chair, she ruefully rubbed the muscles in her human-like, albeit super-sized forearms, as she watched status reports scroll across her screen. Status reports were just about the only new reading material she was getting while in transit... and they did little to ease the monotony. She wished Setter Caine was nearby, but the First Lord of the Admiralty and Ursla's best friend had stayed on Earth to oversee the rebuilding of the ships that had been lost in the Church attack.

So she didn't have much to do, and she had no one to commiserate with. At least her new flagship, the 150-gun First Rate ship of the line *Agamemnon*, was large enough to give her adequate head room when walking the decks — her old command, the Fifth Rate frigate *Cerberus*, had not been so accommodating, and she still had the headaches to prove it...

The entry chime sounded, swiftly shifting her back into reality, and Ursla swiveled her chair to face the door before offering a greeting, "Come on in."

The sliding doors to her cabin parted, and her Flag Captain, Artemis Tigar stepped in. An orange-and-black striped feline, Tigar was well experienced in the workings of a fleet, and had served under Ursla when she'd been Captain of the Earther flagship, *Orion*. He'd been with *Agamemnon* for six years, three of those as Captain, and his experience with the ship had been quite helpful. In any case, they were good friends, even if she didn't count him as close a friend as Caine.

"Andra," he nodded in greeting.

"Nice of you to drop by, Artie. What's up?" she waved him to a seat.

The tiger, measuring only slightly more than half Ursla's standing height, slowly paced across the main cabin of Ursla's quarters and sat on the oversized couch. He sighed deeply and locked eyes with his Admiral.

"Just had another look at the info packets we got on the Kroggs... have to admit, I should have taken a closer look at them before we left, but I never had the time to really digest it all. What's starting to come together in my head isn't exactly... *settling*. I mean, it's not what the notes say but what they *don't* say... have you noticed anything?" Tigar bobbed his head at Ursla's desk terminal.

Ursla cocked an eyebrow and shrugged, "I've been through everything Sarah sent me a couple of times, and I get the impression the Kroggs aren't going to be major factors. They maintain three small planetary embassies and a few sloop-sized ships, I think. The Larosians don't seem to commit more than a couple of squadrons at a time... and they only seem to do that every few years..."

Tigar's head tilted slightly, "I know that's what they reported, and I'm not suggesting they're trying to hide anything from us. But something in the data they sent doesn't add up... and the humans may not have noticed. I mean, I didn't — not until I really started brooding over it."

Curious and slightly surprised, Ursla turned her eyes to the bright holo display on her desk and started scrolling through the files in her holo tank. Opening the data packet, she watched the information scroll through the holo screens.

The first image the packet revealed was of a two and two-thirds meter tall black creature with a humanoid form and large, intimidating blades on his arms, shoulders, and legs. Four arms hung from his shoulders, a crown grew from his skull. His covering seemed to be a solid carapace, jet black and shiny. He looked as sinister as a black widow spider, one of the few insects that Ursla thought had a truly menacing look, even though Earthers were immune to its venom. The very appearance of him made Ursla shiver.

"Don't much like the look of these fellows," Ursla said quietly, and Tigar nodded.

By Earther standards, Ursla was big, but this Krogg made her look average-sized. She glanced down at the caption beneath the image.

"*Standard* Krogg warrior," Tigar recalled aloud.

Ursla nodded, "And that's the grunt. They have tougher officer-types and even some with telepathic abilities."

Tigar ground his jaw, "Their ground forces are bad enough, but that's not what I'm worried about."

Ursla frowned and looked up at the Flag Captain, who obliged her with a clearer explanation, "Look at them, and read about their track record. Why are these things letting Genesis do their fighting for them? They're clearly much more advanced than the humans... even without having seen much about the Larosians, I'm willing to bet the Kroggs could handle these incursions on their own. So why involve the Church, and force the humans to stop those 'Warcruisers'?"

The thought caused Ursla to frown, but she offered a nod prompting Tigar to continue.

"Now I have no frame of reference for Krogg thinking, but if it were me, I'd be using the humans as a front. That way anyone who arrives at Genesis meets resistance from the humans, not the Kroggs. They don't realize the area is occupied, and assume they've run across a small alien race not worth paying attention to in such a big war."

Tilting her head thoughtfully, Ursla sat back and nodded, "I could buy that..."

"But," Tigar leaned forward on the couch, "would you leave the Genesis Navy alone to hold a front against the Larosians? We've heard the stories about the way the Warcruisers continually exact high tolls in action. If the Larosians sent a large force, they could bowl right over the Navy into an open Krogg flank..."

"Unless there's a strong holding force nearby," Ursla finished the thought with a nod. "And I doubt that sort of force would be glad to see us trying to dethrone the Church."

"Exactly."

Releasing a deep sigh, Ursla folded her arms across her chest, "So... if the Kroggs are in strength in the area, why are they hiding? I'm getting a sinking feeling this'll be *very* complicated."

Tigar smiled, "That's why you're the Admiral, Andra."

Ursla cracked a smile of her own, then scratched her chin thoughtfully. These thoughts were all referring to a hypothetical potential based on some form of clever logic that may have never occurred to the Kroggs... but it was something she had to consider. If the Kroggs had a large force nearby, and the Church had looked the other way for two centuries... the humans were the unfortunate pawns in a dauntingly large game of chess.

"So, what do you think we should do? Turn around and bring up the First Fleet with us?"

Tigar smiled and shook his head, "I'm suggesting we stay on our toes. The packet doesn't say much about fleet sizes, but I think we're pretty well equipped to deal with whatever they have. Based on the number of ships the Larosians have been sending this way, I can't imagine the Kroggs having more than 1,000 vessels in the area anyway."

Ursla nodded and scrolled through the holo screen, watching as it filled with itemized information on the nature of Krogg ships. She'd didn't really want to deal with 1,000 *Krogg* ships — frankly, she found their very nature to be most unnerving. To begin with they were biological, and as near as the humans could tell, they were bred and raised like horses had been in Earth's past. Different species made up different classes, with 'Destroyers' being the smallest and 'Motherships' the largest. It was a type of Naval development entirely foreign to Earth science and philosophy, but it apparently served the Kroggs well.

Living ships... and impressive living ships at that, "Their carapaces resist laser energy — most forms of focused energy bounce off with little or no collateral damage. Chemically-propelled weapons are ineffective... I don't know that I want to handle 1,000 of these, Artie."

Tigar's ear twitched, "There *is* that attached note. Raw energy might be enough to crack them — if we turn off the safeties... you know what I mean. The bayonets won't touch them, but our shields..." Tigar paused as Ursla scrolled to the Earther-added insert.

"Our shields will act like armor. So if our shields are up, we can *physically* fight them," Ursla finished the thought in grim tones. "I had thought a bit on *that* part."

Ursla winced as she recalled the last time she'd had to fight hand-to-hand with her shield. It had been on the Antarctic Plains against a company of Crusaders, and they'd lost — *badly*. The shield had stopped their bullets — and their blood — from spraying all over her.

"Well... hypothetically speaking, the Kroggs could've been much worse than this," Ursla noted.

Tigar stared at the holo but gave a nod, "Much worse, I suppose."

But they were dealing with Naval matters right now, so Ursla enlarged the window displaying the vessels and returned her attention to it. Because the ships were alive, it seemed the only way they could be controlled was by way of one of the Krogg Telepaths. They didn't have many classes of ship, but some of them were just so huge.

The Genesis Fleet's Colonizers — ships which carried a million Crusader marines between planets — were perhaps a tenth the size of some of the Krogg fighter-carrying Motherships.

"Make sure all the skippers in the fleet have read this closely. And suggest they encourage their crews to practice their sparring — if the only way we can really meet these Kroggs is hand-to-hand, we're going to have to be at our best."

"I'll get the word out..." Tigar gave a short nod of agreement, then stopped with a thoughtful frown. "This probably isn't even a question, but we're definitely declaring these Kroggs as hostile?"

Ursla met her Flag Captain's eyes and blinked. As much as she'd read about these Kroggs, she'd never actually thought of them as anything *but* opposition — both Liz and Sarah had made it clear that the Genesis Navy was forcibly going to remove itself from its 'alliance' with the Kroggs. And since the Earthers were pledged to help the Genesis Navy, conflict with the Kroggs was almost a foregone conclusion.

"We're allied to the Genesis Navy, and the Genesis Navy has declared them hostile. I think that rules out any other options," she said slowly after a thoughtful moment.

Tigar offered another thin nod and then pulled himself to his feet. Tugging his uniform into order he turned to face Ursla, "And if we don't support the humans, they might never get out from under the Krogg boot. I just worry sometimes that once we deal with the Kroggs, we might be misrepresented to the general Genesis public — we might be made into new Kroggs. Us being a strong third party and all."

Ursla heaved a heavy sigh, "Maybe... well, it's a possibility. But I'm hoping that when they see we're true to our word we'll have proved our character. Some will probably believe we have a hidden agenda, but it's still our duty to help. We promised our human friends we'd try — *I* promised Liz Hastings, Sarah Manchester, and Setter that we'd free Genesis. We'll do whatever we must to make good our promise."

Tigar nodded gravely and left.

Alone again in her quarters, Ursla let her mind float. At some point in the past, Earther scientists had considered telepaths, organic vessels, and just about everything else in the packet in case the humans had created them for their returning Quest. But the potential threat of humans making use of those tools paled in comparison to the present state of uncertainty. Humans with telepathy or biological ships could still be expected to act something like the humans in Earth's history books.

But the Kroggs... well, that was a separate matter. There was no context for understanding, no way to predict how these aliens might act. Ursla could guess forever and never come close. Totally alien... and equipped with technology that could pose a serious threat to the Earthers.

For all their contemplation about the return of humanity, the Earthers had never seriously studied the possibility of a powerful alien race intervening in Genesis affairs, and had certainly never considered the prospect of mounting a campaign against an alien Navy. Interference with the Kroggs could conceivably bring about the destruction of the Earthers — if Ursla's 603-ship Second Fleet and Sarah's accompanying 900 ships attacked the Kroggs and were decisively defeated, Earth would suddenly become a target.

With only 1,000 Earther ships left at home, many in varying states of repair, a successful defense would be difficult, if not impossible. Indeed, if the Kroggs could blast the Second Fleet from space as a matter of course, it might be impossible for *any* Earther force to stop their advances on Earth.

Awaken a sleeping giant, why don't we? If they're that powerful then Earth is in trouble... but that's not a relevant point, is it? We promised to help the humans, and we will. Even if it puts us in danger, we must stand by our pledge. This is all premature anyway. We don't know anything about the Kroggs firsthand — not yet, anyway. We'll just have to wait and see...

Wait indeed. Ursla rubbed her head silently and leaned back in her chair. For better or worse, she wanted to get into the action soon.

Three squadrons of Genesis Battlecruisers began to decelerate three days ahead of the main fleets. Screening for the main force, they were supposed to deal with any Krogg picket problems before the returning vessels — and more importantly, the Earthers — were detected. Both Sarah and Ursla wanted to keep the Second Fleet's presence a secret for as long as possible, lest they lose the advantage of surprise in their opening encounters with the Kroggs.

Commanding the screening squadrons was ArcBrigadier Patrick Conroy, formerly ArcColonel of one of Sarah Manchester's pre-defection Battlecruisers, *Harbinger Bishop*. He had risen up the promotion ladder quickly after the fall of the Church forces — as had many Genesis Naval personnel — and was well respected in both fleets as an exceptional cruiser commander.

Just before boosting for Genesis, he'd even finished some training with Dran Nightclaw's 111th Flying Squadron, the force of eight Fifth Rates once commanded by Ursla herself, which was recognized as the premier frigate squadron in the Earther Navy. Pat had given good old Nightclaw a close run in a number of cunning actions, well reinforcing his reputation as a fighting ArcBrigadier. He was obviously the best man for this job... but just now his credentials were irrelevant, because his squadron was facing an unpleasant surprise.

"What exactly is a Krogg picket doing *four days* out of Genesis?" his Irish accent, passed down with remarkable accuracy through six centuries of Genesis history, emphasized his displeasure.

His Flag ArcColonel, Jessica Forbes, shrugged absently, "They're probably wondering what happened to that big fleet that left a year ago. I'm surprised they didn't have pickets closer to Earth."

"Aye, you'd expect they would," Pat nodded.

The picket to which they referred was a diminutive Krogg Destroyer — a small thing with a reasonably light armament. It had no chance of surviving an encounter with three squadrons of Battlecruisers; indeed, a lone Battlecruiser could probably knock it out.

The main problem rested in the fact that the Destroyer, if not eliminated swiftly, could alert every Krogg in the galaxy to the Genesis Fleet's approach. That would cost the Allied Fleet its advantage of surprise, and might just bring Krogg reinforcements into Genesis — neither alternative qualifying as particularly acceptable.

"Well, whatever brings it out this far, it's not going back," Pat said rather coldly.

Forbes turned to face her commanding officer with a frown, "If we attack, it'll probably get off a signal."

Pat huffed out a sigh and glared at the tactical plot on the main screen.

Leave it to the Kroggs to screw up his day... *Harbinger Bishop* was at the point of the Genesis Battlecruiser vanguard, and the Krogg Destroyer was about two minutes ahead.

"The way I understand it, when a Krogg Telepath goes into message-send mode, he has to tune out the universe and gather strength for a minute... especially if he's not expecting to have to do it. I imagine this poor devil's got such a backwater job that he's damn near asleep. I'm sure our laser crews are fast enough to pick him apart in that time," Pat rubbed the back of his neck thoughtfully.

Forbes cocked an eyebrow, "Yes, but getting into laser range will be a little... *tricky*."

A fair point... they'd have to bluff the Krogg somehow. "They can't do direct thought reads between ships, right?"

This time Forbes frowned, "I'm pretty sure it's direct line of sight... don't think they can read your mind over the comm... but you'll need a hell of a lie to get him to ignore us."

Pat began to nod and then stopped himself, an idea playing in his mind, "You leave the lying to me lass... have you ever pretended to be hysterical before?"

The Krogg Destroyer was not a large ship, nor did it have a large crew. The Telepath who controlled the living beast was in his isolated chamber in the ship's center, and he was very much aware of the human ships now approaching. Their weapons weren't armed, but they had a sinister air about them... yet the instinctive warning was so obscure that it was difficult to sense clearly...

The Destroyer turned to face the newcomers just as they completed their deceleration, and its transmitter flared.

"Signal's coming in," *Bishop's* Comm Chief reported, and Pat rubbed his hands together expectantly. He was actually looking forward to this, Gods help him.

"Good then, let's seem hysterical folks. Remember, most *terrible thing* we've ever seen in life, alright?" he dropped into his chair and turned to face the bridge monitor.

The signal took a few seconds to go through the translation buffer, as the telepathic-energy transmission was not completely compatible with Genesis systems. After a moment the Krogg Telepath appeared on the screen.

Pat didn't bother to hide his shiver when the creature appeared, as he doubted anyone would — after going through what he'd 'gone through' anyway.

"Identify yourself, ArcBrigadier," the Krogg's voice was an unsettling hiss, translated into a gravelly, almost devilish voice by the computer. "Your absence has been–"

"Dammit, just shut up and listen! We're being pursued by some beasts I've never seen! The things spawned on Earth... they blew the whole fleet to the unholy gulags!" Pat snapped, nearly flinging himself forward out of his chair.

Easy Pat-my-boy, don't give yourself a stroke.

The Krogg Telepath was taken aback by Pat's vicious statement. Humans were generally inferior, but this report could prove important and seemed to be confirmed by the ArcBrigadier's emotional instability.

"We're under pursuit! And they're coming with at *least* 1,600 ships! They could wipe out Genesis! *All* of Genesis! You need to do a general broadcast — long range! Warn the system!"

The Krogg was shocked by the suddenness of the outburst, and instinct compelled him to simply nod. Even had he been suspicious, he would have been required to warn his masters.

"I will send the signal. Wait as I gather my strength!" the hiss made Pat's hair stand on end.

But inwardly, he was pleased — this was exactly the sort of reaction he'd been hoping for... and he enjoyed acting a bit insane every now and then.

"We'll form around you to cover. They weren't far behind!" Pat half yelled, hoping his face was bulging and bright red.

The Krogg hissed something untranslatable and vanished from the screen. Pat turned his chair around to face the balance of the bridge crew, miming an award statue in his hands, "I'd like to thank the academy for this award, and my mother..."

One of the ratings shot a confused glance at another, and then the whole bridge crew turned to him with curious expressions on their faces.

"Oh Gods wept! Have none of your read up on Earth history yet?"

The three squadrons of Battlecruisers closed on the Krogg Destroyer with icy precision, their laser mounts charging to engage the small ship.

Had the Telepath been paying attention, he would have noticed their unsettling behavior, but he was isolating his mind, preparing to send a telepathic message to his comrades in the Genesis system. The ship's small unthinking crew of warriors silenced their low-level telepathic chatter to let their master concentrate in peace, and energy began to swell slowly in his mind.

If this enemy force was able to reach Genesis, the Krogg plans would collapse. It was surprising that a human force could remain so well organized after a flight as harrowing as the one the ArcBrigadier described... with perfectly repaired ships and exactly three squadrons...

Wait.

The Krogg Telepath released his concentration just in time to see the sphere of thirty-six human Battlecruisers envelop his Destroyer. He immediately started the emergency burst-transmission routine — the process that would allow him to broadcast a quick message indicating danger to Genesis — but it was far too late.

Never before had Pat Conroy been given the opportunity to actually open fire on a Krogg ship, though he'd desperately wanted to many times. Now he had that chance, and while his use of thirty-six Battlecruisers against a Destroyer legitimately counted as massive overkill, he wanted all his crews to be involved.

"Oh sweet justice..." he muttered, then louder: "All ships, fire as you bear!"

The battle group fired in almost perfect unison. Laser crews had been very careful in their targeting, and now enjoyed their rare chance to engage a ship — indeed, a *Krogg* ship — at point-blank range. These were the sorts of days laser crews lived for... and the Destroyer rather abruptly ceased to exist, long before the Telepath could send off his message.

Pat smiled — it was about time the Kroggs got a bit of their '*compassion*' back. The Genesis Fleet was done being ordered to its death by these bastards.

"Right, let's get back into flux. We can't slow down too much!" Pat settled himself in his chair and took a centering breath.

The thirty-six Battlecruisers of the forward screening force began their acceleration routines, readying themselves to enter flux.

They left the spinning fragments of the dead ship and crew in their wake.

CHAPTER 2

ArcColonel James Stanton sat in his chair on the bridge of the recently recommissioned Genesis Battlecruiser *Archangel Sword*, rueful thoughts filling his mind. Such thoughts were nothing new to him — the past eight months had been full of unhappy sentiments and uncomfortable feelings. Today seemed even more desperate than any day before, however, because Stanton and the crew of *Sword* were at last making a move that reflected their concerns.

The technical term for their course of action was *desertion*, though the crew had caustically come to call it *liberation* — as far as they were concerned, it marked the end of a long and tiring ordeal.

Archangel Sword was technically a Genesis Navy Battlecruiser, one which had been part of Sarah Manchester's squadron during the defection from the Church months before. *Sword* had been with ArcGeneral Manchester during the action at the asteroid belt, and in that battle had been painfully carved up by a few Church Superdreadnoughts. It had been a distinguishing action, one the crew had been lucky to survive, and it had sent *Sword* to Earther yards for reconstruction over the past eight months.

But the Earthers hadn't simply repaired the damage. They'd offered to *enhance* Stanton's ship, and while he'd wanted his old ship back to normal, Liz Hastings had flexed her muscle from the top. Maybe it was her new leg, maybe her new Earther friends, but she just didn't seem to be able to say no to their kind offer. So the Earthers went ahead with their changes, turning *Sword* into a test-bed project.

James had watched unhappily as the Earther yards bastardized his ship, mounting their carronades instead of lasers, augmenting his traditional energy armor with their energy shield, upgrading his flux drive with their Wyndhymn generators to create an ultra-efficient hybrid, and so on. He had complained to Hastings, and then he'd met with Vice Admiral Savanna Felix, head of the Earther reconstruction efforts. Felix had been much more understanding, but he couldn't overturn Hastings' orders — *Sword* was a Genesis ship, after all. So the job was finished as Hastings had wanted it.

And the ship that James Stanton and his crew had traveled in from Earth to Genesis wasn't the same. Technically it was a better ship, but it wasn't the ship they'd fought in, and it represented trouble at the top of the Genesis Navy, at least as far as James was concerned — the lack of a singular vision, of a goal for the human ships.

Hastings at last had freedom from the Church, but she now seemed keen on handing influence over to the Earthers... who didn't even *want* it. Admiralty House on Earth was definitely avoiding getting too close; squadrons were never mixed, as that would eliminate the tactical strength that a homogenous force provided. But Hastings persisted in trying to close ranks with the Earthers, and *Sword* was proof of it going too far.

The Battlecruiser hybrid was a one-off that existed in the gray area between Dreadnought and Battlecruiser. After a minor shouting match with Hastings, James had discovered the reason it hadn't shipped for Genesis with its old squadron mates in Pat Conroy's force: *Sword* was *too* Earther for duty in a Battlecruiser squadron, but not Earther enough for an Earther frigate squadron.

James and his ship and crew were effectively confined to Earth space.

At first James had been convinced he was alone in his anger at *Sword's* marginalization, but in talking to his colleagues he'd realized they felt the same. This... *alliance* wasn't right for them. Not the way Hastings saw it. And until an alternative surfaced... His officers had talked it over in his wardroom two days earlier, and the unanimous decision had been to abandon. Again.

They'd spoken privately with every member of the crew, many of whom were bitter to see their ship changed by Earther enhancements, and to be left behind. About seventy had elected to be put off the ship, but even they had been sympathetic enough to swear silence until after *Sword* left Earth space.

Indeed, crews from a number of ships had already expressed their unhappiness with the situation — it was common if unwelcome knowledge that a handful of human ships had left the ranks of the combined fleet over the past months, and the Earthers had wished them well. Genesis Fleet Command had resisted more vocally, but the Earthers, operating as a separate Naval service with no responsibility for the deserters, simply queried the departing ships. When an Earther Captain asked an abandoning ArcColonel under whose authority he or she was acting and the reply of 'our own' came back, the Earther nodded with a serious expression, said they'd be missed and welcomed in Earth space if they ever chose to return, then wished them safe journey.

It was unorthodox by human standards, but the Earthers just let the deserters go.

And go *Sword* was about to — the ship was now returning to open space, with a large sum of its old crew still aboard and a healthy crop of other carefully selected Genesis spacers filling the holes. Cruising out into deep space without orders from above, and with no clear idea of where they'd end up. A gamble, to be sure, but James couldn't stand to be in the company of his Navy anymore — he'd go make his own war on the Kroggs if it came to that. And *Sword* would not be made a white elephant, never to see service. No one was going to stop them from leaving today.

• • •

The 74-gun ship of the line *Apollo,* under the command of Captain Draco Maximane — a good-natured lion who had an interest in human nautical history — halted *Sword* on its outward journey. Courteously keeping his gunports closed and crew stood down, Maximane brought his ship up alongside the hybrid and matched speed.

Maximane truly hated to see good ships and crews like *Archangel Sword* and its complement go, but he acknowledged their right to do so — the psychological stress of being flung from the clutches of the Church into the foreign Earther lifestyle had to be immense, even if some of the humans were handling it well.

Although he couldn't pretend to understand them entirely, Maximane was willing to give these humans the benefit of the doubt. They'd proven their good character with spilled blood a year ago, and the Earthers had no right to ask anything more of them.

What would the Genesis Fleet Command say? Well, Maximane couldn't worry about that, "Query them please, Signal Officer. Master, keep us alongside."

A signal lanced across the gap between the two ships, and James indifferently watched a lion appear on his bridge screen, "Good day, Captain."

The lion nodded with customary Earther courtesy, "And to you, ArcColonel. Might I inquire as to your mission today?"

James Stanton paused ever so briefly, assessing his reply, "Captain, my ship and I are intent on leaving the system, under our own initiative."

Maximane paused as well, then nodded, "It'll be a shame to lose a good ship and crew such as yours, sir. But all the same, good luck to you — take care of yourselves out there."

James' expression remained neutral, and he offered a quick nod in reply, "Thank you, Captain. Good day to you."

As the screen blanked and the Sensor Chief on *Sword's* bridge reported the large 74 to be moving off, James felt a momentary stab of uncertainty. He could honestly see himself fighting alongside the Earthers — playing a role in the liberation of Genesis — but damned if his own Navy would let him.

It was not an easy thing, to walk away, but he simply couldn't fit into this version of an Earther world, nor could his crew. He didn't know where he could fit anymore.

Draco Maximane was grim as *Apollo* turned back to its patrol route along the belt, but he was still obliged to perform another duty related to the desertion.

"Signal Officer, send to Admiralty House that the Battlecruiser *Archangel Sword* has left the system of its own volition." Maximane turned to his First Lieutenant, a polar bear named Garvin Jardaw who'd been with him for several years in the Third Rate, "Are there any human ships on the *Sword's* base course?"

Jardaw had already predicted the question and was searching through charts of the Sol sector on his screen, "One Dreadnought, *Saint Damian Freedman*, on the Pluto patrol."

Maximane nodded silently — it seemed that the officers of other Genesis Naval ships were not kind to those who chose to leave. Maximane didn't quite understand the sense of possessiveness the Genesis Navy felt over its crews. The Earther Navy was a volunteer fleet; it was the Captain and crew who made the decisions on an Earther ship, and it was the combined commitment of these two groups to the Navy and to the mission that guaranteed the strength of the fleet. No one in the Earther service ever pretended differently, but the humans clearly had a separate set of standards. And unfortunately, Maximane realized, those standards were causing as much division as unity in the Genesis Fleet.

In immediate terms, that sort of division could prove deadly...

Maximane ground his jaw for a second, then turned to his Signal Officer again, "Send to *Castor*, we're going off station for twenty minutes."

It was the meeting with another human ArcColonel that James Stanton had most feared for his outward journey — the Earthers were not abrasive, but another human ship of war might be less inclined to let him leave Sol space with *Sword*. When the Heavy Cruiser *Grendelsbane City* had departed just a month before, the ArcColonel of an intercepting Superdreadnought had actually threatened to blow the ship out of space if it didn't turn back. It had been a tense moment, but the swift Heavy Cruiser had managed to get around the battleship and escape. The Earthers had quietly expressed their desire to keep Sol space free of combat, but Genesis Fleet Command still seemed to have its blood up.

As did most of the patrolling ships' ArcColonels — that's why Hastings posted them out there, to discourage desertion through threat of conflict.

Sword could likely outrun or outgun any human ship it came across, but Stanton had never been one for trading threats with his own officer cadre. Now, as *Saint Damian Freedman* loomed in the space before them, James doubted if he could get away without such an exchange.

The two Genesis ships slowed to face each other just inside missile range, and a standard hail came from the larger Dreadnought, asking for course and mission. James watched the text message scroll up on his screen and tapped back an equally impersonal reply:

ArcColonel James Stanton, Archangel Sword
Course: Outward as bearing 188 by 232 by 112
Mission: None

He keyed the 'send message' button and waited as the Dreadnought processed it. A few seconds later a visual hail came from the larger ship, and James sighed and told his Comm Chief to put it on the main bridge monitor.

Seconds later, an angry-looking oriental woman filled the screen, "This is ArcColonel Hoshi Chen to *Archangel Sword*. What in the name of the Gods are you doing?"

James recognized Hoshi immediately — she'd been junior to him only a few months before, the exec on one of Manchester's other Battlecruisers, *Paladin Saint*. She'd obviously gotten a nudge up to ArcColonel and had been given a Dreadnought. It seemed a mixed blessing — the battered old battlewagon was probably too badly damaged to accompany the mixed fleet heading for Genesis, so it'd remained in-system.

"Good day, ArcColonel. It's been a while. How goes the shakedown cruise?"

Chen's eyes flamed. Her expression was dark and the scowl on her face held an unpleasant message, "Damn you, James! You can't leave us too! What in the gulags of hell do you think you can accomplish on your own?"

"Well, *Hoshi*, I don't hope to accomplish anything in particular, but I know I'll be a lot more comfortable with my ship and my crew. Maybe we'll actually get a chance to do something out there. But we're not sitting on our hands anymore, with our own fleet refusing to give us a job."

Chen's face flushed crimson and she glared lasers through his monitor, "I can stop you, ArcColonel. Don't make me. By Gods, I'm loading my tubes–"

A chirping on both bridges cut off Chen's words, and James frowned and glanced at one of the nearby screens, almost feeling his mood shift to pleasant.

Apollo slipped out of energy drive alongside *Sword*, linking immediately into the comm conversation. Captain Maximane appeared on *Sword*'s bridge monitor, splitting the screen.

"Is there some trouble here, ArcColonel Chen?"

Hoshi's eyes were burning, and James' eyes narrowed as he offered an absent nod of greeting to Maximane, "Nothing to trouble yourself with, Captain. The ArcColonel was just giving us her best wishes as a sendoff."

Maximane cocked an eyebrow, "I find that rather hard to believe. ArcColonel Chen, I must ask that you stand down from action stations and return your missiles to your magazines. I believe you know standing policy for Sol space."

Fleet Command and Admiralty House would *love* this, James decided with a grim wit.

"We'll get out of your way, Captain," James said quietly, and Maximane nodded.

"Safe journey, Mister Stanton."

"Don't *ever* show your face in our space, James, or by Gods we'll *remove* it. You got lucky today... don't expect that to continue," Chen cut her link first, and then with raised eyebrows and a last brief nod, Maximane cut his link too.

James took a deep, cleansing breath, then looked to his executive officer, "Well, let's keep moving before we get those two shooting at each other."

Archangel Sword accelerated outwards from the Sol star.

CHAPTER 3

"He did *what?!*"

The officers' mess of Lazarus Base — the central Genesis Navy base on Earth — collapsed into sudden silence at the outcry. A few dozen pairs of eyes turned towards the heated face of ArcGeneral Elizabeth Hastings, then quickly looked away as her glare began to track back to their owners.

"*Archangel Sword* left at 08:00 hours, ma'am," Hastings' aide, a recently promoted ArcMajor, appeared calm — probably through the application of much fortitude.

Hastings, as always, was disarmed by her adjutant's stoic tone. Indeed, he had realized months earlier that handling the ArcGeneral's moods was an art, and he'd perfected his skills in that regard. Of late she was increasingly irritable, and that could doubtlessly be blamed on the crisis her Navy seemed to be facing. It was having a hell of a time staying together...

The Navy had been a stable force in Hastings' life, but now she watched fragments of it go rogue as she tried to sort the rest into active units, all while dealing with ship skippers who were desperate for commissions to whatever vessels came out of the yards. There was a vast surplus of human crews in Earth space, and the Earthers could only repair ships so quickly. Forming and crewing installations like Lazarus Base had emptied some of the pool, but nearly 600 complete ship crews remained unemployed, left to idle about. It was a nightmare — so many qualified spacers with no ships for them to crew.

It was the sort of situation that bred dissent, and Hastings had known it from the outset. From the beginning of her cooperation with Admiralty House, Liz had entertained a dark uncertainty about her people — there would inevitably be different visions of the future without the Church. She'd retained absolute control of her Navy for fear that some would see her as replacing the Church with the Earthers, but that association had still been made many times. Some people didn't seem to realize the reality of the situation — the Earthers were offering technology that could help Genesis free itself from the *Kroggs*. But some Naval types had decided early on not to trust the Earthers, and they'd been the first to leave. Now people like James Stanton were deserting... presumably because they didn't like the way the relationship between the fleets had developed.

Well, for James it had probably been a matter of his particular ship's plight.

Nonetheless, it was symptomatic of a larger problem. The Earther Navy was carefully staying out of Genesis affairs in this region of space, except for refusing Liz's ships permission to fire on deserters in Earth space, and suggesting that she not send out hunter squadrons. But even with that visible separation, suspicions of the Earthers still remained in some of the Genesis Fleet's darker corners.

Such was the nature of the post-Church Navy.

And Liz Hastings was sitting at the top of the whole structure, trying to hold everything together while pioneering a new friendship with the Earther Navy without looking like a sell-out and a traitor... it was exhausting. She was determined to hold firm, and to shape the Genesis Navy into an even more modern fighting force, but the resistance from within was damning.

Sitting in front of her salmon and potato meal, the ArcGeneral realized she'd lost her appetite. Reactions were merging and melding in her mind — anger, sorrow, confusion and *shame*.

She'd brought a unified force to the Earthers and convinced the new allies to support them in a struggle against the Church. With the Church neutralized and Earth safe, she'd expected duty and loyalty to bind the Navy through the rough period of reconstruction. But the bonds hadn't been nearly as strong as she'd expected. Gone was the loyalty between officers that had prevailed when Crusaders had overshadowed fleet operations... what remained was as divided and unpleasant as anything Hastings had encountered in Genesis society. She could only wonder what the Earthers thought of them... and of her.

It couldn't be anything good.

Hastings thrust herself to her feet, turned away from her aide and stormed out of the mess, leaving a group of shocked officers in her wake.

The Earther war-gaming season was just about to get started, and *ENS Orion* sat at anchor in Earth orbit, preparing for its first simulated action since before the Battle of the Pluto Orbital Plane. Though command of *Orion* would belong to Captain Labrador Forepaw during the coming games, it would be up to another officer to command the 101st Battle Squadron for the actions.

First Lord of the Admiralty Setter Caine sat back in a chair in *Orion's* number six briefing room, looking over two reports on glowing screens in the holo tank at the table. He really didn't want to be worrying about these matters right now — he wanted to be working with his squadron Captains on tactics — but his *actual* job (running the Earther Navy) did take precedence. So he was going over some rather serious matters with the chief of the new Naval Expansion and Integration department, Vice Admiral Savanna Felix.

"James Stanton actually *left*?"

Felix nodded slowly, with a grim expression, "You remember his name then?"

"As I recall there was quite a fuss about his ship. It was one of Liz's projects,"

Caine let his voice trail off. It seemed the human situation was getting more complicated by the day — Liz's efforts to bring the Earther and Genesis Navies to a common technical standard were being met with resistance by some of her best officers. Reactions were seemingly mixed, at least among the crews left now in the Sol system, as to the benefits of Earther tech in human ships that hadn't been designed for it.

And crews were abandoning because of this difference in opinions.

Liz was having a difficult time trying to keep all those different positions from ripping her fleet apart, and Caine didn't envy her the task. The Earther Navy had been through its share of paces lately, the slaughter of millions of Crusaders in the last year not least in any Earther's mind. But the Earthers had no problem maintaining cohesion — they were together by choice, and they trusted the judgments of their senior officers. Because of their mutual commitment, Earther Captains and Admirals never had to worry about desertion, and thus the disciplinary system in the Earther Navy was entirely one of self-control.

Now the humans seemed to be attempting to take on that self-control system, without the uniformity of purpose that made it possible in the Earther Navy.

Teething problems for the new Alliance. Pains that the Earthers needed to sit back and watch with crossed fingers...

"Well, any reason it bleeds into our sphere, Savanna? It being one of Liz's ships and all..." Caine let go a light sigh and leaned back, looking to his companion.

Felix shrugged and then offered a nod. There were *always* complications with these things, Caine realized... the humans seemed to have a reservoir of spite held specifically for use on each other. He was *almost* ready to concede that they were psychologically incapable of accepting anything that seemed good — unless, of course, they recognized strings attached.

Grimacing at that thought, Caine looked across the table to his companion, "Why do you think he left, Savanna?"

The cat leaned back in his chair and looked up over the head of his senior. He wasn't sure what was driving the humans — it seemed painfully clear that no Earther could easily climb into a proverbial pair of human shoes. The humans had a safe, welcoming home here — they were treated as any other Earthers, and many of them seemed to be adjusting well. But some simply couldn't adapt, and James Stanton had been one of them. A good officer by all accounts, he'd had some spectacular arguments with Liz, and Felix had mediated many of them.

"Stanton was bitter about what had been done to his ship without his crew's consent, and he was very unhappy when Liz pulled his ship out of Sarah's fleet," Felix said quietly, meeting Caine's eyes. "But there's obviously more to it than that... it's a matter of feeling as though they don't fit. James said it to me a couple of times — he felt like he was imposing, he felt like we were doing all the work, and he didn't want to have to rely on us for everything... I think there's too long a history of foreign intervention in that Navy. The crews want to prove they can fight their ships without the Church and the Kroggs pushing them around. Our help gets labeled *charity*, and if we give too much then we get labeled 'too good to be true' and suspicions about our agenda starts growing."

Caine cocked an eyebrow at the human colloquialism. He'd heard it a lot. It had bothered him since Pat Conroy had been talking with Ursla before the defection, and he'd kept it in mind ever since. He supposed it made sense on one level — so accustomed to their divided and sometimes deceptive lives, the humans couldn't simply accept the Earthers as benevolent.

And the Naval personnel, strong and professional to a fault, were melding with that a deserved sense of pride and an unnecessary fear that the Earthers didn't respect their fighting abilities. All Caine could do to prove the Earther opinion was treat the Genesis Fleet as an equal ally, which he was doing. But as much as he kept Earther and Genesis structures divided, complications could drag the Earthers in at any moment. Admiralty House had made it clear that no combat between Genesis ships would be tolerated in-system — two ships fighting at random might literally split the Genesis Fleet and start another mutiny... a civil war, even.

So as much as Caine was being careful not to unduly influence Liz's command of her fleet, there was by necessity a certain amount of caution on the Earther part. It was extremely complicated...

As though he was listening to Caine's musing, Felix leaned forward and tabbed the holo tank, bringing up a schematic of *Apollo*, "Draco Maximane had to put his ship off *Archangel Sword*'s beam to make sure ArcColonel Chen didn't fire into Stanton. No shots fired, but I don't imagine Chen gave a glowing review to Liz."

Caine ground his jaw and nodded, "Liz is definitely on side with us... which is part of her problem I suppose. But anything *we* could do would probably just make things worse, so we have to leave it to her..."

Then a strange notion occurred to Caine. The Earthers might indeed be facing unfair associations to the Church... why not bring the Church *back* into the picture? Oh it was a dangerous thought... but what if it did work...?

"What about Harvey Bingham," Caine frowned and spoke in low tones. "You think he might be able to... well, add a different perspective?"

Felix's ear twitched at the mention of the High Chancellor. Now recovered from his general amnesia, and presumably free from his fanaticism and megalomania, he was being eyed curiously by the Earth Consulate as a potential leader for the ex-Crusaders now living on Earth.

"Well I'll look into that anyway... I think I'd try just about anything right now," Caine read Felix's reluctance on his face as he spoke. "In the meantime, I think we should use the war-games as an excuse to change our patrol schedules. Try to get the hotter element like ArcColonel Chen off the outer line…"

There he went, making decisions for Liz…

"Or," Caine's brow creased in a deep frown, "I'll leave that deployment up to Liz. But we'll have Battle Squadrons out there on maneuvers for the next three months, so we can keep Genesis ships to the inner ring, at least."

Felix nodded slowly, then scratched his chin thoughtfully, "You want me to talk to Bingham?"

Caine blinked at that thought and then slowly shook his head, "It should be me. After our history with him I can't justify sending anyone else in my place. Besides, you're due at war-games this afternoon anyway, aren't you… aha."

A smile formed on Caine's face, breaking the darker mood, and Felix tried to frown innocently, "What?"

"You're not using this as an excuse to get out of war-games, you old desk Admiral. I know you don't like the command chair, but we're all obliged to take our turn."

It was true that Felix felt uncomfortable on a bridge, but it was standard practice that every decade all flag officers had to command at least one force for a round of war-games. Having gotten his flag rank ten years ago to the day, Felix was out of time — either he went to war-games this afternoon or he would be in violation of standing Earther procedure. What that meant… well, nobody actually knew — it had never happened. And frankly the Admiralty probably wouldn't care too much, but Savanna Felix would. It was part of the job — a part he couldn't legitimately dodge any longer, and so a duty he would indeed perform.

This afternoon he was boarding a ship.

"They want me on *Tonnant* in three hours," he smiled finally. "I'd best go, then."

Caine grinned and nodded, "I get the sense you'll do very well, my friend. I only hope I do as well with the High Chancellor."

Lord High Chancellor Harvey Bingham sat in a comfortable armchair and read his book. *War of the Worlds* was apparently a classic salvaged from the early twentieth century, written by someone named Wells. An interesting book indeed, though somewhat cryptic given the manner in which history had played out 150 years after its writing.

The den of his home was cool and shady, built from unfamiliar timbers, and he found it an agreeable place. He'd decided to spend much of his recovery time over the past months reading in this room — classics, neoclassics, and Earther-classics had all passed through his hands, helping him re-learn the fundamentals of human decency… and perhaps a little of Earther morality too. He was beginning to feel balanced, unlike the man he'd been. The Earthers seemed pleased with his progress, and the Earth Consulate was becoming adamant that he return to the public sphere soon, to lead the millions of ex-Crusaders and the relatively few shipless Naval types who now lived in a similarly reformed state on the planet.

The soft chime of the doorbell made Harvey blink. He marked his page and laid his book aside, stood up and climbed the stairs from his den onto his well-lit, glass-enclosed, above-ground floor. He'd elected to live in Newfoundland — a truly charming, rugged place — partially because he marveled at the water which was icy cold and had an acidity so agreeable that it didn't burn skin as the Genesis seas had. His home also put him near his doctor, Elandra Caine, who had actually gone through the 'claiming' process. Harvey still didn't quite understand how the Earther system worked, but from what he did grasp, Elandra had simply found a piece of land no one else had any need of, 'claimed' it and called in a contractor to build the house.

With *no* currency changing hands, no deeds or written contracts... the home and surrounding area was now recognized as *Bingham's*, but he still didn't know if that meant he *owned* the land or was just seen as the most influential squatter on it. He didn't bother the wildlife; they didn't bother him.

In any case, it was probably Elandra at the door. She was his best... his only friend, and since he had no duties to carry him beyond his simple beachside home, he seldom had contact with anyone else. She visited as often as possible to alleviate his solitude, but so long as the database had files to run through his Home-Book Printer Unit, he was happy.

As the bald, average-height High Chancellor neared his door he saw the customary fur and perky ears through the frosted glass, but this wolf's build, color and dress was different. Elandra was slim and feminine — in a surprisingly human way — but this wolf was broader and clearly male.

With the blue uniform of the Navy.

Curious and slightly nervous, Harvey opened his door with a keystroke, and nodded to greet the newcomer.

"Good day," he said with a pleasant smile. "Can I help you?"

The wolf turned to him with a matching, if somewhat more conservative smile, "Good day to you, High Chancellor. I trust you're well."

Harvey froze in place.

The last time he'd been face-to-face with First Lord Setter Caine, he'd threatened to massacre the entire Earther race and take the planet in the name of the Church. Since then the two had literally stayed at least 100 kilometers apart at all times. Harvey had been recovering, of course, which gave him an excuse to keep away, while Caine was trying to build a new cooperative alliance of the races.

They hadn't actually seen each other since that last day on the Pluto Orbital Plane... and in point of fact, they'd only ever met in person once. On *Orion*, a *lifetime* ago. And that time they'd nearly come to blows. Not for trivial reasons, either, from what Harvey remembered — had he been Caine, he would have torn himself limb from limb...

So what was Setter Caine doing here today?

"Might I come in?" Caine's voice was polite, even comfortable.

Harvey gurgled his attempt to reply, nodded awkwardly, and let the wolf in.

CHAPTER 4

The Allied Fleet assembled just beyond the outer reach of Krogg pickets around the Genesis system. The 1,500-ship force had been traveling in a single-mass formation for the past two weeks, and even though the Earthers could have easily outpaced the humans to the rendezvous, Ursla and Sarah had decided the unity of movement would have a positive impact on morale — particularly *human* morale.

Loyal crews — those not wanting to leave the Alliance — had been stationed on Sarah's 900-odd ships, and though she knew they'd remain steadfast in their commitment to the Earther partnership, neither she nor Ursla wanted to make them feel as though they literally couldn't keep up. The Genesis ships attached to this force were to be full participants in the mission — they'd have the chance to prove their abilities to the Earthers, even though they didn't need to.

The so-called 'Retribution Fleet' brought itself into squadron and task force order after its deceleration from flux. Sarah watched from the bridge of her Superdreadnought, *Joseph Barron*, with some impatience. It was a slower process than she would have liked, but it was an inevitability of flux travel — formations got jumbled after two weeks in transit.

The Earther Second Fleet had come out of energy drive in battle order, but such was the ability of the Earthers. They didn't mock the human plight — they commended the maneuvering ability of the ships that had to work for their formations. While there could be no doubt of their sincerity in the compliment, Sarah's reaction — and that of many of her officers — was a frustrated one. The Genesis officers cadre was hell-bent on pulling its weight, and seeing the Earthers pause patiently to let the human ships order themselves was just another one of those things that spawned some illogical irritation.

In any case, Sarah was too busy scanning her screens to spend any more time mulling over the moods of her crews. Pat Conroy's Battlecruisers would be somewhere nearby — it was their signal, received a day before, that had stopped the Allied Fleet short of its destination. They'd been out ahead stirring up trouble, and as such she hadn't heard from the Irishman in over two weeks — a surprisingly unsettling experience after being forced into his company, more or less willingly, for almost a year.

Aside from Liz Hastings, Sarah had no friend she could confide in as much as she did Pat Conroy. Now she was forcing herself to again become accustomed to the natural, solitary life of a Naval flag officer. But so many things had changed in her life since the Quest, it was *impossible* to simply sever the ties of friendship.

"Sensor Chief, do you have a fix on *Harbinger Bishop* yet?" Sarah's question was tighter than she'd have liked.

Barron's Chief — a veteran spacer who'd joined the ship alongside many of the crew from Sarah's old Battlecruiser, *Warlock Prophet* — shook her head briefly, "Not yet, ma'am. I'll tell you when I see it, you know."

The woman's tone carried a dry wit, and had Sarah been through less with the crew from *Prophet* she might have had a mind to call it insubordinate. But of course she didn't really mind the tone, even though she didn't understand the reason behind it.

Oh well, spacer humor, no doubt.

"Thank you, Agitha," the ArcGeneral's tone was equally dry, and the Chief smiled and continued pouring over her ship-clouded screens.

And then the icon she'd been waiting for appeared on the very edge of the Superdreadnought's sensors.

"There's *Bishop* now," Agitha was irreverent.

"Comm Chief, send a sig–"

"Sent, ma'am," the Comm Chief was another old hand from *Prophet*. Sarah almost frowned — two-thirds of her bridge crew had come over from the Battlecruiser, were they all going to be so in tune with her wishes this whole time? Oh well, they were probably just as eager for news as she was.

Sarah waited for the message to reach her friend and be processed. It occurred to her that Pat might not be on *Bishop's* bridge, but she dismissed the doubt as she decided he'd want to retain personal squadron command when his Battlecruisers were reintegrated into the fleet.

"Message coming in, ma'am, from ArcBrigadier Conroy."

Sarah smiled inwardly — right on time, "Put it on."

The screen at the front of *Barron's* bridge flickered to life, and Pat's head appeared. He smiled at Sarah in a familiar way, "Good day, lass! Pleasant trip?"

Sarah frowned in good humor, "I'm glad you haven't grown too formal in my absence."

The big Irishman chuckled and shook his head, "I'm sure formality matters to someone. Was it an interesting trip then... or were you bored to tears?"

A smile formed on Sarah's face, "I wasn't *actually* weeping, *thanks* Pat."

From Sarah's perspective, Pat was lucky: his message of the previous day said his Battlecruisers had seen action against a number of Krogg pickets between the rim of Earther territory and the Genesis system. She'd seen a lot of nothing, quite a lot of nothing.

"I managed," she continued, and he cocked an amused eyebrow. "I suppose I'll see you in an hour or two — when senior officers meet aboard *Agamemnon*."

Pat chuckled, "Now we know I'm not senior to Caitie Hargreaves or Bill Masters, so I won't be there. Unless I'm getting a raise…"

Sarah's smile persisted, "No, you aren't. But don't you think we might need a report on the mischief you've been up to over the past two weeks?"

Pat assumed a thoughtful expression and scratched his chin, "Well I suppose that might be important. Just want me to show up and tell my story then?"

"Well can you do any tricks? I'm sure we'd like to see that too," Sarah was grinning now.

A mock-frown crossed Pat's brow, "Oof, I'm wounded, woman! Fine then, I'll just be seeing you there, won't I? Torturous though that'll be!"

Sarah chuckled to herself as the screen blanked, completely unaware of the conclusions drawn by the entire bridge crew about the exchange. She wouldn't have wanted to know what they were thinking anyway.

Agamemnon's main briefing room was neither small nor unimpressive — it could easily seat thirty officers, plus an additional twenty in a pinch. Its large central table was surrounded by the dangerously comfortable Earther chairs, and as Sarah decided every time she came aboard, it made *Joseph Barron's* main briefing room look like a bare, artificial closet.

In the chamber, almost a dozen officers mingled, some of them Earthers, many others human. Admiral Varnon Broadpaw, Ursla's second in command, was a good-natured wolf, who Sarah had first met briefly just before the Battle of the Pluto Orbital Plane. Junior to him were Vice Admirals Andrea Talone and Jax Furgus and a handful of Commodores. ArcLieutenant-Generals Bill Masters and Caitlin Hargreaves joined Sarah, as did a few ArcBrigadiers including Pat.

Ursla would preside over the gathering as soon as she arrived, but in true Earther-fleet-commander style, she was running just a tad late. Having been third to reach the room, Sarah had waited impatiently for Pat to arrive. She'd hurried over to him as soon as he'd come through the door and collapsed unceremoniously into a comfortable chair.

"Nice of you to finally join us," she greeted him with a dry smile as she leaned against the table.

Pat laughed and sat back, closing his eyes briefly, "I got lost — seriously, I've never been aboard *Agamemnon* before!"

Sarah chuckled, relieved to see him again and oblivious to the knowing glances from all around her as she fell into conversation with her friend.

On the other side of the room, ArcLieutenant-General Masters turned his glance from the pair and smiled with raised eyebrows at his fellow ArcLieutenant-General Hargreaves and at Jax Furgus, "So what does it mean on Earth if you spend all your free time with someone, nearly get killed together a bunch of times, and then start briefings like that?"

Jax grinned, "When I started looking at my wife like that, we looked for a nice ship and moved in together. But that was on Earth…"

His companions chuckled and nodded.

The main hatch slid open and Ursla ducked — literally, thanks to the slightly lower doorframe — through it. On a Genesis ship, standard practice would have brought every officer in the room to attention, regardless of rank. The commander of the fleet — or, officially, co-commander — had arrived. But this was an Earther ship, so the Earthers waved and a couple offered jovial jeers.

"Good of you to descend to our level, Andra!" Furgus roared in his friendly lion's voice.

Ursla grinned at her subordinate, "With you here, Jax, I deserve a medal for my fortitude."

The room bubbled with laughter and people began to find seats at the long table. As was customary, Ursla took one head and Sarah the other — the two fleet COs were in their places. Pat was in the seat to Sarah's right, and as the flag officers settled themselves, Ursla looked to him.

Normally a Genesis meeting would have opened with some sort of summary statement and an outline of things on the agenda, but Sarah had found that the Earthers didn't adhere to strict timetables for these sorts of meetings. They also seemed to remember everything, and never wrote anything down… so true to form, Ursla just began.

"So, Pat, we've been passing debris. I suppose you've been busy."

The burly ArcBrig nodded with a smile, "I got them all with the same act — a lovely performance, supported of course by my bridge crew. I start by pleading with them to signal Genesis and warn them that an evil, massive force is coming to give them their comeuppance. Quite hilarious… from my perspective anyway. The Kroggs had put out six pickets from what we've seen. The first two were lone Destroyers, the next two were groups of three, and the last two were groups of six. We polished them all off without much noise. From what we can tell, no one in Krogg HQ knows what to expect from this direction… probably due to our silence of late."

As Pat spoke, Ursla tapped some of the selected mission recorder logs from *Bishop* onto screens projected in the table's holo display. One of his red-faced performances drew some chuckles, and he grinned before going on, "We moved a little ways in from where we are now to check out the state of Genesis, but we couldn't get any further without being noticed — they have a Mothership and a few Superdreadnoughts on their in-system perimeter."

The room sobered with those words, and Pat paused to let everyone digest the information. A strong picket towards Earth might reasonably have included a Superdreadnought or a couple of Dreadnoughts, but a *Mothership*? Perhaps the Kroggs had become concerned, wondering why their pickets had fallen silent. There was no way to be certain of how frequent their contact with their outlying patrols usually was, but it was possible they'd grown suspicious.

Krogg Motherships were massive — almost ten times the size of a Genesis Colonizer, nearing twenty times the size of a regular First Rate. They carried vast numbers of 'corvettes,' ships that were a cross between Destroyers and pinnaces, and thus were like small fleets unto themselves. Backing them with Superdreadnoughts suggested the Kroggs might be expecting trouble — where Motherships were devoid of major ship-to-ship weapons banks, the Superdreadnoughts in close support could hammer at any assailants while the corvettes launched.

But what concerned Ursla most was what such a presence meant for the system's garrison — in order to detail that many ships specifically to watching the Earth approaches, a presumably large fleet reserve had to be nearby.

"So," she followed that line of thought, "we don't know what's waiting for us in-system?"

Pat shook his head, "Sorry, Andra, I couldn't figure out a way to slip in."

Ursla nodded in reply, "You did quite well, Pat. Nothing you could do about the scouting situation... I think a sloop might be able to get in there though. What do you think, Varnon, anyone we have up to it?"

She turned to Broadpaw as she spoke, and the wolf nodded, "We have a number of particularly good and *eager* sloop skippers. I'm sure quite a few of them are fit for the job."

Ursla nodded and panned the table in search of ideas, "Thoughts?"

There was silence — the concept of scouting the Genesis system was hardly a new one, and it had been decided well back in Earth space that if Pat ran across a significant picket, an Earther sloop would have the best chance of running reconnaissance undetected. While a Genesis Destroyer might be written off as regular system traffic if it were detected, it would have to get awfully close to quite a few Krogg vessels to gather the intelligence required for this operation. They needed a vessel that could become all but invisible to perform this duty properly, and since the Kroggs had no concept of Earther technology, the best chance for a successful mission lay with the ships of Ursla's Second Fleet. An Earther ship's readings might get written off as an odd blip... or could draw unwanted attention. So the commander of the sloop would have to be quite good at *not* being noticed.

"Right, then we'll reconvene when our sloop gets back. I'll send all of you data packets on what ship we're sending... once I decide that myself. If there's nothing else, we're all done, I think."

Varnon Broadpaw's brows arched, "But I didn't even get to argue with Jax once."

Furgus grinned, "In the corridor, right now — let's go!"

There were closing chuckles and the room cleared relatively quickly — most of the commanders disliked being away from their battle groups, especially with

Kroggs in the general area. Sarah and Pat were left alone to chat briefly and catch up on the two weeks they'd been apart. They left half an hour later, chuckling all the way to the flight deck.

CHAPTER 5

Commander Fox Magnus wasn't entirely sure who had volunteered him for this mission, but he was certainly going to find out. Someone had decided he and his cherished sloop, *Flame*, were to scout the Krogg positions in the Genesis system. The mission was a difficult challenge to some, virtual suicide to others.

He'd have to send a gift basket to whoever had assigned him to it.

No, that wasn't a sarcastic thought — *really*, a nice big gift basket with scented soaps and some greenery, because this was just the sort of crazy mission he secretly craved.

Fox Magnus always loved a good challenge, and this was just his style. His sloop, crewed by a mere ninety-eight Earthers, mounted a light armament of eighteen guns. In Earth space, *Flame* had seen limited action for that very reason — joining Ursla's Exodus Battle Group, the ship had done everything possible to shield Naval small craft during the defection, but had been left to harass Superdreadnoughts a bit ineffectually during the Battle of the Asteroid Belt. Neither of those jobs had taken advantage of *Flame's* virtues, but this one surely would.

In a reconnaissance role, no one could do better than Fox and his crew. They trained endlessly to ready themselves for missions like this, and now they'd get their chance, at long last, to prove how vital the diminutive little sloops could be. The Kroggs wouldn't catch them, no matter what!

This confidence was permeating the small bridge of *ENS Flame* as Magnus finished explaining the situation to his crew. He'd been holding down the intercom key on the arm of his chair for about three minutes now, explaining objectives:

"...So the Admiral wants us to slip in and — forgive the pun, *ahem*, here — *sloop* around a bit. Nothing we can't handle."

Lieutenant Chronos Claw and Midshipman Lang Sandpelt, Magnus' full complement of officers, were both old friends, and they shared his confidence, as did the crew. It was just another factor that would aid their success in this mission.

"We're moving immediately, so all hands to action stations. Rig the ship for stealth routine, please. That's all."

Lifting his finger from the intercom key, Fox leaned back in his chair, "Well, I'm excited."

Chronos Claw grinned, "I suppose *you* are. They're *my* engines you're going to put all the stress on, eh?"

Descended from a cougar, the Lieutenant was smaller than most cats in the Earther service, though bigger than Magnus himself, and now Fox grinned back, "How is it *my* ship and *your* engines?"

"Laws of the engineer. Lang will back me up, won't you Lang?" Claw grinned and jabbed the Midshipman softly in the ribs with his elbow.

"You two do whatever you like, I'm shutting up until I have a commission," Sandpelt said with mock defensiveness. "Besides, if I let you two fight it out, *Flame* will be mine!"

Fox and Claw chuckled, the Commander patting Sandpelt on the shoulder, "You'll have your day, but not now. Anyway, we best get to work. I got these orders direct from Ursla."

"I'll head down to the engines then," Claw said with the hint of a smile.

"Do you want me here or with the guns?" Sandpelt straightened his posture and sobered.

Magnus pondered for a second and shook his head, "We won't need them. Well, that is to say if we did need to use them I don't imagine the odds would be in our favor, so there wouldn't be much point in using them."

Lang smiled and nodded, "True enough."

"Ship is at action stations, skipper," the Cruising Master reported from his post in front of the officers. "Now reporting silent routine, all decks."

"Very good, Master. Take us ahead, 50 pls, if you please."

Flame slowly slid away from the thick cloud of Earther ships towards the presumably Krogg-infested Genesis system.

"Clearing the fleet, sir," the Sensor Chief reported from behind.

"Very good, helm, activate energy drive, bring us in at 1,600 pls. You know the routine — avoid *everything*."

Ursla sat back in her chair aboard *Agamemnon* and watched *Flame* slip away from her fleet. A single sloop prowling about a system full of potentially — *likely* — hostile alien ships, not sure of what it'd find… in the estimation of some it might have been a suicide mission. But for Fox Magnus, and his handy little *Flame*, it would simply be a challenge, while for Ursla it would provide a good benchmark for the comparison of Krogg and Earther technology.

Fox would do well — that's why Ursla had chosen him for the operation. She'd kept her eye on him as he'd come through *Orion* as a Midshipman almost twenty years before — she'd been the Captain of Caine's flagship then, and Fox had been a remarkable young officer. Then he and *Flame* had fought Church Superdreadnoughts at the asteroid belt, managing to harass several of the much larger ships without sustaining any severe damage from their fire. In quiet upper circles, he'd earned the certain reputation of being a high-stress performer. Now he again had a chance to prove both his own and his ship's abilities.

Agamemnon's long-range tracking sensors were able to follow *Flame* as it approached the outer sphere of Genesis pickets. The sloop was virtually invisible to anyone who didn't know the signature of Earther energy drives, and as such it drew closer and closer to the system without the pickets' notice.

As the rim of the Genesis system finally appeared in front of it, *Flame* dropped from energy drive — and from *Agamemnon's* sensors.

Good luck Commander Magnus.

"Silent routine established, sir. We're giving off point oh-three percent energy emissions," the Master's words were calm, but Earther instinct conveyed his underlying excitement to everyone on the bridge.

So far it had been effortless. But they'd only just slipped in and running a picket was exactly the sort of job *Flame* had been designed for. Now they had to remain invisible as they scurried about, picking up as much data as possible without being seen. That would be the fun — and of course, the *difficult* — part.

"Watch room, Magnus here. Ready on your sensors?" Fox spoke quietly. No one could hear *Flame* through the void of space, but it seemed wrong to yell while sneaking around.

"Ready sir," the operator in *Flame's* deep-range sensor lab answered in equally discreet tones.

"Very good, begin scans."

All Earther sloops were equipped with hefty long-range sensor suites. The old doctrines upon which the Navy was built delegated sloops to the task of scouting, so it had made sense to give them even better sensors than those mounted on frigates. That way they could see something coming with enough advance warning to get out of its way.

Now *Flame's* sensors stretched inward towards Genesis itself. The energy pulses were of such a low bandwidth that they were virtually undetectable, but the information they provided was remarkably accurate. Data began flowing into the sloop's processors.

Magnus smiled as his crew proved correct his predictions of success. *Flame* would not be caught.

Then the 'alert' chime began to sound.

"Ma'am, I'm picking up increased comm traffic from the pickets... it's directed toward Genesis," *Agamemnon's* Signal Officer made his report darkly.

"Unusual chatter?" Ursla asked, turning her chair to face him.

He listened through his earpiece for a moment, adjusted a dial in front of him, looked up and nodded, "The messages are on their telepathic frequencies. The bursts are more intense than any we've observed so far... I couldn't tell you what they're saying though."

"Any increased emissions from the pickets?" Ursla turned back to her Sensor Chief.

The cat frowned momentarily, "Looks like they're increasing the strength of their sensor pulses. No movement yet."

The Chief paused again and looked up, "Ma'am, with the intensity of the scans the Kroggs are deploying now, I don't see how a fly could get through there undetected."

Ursla nodded slowly and suppressed a minor growl. The Kroggs had gotten wind of something — they must have seen the unusual energy signature as *Flame* entered the system. Magnus had either been caught or he was walking into a trap.

"Fleet, beat to quarters. Stand by for action. We can't move in until we know what's going on, but I want to be ready if the Kroggs come looking for us."

"Three Destroyers coming this way now, skipper. Looks like they're flying a general search pattern. Nine more are doing the same thing along our flanks. They might've made us on system entry... though they don't seem to see us right now. But it doesn't look like we have a clean way out."

The report wasn't encouraging, but Magnus wasn't ready to give up just yet. Or ever, for that matter. He was determined to find an escape route, even if he ended up having to manufacture one himself. As a last resort he could cut and run, spinning his drives up to 2,000 pls and visibly rocketing out of the system. That would be his fallback... but he might still be able to figure a stealthy way out of this.

"Very well then. Not so easy as we'd like." He turned to Sandpelt, "Lang, I want you with your guns after all. I hope you don't have to use them."

The Midshipman nodded and briskly trotted to the lift.

"We'll be in detection range in three minutes sir."

Magnus laced his fingers and settled back into his chair.

"All hands, stand-to for action."

CHAPTER 6

ArcGeneral Elizabeth Hastings drummed her fingers on the desk before her. From time to time, the impact would approximate the rhythm of a familiar tune, but for the most part the beats were irregular and haphazard. Perhaps they suited her frustrated mood; they seemed to be as jagged as the Navy she was trying to hold together.

She stopped that bitter line of thought immediately — she couldn't simply blame the fleet, which was fundamentally loyal, if moderately divided on the particulars of cooperation with the Earthers. Only a few irrational individuals were causing the most visible trouble, and yet because of those few, Hastings had wanted to threaten *every* human in Earth space into submission — there would be no more desertions, or she'd take what ships she had left and hunt down every single traitor out there.

Caine was more conservative in his approach, and of late had been gently nudging her not to become a reactionary. He politely pointed out that she'd just make more enemies, and in customary Earther style, was subtly twisting her arm. Instead of coercion, he suggested that absolute loyalty could be *earned* — get the crews on her side, and they'd stop themselves from deserting.

Sounded great — for the Earther Navy. But in her current state of mind, she didn't expect it to do much good in the Genesis Fleet.

She'd already tried incentives, threats and anything else she could come up with to get through to her crews. Nothing had worked, and she had to try something new; a reasonable, logical, typically-Earther philosophy might be her only chance. If she didn't find a solution, the Genesis Fleet at Earth would turn into a spectacular joke.

The most recent idea from Caine's desk was to deliver an address to all the Naval personnel in-system, clarifying the Genesis Fleet's displeasure at desertion but leaving it open as an option. Caine thought it best to let the humans feel as though they had an 'out' — they couldn't feel trapped in Earth space, or the Earthers would doubtless take the blame.

So Liz would give a speech, talking about the divisiveness she loathed with poise and good manners. Apparently the Earthers were rather adept at public broadcasts... but Liz had never done more than address her crews over Fleetcomm. Many of those addresses, in fact, had taken place back when she'd had to restrain her crews because the Church had been causing immense problems for the fleet... as they were doing in a different way today. It was ironic, the Church was going from horrible oppressor to civilized competition. Caine probably hadn't realized just how ironic the situation was when he'd suggested they *split* this address.

Because there were to be two speeches, or perhaps more precisely, one combined speech. The Navy couldn't feel as though it was being singled out among Sol humans for a wrist-slapping when there were millions of ex-Crusaders living in cities across Earth. Surprisingly enough (at least from Liz's perspective) these Crusaders were quickly becoming model citizens in Earth society. Earther kindness was much more persuasive than Church discipline, it seemed, so the Crusaders were quite happily living on the planet their Quest had sought, simply sharing it with its new owners. It was fulfillment of their Prophecy, just with an Earther complication.

And there hadn't been a delicate incident involving Churchers for *six months*.

In any case, Caine had thought it best that the Churchers give an address at the same time as the Navy, so it didn't appear the Navy was being scolded.

Liz hoped it would work.

The speeches would simultaneously air on Fleetcomm and Earthcomm. The ArcGeneral would tell her people she supported their right to desert if they wished, but that she hoped they would stay and help humanity build a free and strong society. Then, a religious representative would speak — to try to 'convince' the Crusaders to continue living happily and equally on Earth. Hopefully it wouldn't sound as lopsided as it did in Liz's head.

She had yet to meet her co-speaker — that was the purpose of this eleventh-hour meeting. Caine had apparently been hard-pressed to find someone to do the talking... or perhaps he just didn't want to give her time to back out when the Churcher arrived.

"He better be able to get people to listen," she muttered quietly to herself, her fingers drumming on.

"Ready, High Chancellor?"

To Harvey Bingham, the question was an absurd one. Of course he *wasn't* ready. He'd spent months in virtual solitude — how could he be ready to address hundreds of thousands of people? He'd been a great orator once, but he'd had a *cause* then, and an unwavering belief in his own righteousness. It was entirely different to contemplate delivering a speech when you weren't divinely sanctioned and inspired. How could he effectively deliver the message when he didn't believe in his own authority?

But First Lord Caine was being sensitive to his situation, and Harvey deeply appreciated the Earther's compassion. The High Chancellor was terribly ashamed of his history with Caine, and was still surprised the First Lord was willing to give him a second chance.

The past days had been spent discussing how to deal with the persistent desertions. The First Lord had thought an address targeted at all human citizens by Elizabeth Hastings would be the best method, but Harvey had been acutely aware of how the ex-Crusaders might respond to an exclusively-Naval address. Earther kindness had helped them turn from their fanatical past, but tensions still existed between their group and the Navy. Even if the Crusaders wished to stay with the Alliance, they might start a movement of class-based violence against the Navy, accusing them of being traitors of this new-found paradise.

As his personal experience so aptly proved, people with firm religious convictions could turn to patently wrong acts. Despite his personal uncertainties, he would have to lead them away from this path.

Civil unrest was in no one's best interest, so Harvey had suggested a message of freedom under the Gods be added to the broadcast — to show the Navy how the Genesis faith had evolved. Over the past months Harvey hadn't been privy to the personal lives of his once-Crusaders, but the Earthers made it clear they were reforming... the Earther Consulate seemed to believe that they would be ready to accept his new brand of leadership, and perhaps rebuild the positive aspects of their old faith to support an integrated society. No longer an overbearing monolith, the Church could promote human solidarity and offer a united front with the Navy to encourage Crusaders and Naval persons to cooperate. It was a small step, but a most important one — humanity would begin to find unity.

Caine had been pleased with the idea when he'd heard it. Complimenting Harvey's attention to detail several times over the past few days, the First Lord was beginning to help restore the High Chancellor's faith in his own abilities. But there was a long road ahead before Bingham would feel ready... indeed, he would probably never have the confidence he once had. Instead, he'd have to make do with reassurances and hope...

"Harvey?"

Bingham blinked, returning slowly to reality, "Sorry, Lord Caine. Just thinking."

Caine nodded with a brief smile; he'd been guilty of off-track thinking himself. He could hardly blame the High Chancellor — after all, he was about to do his first public address since before he'd *reformed*.

And 'reformed' barely scratched the surface of the metamorphosis that had seemingly taken hold in the High Chancellor. Caine was actually growing to like the man — something he'd never dreamed possible. For the first few days he'd feared the affinity he felt for Bingham was premature, but in addition to the high esteem in which Elandra seemed to hold Harvey, the Chancellor's attitude and contributions of the past days spoke for themselves. He was certainly different — now time would tell whether he could make good his past mistakes.

Caine managed to catch himself before his thoughts spiraled away as Bingham's had, "Well, we should go meet ArcGeneral Hastings before we head to the broadcast booth."

Harvey stiffened, then consciously forced himself to move forward, "Right. Let's do that."

Hastings heard the door open — finally — and turned her chair to face the newcomers. She froze as she saw the pair enter the briefing room. Then anger forced her immediately to her feet.

Harvey Bingham, wearing the traditional crimson cape of the Church uniform, and looking the same as he had aboard the bridge of *Genesis* a year before, cut a menacing shape. It really was her once-nemesis...

Caine quickly interposed himself between the ArcGeneral and her past enemy, "Liz, you know the High Chancellor."

Bingham stiffly edged around the First Lord, offering Hastings a nervous nod. The ArcGeneral had not seen him since that encounter in the Sydney hospital eight months before. Since then she'd been told the man's memory had returned, and that Elandra Caine had been his only real companion and friend. But she'd never believed the rumors she'd heard about him being a different man — his absence from the public eye had suggested to her that he was trying to hide his continued fanaticism until he could find a way unleash it.

It was a rash conclusion, to be sure, and she realized that as Caine locked eyes with her and gave a reassuring nod. Liz ground her jaw and forced herself to admit why she was so angry: aside from a long-held hatred of this man, it was the chance that he, his Church, and his Crusaders would be better prepared to advance human society in this system than would her Naval personnel. She thought so highly of her crews, her loyal Navy... she didn't want to believe Crusaders could actually be better citizens. But the Earthers were turning the Crusaders into a progressive human demographic, using only gentle persuasion, patience, and an inundation of Earther culture for millions of men who'd been settled provisionally in Earth's major cities. While the Navy fought over how best to work with the Earthers, the Church was *working*... and here was Bingham, a symbol of everything Liz wanted to despise, and now everything she feared.

As Bingham slowly edged around Caine, Hastings caught his eyes. Just as had been the case months before, they didn't bear the cunning and malice she expected to see in the man she'd readily call her mortal enemy. They were tired, kind, determined eyes... A part of her still wanted to scream at him, to exact *some* justice for all the people he'd killed. But reason was much louder than anger in her thoughts. Truly reformed or not, she could use this man — make him work to create justice in the wake of his destruction, compel him to redeem himself by helping the Navy. If his agenda turned out to be suspect, neither she nor the Earthers would tolerate his public return for long before seeing him sequestered again.

Hastings' eyes fixed on Bingham's, and he stared back apprehensively, unwilling to look away. Could he really have changed?

If Caine trusted him with this address, then perhaps he had. Perhaps in regaining his memory he'd learned something more about himself... perhaps the influence of the Earthers had helped him cast his life in a different light. It was a possibility, at least.

So Hastings slowly forced the tension from her muscles, backing down and offering the High Chancellor a civilized nod.

"ArcGeneral, it's been quite some time," Bingham's words were soft.

Hastings eased herself down into her chair and nodded, "It has, High Chancellor. I can't honestly say I've missed you."

Bingham's expression remained neutral and he offered his own nod, "That is perfectly understandable."

Caine gestured Bingham into a chair on the opposite side of the table from Hastings, then seated himself on a third side. Hastings watched the two find their places, then turned to the First Lord, "We're still broadcasting in an hour?"

"If that's alright with you, yes."

Hastings nodded and looked across the table. Bingham met her gaze once again, his expression showing strength — as far as Liz could see, his transformation, assuming it was legitimate, hadn't erased his ability to appear assured. But in Harvey's mind it was a most spectacular bluff. He was ashamed to see Hastings again, ashamed to share a room with her and ashamed to meet her eyes. There was much that he had done which he expected could never be forgiven. Now all he could do was remain calm, maintain his presence of mind, and do all he could to earn some acceptance from a woman who had no obligation to be civil with him.

In what seemed to Bingham a testament to her character, though, Liz Hastings was being equally — *painfully* — polite. Sitting as a third party who'd gone from hating to at least respecting Bingham — and not without difficulty — Setter Caine could see her doubt. That was understandable... but hopefully it would fade.

"How are we to be seated when we broadcast, First Lord?" Bingham spoke, eyes remaining on Hastings. "Side by side? The ArcGeneral speaks and then I do?"

Caine nodded, though neither human was watching him. "We'll keep you both in the same shot for the visual broadcasts, and when you introduce yourself Liz, you should probably introduce Harvey... it would mean a lot coming from you," Caine's words were quiet.

At the mention of Bingham's name, Hastings broke the stare and looked quickly to Caine. It was awkward to hear an Earther refer to Bingham by his first name — she would never have used it in the past, except perhaps to mock him...

"Right. Introduce High Chancellor Bingham."

Caine nodded again, the gesture being received more positively the second time, "Very well. Let's go over our notes. We're due in the booth in fifteen minutes."

The bear behind the camera was outgoing and friendly as the two humans entered his broadcast booth. The area was filled with typical Earther furnishings — a simple gray desk in front of two comfortable chairs, backed by a glass window overlooking London.

Hastings took a moment to gaze over the Earther-refined city. London wasn't the same metropolis that had once been the home of Sarah Manchester's ancestors, but the Earthers had tried to revive as much of the old city's character as possible in their new construction. Most of the human buildings had been eliminated by a small nuclear device set off during the chaos brought on after the release of the Omega Virus, so the Earthers had rebuilt it from scratch. Now it served as the home of Earther Admiralty House, and it made the perfect backdrop for her broadcast. *Their* broadcast.

Hastings glanced at Bingham. He was getting properly seated in his chair, thanking several Earther stagehands for their help with his awkward cape. He'd finally elected to remove the damned thing, and now he was even loosening the top snaps on his tunic — things no High Chancellor would have ever dreamed of doing before. His appearance turned from formal to friendly with the opening of two snaps, and again Hastings wondered about this supposed change.

"We're ready for you, ArcGeneral," the camera operator called, and Hastings turned and offered a polite smile to the industrious-looking black bear, then found her seat.

Fifteen minutes later, Caine sat half-on, half-off his desk. He'd spent surprisingly little time in his office in London; it was perched in the sunniest quarter of Admiralty House, but of late he hadn't been planetside long enough to enjoy it.

"We now bring you a special message from the Office of the Genesis Navy and from the Office of the Genesis Church," an anonymous voice came over Caine's viewer.

Hastings and Bingham appeared in Caine's holo tank, side by side and smiling politely.

"Good day, human citizens of Earth. As you know, I'm ArcGeneral Hastings and I'm here with High Chancellor Bingham..." Bingham nodded and broadened his smile at Hastings' words, "... and we wish to address an issue which has been coming to the forefront of our society lately. High Chancellor, would you like to begin?"

Caine frowned. Then he blinked and frowned at the invitation. What exactly was she doing?

They'd planned to let her speak first, set everything up. Was she comfortable with his presence, or was she testing him? Bingham started speaking immediately, the change in his character reflected in his friendly tone and kind expression. He and Liz would probably never be comfortable together in the same room, but at least they'd both do their jobs.

For the next half hour Caine joined a captive audience of Earthers and humans as two old nemeses spoke to all the inhabitants of Earth about the role of humanity in Sol, and of the Church and the Navy on Earth.

CHAPTER 7

"Okay, what do we know about Krogg sensor systems?" Fox Magnus watched the time tick down as he asked the question — the Destroyers weren't far from detection range.

No one answered, and he realized he was the only person on *Flame* who'd been given the info packet on Krogg ship capabilities. It didn't matter anyway because the question had been essentially rhetorical. Krogg ships were bred to fight and all their systems were based on 'natural' body functions... some more loosely than others. That meant their sensors were a modified sort of semi-telepathic sonar system — the same kind of sonar that let bats and dolphins navigate back on Earth, just using different forms of energy. These ships sent out some sort of tele-pulses in all directions and then detected any reflections. He had to find a way to use that to his advantage.

Of course, the telepaths running Krogg ships could also sense the presence of foreign objects — there wasn't much he could do about that. But hopefully they couldn't target their weapons based on that telepathic sense alone, so as long as he could evade the sonar...

The revelation hit Magnus like a fast-moving piece of timber, and as it did his finger stabbed the intercom key, "Chronos, can you start our energy drive and keep us stationary?"

The Lieutenant in the engine room paused a moment at the abruptness of the question and then quickly consulted the ratings in *Flame's* engine room, "We *can* — what are you up to Fox?"

Magnus grinned as the affirmative came back, "The Krogg ships use a type of tele-pulse sonar — if we can go to energy drive, the pulses might pass right through us."

Another pause over the intercom as Claw consulted with the ratings, "The intensity of our energy field might warp the sonar readings — we might still be detectable."

Magnus frowned... how could they lower the intensity? His hand clenched into a fist and he ground his jaw. He was so close — there had to be a way! Forcing his hand to open, he watched the range tick down further. They'd be detected in about a minute and a half...

Then his stare fixed on his hand, a fragment of an idea beginning to form — it had been a fist... now it was open. He started to visualize *Flame* as a swirling ball of tightly packed energy, plainly visible and easy to detect. His mind then watched the figurative hand open... extending the field, making it much less dense... much tougher to detect...

"When we're in energy drive, our energy composition is held together by a force field, right? We're packed into a tight ball to maximize our acceleration," he was talking as soon as his finger jabbed the intercom. "What if we expanded the size of the field — we could spread our energy over a larger area and minimize its intensity..."

Claw, quick on the uptake, picked up his Commander's words, "Like unclenching a fist, you mean? From a tight ball to a more spread-out field... I'm guessing we'd be a lot harder to detect..."

"Exactly!" Fox couldn't help but smile at Claw's example.

And they said Earthers weren't telepathic... Ha!

"It'll put a heavy strain on the force field generators — if they give out there'll be nothing to keep the ship together and we'll disintegrate," Claw warned evenly.

The possibility didn't phase the young fox. He knew his ship and his crew would keep things together... literally, in this case.

"A chance we have to take. Do it," Magnus watched the Destroyers close on his position, his heart rate increasing along with that of the rest of *Flame's* crew.

"Drive coming online..." Claw's voice came over the intercom.

The energy drive hummed soothingly, and from the outside it appeared as though *Flame* had collapsed into a swirling ball of light blue energy.

"We're guessing we can stretch the field to about 250 percent of normal, Fox. Any more and the generators will blow," Claw continued. "We're starting to open the field now."

"We estimate one minute to detection range," the Sensor Chief reported, receiving a nod in reply from Magnus.

"We're at 125 percent and increasing... 130 percent," Claw's voice became more urgent.

Fox was picturing *Flame's* light blue energy ball expanding into a thinner cloud, then spreading further and fading against the black canvas of space.

"A little faster if you can, Chronos," he said as the Krogg Destroyers drew ever closer.

"Forty seconds, sir."

"Right, 180 percent, and spreading..."

"Thirty seconds, sir."

"200."

"Twenty seconds, sir."

"220."

"Ten... nine... eight... seven..."

"Increase the rate, we've got no choice... 235 percent, Fox..."

Flame began to vibrate slightly as the force field surrounding it spread out even further at a heightened speed, the ship (in energy form) expanding to fill the energy bottle.

"Four... three... two... one..."

"That's it! Lock the field! We're out at 250 percent, Fox."

The vibration eased as the sloop stabilized, its drives humming more noticeably because of the excess strain.

"We're in sensor range, sir. If they can detect us, it'll be now," the Sensor Chief's voice was tense, and the entire ship seemed to tremble with apprehension.

"Bridge to gun deck; Lang, be ready if we need you," Magnus gave the order despite his hopes.

"Fox, to disengage the drive, we'll have to pull the field back to 100 percent or we'll return to regular matter in pieces spread over this large an area," Claw interjected over the intercom.

Magnus sighed and nodded to himself. They couldn't fire while under energy drive, and since reintegrating would take time, having the guns crewed likely wouldn't do much good. But somehow, it *felt* better to have them ready, even if it would ultimately feel *much* better if they weren't needed...

Fox turned to the Sensor Chief, "Any sign of detection?"

The Chief shook his head silently, watching his monitors hypnotically, "No change in base course or scanning intensity. They're going to pass us, sir. Soon."

As the Chief said this, Magnus watched the icons of the Krogg Destroyers come into relative pistol-shot of his sloop. They weren't deviating from their standard pattern... they were just coming straight on...

And passing little *Flame*, now a faint blue haze against the stars.

Magnus let out a well-deserved sigh of relief and *Flame's* crew joined him.

"So, how much speed can you give me in this state, Chronos?"

Claw pondered the question momentarily, checking the gauges in his engine room, "About 400 pls, I think."

"Good, helm, let's head in-system, 100 pls for now," Magnus gave the order with refreshing confidence, and *Flame* began to close with the planet Genesis.

"Skipper, long-range watch here. You might want to come take a look at this."

Magnus was watching *Flame's* progress on the bridge's center holo tank when the call came in.

"Cruising Master, you have the ship," Fox ordered as he got to his feet. The operators of *Flame's* long-range detectors wouldn't be calling him unless they'd found something important.

The Commander quickly crossed *Flame's* small bridge and stepped into the lift. After a few moments and a short journey across his small ship, he found himself in the sensor suite.

The head sensor technician was leaning over her readouts, consulting her two fellow operators. She turned to see Magnus as he stepped into the room, "Sir, there's something very odd out there."

Magnus quickly came to stand beside the coyote at the central holo display. The three-dimensional projection showed a fairly detailed map of the Genesis system, including the asteroid belt that surrounded its outer rim — thousands of black icons, and...

"What is *that*?" Magnus' finger stabbed into the projection and pierced a distorted blob just beyond the inner perimeter of the asteroid belt.

"That's what we wanted you to see. It's distorting our pulses pretty badly, and the Krogg ships seem to be in a defensive pattern around it," the Senior Chief explained.

"Some sort of black hole?"

The coyote shook her head, "Not enough grav shear. We're thinking some sort of spatial anomaly — a wormhole, maybe."

Magnus eyed the blob closely, "Something a lot like that I'd bet, Chief. How many Krogg ships do you count in-system? Looks like a lot."

The Chief nodded again, keying a few of her controls to make the black dots in the projection flash, "We were expecting about two, maybe three hundred based on what the Genesis people told us. But so far we see about *3,000*."

Fox had seen the same Genesis estimates. The assumption had been that the Kroggs might move in some larger forces to protect the system while the Genesis Fleet was gone, and Ursla's recent warnings had suggested even as many as 1,000 ships. So she was only *2,000* short in her guess. *Oops.*

Magnus cocked an eyebrow, "So either the Genesis intelligence was very wrong, or the Kroggs are planning something. I bet on option two. You?"

The Chief nodded, "The reports we have from the Genesis intel say that anomaly... *whatever* it is... is in space that belongs to the Kroggs. That's where they've been keeping their base, near as we can tell."

"So now that the Genesis Fleet is out of their way, they're doing something untoward," Magnus paused in thought. "Very well. Have you covered the entire system?"

"Yes sir, good images clear to the other side, and a few nice close-ups of the base."

"Alright, pay attention to their pickets as we leave."

Magnus left the sensor suite, knowing the knowledge they'd gathered would give the Admirals and ArcGenerals plenty to think about. As he walked to the bridge lift, he reflected on the size of the fleet guarding that unidentified *something* near the asteroid belt. It would doubtless prove important to the upcoming operations in Genesis... not too bad for a day's work.

The flag officers would need this information quickly, and recognizing that fact, he barked orders as soon as he emerged onto his bridge, "Helm, get us out of here, 400 pls."

CHAPTER 8

Archangel Sword decelerated from flux drive more efficiently than any other human ship. The combination of Earther and Genesis technologies had given the Battlecruiser a certain immunity to many of flux drive's original problems, something ArcColonel Stanton did have to admit he was happy about. Decelerating from flux had never been a favorite part of his Naval career.

Now, as his ship arrived in what had been dubbed 'Renegade's Belt', he was gripped by the reality that his Naval career was over... He wasn't with the fleet anymore.

"Deceleration complete, sir," Stanton's Helm Officer reported, nudging the ArcColonel from his brooding.

"Any sign of other Genesis ships in this region?"

There had been rumors that the Genesis ships coming out this way had formed something of a Coalition, and that interested newcomers could rendezvous at the Belt to investigate joining. A couple of days outside the Sol system, but far off the direct path to Genesis, it was out-of-the-way enough to be safe from angry human patrols.

"I don't have any ships on sensors, sir, but I do have debris fields... four separate ones," the Sensor Officer reported slowly.

"Transponders?" Stanton asked in reply.

"Three fields have surviving transponders, yes sir. The ships *Vanguard Paladin*, *Vandercamp City* and *Dornier Town*. The fourth field is big enough to be a Light Cruiser."

Stanton pondered the report briefly — a Battlecruiser, Heavy Cruiser, and two Light Cruisers lost at this rendezvous point. Was it a trap? His mind piqued with the thought of having been baited into danger.

Could the rumors have been spread by the Navy? A vengeful squadron of Genesis Dreadnoughts could be lurking somewhere, waiting for their moment of surprise... Well, there was nothing keeping him here, and *Sword* was faster than any Genesis ship in space...

"Engineering, get the drives spinning back up, get ready for flu–"

"Sir! Ships decelerating to starboard!" the Sensor Chief came out of her chair slightly as she barked her report, and Stanton quickly turned his chair towards her.

"What do you have?"

"Genesis construction... a Superdreadnought, three Battlecruisers... two Heavy Cruisers, a Light Cruiser and four Destroyers. Closing with us fast, sir. Make it .55 cee."

Stanton spun to the main monitor as the ships' icons appeared, "Battle stations. Engineering, get me those drives."

"Another ship is coming in port. It's a lot closer... it's *Grendelsbane City*... closing at .78 cee... Looks like it's taken some damage."

Stanton called up the sensor plot on his personal screen, "ETA on that squadron?"

A pause, "About four minutes to weapons range sir. *Grendelsbane* is almost in range now..."

What in hell's gulags was going on here? Had he tripped over a picket or what? *Grendelsbane* had deserted and was now *damaged*... perhaps it was another victim trying to spring *Sword* from the trap...

"Signal coming in from *Grendelsbane City* sir, it's ArcColonel DeBrooke," the Comm Officer cut in hurriedly.

Stanton ground his jaw, his question about to be answered.

"Put it up," he replied.

It took a second for the message to come through space, be received and piped up to the monitor buffer, but in a relatively short space of time ArcColonel Audrey DeBrooke appeared on the screen. She and Stanton had been in the same provisional squadron during the battle with the Church Fleet, but he didn't know her well.

"Stanton, thank Gods! You have to get away from that fleet *immediately!*" DeBrooke wasted no time on niceties.

"What the hell is going on?" Stanton's question was demanding and almost angry, but DeBrooke didn't seem to notice his agitation. She had a recently-healed wound on her forehead — a shrapnel gash by the looks of it — but it was unclear what that might suggest in terms of her allegiance.

"Those bastards are the *Coalition* we heard about. They set up a raiding force to attack Genesis and Earther shipping — they'll try to recruit you and if you say no they'll blow you to bits... unless you're interested you'd better get out of here!" DeBrooke's warning was the sort of clear and direct assessment Stanton expected from a professional Naval officer, and he greatly appreciated it just now.

And of course he wasn't interested in making war on Genesis and Earth. He'd found it hard to believe all the deserters would cooperate towards a productive end — things were altogether too complex for that to happen so soon. These Coalition members must have been the most disloyal of those who'd left. Unfortunately, they were very well armed for dissenting mutineers...

So *Sword* would have to cut and run... but why hadn't *Grendelsbane* already done that?

"Why are you still here, Audrey? Surely they're after you, with what you know," Stanton voiced his question, and the junior ArcColonel shook her head sadly in reply.

"They knocked out our flux drive when they first hit us. We managed to limp into a nebula and evade them at sub-light, but all we've gotten back is short-jump capability. We'll try to slow them down — you have to get word of this back to Earth."

Stanton cocked an eyebrow at the young woman, "You don't have a chance of holding them..."

A sad smile formed on her face, "Speak for yourself, ArcColonel. We've got our eyes set on the Superdreadnought, and believe me, we'll give them hell. Your drives are good; there's no point us both dying out here."

Stanton frowned and leaned back in his chair. What she suggested was logical, but it struck him as entirely wrong — she'd kept her ship alive all this time for a reason, and that reason had to be better than simply saving *Sword* and getting a brief word to Earth about troubles out here. No, even without the bonds of a common Naval service left to tie him to *Grendelsbane*, Stanton wouldn't leave the courageous cruiser to die. If nothing else, he'd help set a new trend for behavior among deserting ships. And it wasn't a hopeless mission; if he had his way, both ships would live... Stanton quickly scanned his star charts and found a nebula nearby.

"You hid in nebula XK41-1 before?" he questioned abruptly.

DeBrooke frowned and then glanced off her screen before nodding.

"Jump back there. We'll slow them down and join you. We're carrying replacement parts for flux drives — we can fix up your engines–" Stanton was already turning away from the screen to begin giving orders, but DeBrooke's words brought him back to her image.

"How can you hold them when we can't? It's better to save the intact ship, James!"

"Audrey," Stanton said with a twitch of a smile, "*Sword's* become a hybrid. We're a mix of Earther and Genesis tech now. We can hold them for a bit, trust me. Get out of here. We'll follow you presently."

DeBrooke stared at her counterpart for a few seconds, a certain respect filling her eyes. She wouldn't even have expected this sort of selflessness from a fellow ArcColonel when she was in the Genesis service — it was hard to know what to say to James Stanton right now.

"Thank you, ArcColonel," her words were much less edgy than before. "Good hunting. Good *luck*."

The two rogue commanders exchanged nods and then DeBrooke vanished from the screen. Stanton forced the fears that she was right to the back of his mind — it was *Sword's* turn to perform.

"*Grendelsbane City* is moving off... it's accelerating into flux. The squadron is closing fast now... standard battle formation," the reports came from the Sensor Officer.

Steepling his fingers, James watched the approach on the main screen. These Coalition bastards didn't know what *Sword* could do... he'd play by unconventional rules and they'd have no idea what was going on...

"Good. Load tubes and charge carronades. Activate shields and armor. Bring us up to full speed, oblique vector relative to their base course," James' instinct for command began taking over. "We'll swing in fast and hit the Superdreadnought, try to get them off balance. They'll probably try to run us down with their cruisers... make sure the stern chasers are standing by for missiles. Engineering, keep the drives ready."

"Getting a hail from the Superdreadnought, skipper," the Comm Officer's report followed smoothly, and James took a breath.

"Send text in reply..." now what could he say that was appropriate?

The bridge crew exchanged understandably nervous glances — they were about to tangle with a rather powerful squadron, after all.

What to say... hmm... aha...

"Send to them: 'Surrender to my independent authority or you will face the consequences.' And don't accept any further replies."

The bridge crew was slightly surprised by the bravado, but slowly a wave of good cheer swept over them. They might be dead in ten minutes, but that was no reason to disgrace the dignity of the ship.

A few acknowledgements came from the appropriate officers and spacers as battle systems came online and the message was sent. And then *Sword* leapt forward, hybrid energy flowing through its shields and weapons.

"They just received the message, sir... and they're bearing down on us. Closing to weapons range now. About twenty seconds."

"Our acceleration is up, sir. Our course is ninety-seven by forty-six by twenty-two."

"Tactical systems are live."

The crew's confidence reassured Stanton, not that he was particularly uncomfortable with the situation. He was completely confident in the abilities of his people and this ship, even though the Earther enhancements had never been tested in action. Now, as he watched the Coalition ships close, a sense of mild excitement began to flow through the bridge — for better or worse, this was the start of their new, independent life.

"Closing now, sir. We'll be in range of the SD in nine... eight..."

"Incoming missiles... point defense active."

The outer elements of the Coalition Squadron had flushed their tubes at him. So be it — *Archangel Sword* handled even more neatly than a human Battlecruiser, and its carronades had triple the protective coverage of standard human lasers.

"Shift course nineteen points to starboard, up angle fifteen. Take us right at the SD," Stanton's words were cool and the crew's response immediate.

Sword surged ahead at blistering speed, missiles driving past it as its vector changed. The Coalition Superdreadnought had not been expecting the smaller vessel to aim directly for it — it would have made more sense for the Battlecruiser to challenge a ship of equal or lesser class.

"Weapons range on the SD... *now!*" the report was excited, and the response was swift.

"Hold missiles to point blank. Carronades stand by to bombard as we pass. I want that son of a bitch out of action!" Stanton bit his lip at the outburst, and resolved to curb his eagerness... but if they could cut the head off this Coalition, chances of them chasing *Sword* and *Grendelsbane City* would be slim.

The Battlecruiser rocked now as the lasers of the ships closer to the Superdreadnought pounded its shields. Had *Sword* been a standard Genesis ship, it'd have been carved up quite effectively by the withering fire, but as it was, Earther shields stopped each beam in space, halting the shots 100 meters from the outer armor.

"Point-blank range in three seconds, sir."

Stanton let a thin smile form on his face, leaned forward in his chair, counted to three, and then snarled the order: "*Fire!*"

Sword, like most human Battlecruisers, had sixty missile tubes, all aiming forward. Unlike most human ships, however, its launchers were augmented with Earther 'catapults' — vastly improved versions of those mass driver rigs which lobbed the missiles out at high velocity like bullets, giving them an extra surge of acceleration before their own drives kicked in. Now inside point-blank range, *Sword's* missiles rammed into the Superdreadnought's hull before their onboard computers even tried to fire internal drives. They hit at almost .97 cee.

The Superdreadnought seemed to collapse in on itself, the skin on its starboard side evaporating and leaving the hull without a great deal of support. The massive warship's velocity dropped off and it began to somersault toward its consorts as its drives imbalanced.

The ships in the Coalition Squadron seemed to collectively freeze in shock at the destruction, their fire halting and their helms going hard over to avoid the flailing capital ship. In the four seconds of inattention, Stanton ordered *Archangel Sword* into flux. They would meet *Grendelsbane City* in nebula XK41-1 and decide where to go from there.

CHAPTER 9

"Three *thousand*? Gods wept!"

Pat didn't even attempt to contain his surprise as he sat in *Agamemnon's* briefing room. The Earther and Genesis Fleet commanders looked at him with half-relieved, half-amused expressions, appreciating his frank assessment of the circumstances.

He shrugged, "Well what do you expect me to say? 'Ooh, Kroggs, *lovely!*'?"

Pat's attitude helped lighten the mood in the room, and ease some of the tension that had been building steadily since Fox Magnus started presenting his sloop's findings. The intrepid Commander had joined the meeting to explain all that had gone on during *Flame's* mission, beginning with the method he'd used to evade the search squadrons of Krogg ships. His quick thinking had rightfully impressed a room full of the Alliance's best Naval officers.

After gathering his data, *Flame's* 400 pls run out of Genesis had been easy. Fox had chosen a relatively 'upward' course for the trip, then had dropped out of energy drive just beyond the Allied Fleet's outer picket. Now, six hours later, the news he brought was reaching the senior officers. As the room sobered, he continued his explanation, aided by a holo projection of the system he'd brought from *Flame's* long-range sensor suite.

"Yes sir, 3,000. But that's just the start. We detected some sort of significant anomaly here," Fox's finger directed the attendees' attention to the blob he'd first seen in the sensor suite. "As you can see, the fleet seems to be mainly arrayed to defend *that*."

"From something in-system or from what might come through?" Vice Admiral Talone asked quietly, and Fox shrugged.

"At this stage no one can really know, I'm afraid. Their formations appear haphazard at best, and they didn't shuffle their order at all while we were in a position to watch. The good news, sirs, ma'ams, is that our path straight into Genesis — the planet that is — is relatively clear. Other than the Mothership, the pickets and internal squadrons only total about fifty ships, most of them light," Magnus slowly brought his finger through the holo from the system edge to Genesis itself, then looked up.

"Now, I've been mulling this over since I first saw the scans, though I may not have all the info you folks do. Still, my own impression of their deployment is that these–" his finger returned to the ships surrounding the blob "–were wedded to that position. All those ships could have made their sweep for *Flame* much quicker, but they didn't budge. My instinct says they've got fairly serious concerns and they have no intention of leaving that patrol zone."

Varnon Broadpaw scratched his chin, "You're thinking they'll stay there if we move in-system — even if we blow through their pickets to do it?"

Fox tilted his head and half-shrugged, "I can't speak with any authority on it, sir. But that blob is obviously important to them…"

Jax Furgus leaned forward, "And, Varn, I imagine 1,500 ships would make them think twice about moving. They don't know who we are, after all, so they'd have to send everything to be sure — especially if we're clean about handling the pickets. I don't get the impression they'd gladly strip that thing's defenses when they don't know if there are more of us. Better for them to wait and see."

There were a few nods of agreement, but Pat cocked an eyebrow, "That's all true Jax, but you forget they know *us*. Genesis ships, that is. If it weren't for you lot being here, they could send 100 ships and damn near bludgeon us."

"But why would they move to kill a returning Genesis Fleet, Pat? You got rid of their pickets cleanly, so I'd imagine they'd be more inclined to ask first and *then* shoot…" Varnon looked to Pat and the Irishman ground his jaw.

"Fair point, I suppose. Just too used to blowing them up already," Pat offered a pleasant smile.

Varnon chuckled, "Well it doesn't even matter so much, because we *are* here. So we'll just have to look bigger and scarier. Even if they got wind of what you've been doing to their pickets, we can hope they aren't arrogant enough to assume they can simply wipe us out… because they may think they can."

There was a pause at the table, and Fox began to feel a little awkward — witnessing a debate between flag officers generally fell outside the purview of a sloop commander's job.

Sensing his discomfort, Ursla nodded to him, "Thanks Fox. Well done. You should head back to your ship."

There were murmurs of agreement from everyone around the table, and Pat offered the Commander his hand, "Damned fine work. From one cruiser skipper to another."

Fox smiled with pride as each of the flag officers shook his hand as he rounded the table; he came to Ursla last.

"We'll need you again, I think, Fox," she said quietly.

"*Flame's* ready ma'am. Just give the orders," he nodded in solemn reply and she smiled.

With that, the young Commander left the briefing room, and headed directly to the landing bay for a return flight to his ship.

"Well, I'm betting he gets a squadron of 74s in two years or less," Pat grinned, and there were a few chuckles from the assembled officers before matters turned more grave.

Ursla leaned forward in her chair, "So, we think the Kroggs are wedded to that position, but it could just as easily be a mundane rally point, commanded by an officer not too interested in sensor blips. If it were *me*, I'd turn on any force half my size and eliminate it quickly..."

Broadpaw leaned forward but Ursla waved him back for a moment, *"First,* I think we need to figure out what exactly that thing is. Sarah, any ideas?"

Sarah had been wondering about the anomaly since the Commander had displayed the projection. She cast questioning glances at Pat and her two ArcLieutenant-Generals, but all returned baffled looks.

"We thought that part of space was open," Sarah paused, studying the figures on her pad. "But from the sorts of characteristics *Flame's* scans picked up, I don't think our sensors could have seen it. The Kroggs designed most of our detection gear, and it looks like the... *rift* is invisible to our scans. And that area of space is restricted to traffic by the Kroggs, so no ship ever gets through there without escort. I suppose now we know why. We used to think the Kroggs were mining the asteroids in the region, but we never got to have a look. This thing could have been there since we landed on Genesis and we wouldn't have known any better."

Ursla frowned thinly, "If they didn't want you to see it, it could be significant to them..."

"They're sure guarding it well. They have more firepower watching it than we have here *and* in the Sol system," Bill Masters noted quietly. "They obviously do care about it."

The room fell silent for a moment, as stares pierced the projection of the rift in a futile attempt to gain some additional insight into its nature.

As Pat leaned forward and squinted at the holo he recalled a battle he'd been part of as an ArcEnsign.

"Umm... hate to state the obvious, but what about the Larosians? If I'm not too far off, Sarah, that's the vector most Larosian squadrons come in on. Draw a line from it to Genesis, and that's the axis most of our battles are fought on," Pat's finger entered the holo and traced a rough line from the rift to the planet. "There's the 'Divinity' Battle site... and here's good old 'Holy Light'."

The Earthers looked curiously from Pat to Sarah, and the latter frowned, then nodded, "Indeed. That's the direction they always come from..." her mind shifted gears as she contemplated the new variable. "It could be some sort of fixed defensive structure... but that wouldn't make sense, it'd be readable if it was, and the Larosians could just go around it."

Again the room grew quiet as everyone present tried to tie two unrelated universes of thought together... Sarah blinked.

Tie two unrelated universes together... galaxies together... we're talking wormholes here!

She spoke up immediately, "If that's some sort of interspatial wormhole or rift or... well it doesn't matter specifically what... it could be a tie to a war in a completely separate section of the galaxy. And that could explain where the attacks have been coming from. But they've never had so many ships in-system before. No matter how badly they handicapped our sensors, they couldn't hide that many dynamic drive signatures from our scans."

"Maybe they were waiting for your fleet to leave — they could be mounting an assault on the Larosians while there's no one around to interfere," Broadpaw suggested.

There were a few thoughtful nods, but Ursla was already drawing on her conversation with Artemis Tigar, "No, they're mounting a defense."

The comment earned her the room's attention.

Somewhat surprised at the reaction, she explained herself, "While we were in transit, Artie Tigar and I spoke about why the Kroggs would be using the Genesis Fleet to defend this system, instead of their own force. He concluded — and I now completely agree — that they didn't want the Larosians to realize that Kroggs actually held the system. But now that the Genesis Fleet isn't at their disposal, they've got to compensate with their own force. The fact that they've deployed 3,000 ships must mean they're expecting company. Look again at their fleet's order — those ships aren't in any formation I'd use if I was going *through* a thin corridor. But that sort of inverted sphere..." Ursla's finger lifted and pointed out the thick mass of Krogg ships, "...is ideal for putting a lot of fire down onto anything that comes out."

"You think the Larosians are coming through?" ArcLieutenant-General Hargreaves offered the question. "Genesis is a trap for the Larosians?"

Ursla let one of her eyebrows climb, "Think about it. If all the Larosian survivors ever sent back was word of a — and pardon this, but I'm thinking from their perspective — a crude, local, space-faring civilization, they'd never expect to find a Krogg battle force out here."

Sarah frowned, "But why would they come through now?"

Ursla paused and ground her jaw, trying to imagine the plans developed at the strategy table for an interstellar war...

Jax Furgus was a shade ahead of her, "They must know something we don't. There's a war going on, according to what the Kroggs told you... so if the Larosians are getting pushed back on the other side of that thing, there's a good chance they might try to retreat through it..."

"So hypothetically," Broadpaw picked up his junior's thought, "the Kroggs are drawing a Larosian Fleet into the grinder. They'll destroy the scouting squadron and suck the entire fleet into a bottleneck. Then they can probably counterattack against an open flank."

Ursla nodded, "The Larosians would think Genesis isn't a threat, and then they discover a very large fleet here... and I imagine we'd see a battle much larger than anything we've experienced."

The room dropped into another uncomfortable silence. If — and it was a *very* big *if* — this was the case, they'd managed to stumble back to Genesis at precisely the moment when two galactic titans were rolling up their sleeves and getting ready to hammer each other to pieces.

If the Genesis Navy truly was serious about ejecting the Kroggs from its home system, this could be called a spectacular opportunity, assuming their suppositions were correct. What that meant for the Earther Second Fleet was a separate matter. Ursla knew full well that if Genesis held firm in its resolve against the Kroggs it would mean the involvement of the Earther Navy in an interstellar war.

"I'll be damned if Genesis is used against the Larosians any longer," Sarah's words were cool and firm. "The Kroggs have sent us to kill Larosians and die in their stead for centuries, and we came here to put an end to that. If we're right about this, the people of Genesis have been nothing more than pawns for all that time. No, my ships will be after those Kroggs as soon as I see Larosians in the area."

The Earthers at the table exchanged quick glances, and Varnon caught Sarah's eye, "And if we're totally wrong?"

Sarah looked to the Earther wolf, silently considering the question. What if they over-committed based on non-intelligence — on the gut feelings of fleet officers. It was a very pertinent concern.

"I don't mean to speak for you, Sarah," Ursla nodded to her human friend, then looked to Varnon, "but the Genesis Fleet's core mission is still to get the Church out of power, and one component of that comes in dealing with the Kroggs. Any potential Larosian involvement is a secondary issue."

Pat leaned forward in his chair with a mild frown, "It'd just make our lives a bit easier if they came, perhaps."

Sarah nodded slowly, "Agreed. We can't afford to cruise in with all guns blazing, just because we feel we ought to kill as many Kroggs as we can..." She paused and swallowed thoughtfully. "As far as I'm concerned, if we get the chance to help the Larosians we should take it. You all know I'm of that opinion — we owe them at least that much after killing so many... but right now that's not an issue. We must focus on getting control of Genesis."

"If we can get to the planet, we can use it as an operational base," Pat was already exploring the options attached to that line of thought. "The six orbital battle stations each mount more firepower than Colonizers, and then there's the separate planetary defense squadron of a dozen Superdreadnoughts. Though the civilian population might be put in danger if we come under fire... well, the Kroggs only have three planetside installations, and I'll bet cash they won't be expecting Earther marines. We could secure the planet from them and hold it."

There were nods around the table, but Jax Furgus interrupted them, "Hold for how long? We can hope that the Kroggs won't care when we move in, but unless we're right about the Larosians there's no reason for them *not* to come in to restore the status quo. We can summon the First and Third Fleets from Earth, as well as any more of the Genesis ships they've brought online, but even with those additional numbers we'll only have about 2,200 ships."

Ursla was already considering the problem, "Yes, if the Larosians don't show, we'd have stepped into it..."

She paused. What were the Kroggs actually protecting? That many ships, and yet none of them were orbiting the planet. Would they pounce if someone took control of Genesis orbital space... or would they stay out there?

Varnon Broadpaw leaned forward with his thoughts, "If they were worried about the planet, they'd be there. I think they're protecting something else. I think, if we move in and stay safe in Genesis orbit, they won't come at us. Because whatever they're guarding is more important to them than Genesis is. And they don't know who we are, or what we're after. Why risk a fight with unknowns who aren't going out of their way to fight you... if you're guarding something very important? Why move away from your center of gravity?"

The wise wolf Admiral's assessment was welcome, though a small smile came to Ursla's face, "I do believe we moved to intercept our human friends on the Pluto Orbital Plane, even though we were protecting Earth."

With an ear twitch, Varnon drummed his fingers on the table, then smiled, "Well. There's that too."

A few nervous chuckles followed the observation, and Ursla sat back in her seat. A risky decision... but there was one clear point to remember: the Earthers couldn't keep their word and help the humans on Genesis if they didn't actually go to the planet. So it was time to go out on a limb, and hope the Larosians were coming...

"We go in," she said as that thought settled in her mind.

Slow nods came again from Earthers around the table.

"So are we making the assumption, then, that the Larosians are going to keep the Kroggs' attention long enough for us to get to Genesis?" Pat leaned back in his chair, eyeing his comrades thoughtfully.

Jax Furgus shrugged, "If we're wrong, the Kroggs will probably come right after us once we get in-system. Then we run, far and fast."

A grin formed on Pat's face, "Nothing to lose then. Well, that's not quite it. Worth the risk to find out, eh Sarah?"

A nagging concern still spawned reluctance in Sarah's mind, but everything did seem to fit. They'd known from the outset that they'd have to take risks to get the Church and the Kroggs out of Genesis, but she hadn't expected them to be so grand. Nonetheless, if their predictions were right, it could be worth the chance.

"I agree we should move in," she said after a moment, looking immediately to Ursla.

The three meter tall Admiral nodded to her friend, and then turned her eyes to the rest of the table, "Alright, there's no point waiting. If we're to have Larosian company I'll want to be in position at Genesis before they get here. The Second Fleet can move against Genesis tomorrow, Sarah, if you're game," Ursla met her counterpart's eyes, and Sarah nodded.

"We'll set it up. I'll get Gillian Hodge to send information on the Krogg ground facilities to General Grieve so your marines can take them."

Ursla offered another nod, "I think the Second Fleet should spearhead the strike — the Kroggs quite literally won't know what hit them. We'll probably be able to get through without casualties. When we get to Genesis orbit, though, we'll need you to tell your comrades that we're friendly."

Sarah nodded silently as Ursla spoke, mentally noting the tasks she'd have to complete.

"Alright then, we've got to figure out who goes first... Varnon, Jax, you going to flip for it, or do I have to listen to both of you prattle on?"

The two officers looked at each other with grins, but Varnon spoke up first, "I had *Algenon's* drives overhauled the week before we left. We're faster, so if it goes bad we're better at running away."

Jax Furgus cocked his eyebrow, "Now wait just a minute, First Rates can't run as fast as 64s and you know it..."

"Glad there's confidence in the plan," Ursla interjected pleasantly, and there were nervous laughs.

Tactics began to unfold.

CHAPTER 10

General Andros Grieve was glad to be doing something useful again. As the Earther Marine Corps' senior commander on the expedition to Genesis, he'd had relatively little to do on the journey between the star systems. He'd sparred with his marines on a regular basis, and re-read his files on Genesis many times, but for the most part he'd found the time very monotonous.

Most frustrating perhaps had been the knowledge that the situation was going to become particularly hectic after this long period of inactivity. Grieve and his marines — the entire First Division, spread across several squadrons of the Second Fleet — would very likely be required to land on Genesis in support of Gillian Hodge's human Naval Marines Corps, and that sort of operation would demand plenty of planning and coordination. However, he hadn't been able to pre-plan because there had been no way to know where planetside Crusaders would be deployed.

So today he needed to choose objectives, assemble strike packages, and sort out all the details of a successful assault landing.

And for the record, he'd never conducted a real combat drop before.

He was aboard *Algenon*, Varnon Broadpaw's 125-gun flagship and one of the other oversized First Rates in Ursla's Second Fleet. He'd elected to travel in this ship to free Ursla of any concerns about landing operations on Genesis — he didn't want to force her to put *Agamemnon* into Genesis orbit to drop troops when she might need to take the fleet elsewhere. Most of his troops were thus traveling with Varnon Broadpaw's squadrons, which had apparently given that Admiral the edge in a debate with Jax Furgus over who was to charge in-system first.

Of course, those were all Naval matters of limited consequence to Grieve's duty. He faced something of a hurdle in overseeing landing operations such as these — with Kroggs *and* Crusaders *and* civilians all over the place. Admittedly, though, he was looking forward to this challenge, despite the pang of uncertainty when he considered the possibility of action against the Kroggs. He trusted his marines — they were all veterans of Antarctica — but they had no first hand experience with this alien race. Reading files about their prowess could never fully prepare his troops for field action against hardened soldiers... he'd have to assume that Krogg capabilities were more significant than even the briefings suggested, and rely on his marines to rise to the occasion.

So the planning had to be meticulous. Indeed, Andros Grieve was being very deliberate with the operational layout as he sat across from Commandant Gillian Hodge in one of *Algenon's* briefing rooms. Hodge was an adept and cunning soldier, and had been commander of the marines aboard Pat Conroy's Battlecruiser during the defections from the Church. After her promotion to command of the Genesis Naval Marine Corps months before, Grieve had begun to work closely with her, and today considered her a good friend.

"Well, I wish I had better intel for you Andros, but this is it. They never let us close to the bases, and *Flame's* scans of the planet didn't give me anything more detailed to work with," Hodge slid a pad across the table into Grieve's hands. Like many other officers in this fleet, she was young for her rank, under thirty and sporting the military's traditional short-cropped hair. She looked altogether too small to be a marine, but then, to a bear like Grieve, most humans looked too small.

Staring at the pad Hodge provided, Grieve let his eyebrows rise and fall as if to punctuate his thoughts. The Kroggs seemed disinterested in the surface of Genesis, as they kept only a small ground presence there. Their three bases were on isolated islands well away from the main continent, with the largest being on the opposite side of the planet from the capital. It was estimated that this large installation housed 200 Kroggs within its building structure... and there was no telling what sort of fixed defenses it held. The other two were only outposts, with perhaps thirty Krogg soldiers and a landing pad each. Compared to Antarctic Base they were *tiny*, but they were defended by Kroggs. And Grieve had read more than enough of the Genesis Fleet's information to have a healthy respect for their potential combat capabilities.

"Well, not a whole lot I hadn't read already then. Too bad we can't slip in and drop a couple of recon squads to gather better data... I specifically took Beckett Lupus off *Cerberus* because I thought we'd have time to do some serious examination of the situation," Grieve scratched his head with his free hand.

"As I hear it Naval matters have forced us to compress the timetable," Hodge's tone reflected slight disappointment.

Grieve nodded, "Andra thinks the Larosians are on the way, so we need to conclude this business quickly. She's got some suggestions to that end — she wants us to drop after they've saturated the bases with fire from pinnace pulsars. But Kroggs would have fair warning that we're coming if we do it that way."

"More fun and excitement for us, I suppose. But I really doubt we'd catch the Kroggs napping anyway — I can't picture one of their soldiers dozing on picket duty. I doubt it'll make much of a difference if we try to soften them up. Might make things a little more conducive to survival," Hodge paused and sighed. "Frankly, none of my marines can really... well, the Kroggs are a *lot* tougher than my troops."

Grieve put the pad on the desk and looked up, lacing his fingers, "I agree.

So I think this needs to be an exclusively Earther landing — at least against the Kroggs. Your marines can stand by in case any Crusaders try to make trouble, but if Ursla pulls off her plan, the Crusaders will be on our side, for whatever that's worth. Now for the Kroggs, near as I can figure, the best shock troops in this fleet are bears. Do you mind if we take on this task ourselves? I think I can pull together a crack force from the Guards Brigade of the First Division."

Gillian didn't like the idea of letting the Earthers do all the hard work... but she also didn't like the prospect of seeing an entire regiment of her best being completely annihilated in a desperate bid to deal with the Krogg bases.

And there was no doubt the Earthers were capable in the field. The best Crusader marines — admittedly not as good as their Naval counterparts, but human nonetheless — had folded beneath the pressure of the Earther marines on the Antarctic Plain. Ursla herself had defeated a company, hand-to-hand, in open territory. She'd become a legend among the troops for her prowess, and she'd clearly demonstrated the advantage bears had on the ground. Indeed, her performance was such that Grieve was beyond considering non-bears for direct action against the Kroggs in their first encounter — raw physical power provided a certain safety net in case the encounter went badly.

So Gillian nodded with only the tiniest shred of disappointment, and the General shifted in his chair and sat forward, looking at the pad again.

"I'll call up the bears. Probably about 500 of the bigger ones. Don't want them getting overpowered by these *soldiers* of theirs," he tapped the daunting image of a four-armed Krogg soldier on the screen. "We can put everyone else in reserve. And we'll need your troops on standby to cover our flanks. Like I said, Ursla is looking into getting the Crusaders on our side, but if some of them get enterprising and want to help the Kroggs, it'll be up to you to stop them."

Activating the desk holo, Grieve brought to life a glowing three-dimensional projection of Genesis. The Krogg posts were pulsing black dots, contrasting with the light green of the planet's surface. Hodge examined the map with thoughtful eyes, "I'm guessing even if the Crusaders think you're hostile, it'll take them too long to deploy to cause you any trouble. That being said, the rash part of me wouldn't exactly mind the chance to take a few shots at them... if it comes to it I'll have regiments poised at their rally points."

Even though she wasn't desperate to get a crack at the Kroggs, Hodge was still eager to see action during the liberation of her home. And if she got the chance to put some Crusaders to rights, more the better. Her marines could easily slice up any Church force, and she wouldn't mind the chance to prove that. But her reasonable side was highly compelling in pointing out the virtue of maintaining the Earthers' advantage of surprise over both Kroggs and Churchers.

"So, we simultaneously drop 100 marines on each outpost and 300 on the central complex," Grieve continued, sensing her veiled eagerness but deciding not to comment on it. "If we're lucky, we should be able to knock them out before they get a chance to call for help."

Hodge frowned and thought of numbers — bears were tough, but on a few rare occasions she'd seen Kroggs in action. One terrorist had been quartered — literally — and then each piece halved. All before he'd hit the ground. The Earthers had their work cut out for them...

But Grieve knew what he was doing.

"So long as you keep the ratios as heavy in your favor as you can, that should work. Remember though, it may come to a lot of hand-to-hand. Better to have plenty more than you need if it turns into a brawl."

Grieve nodded, "Indeed. Alright, I'll pick my best and *biggest*. Now, we need good landing sites..."

Ursla and Sarah sat comfortably in Ursla's quarters, reviewing projections and data pads as they sorted out the best strategy for eliminating the Krogg pickets. The gravity of the situation was unmistakable and the atmosphere held a certain but unspoken undertone of seriousness. This would be their first encounter with the Kroggs, and if they handled things incorrectly there was a fleet bigger than theirs nearby, ready to crush them. So they'd already been through the plan twice, and now just the third and final reviews remained.

"So we lead with First Rates..." Ursla pointed to the simulated spearhead of the Second Fleet in the holo tank.

Sarah nodded absently, trying to envision the action as it came to pass. Thanks to the intrepid Commander Magnus, the Earther Fleet could leap off ahead of its human companion force and reach the picket ships undetected. *Some* of the Second Fleet, anyway.

The Second Fleet's entire complement of First Rates — two squadrons of eight — would go ahead, backed by three additional squadrons of 74-gun Third Rates. The force would include fewer than a third of Ursla's capital ships, but it would make a hell of a hammer. Heading straight into the inner perimeter, they would come out of energy drive within point-blank range of the Mothership squadron, and then forty-five Earther line of battle ships would smash every Krogg vessel in the area. The Genesis Fleet would slip in-system, supported by the rest of the Earther Second, sweeping up any Krogg Destroyers untouched by the first Earther strikes.

Ursla's advance strike group would hold and wait for Sarah to catch up, then enter Genesis orbit as quickly as possible. Sarah would have to alert the defense grid deployed in the space around the planet, and make sure the Earthers weren't fired upon. As soon as the defenses recognized them as friends, Grieve's marines would drop to wipe out the Kroggs planetside. Then, before the Crusaders on the planet were able to mobilize, Sarah would have to speak to the Lord Second Chancellor about how successful the trip to Earth — the

Quest — had been, and how the Earthers were helping to fulfill the great destiny of the human race. She'd come up with a number of versions, each subtly keyed to play on a different mood in Chancellor Argyle...

Whatever it took to keep the Church from resisting, and forcing a spectacular planetside confrontation. They could diminish the Chancellor's power another day, for now they needed his cooperation to defeat the Kroggs.

Altogether, things seemed fairly well in hand — or, more precisely, the *plans* seemed well-founded. They hoped to carry everything off without casualties, and with the edge of surprise that was not a total theoretical impossibility. But plans weren't prone to surviving contact with the enemy... so they'd just have to do the best they could.

Stretching her arms over her head, Sarah allowed a long yawn. Ursla cocked an eyebrow at the action and smiled, "Tired, are we?"

Rubbing her neck gingerly, Sarah shrugged, "To be expected, I suppose. A lot of work in a short interval. I thought I'd be ready for it all after so much downtime, but I suppose I'm a bit out of condition."

Ursla unconsciously let out a relaxing breath and nodded, "Near as I can tell, that's the problem with interstellar campaigns — too much time in transit. Of course I'm an authority on interstellar war, having fought so many..." she and Sarah shared a wry smile. "But I guess it's the same with all campaigns... no matter how ready you are, you still have to force a great deal of preparation into a short space of time."

"Hmph," Sarah flopped back in her seat, her face taking on a more drawn and exhausted look as her focus dwindled. "Still thought I'd be more fit for it."

Ursla chuckled and absently piled a dozen pads into some sort of order on the table, "I'm sure we're doing just fine for amateurs. But I think we could both use sleep — I'm not keen on being so fatigued when going into battle. Not when I've got an alternative, anyway."

A long blink and a jaw locked determinedly against a yawn marked Sarah's silent agreement, "Then I suppose I'll find my way back to *Joseph Barron*."

Standing stiffly, she tried to stretch as many appendages as she subtly could, then took a deep breath, "I'm looking forward to getting this done with, though. Bloody tired of the stress. If it kept up I'm not sure exactly how I'd cope with it all..."

Ursla leaned back and cocked an eyebrow at her counterpart, "I don't think you're giving yourself enough credit. But don't worry, we'll have Genesis tomorrow, and then we can deal with the Kroggs. One thing at a time."

"Right," Sarah made an effort to sound convinced, then offered a parting nod to her colleague and turned for the door.

Ursla watched her go, suppressing the urge to simply tip to one side and go to sleep. She was still having a hard time believing that only a few days earlier she'd been craving something to break the monotony. This had all come together reasonably well, and Sarah seemed to be handling things decently enough — despite the fatigue and stress. They'd all need their best games for tomorrow, and if the Larosians arrived, that would present an entirely more complex challenge...

Well, the matters at hand were more pressing than the potential arrival of new aliens on the scene. What happened tomorrow would inevitably shape the course of Earther-human relations for decades to come.

"Better not mess it up, then," Ursla muttered to herself with a sardonic smile.

Then she went to bed.

CHAPTER 11

"It's directly to port, sir. About forty degrees down angle," *Archangel Sword's* Sensor Chief had finally reported the location of *Grendelsbane City*.

Stanton had been impatiently drumming his fingers on the armrest as he'd waited, wondering whether Audrey DeBrooke had run into something else on the way to XK41-1. He was relieved they'd finally found her.

The Coalition Squadron hadn't given chase once its Superdreadnought had gone down — not surprisingly, since *Sword* could have easily taken any three of the remaining ships. The trip across the short gap of space to the nebula had gone without incident, but finding DeBrooke and her cruiser had been a challenge.

The ArcColonel really knew how to make her ship disappear, which likely explained why she and her crew were still alive.

Not wanting to give away *Grendelsbane's* position in case the Coalition ships were trying to follow them, Stanton had elected not to attempt long-range signals, deciding instead to find DeBrooke the old fashioned way — by looking. The nebula interfered with normal sensors, so it was left to close-in sensor pulses to find the ailing Heavy Cruiser. DeBrooke would hopefully realize *Sword* was a friend if it popped up on her screens — he had his transponder codes blaring the ship name on all channels, so her Sensor Chief should be able to recognize the Battlecruiser before *Grendelsbane* attempted to open fire...

"Helm, take us to it, 0.1 cee," Stanton ordered, watching on his monitor as the icon of *Archangel Sword* slowly turned and dove towards the smaller ship. "Communications, can we tightbeam them a signal?"

"Yes sir..." the Communications Officer replied, then paused. "Sir, they're tightbeaming us."

Stanton nodded — DeBrooke was obviously as glad to see *Sword* as he was to see *Grendelsbane*. The old adage about safety in numbers seemed to ring true, even if the number happened to only be *two*. Dealing with bandits like those in the Coalition called for a stronger hand than any single ship could provide...

"Put it up," Stanton brought his mind back to the immediate circumstances and shifted in his chair.

A smiling DeBrooke appeared on the screen before him, "Did we see that right? Scratch one SD?"

Stanton shrugged in reply, "The Earthers knew what they were doing when they changed my ship. Too bad for Liz Hastings that she didn't give us work, I suppose."

DeBrooke nodded, her pleasure at the Coalition defeat all too obvious. After a month of avoiding them in a battered ship, she was clearly glad to see those traitors — not only deserters, but individuals bent on killing their *own* — put to the sword. And indeed, Stanton was glad his *Sword* had done the damage. Collaborating, they could probably get out of the situation completely.

"I'll get engineering teams together and send parts across to you, Audrey. Perhaps you'd like to join me for a meal, we can discuss what we do next..." The last offer had to be an irresistible one. A Heavy Cruiser normally lacked the luxuries of a Battlecruiser, and after a month of constant strain, *Grendelsbane* couldn't possibly have any of its amenities left intact. With that much damage, the ship's crew had to be living off cold water and bad rations.

Unsurprisingly then, DeBrooke agreed with a nod, "Thank you, James, that would be utterly fantastic! I'll be over presently."

As the screen blanked, Stanton leaned back in his chair. DeBrooke was quite an impressive ArcColonel, keeping her ship alive in all this mess. Took a cunning and daring sort of person to pull that off — all in all a remarkable woman...

Stanton stopped that train of thought — it wasn't the sort of internal dialogue he needed right now. They were being hunted, and half his would-be squadron was crippled. There was a lot to do.

But he hadn't felt this alive for a while...

"...so we carry parts for both flux and energy drives, plus techs trained on both. Our hybrid drives are a bit of both, so the Earthers thought that would be prudent," Stanton finished his explanation of *Sword's* situation.

His fellow ArcColonel nodded and sipped her water, "A good thing too. My Chief Engineer has been trying to jury-rig something for weeks, but like I said, all we had was short range."

Stanton leaned back in his chair and nodded. His cabin was the site of this meeting, and DeBrooke, looking a bit haggard, was graciously inhaling every bit of food his steward could offer her. *Grendelsbane's* hydroponics bays had been swimming in radiation since its engines had gone offline, so they'd been eating rations during their long expulsion. With the right components, that could be rebuilt as well — and it would be.

"So, the question is what to do now, isn't it?"

Stanton sighed at his counterpart's question — he'd been considering the difficult issue for the past few hours. They couldn't simply wash their hands of this Coalition — other Naval crews could be killed, and if piracy became an issue, *every* nonaligned ship might draw the Earther wrath, including innocents like *Sword* and *Grendelsbane*. Well, the Genesis Fleet's anger, anyway — Gods knew the Earthers would probably have some benevolent, enlightened solution...

"I think we should send a drone to warn Earth about the Coalition," he said thoughtfully. "We can tell anyone who wants to defect to head elsewhere... I'm pretty sure the Earthers would let that message circulate. As for us, I think we should move together, maybe head for a different sector. We can try to find others and get them to join us..."

DeBrooke cocked an eyebrow, "And form our own raiding group?"

Stanton snorted a laugh and shook his head, "There has to be somewhere else in this galaxy that's worth settling. We can try to build a colony, live our own way. Our ships would be strictly for trade and defense."

And for some reason, 'make our own war against the Church and the Kroggs' had dropped off the bottom of his list. James had left Earth partly because he'd been angry at not being deployed on the Genesis campaign, but perhaps this brush with the Coalition had taken some of the fire out of his blood. The appeal of escaping the politics and just *living* was beginning to take hold. And it was worth exploring, at least as *Grendelsbane* and *Sword* got accustomed to each other. If they wanted, they could make their war later on.

DeBrooke took another long sip of water and leaned back in her chair, "And our relationship to the Earthers and to our people?"

Grendelsbane's skipper really wanted everything figured out quickly... but then, she and her crew *had* been marooned out here for a month, at the mercy of a band of pirates.

A mild frown formed on Stanton's face, "I think we can ultimately let them dictate that. The Earthers won't give us trouble, but our people... well, *we* shouldn't shoot first."

DeBrooke pondered the statement for a moment, nodded, and emptied her glass, "Sounds good for a start. It'll take a week or two to get *Grendelsbane* fixed up. Until then, I guess we just take it easy. Let our crews get to know each other, start developing a sense of camaraderie."

"Sounds good to me," Stanton agreed with a smile, and then, not quite believing what he was saying: "We can catch up too. I haven't seen you since... Gods, since we were part of Manchester's fleet at the belt!"

There was a chill as Savanna Felix took his seat on *Tonnant's* bridge. The 80-gun Second Rate was one of the oldest commissioned vessels in the fleet, but it remained formidable enough to serve as a Vice Admiral's flagship during war-games.

It was also a bit drafty... no, those chills were actually brought on by *nerves*. Right, Felix *really* didn't want to be here. He liked his desk, he had no interest in throwing squadrons at the enemy... that was for Caine to do! But no, this morning it was his job.

This was the second time he'd boarded *Tonnant* for these games — that afternoon session he was supposed to attend had been cancelled abruptly, just as he'd taken his seat, due to a hurricane in the south Atlantic. Admiral Kella Felar, his opposing commander, had rightly left her ship to batten down her house, so they'd rescheduled the war-games. And now Felix was technically in violation of Admiralty policy.

No one actually cared about that, of course. Flag officers were required to take a turn at the war-games every decade, just to make sure they had some line command experience in case of a crisis. Felix was such a fixture on the administrative side of the Navy that no one worried about his abilities with a squadron or two — except, of course, for him. He feared he'd embarrass himself and his crews, and being forced to wait after his first appointment with fate had done little to lessen his anxiety.

At least Kella Felar was back in command of the opposing force — her house safely shielded from the hurricane — and she'd promised she'd make it quick. Playing the role of the offensive force, she would have three Battle Squadrons and a Flying Squadron under her charge. That meant she had eight First Rates, sixteen 74s, and eight Fifth Rate 36s... to his single Battle and Flying Squadrons — an 80, seven 74s, and eight Sixth Rate 28s.

He'd be eliminated rather quickly...

"Games are starting, sir," *Tonnant's* Second Lieutenant was standing at the Signal Officer's console. "Admiral Felar sends her compliments."

Felix ground his jaw — at least *Tonnant's* crew was being kind to him. They knew he was an administrative branch Admiral, and they probably didn't really want him commanding them any more than he wanted to be here... but it was necessity...

In any case, his task was to ensure his two squadrons protected the Earther base at Io from Felar's marauding attackers. Felix just needed to figure out how he could begin to attempt it.

Since size wasn't on his side, he'd need to think about maneuverability...

Admiral Kella Felar frowned slightly at the battle plot as *Endymion* and its accompanying squadrons edged towards Io. There was no sign of Felix at all — his frigates, his 74s... everything was missing. Surely he hadn't backed out... he'd only have to come back again.

No, he had to be around here somewhere...

"Send the frigates ahead, open order. Do a sweep around the moon..."

A beep sounded.

Felar frowned and turned to her Sensor Officer, "Lieutenant?"

The wolf leaned over his Sensor Chief's shoulder and frowned at the screen, "I'm not sure ma'am... something just came around behind us at over 200 pls... it can't be energy shot but... by the *Earth!*"

Felar's eyes shot to the main battle tank, and the holographic projection told the story. Sixteen Earther warships flying Felix's pennants escaped from energy drive in the attacking force's wake. Their simulated broadsides flared angrily, then the ships accelerated up to 200 pls as they returned to energy drive.

Endymion rolled hard to avoid incoming fire, but many of the Earther ships registered simulated damage in the strike.

And Felix was gone again.

Felar's eyes narrowed at the plot... where had he come from? He'd popped in and out of material state like a gopher coming out of a hole... but there had to be somewhere she could pin him! There was nowhere to hide... except behind Io...

"All ships, best speed to the moon," she said in a soft but firm tone.

Three of her 74s couldn't follow their orders, their drives having been shut down due to 'damage'. The rest of the battle group advanced unevenly, many ailing ships lagging behind, and they neared Io cautiously.

"Frigates ahead — get them around the other side to have a look," Felar was curious to see whether that was where Felix was, tucked into the sensor shadow cast by the moon. The Fifth Rates lunged forward to investigate, and detailed scans of the space behind Io came up in her holo tank... empty.

Felar frowned — well this could be beginner's luck, but Savanna Felix flew a desk. That was his career. No one but line officers got the best of her... The objective was Io, and soon the interesting tactics Felix was using would see his objective fail; her squadrons would be in range of the moon, ready to drop marines and thus end the war-game with a successful assault and victory for her...

They came from the far side of Jupiter, slingshotting around the massive planet under energy drive at 350 pls. The eight frigates of Felix's Flying Squadron appeared above Felar's 36s, and catching the attackers unaware, successfully disabled the larger vessels with the loss of only one of their own.

Felar blinked in surprise as the icons of those ships winked out, and then her mind froze as Felix's eight capital ships dove into the center of her formation. They returned to normal drive with guns running out, and their broadsides hammered away at her unprepared ships without reply. Diving back into energy drive, Felix's 74s rushed back towards Io, and meeting the Sixth Rates, his combined force formed a battle line between Felar's ships and the moon.

It took a second for Felar to realize *Endymion* was decelerating, and another to note that her flagship's icon had winked out on the main battle plot. Along with *fourteen* other attacking capital ships. The remainder, six First Rates and four 74s, were all damaged to varying degrees, and probably wouldn't be a match for Felix's force.

With over fifty percent losses, the commanding officer of the surviving squadron ordered the retreat.

You could have heard a pin drop.

• • •

Aboard *Tonnant*, Felix glanced around at the astonished faces of his bridge crew.

"What? I cheated a little... that's all... come on, I wanted to get it over with, so I figured I'd do crazy things that no one does..."

The Captain nudged him with her elbow, "You know full well that the only one ever to beat Admiral Felar in these games is the First Lord and sometimes Admiral Broadpaw."

Felix frowned and opened his mouth to speak, but the Signal Officer cut him off, "Admiral Felar for you, sir."

The commander in chief of the Earther First Fleet appeared in the main holo tank, "Savanna Felix, don't get any ideas about this... your unconventional tactics, or... I mean..."

Felix held up a hand, "I know, I wasn't exactly fighting by protocol... I'll go back to my desk..."

"You try to leave that ship and I'll send pinnaces out to drag you back. I'm calling Setter right now, and if I have my way you'll be commanding a battle group by this afternoon. Start grooming a replacement for Antarctic Base... hmm, come to think of it, with Varnon gone, you want the Third Fleet, when we finish rebuilding it?"

Lowering his hand slowly, Felix shrugged, "How about my desk for now?"

A laugh rippled through the bridge, and Felar smiled and vanished from the plot.

Felix looked at the bridge crew around him, and after a moment's pause the First Lieutenant, Varnia Broadpaw — daughter of the Admiral, and once Gun Captain for *Orion's* lower port side gun deck — spoke up, "Well, let's hear it for the Admiral's pending promotion!"

There was a cheer, and then the Captain came to her feet, "Somebody get a desk out of storage — we'll bolt it to the deck next to the plot!"

Felix smiled nervously and looked around at the crew. This wasn't exactly the sort of morning he'd been expecting, and now he'd be a line officer by the afternoon. Caine respected Felar's opinions, and the First Lord had always seemed to have an unnatural confidence in his leading desk Admiral's potential with the ships.

Just *wonderful*.

All Savanna Felix could do now was hope he was up to whatever they handed him, and send a goodbye note to his desk...

CHAPTER 12

Sarah was still exhausted when the morning of the attack came, but anticipatory adrenaline was compensating for her lack of sleep. Indeed, the battle rhythm that overtook her senses was almost as familiar as sleep itself — she could trust her mind to act sensibly under its guidance.

"Signal from Admiral Ursla; she's ready to move in with her strike force," the Communications Officer spoke behind Sarah, helping her focus.

"Very well, signal the fleet to make ready for acceleration. All ships to action stations," the process of delivering orders managed to eliminate the last of Sarah's fatigue.

"Ma'am, signal coming in from ArcBrigadier Conroy."

Sarah glanced at the Comm Officer with unconcealed surprise, "Really? Put it on my screen please."

Pat's face appeared on the small screen that usually offered Sarah an unabated view of the battle, "Pat?"

The Irishman offered a smile, "Just checking that you're still awake, girl."

Sarah's face reddened slightly, then her expression shifted to one of mock anger, "I'm only slightly exhausted, thanks..."

Pat held a hand up with a grin, "I figured. Keep safe, Sarah. No charging the guns this time."

The remark sliced off any reply Sarah was going to give — she couldn't even count the number of times she'd rushed into risky situations. Her results were always positive; she either exploited a weakness the enemy hadn't expected to defend or had help show up at exactly the right moment. That help, surprisingly enough, was often Pat. Still, his tone told her that he was worried about this action. The Kroggs were the enemies of the Larosians and the *masters* of the Church, and by no means could she consider them an easy foe.

"Don't worry, Pat. I'll take care of myself — you make sure you do the same though."

He noted her concern, and Pat's grin became a solemn smile, "Aye. See you in orbit."

The screen blanked, and the entire crew of Sarah's flag bridge snapped their heads back to their stations before the ArcGeneral could notice their surveillance.

Behind Sarah at tactical, one tech poked another, "They're talking like this over Fleetcomm and they still can't figure it out, can they? Gods help their children..."

Ursla watched the readings on her console as the Alliance Fleet brought itself to readiness. The five squadrons of ships of the line detailed to this action were already formed into a vanguard ahead of the fleet, slowly leaving their compatriots behind as they crawled forward at 50 pls. Ahead of *Agamemnon* and the van, a thin line of Krogg pickets didn't even know what was coming.

"Strike force clear and signaling ready, ma'am," the Signal Officer reported.

"Very good. Strike force to activate energy drives and set for stealth mode. Hold formation and accelerate to 400 pls."

Ursla watched as the icons of her force, once in a neat formation on her three-dimensional battle plot, evaporated into a fog. Their transponders still marked a neat series of lines abreast as they held their formation reasonably well, and their drives pushed them forward far more quickly, leaving the rest of the fleet behind them.

"Strike force accelerating, ma'am. ETA, twenty-two minutes."

Ursla nodded silently. They were slipping through lines of defense without the Kroggs having the slightest idea they were doing so. A good start to a long day — a day that she hoped would remain so positive.

Pat watched silently aboard *Harbinger Bishop*. Ursla's force was accelerating away at 400 pls, her ships undetectable to the Kroggs. Part of him wished he could be with her, to surprise the arrogant bastards and pounce on their Mothership, but another, stronger half was glad to be with Sarah's fleet.

Someone had to look out for her after all. Her history of risk-taking had many defining moments — dueling tube-to-tube with a ship that was a class and a half better than hers, rushing a room full of Crusaders with only a squad of Earther marines behind her, and challenging a large, well-trained Crusader Shappa to a fist fight. These risks had all met with success, but Pat had seen how narrow Sarah's margin of survival had been in each of the misadventures. He worried now that the Kroggs could close that margin, and that any such risks on Sarah's part could prove fatal.

Hell, *eye-to-eye* contact with a Krogg could prove fatal. Breathing the same air, seeing the same *color* — Kroggs seemed good with death... well, Earthers were hopefully much better.

Grinding his jaw, Pat leaned back in his chair and waited for the order to accelerate.

The range closed steadily, and a gap of over twenty minutes was swallowed up in what seemed to Ursla, like seconds. Her instincts were heightened, and she could sense the anticipation that seemed to be filling *Agamemnon* as the

First Rate raced to action. The Earthers were going back into battle, against an essentially unknown foe...

The instincts of the hunter — the drive which had been a means of survival for the predators of order Carnivora barely 700 years before — remained with the Earthers, buried deep in their psyches. When action came it resurfaced, and turned Earthers from the friendliest sentient species yet known in the galaxy to one of the deadliest. It was a powerful combination — an ability to mix carefully honed logic with inexplicable foresight and feeling. It wasn't telepathy or a mystical universal force, it was pure *instinct*, and it would hopefully serve them well today.

The test was about to come.

"One minute, Admiral."

"Very well. Strike force to bring fields in to 100 percent and stand by to disengage drives," Ursla's sober tone reflected the calm of her tactical mind.

Forty-five Earther line of battle ships, the mightiest in the Alliance Fleet, began to draw their energy drive fields in from 250 percent to 100. The loose vanguard was being tightened as energy fields became more compact, and from the outside it would have appeared that there was a First Rate's broadside hurtling toward the Krogg Mothership sitting on the system picket line.

The reality was infinitely more deadly.

"All ships standing by," the Signal Officer, a veteran of the Church battles, had no difficulty keeping his voice calm.

Ursla watched the battle plot before her as the force closed rapidly. They would come out of energy drive and run out their guns immediately, so they needed to be in good range...

"At my order, Signal Officer..."

Almost...

Just a little more...

"Now."

The Earther strike force of forty-five ships of the line thundered into existence off the port beam of the giant Mothership. Their guns ran out as soon as they returned to their normal matter states, and no fleet order needed to be given.

The First Rates — the biggest and toughest ships in the Allied Fleet's order of battle — released their withering broadsides first, before the Mothership even realized it was under attack. The massive ship was impossible to miss. Bulbous and with what outwardly appeared to be an eyelid on its upper half, it could have outmassed a small moon.

The broadsides slammed home violently, cracking the armor of the ship's side and spilling what Ursla could only guess was blood into space. The Third Rates — all 74-gun ships — fired their own formidable broadsides a split second after their bigger cousins. The crevice made by the First Rates seemed to bubble with gore as their shot struck home.

The Mothership began to roll, trying to hide the damage from its attacker, and the giant eyelid began to slowly open.

"They're trying to launch corvettes; 234th and 236th, target their launch bays; 230th, cover the First Rates against Superdreadnoughts." Ursla's orders were quickly passed along by the Signal Officer, and each squadron leapt to its particular duty.

Two of the units of 74s turned their broadsides against the eyelid. On the Mothership, that eyelid was like a hangar door, and within the mammoth's hull, six or seven hundred small corvettes waited to launch and attack the enemy like an angry swarm of bees. The intel provided by the Genesis Fleet recommended not letting that launch take place, and indeed, it wouldn't be allowed here.

Sixteen ships' broadsides laid fire straight down on the immense door, and the shot pierced it quickly. Within, corvettes lined for launch were disintegrated as rolling energy fire hammered home again and again.

The First Rates fired heavy blows from the flank, their broadsides systematically tearing the ship to pieces, gouging out its organs, spraying blood into space to form a crimson mist around the action.

Then it came.

Wounded fatally and in what must have been immense agony, the beast that was the Mothership cried out, the shriek translating through space in some brand of sub-telepathic waves, permeating every ship nearby. Ursla cringed as the savage cry slammed through her flag bridge, and it inspired her to quickly end the Mothership's existence — to put it out of its misery.

Two squadrons of 74s and two squadrons of First Rates seemed to share her determination, and their guns flared together. The Mothership's scream ended, the vessel disintegrating in a cloud of unimaginable gore.

The Earther ships turned from the bloody remains to engage the Krogg Superdreadnoughts that now came forward to issue a challenge. These were more conventional fighting ships, at least by Earther standards, but there were only a half dozen of them — no matter how technology seemingly stacked up, the Earthers clearly had the advantage in numbers.

The Kroggs came in a vanguard, their ships reacting together with a mixture of inherent instinct and overlaid telepathic instruction. Projectile batteries aboard the Superdreadnoughts began to spit — literally. Hollow spines holding caches of ultra-concentrated acids erupted from the vessels' carapaces, targeting the Third Rates of the 230th Earther Battle Squadron. Carronades swept into action, the 74s fighting as a unified force, drawing on their battle experience of months before as well as the crews' honed Earther instinct. The spines were wiped from space as even more erupted. The 230th focused itself on drawing the Superdreadnoughts' fire while the ships of its sister squadrons of 74s came to its side to empty their broadsides at the Krogg ships.

The Superdreadnoughts scattered quickly, managing to evade most of the tide of energy, and accepting little damage while their spines continued to erupt from hull orifices. They evaded upward, dancing out of the way of the 74s' shot, but then ran across the sights of the First Rates.

Sixteen of the Earthers' mightiest ships hadn't opened fire on the fast-moving Kroggs at long range. Instead they'd used their own impressive maneuverability to close range with the Superdreadnoughts. Now, Krogg versions of lasers — focused neuro-electrical blasts similar in principle to the shocks from an electric eel — stabbed at the First Rates' shields until the Earther guns thundered from point-blank range. Telepathic shrieks of agony filled the silent vacuum for another brief moment, and then the Krogg Superdreadnoughts vanished into oblivion.

And that was the end of the Krogg picket.

On the flag bridge of *Agamemnon*, Ursla heaved a sigh of relief — her ships had survived an encounter with Krogg warships, albeit with overwhelming odds in their favor. And they'd opened the door to Genesis.

"All ships form vanguard by squadron," she ordered.

Her eyes drifted to *Agamemnon's* main battle tank.

Now we wait for Sarah.

CHAPTER 13

"Great Gods!"

The night watch on *Genesis One* was usually quiet, but something had just disturbed the orbital base's calm sleep period.

An ArcMajor supervising the technicians in Sensor Control turned to the surprised non-com as he blasphemed, "Damn you Bill, stop swearing!"

The tech turned his chair away from his screen, "Ma'am, look at this!" His panicked voice instantly changed the ArcMajor's mood, and she rapidly rounded the stations between the main sensor console and her desk.

"Some sort of massive volley of energy weapons, heading towards the Krogg in-system picket... they're getting more concentrated as they get closer!" the tech roared.

The ArcMajor's eyes widened as she saw the forty-odd pulses cruise in-system at 4.0 cee. How in hell's gulags could *energy bursts* move four times the speed of light?

Without hesitation, the ArcMajor spun, jogged back to her desk, and slammed the 'General Alarm' key. The crews of the six *Genesis* orbital stations sprang to battle alert.

"Bloody! Bloody! Bloody!"

His collar buttons kept unsnapping! Dammit!

The ArcBrigadier commanding the *Genesis* stations trotted through the corridors of *Genesis One*, hastily trying to make himself presentable. He'd managed to get his uniform on within a minute of the alarm, but he was hardly fit for a parade.

Reaching the Command and Control Center aboard his station, he stopped fiddling with his uniform, "What in Gods' names is going on?"

The ArcColonel commanding *Genesis One* quickly turned to him, "I can't believe it sir! The Krogg picket is under attack!" Desperately, the man stabbed his finger at the Genesis system map on the C&C's main screen. "Ships like we've never seen before just *appeared* in front of the Mothership and blew it apart! And now they're cooking the Superdreadnoughts that were with it!"

The ArcBrigadier's jaw dropped as he stared at the monitor. With the fleet out of system, he was the senior line officer of the Genesis Navy — if these were hostiles, and they surely appeared to be, he had to deal with them...

The last Krogg icon vanished.

Not even at the Battle of Glorious Saviors had the Kroggs been so ravaged... and the Larosians had gotten through to a Krogg picket that day.

"Gods — there are *more*! Hundreds... coming in-system..." the Sensor Officer cried, and the ArcBrig immediately saw them, a cloud of ships rushing from the rim of the system, brushing away Krogg pickets as if they weren't there.

The Krogg Fleet wasn't even reacting! What the hell was going on? Their alien 'allies' had at least 100 ships in Genesis — he only had a squadron of Superdreadnoughts. *Human* Superdreadnoughts... and the six *Genesis* orbitals. Not enough. If these intruders could crush a Krogg Mothership so handily, his stations would be toothpicks by day's end.

Gods, I wish Sarah was here.

The ArcBrigadier turned to his Communications Officer, "Alert ground bases to stand by for orbital attack. Defcon Omega! Alert the Krogg bases groundside — tell them we have unknowns incoming, presumed hostile. Maybe they'll send something to stop them. Get the SDs to power their drives..."

And do what?

"Sir, the Krogg Fleet is rendezvousing with that picket group... detecting ten Superdreadnought *squadrons* moving out from their sector..."

"*Ten!* They don't have that many ships in-system!" the ArcBrig barked, but the main screen proved him wrong.

One hundred of the horrid Krogg warships appeared on the fleet's flank, racing down on it with bitter speed. Nothing the ArcBrig knew of could survive that kind of onslaught — the entire Genesis Fleet, built to Krogg specifications with Krogg-assisted technology, would be hard pressed to fight them off...

Not relevant right now!

The red icons of the Krogg ships hurtled towards the intruders, and then the yellow icons of that unknown fleet split apart. One group of about 900 hurtled towards Genesis while another 600 went to meet the Kroggs. The ArcBrig mentally crossed his fingers — if the Kroggs could stop the smaller group there was a chance...

"The larger group will be in range of us in four minutes, sir! They're running under a stealth system that reads a *lot* like our own."

"Well they can't bloody well be ours!" the ArcBrig barked to no one in particular. "If we could knock off Krogg Motherships we wouldn't need the bastards!"

The 600 ships suddenly stopped in space and seemed to turn ninety degrees to one side. The Kroggs sped down on them.

"Projectiles from the Kroggs, sir... three volleys."

That meant they'd flushed their ready spines. It'd take them forty seconds to grow another three volleys into the launchers. That was a *lot* of spines... there was no fleet he knew of that could–

"Energy spike... oh Gods..."

The monitor filled with a cloud of energy, rushing from the intruder fleet into the Krogg volleys. A second, much more concentrated wall of energy followed scant seconds later. When the first cloud crossed the Krogg volley, the acid-spines seemed to vanish, and the second wall of energy accelerated through the cloud, slamming wholly into the Krogg Superdreadnoughts.

Forty of the massive Krogg warships disappeared from sensors.

The breath caught in the chest of every human who saw it. Not even *Larosians* had done that much damage to the Kroggs. These intruders...

The rest of the Krogg Fleet turned tail, running ahead of the tides of energy sent at them by the 600. Not *one* of the newcomers had been destroyed. The ArcBrig somehow doubted they'd even been touched.

"Alert the SDs. Tell them to form around the stations and add their missiles to ours. We'll see if we can slow them down..." the knowledge that his death was inevitable almost calmed the ArcBrig. "Load our tubes, we'll select targets based on size. Alert the ground anti-spacecraft batteries that they'd better go to independent fire control. We won't be up here long to pick their shots for them."

The room was frozen by the terror thundering towards them. The ArcBrig turned to his crew, "Move, all of you! We may not have much of a chance but we'll do what we bloody well can! Clear?"

His clipped British accent seemed to make the orders resonate in the C&C chamber. Non-coms and officers leapt into action, and the six *Genesis* stations and the local Superdreadnought squadron prepared to go down fighting.

"The large group will reach weapons range in two minutes, sir."

The ArcBrig found his chair and sat in it, displaying a calm facade to settle his crew. It was the way an officer should act. His was a family of officers, a proud Naval family. Mother, father, sister — right through the 'great-great-great-great...' generations — they'd all been officers.

And now he'd die with as much honor as any of his family, and as his sister would want of him, if she ever heard of this while she helped guard the Quest...

Wait a moment... these intruders had come off the vector from *Earth!* The Quest path! Gods, he hadn't realized that before. Had they annihilated the fleet? Killed his sister? ArcGeneral Hastings? The High Chancellor? Well, he wouldn't shed tears for a Churcher, but great Gods, this could be the end of humanity...

"Umm... sir?"

The ArcBrig snapped back to reality, turning his chair to his Comm Officer, "*Umm?* Let's have a bit more professionalism in the face of death, if it's not too much trouble."

He realized that must sound absurd, but it made perfect sense to him.

The ArcLieutenant looked up, altogether too pale, "A signal coming in, sir."

The ArcBrig rose impatiently from his chair, "From who, man? If the Superdreadnoughts want to run tell them to–"

"From the intruders, sir. The bigger group. It's on Fleetcomm Omega."

The ArcBrig blinked. That was a secure channel for fleet business — encrypted against Crusader surveillance. Either the alien intruders had figured out Genesis channels from wreckage, or…"

Sitting down and turning back to the main screen, the ArcBrig collected himself, "On the main screen, if you please."

There was a short delay — one which seemed altogether too long from the command chair — as the signal went through the decoder, and then a face appeared on the screen.

The entire C&C staff let out a collective sigh of relief as a familiar face appeared… wearing *ArcGeneral* stars. *Full* ArcGeneral stars.

"Planning to blow something up Graham? I must say, missiles aren't quite as friendly as a hug for a homecoming welcome."

ArcBrigadier Graham Manchester managed to let out his breath, "Gods, Sarah! Just as well to kill me as to scare me to death like that!"

Sarah chuckled, "You know I love to make an entrance. Anyway, do *not* mark the fleet coming in behind me as hostile. Stand down from action stations, and do *exactly* as I say."

The junior Manchester sibling frowned briefly, then turned to his command crew.

"You heard the orders."

The *Genesis* stations stood down.

CHAPTER 14

"So you're sure he won't shoot us down?" Ursla asked with a half-grin, staring out the pinnace window as the large orbital station — *Genesis One* — grew before her.

"He knows it's us!" Sarah's mock defensiveness caused Ursla to chuckle.

"Sibling rivalry?"

Sarah's glare stopped the Admiral's remarks, though Ursla still shared a laugh with Pat, who sat beside Sarah on the flag pinnace from *Agamemnon*. This small ship had been selected to bring the trio to *Genesis One* — Ursla would never have fit into a Genesis craft.

"So why am *I* here exactly?" Pat asked as his laughter subsided.

Sarah glanced across at him, "Graham knows you. It'll make it easier for him to believe me."

Pat cocked an eyebrow, "I suppose. But if he doesn't trust his own sister…"

Another well-timed glare from the ArcGeneral convinced Pat to intently examine the quality Earther carpet beneath his feet.

They sat in silence, watching the station grow to engulf the small craft. Sarah had told her brother to lock down every Naval installation and ship in orbit of Genesis, pinning down their Crusader garrisons to keep them from interfering with the upcoming meeting. The last thing they needed was a fanatic calling Ursla a demon or worse — it would complicate matters even more, and violence might ensue.

Graham had never seen a ship like this pinnace. It was bulbous but elegant, far bigger than anything in the Genesis small craft line, save maybe for a cargo hauler, and it maneuvered so handily! The directing lights on the inside of *Genesis One's* main launch bay guided the Earther *small* craft to a landing slot, though as it descended to the deck it easily filled the empty one next to it as well.

As the humming from the alien engines slowly subsided, Graham took nervous steps toward the craft. His escort of ten marines followed a short distance behind, warily holding their weapons as they eyed the craft suspiciously.

Aside from that escort, the bay had been completely sealed off from the rest of the station.

A hatch opened on the side of the craft and a slim embarkation ramp slid to the deck. He walked to the bottom of it, waving his marines to stay back. They spread out naturally in a defensive pattern, their rifles aimed at the hatch.

Graham held his breath — this could all have been a ploy to get aboard... What if Sarah had been forced to say what she'd said? What if the image he'd seen had been an alien body double? This could all go very badly if his rash first instinct to cooperate proved wrong...

And then Sarah stepped out of the hatch, with Pat beside her!

Could it be two body doubles... oh get a hold of yourself man!

They descended easily, smiles on their faces, and Graham remembered to breathe. Lack of oxygen and extreme muscle contraction were making his chest hurt.

"Graham!"

Sarah's greeting was more than affectionate, and as she reached the bottom of the ramp she threw her arms around her younger brother. He smiled in reply, wrapping arms around her. The marines relaxed. Slightly.

"Sarah. Gods, you better explain this, sister!" He drew back and shook Pat's hand, "How are you, Pat? Gods, an ArcBrig now? Well done! And what's this ArcGeneral stuff, Sarah?"

"I can boss you around again, and Liz says so," she smiled.

"Not bloody likely!" Graham came between Pat and Sarah, throwing arms around both their shoulders. "Now, what are you doing battling Kroggs? Better be a good answer to this one." He tried to slowly lead them away from the pinnace, but they stopped him.

"You better see for yourself, Graham my friend!" Pat turned the slightly smaller man around and grandly waved back at the pinnace. Both Graham and the marines had been so relieved to see two of their own, they'd neglected to watch the ramp.

A huge, brown, hairy beast was silently descending! It was a wild-looking thing... wearing a uniform! And it had two other creatures with it! A shorter gray thing... a *wolve*! The mythical beasts of Earth! Gods!

The marines' weapons rose instantly, and the two smaller beasts replied by leveling their own hefty guns.

"Marines, lower your rifles!" Pat roared, then getting no response, "They're friendly! Do it or by Gods I'll have a piece of the lot of you! Do you really think you'd be standing if they were hostile?" Then looking at the smaller beasts, he offered a wave, "Don't worry, Beckett, they'll behave."

The human troopers exchanged uncertain glances at the loud orders, then lowered their guns slightly. The beasts' guns lowered as well...

Sergeant Major Lupus' eyebrows arched briefly, then he bobbed his head to Ursla, "Should be alright, Admiral. If there's any trouble... well, just put your shield up. We'll watch..."

Ursla smiled at the comment, "I imagine there won't be. Just remember, smiles without teeth…"

She donned that precise expression and walked towards the three Genesis officers. The two wolves remained at the bottom of the ramp and smiled awkwardly.

Three Naval marines deftly got into Ursla's path, trying to keep her from Graham.

"A noble sentiment, but you wouldn't do much good," Sarah announced to the troopers. "She dismantled a couple of companies of Crusaders by herself. Hand-to-hand. And I'm not exaggerating."

Looking at the creature, Graham didn't doubt it. The marines parted nervously, watching as the big uniformed being paced the last few meters to the trio.

Sarah turned to her brother, "Graham, meet Admiral Andra Ursla, Earther Navy."

Ursla smiled kindly, extending a mighty paw down to him, "Pleased to meet you, ArcBrigadier. I wish I could say I'd heard a lot about you."

Graham tried to say something, then the room started spinning. That was just before… he fainted.

"Just a tad more… *surprisable* than you, Sarah," Ursla laughed as Graham came around.

The stricken ArcBrigadier sat up, taking in the surroundings. He was in the storage room adjacent to the hangar, lying on a tarpaulin. What happened?

Then Ursla came into his view and his breath caught.

"Sorry, Graham. Nobody told me I was *that* ugly," the creature said, and both Pat and Sarah laughed outright.

Graham blinked a few times, remembering what happened.

Oh *Gods*.

The ArcBrig stuck out a tentative hand, "Graham Manchester, pleased to make your acquaintance, Admiral Ursla."

Ursla smiled good-naturedly, "Likewise. Sorry about that — Sarah should have warned you. It's 'Andra', by the way."

Graham stared at her quizzically.

"My *name*, Graham. Andra. Feel free to use it."

"Aha. Yes… quite, umm… Andra," Graham got to his feet and dusted himself off. "Right then. Andra. Sarah. Pat. Would someone please explain exactly what is going on here?"

Sarah put an arm around her brother, "A long story, and rather amazing really. But every word of it is true."

CHAPTER 15

Algenon began to shrink behind Andros Grieve as his dropship and five others hurtled from the main bay. The acceleration was barely felt because of the landing craft's grav compensators, but the General knew from experience that he was moving at an intimidating velocity.

Each ship carried a hundred marines, plus an armory enough for 150 troops. They were small and fast, not to mention agile, allowing them to slip in through thick defenses and deliver a full company of infantry.

However, today, they wouldn't have to evade.

Grieve relaxed in his seat and recalled all Ursla had told him. They'd met with Graham Manchester, the commander of the Genesis planetary defenses, and had him stand down the ground batteries. He told all concerned planetside that they'd mistaken the returning Genesis Fleet for hostiles, and that anything entering the atmosphere was friendly. For the benefit of the Genesis Church's political Chancellery, Krogg losses were being quickly erased from sensor logs. Graham was even now briefing his people as to the new state of allegiances.

Altogether, they were peddling a story that was close to the truth.

The ships and stations in orbit were already rallying behind their comrades from the Genesis Fleet, and as their compatriots had, they were responding reasonably well to the Earthers.

The Superdreadnoughts and the *Genesis* stations had all maintained rather large compliments of Crusaders, so Hodge had supplemented their Naval marine garrisons with some of her own, and Grieve had provided half-companies of Earther marines in case the Churchers got unpleasant. So far they hadn't been needed — a state of affairs that would hopefully continue.

But that was only a sideshow. Pacifying Crusaders wasn't a simple matter, but it seemed easy when compared to dealing with Kroggs. The aliens would be the challenge, and no one pretended otherwise. By now the alien garrisons on Genesis would know that something was up, but they wouldn't know exactly what. They had to be aware that an unknown force had come into Genesis space with Sarah's returning fleet, but in the ground installations they wouldn't realize that a hammer was about to fall on them. All they could see in orbit were Genesis ships — the Second Fleet was in a higher orbit hiding in the sensor shadow of the humans.

The Kroggs might expect that battle with these strangers was in the offing, they just couldn't know how soon, or at what targets. And they wouldn't expect the Earthers.

As Grieve watched *Algenon* shrink into oblivion and the planet beneath accelerate toward him, five of the Earther marines' dropships cruised away from their vessels, each with a full load of bear marines aboard. Another transport aboard *Aboukir*, a 74 of the 236th Squadron, held seventy reinforcement bears in case they were needed, and two other dropships loaded with feline and canine marines were ready on that Third Rate's deck as well.

The Kroggs might be tough, but Grieve was hoping they couldn't handle what he was about to throw at them.

The five transports plummeted into the atmosphere of Genesis with blinding speed. Their atmospheric engines began to hum as they were given something to breathe, and the formation shattered as they headed for their appropriate landing sites.

A transport headed for each of the two small Krogg outposts, while the other three flew in a loose cluster ten meters above the treetops of the Genesis jungle, angling for the main Krogg installation. Grieve, among these three, watched the thick canopy of the planet uneasily.

The vegetation on Genesis was very different than that found on Earth. He'd enjoyed trekking through the Amazon, and the jungles of South America and Southeast Asia, but the character of this wilderness was different — alien.

The difference was more pronounced than Grieve had expected — this was far from the planet he knew, and that fact struck him forcefully as the jungle blurred beneath his craft. Everything was a sea-green color — from plants to dirt — and thick humidity filled the air, which he'd been told actually held a mild *sting* due to the nearby oceans' acidity. He was in foreign territory, about to face foreign troops.

The dropships sped onwards, gradually slowing and losing altitude as they neared the base. The landing sites had been pre-selected based on scans made from orbit, and as the installation appeared on the short-range sensors, the craft scattered again, the two ships on either flank accelerating ahead and angling away to land at sites on the far side.

Grieve had determined that surrounding the base would be the best method for assaulting it — without knowing precisely how the Kroggs might react, he preferred the ability to cover the base on any side over a simple concentration of forces. Satisfying this desire, his ships were landing at points on a triangle that he'd sketched over the maps of the area with the Krogg installation at its center. A hundred bears from each side... it would be decisive, he hoped.

The dropship slowed to a hover, finding the landing site exactly where scans had suggested it would be. Lowering its landing feet, Grieve's craft descended to the jungle floor only a half kilometer from the Krogg base.

• • •

Grieve descended the ramp in silence, his khaki uniform clashing somewhat with the surrounding flora and fauna. The marines had gone before him, disappearing from the clearing into the jungle. Their perimeter was well laid but impossible to see.

Keying on his first of three body shields, Grieve hefted his heavy energy gun and swept forward from the ship to join them.

"Two Company, Three Company, position check," his voice was soft as his orders went through his small headset to the other two companies emerging from dropships.

"Two Company in position and ready."

"Three Company in position and ready."

Grieve nodded to himself and smiled inwardly — these troops were the best of his veterans; Earthers who'd fought at Antarctica and who he'd considered hardened veterans even before that action. While he heard that human marines didn't always take well to action in their first few encounters, his marines did very well whenever called on. It was likely part of their predator legacy, and experience would only make them *better*.

Experience like today's.

"Number One Company in position and ready," he replied. "Advance to the base's clearing and take up firing positions."

The Earther force began to move all at once, slipping through the jungle without disturbing its natural harmony. The base clearing was only a few kilometers from their initial perimeter, so it took very little time for them to reach it.

The Krogg installation was black and shiny, much like a black widow's carapace. Its structure was disturbingly organic, with what appeared to be giant black bones reaching upwards and black skin and flesh stretching between them. It was not very large, at least on the surface, but human-supplied intelligence suggested a garrison of about 200.

The clearing it occupied was about 5,000 square meters in size, most of which was open, grassy meadow. The installation was directly in the center, allowing enough room on each side for small craft to land.

In the field, four Krogg soldiers stood watch.

Standing at each corner of the base, these pickets looked outwards, watching for any threats. They carried no weapons, but they needed none. Their four arms were adorned with giant sword-like blades, as were their legs and torsos. Their heads mounted single eyes and bony crests stretching backwards — much like the helms of dinosaurs. They were about two and a three-quarters meters tall, perhaps slightly more, and they shared their installation's shiny-black exoskeletons.

The very sight of them chilled Grieve.

"One, Two and Three Companies, release safeties. Take out the guards on my count," Grieve's order was barely more than a whisper.

Around him, marines raised their rifles to their shoulders, keying the guns to unleash their full energy with each blast. The controlled bursts normally used would disrupt bodily function and cause a coma in the target. When the safety came off, the full-energy blast would instead incinerate the average person. But the Kroggs weren't average, and based on what he'd read in the Genesis info packet, his marines would need to be shooting very cleanly to bring these aliens down.

Grieve listened to the whispers of his bears through his radio — in the Earther service, the General spoke directly to all of his troops, and they could all speak directly to him. He knew better than to try and micromanage them, and they knew better than to swamp him. Such was the case with all Earther officers and their commands.

"Second Platoon, Three Company, sir. We are in position to lay fire down on their main exit. At least we think it's their main."

"Roger, can anyone else back them up?" Grieve looked across the clearing to where he knew that element of number Three Company would be.

"Fifth, Two Company in place, General. We've got a pulsar on it."

"First, Three Company in position as well."

Grieve nodded to himself. Sixty guns plus the company pulsar would be enough for the outset. Each Krogg would likely hold against five or six rifle shots, but if three platoons could keep up a high volume of fire...

"Alright, the rest of you divide up to make sure you can take those guards out quickly. Three platoons to each. Pulsars hold fire and watch the base... be ready for counter-battery fire. Those taking out the guards on the north face move to support the fire on the door as soon as your targets are down. The rest of you, start bombarding the base," Grieve watched as he whispered, and listened over his radio as the platoons coordinated with each other.

The edge of the clearing showed no indication of the kind of activity which might be occurring within. One by one, the fifteen platoons of number One, Two, and Three Companies reported their readiness. Their guns were trained on their targets and they were under whatever cover was deemed necessary by company officers.

Grieve glanced left and right, identifying the khaki figures of number One Company around him. Despite the clash of colors, they somehow still appeared to be part of the landscape.

Looking back at the installation, Grieve raised his gun to his shoulder and looked down its barrel.

"Head shots, everyone. Get ready..." Grieve inhaled slowly, sighted his target's eye, and gently rested his finger on the trigger.

"Fire."

The explosion of energy from the tree line was sudden and dramatic. The meadow was hidden under a cloak of blue-white pulses, and every shot struck its target.

Almost simultaneously, the four guards around the complex collapsed, overwhelmed by some sixty rifles each, their heads splitting off their torsos, fluids and gore splattering the ground around them. The clearing collapsed into an uneasy silence as the firing stopped.

"Fire positions, move!" Grieve's order was unnecessary but he gave it anyway.

Bears were moving swiftly and silently through the woods around the compound, their sight picture never wandering too far from the base. They stopped as they found new positions with cover and a good line of fire on their target, took careful aim, and waited.

Grieve moved with his platoon to the rear of the base. He would be among those bombarding the complex, not those watching the door. He found a thicket of bushes and dropped behind it without ceremony. Three other marines joined him, sliding down and staring over the hedges at the structure.

Defensive hard points seemed to grow from the sides of the frightening complex — launchers for their acid spikes, neuro-electric pulsars, and things he didn't even recognize from the files.

"Pulsars, bombard platoons, take out the defenses. Door team, hold your fire for now," the units to which he spoke were already bringing their weapons to bear when he gave the order, and for his part Grieve was already taking aim at a nearby launcher.

"Sir, Second, Three Company, on the door — looks like two or three of the hard points on this side are out of your line of site. Should we clear them?"

Grieve looked across to the door, noting what would be out of sight to the troops he had strung out around the base. "Wait until something comes out, Sergeant. Then make them your priority."

"Yes sir."

"Good. Pulsars, bombard teams... engage."

Grieve squeezed his trigger and a fountain of energy surged from his gun. Along with dozens of other blasts, the energy slammed into a spine battery and slowly began to wear it away. Two pulsars whined as well, their substantially heavier energy charges tearing angrily at the carapace. The installation's armor was tougher than that of the soldiers, but even tough shells had to give way at some point. The spine battery and many of the Krogg hard points were erased, followed quickly by the rest of the offensive weapons on the installation's shell.

As the firing dropped off, Grieve slowly stood up, "Bombard platoons into the clearing. Pulsars cover. Set energy charges on the walls. Door team, keep us covered."

Each marine on this mission carried a large explosive energy charge — a weapon which was essentially a small Wyndhymn generator without a containment shield to keep the field together when it was in energy state. In the same way *Flame* would have come apart if its field collapsed, the victim of the charge would turn into energy, scatter and reconstitute in pieces. It was a demolitions tool — a dangerous one — and it would have to do its job on the base.

"Door team, we have Kroggs coming out... quite a few, sir. We're engaging."

The face of the installation with the exit hatch was suddenly swamped by untamed energy fire. Krogg soldiers rushed from the exit much like ants pouring from a hill, and they were too fast for the bears on that side to stop.

Soldier Kroggs were not particularly intelligent, and indeed, their only seriously developed skills were those used for killing. Here, those latent abilities, combined with the direction of a telepathic Warlord somewhere nearby, would give Grieve's marines a lot of trouble...

Ragged Earther flanks were suddenly under threat, and disorganized teams of bears turned to try and hold the Kroggs while their comrades attached their charges to the base. Grieve hauled his charge from his pack, tossed it to another marine, and went to join some members of First Platoon, One Company. It was his responsibility to evaluate the threat posed by the Kroggs, and that meant he'd have to personally deal with a few.

Joining a cluster of about twenty Earthers, Grieve opened fire at an oncoming soldier. The blasts seemed to glance off him at first, but as the Krogg continued to charge into them the energy slowed, then cracked, then tore into him. After almost half a minute of steady fire, he collapsed. These aliens did not fall easily — not without 300 rifles concentrating to break their armor.

And with so many coming, his marines couldn't afford to waste thirty seconds on each.

The bears were stringing into a thin line against the Kroggs, screening for their fellows who even now were moving around to the undefended sides of the installation. Charges on remote detonators were slapped against the base's outer skin, nearly 200 in number. As they were placed, the marines rushed from the walls to the nearest lines of Earthers, adding their fire to the melee. One of the pulsar teams rushed from cover, planting its heavy weapon in the open field and sending a steady fountain of energy into the soldiers.

But there had to be 300 Kroggs pressing. Human intelligence had obviously underestimated the installation's garrison.

The first soldiers closed on the Earthers as the lines began to thicken, and the fight hardened.

"Bayonets won't work!" Grieve roared into his radio. "Shields up at full, break them by hand!"

Dropping his own rifle, Grieve activated both his extra shields and launched himself at a soldier charging his section of the line. The alien had not expected the attack — indeed, Grieve hoped he was offering a challenge unlike anything the Krogg had ever seen, human, Larosian, or otherwise.

The general's mass plowed the soldier to the ground as the Earther line dissolved into action and joined him. Grieve leapt to his feet and spun on his attacker. The Krogg was drawing himself up to full height, his mouth twisting into a snarl. He lunged at Grieve with animal ferocity, his arms spread wide and high, blades glimmering in the sunlight. Grieve braced himself and met the charge.

One arm intercepted the Krogg's left pair, the other drove a mighty fist into his breastplate. The soldier staggered back in surprise at the bear's raw strength, but the shock lasted only seconds. The creature came again, arms spread so as to preclude blocking. Two arm-blades whistled home against Grieves shoulder, but his shields knocked them aside. The force of the blow made him stagger, but his arm did not come away in the bloody mess the Krogg had intended.

Damn it had *hurt*.

As the soldier gaped in shock at the unaffected Earther, Grieve pressed in with blinding speed. Two fists balled together into one, and a mighty swing surged up through the General's body, the energy to deliver it coming through his legs, hips and shoulders. The swing rose high, aiming for the soldier's eye.

Realizing what was going on, the Krogg tried to evade, but his recognition came too late. The blow was a crashing wave. The upper skull of the Krogg seemed to collapse, and the soldier dropped to the ground, unmoving.

Grieve's example crossed the field almost immediately, with other Earthers mirroring his action in one form or another. Kroggs did not fall quickly, but they did begin to fall. Some of the marines started to collapse from the shock of broken bones and internal damage caused by Krogg blows, but the shields continued to keep blades out. The wounded were pulled from the field as they fell, often firing rifles with both arms as they went, trying to keep the black aliens at bay.

Another Krogg came for Grieve, ramming him to the ground with an effective tackle. The General was too fast to be finished off, though, as he rolled to one side and hefted a discarded rifle. He fired a single shot at the soldier's head, forcing it to flinch away, then leapt to his feet and slammed the rifle butt into the weak point on the Krogg's skull. Both rifle and bone crumpled with the force of the strike, and Grieve left both on the ground.

Charges were planted, he realized. They could...

"Fall back now — pulsars cover us!"

Only the torrents of energy released by the heavy weapons seemed to persistently crack the Kroggs, so now the pulsar teams raked the field with their fire, distracting the Kroggs while the Earther companies snatched up their rifles and fell back to the shelter of the trees. Small detonator keyboxes were drawn as they ran, and as Grieve slammed into the underbrush, turned and drew his own, he watched the clearing empty of Earthers.

The grassy meadow was filled with Kroggs, many trying to charge at the pulsar positions, but none succeeding. 'All clears' rang from around the tree line, and as the pulsar fire slackened, the soldier Kroggs began to creep curiously toward their complex's walls. Grieve gazed at them and let his finger hover over the button on his detonator.

"Now." His finger clenched the key.

The entire complex and most of the guards around it were instantly swept up by energy drive fields, then expelled from them milliseconds later in clouds of debris that rained on Genesis. When the flash cleared, nothing of the complex remained on the surface, and a crater marked the place where the underground barracks had once been. Only a dozen soldiers remained around the blast site, and Earther fire brought them down as they staggered leaderless through the falling gore.

Mission successful.

"Back to the ships. Let's get out of here. Companies report casualties as you go." Grieve's voice maintained its calm. The marines gave quick words of acknowledgement and slid back into the underbrush.

CHAPTER 16

Ursla didn't often feel uncomfortable, but she did now. Playing the role of loyal supporter of the great Quest wasn't something that came naturally to her, and she found it most disconcerting. Granted, it was necessary; she had to deceive the second-in-command of the Church of Genesis into accepting Earther help — or at least, not declaring holy war on the Earther and Genesis Navies.

The original plan for pacifying Genesis — the one conceived in brain-storming sessions months earlier — had been a straightforward invasion and occupation of significant targets by Genesis Naval marines, followed by a pre-sentation of the evidence of the Quest's true nature to the general public. Ursla hadn't been particularly fond of the abrupt plan, but it was Sarah's to choose and implement, so she'd simply offered some advice as to the maintenance of civil order during what would amount to a coup.

Now, though, the situation was much different. The Kroggs had 3,000 ships in-system, and the Allied Fleet was clearly wary of its intentions. They couldn't afford to attempt an outright capture of Genesis just now — it would require too much focus and might leave an opening for the Kroggs to attack.

Such an attack might never come — were Ursla in command of that Krogg Fleet she wouldn't budge. Genesis itself wasn't worth much, and though the Earther Second Fleet had blasted fifty odd Krogg Superdreadnoughts and a Mothership out of space, there was no way for a Krogg commander to be absolutely certain of the fleet's abilities in action. Of course, they had a two-to-one advantage in numbers, but those ships were guarding a choke point, presumably with no way of knowing when their primary enemy would come through. If the whole Krogg force, or even part of it, moved off station, they could negate their defensive advantage, letting the Larosians come through unopposed. The Kroggs undoubtedly knew and respected the abilities of the Larosian Fleets, and since Ursla wasn't going to give them trouble now that Genesis was secure, she fully hoped they wouldn't risk leaving their station to pick a fight with her — a fight that, as far as they knew, might cripple their fleet.

Essentially, Ursla was relying on something she'd once read about called 'Risk Theory'. She was hoping the Kroggs wouldn't risk their massive superiority in an attack against a numerically inferior enemy, for fear of losing a large number of ships and thus being left vulnerable to other enemies.

And to the credit of everyone in the briefings who'd recommended this course of action, the Kroggs had indeed stayed on their station, even though they'd doubtless been warned about the lost garrisons on Genesis. The Second Fleet and the Genesis Fleet were both sitting with drives ready, prepared to fight or flee if the Kroggs actually did decide to make trouble at the planet, but so far the Earther and human predictions about the alien deployment were proving sound.

Not *right*, just *sound*. That was why they couldn't risk an actual overthrow of the Genesis political Chancellery right now — they needed to cooperate, to get the planet's resources on side, and then do everything possible to get the orbital stations upgraded to tech levels matching those of the reconstructed Genesis Fleet.

Thus, Ursla needed to play a part in a rather spectacular deception. If only for a short time, she'd have to adopt a pro-Quest Earther attitude, and appear to be ready to serve at the pleasure of the Chancellery.

If she failed, they might all be damned, and the fleet could be expelled from Genesis space on pain of reparations against the families of its crews' planetside.

No pressure.

The Chancellor, one Benjamin Argyle, was on his way to *Genesis One* as Ursla sat in one of the station's meeting lounges. Fortunately, the station's ceilings were higher than those of Genesis ships — she'd had to crouch only when entering the room. Perhaps that was why Graham had selected it.

Ursla smiled involuntarily at the thought of Sarah's younger, less *seasoned* sibling. He was positively comical sometimes — no doubt he shared his sister's ability to run a tight Naval operation, but he was surprisingly (and probably involuntarily) amusing while he did it. His sister could use a tip or two, perhaps...

Ursla slowly tapped her foot on the deck. At least Andros' operation had gone well — the Kroggs hadn't known what hit them. Remarkably enough, there had been no fatalities among the Earther troops dispatched against the three bases, though at least forty bears were undergoing regenerative treatment of one sort or another. With the possibility of Krogg interference planetside eliminated, and with the evidence of the unchanging Krogg deployment in Genesis space, Ursla had a decent case for cooperation — whether its validity mattered at all, though, depended on the character of this Second Chancellor.

He couldn't be far off now. His pinnace was probably aboard already.

According to Sarah and Pat, the Second Chancellor was far more pliable than the first — he lacked Harvey Bingham's intense fanaticism and instead was in constant fear that he was doing something incorrect. He had been appointed for hereditary reasons, and had risen to Second Chancellor as a result of seniority, not zealous faith. In Sarah's opinion, he wasn't a great leader, but a man striving to please and hoping to hold things together in the absence of his gloried High Chancellor. As far as Pat was concerned, it was little wonder Bingham hadn't taken Argyle on the Quest.

Ursla hoped there was a chance of getting through to this man. Argyle was still committed to his Church. If he condemned the Allied Fleet in orbit, his Crusaders could march into the Naval districts of all Genesis cities and begin a massacre to exact retribution. Capturing the planet with those two million Crusaders mobilized would probably be impossible — they were in every town and with every Church diocese, and the Allied Fleet simply didn't have enough marines.

So this had to work.

Ursla heaved another heavy sigh, trying to keep herself from appearing ruffled.

No pressure.

Every time Sarah saw the Lord Second Chancellor, she had to stop herself from smirking. Unlike Bingham, the middle-aged, somewhat round fellow carried no air of menace. Instead he seemed to create chaos — his adjutants were constantly reminding him of where things were, what he was supposed to be doing, and so on. Now, as his cutter slipped through the doors of *Genesis One's* bay, it seemed to maneuver as coherently as its faithful passenger.

Ursla's pinnace was still sitting on the deck as the diminutive crimson Church craft tried to find a landing slot. Upon seeing the alien ship, the surprised pilots banked violently, nearly crashing into the bay wall. The dockmaster's tractor pulses snatched the Crusader craft before it could cause any damage, then guided it over the top of the Earther ship and set it down a few meters in front of Sarah and her party.

Taking a steadying breath, Sarah glanced to the right towards her brother, then left to see Pat. She had strong support in this, anyway — two of the best men in the system, as far as she was concerned. The Church pinnace's coolant vents hissed, ejecting fog towards the deck in high-pressure streams. The embarkation hatch opened quickly, and the ramp slid to the deck with less-than-elegant speed.

"Guard, attention."

Sarah had to admit that, despite his occasional eccentricities, Graham had a certain smart way of delivering orders. In the bay behind her, *Genesis One's* entire complement of Naval marines plus several extra platoons from her fleet came to attention. Their appearance was perfectly crisp, though she knew that they were hardly decorative troops — like Earther marines, they were deadly men and women in action.

A platoon of Crusaders suddenly erupted from the pinnace, scrambling down the ramp in what Sarah would once have considered a perfect deployment. After seeing Earther formations move, however, it was a relatively unimpressive display. She tried to force any signs of that feeling off her face, replacing it with a pre-Earther, suitably 'awed' expression as the crimson cloaks fluttered and they raised their weapons.

"All of you must lay down your arms in the name of the Church of Genesis!" one demanded, as his fellows formed a loose line before the assembled Naval personnel.

Sarah cocked an eyebrow. This wasn't Argyle's style — he must have been flustered by the Earther pinnace and told his guard to secure the area. Of course, 'secure' to a Crusader meant 'demand utter submission'. For all the tact she had to show the Lord Second Chancellor, she would *not* start with humiliation.

Graham was of the same mind, "Marines, stand-to, if you please."

The simplicity of the soft remark made Sarah's lips twitch in a smile, and she didn't bother to hide her satisfaction as the Naval marines — a dozen platoons of them — all swept their rifles to their shoulders and drew beads on the Crusaders' heads.

"Crusaders, you might wish to stand down. We are quite loyal to the Church, but we don't mean to be held hostage on our own flight deck," Sarah understood that being so seemingly disobedient to the Church's orders might not help her position with Argyle, but at least she had restrained the urge to yell 'Open Fire' while diving for the deck. That would've been much worse...

Well done.

Supplementing the hundreds of Naval rifles now aimed at their heads, Sarah's remarks convinced the Crusaders. The Church marines remained silent.

"Oh dear!"

All eyes turned up to a surprised character descending the ramp in a mad dash, "By the blessings of the Gods, we were slightly unsettled by the presence of that alien ship! Crusaders, into file! Smartly now!"

Lord Second Chancellor Benjamin Argyle shuffled hurriedly past his guards and approached the three officers before him. He paused a few meters short of them, nodding silently in recognition to Graham, then eyeing the two unfamiliar faces.

He frowned for a second, then donned an expression of triumph and recognition, "ArcBrigadier Sarah Manchester! You were with our Quest!"

For a Churcher, Sarah had to admit that Argyle's guilelessness made him tolerable. Perhaps he could better accept the truth than Bingham had... well, now wasn't the time to test that theory. She couldn't take the chance that he'd turn against the fleet.

Bowing slightly at his recognition, she recalled her old protocols, "Lord Second Chancellor, I am honored that you recognize me."

The man smiled with a slight nod, "You are one of our most valiant warriors. Unlike some of my peers, I do have a certain appreciation for the role you play in our Quest."

Funny, he never stood up to Bingham on our behalf... Sarah silenced her internal bitterness. One didn't stare aimlessly into the mouth of a gift cow, as the old Earth saying went... or was that gift *horse*?

"But, ArcBrigadier, if I am not mistaken, you are wearing *ArcGeneral* pips. You've been promoted?"

Sarah blinked in surprise — few non-military Church members bothered to learn the Naval ranking system...

"I have, Lord Chancellor. By ArcGeneral Hastings."

"And where is she? And the High Chancellor?"

Sarah bit her bottom lip and swallowed. Fiction time.

"This is a long tale, Lord Chancellor. Perhaps we could discuss it in one of *Genesis One's* lounges."

Ursla could hear them coming down the hall, but she couldn't sense the usual tension that accompanied Church personnel. He hadn't refused the meeting, had he?

Well, if he didn't turn up there would be problems. But if he did, Ursla needed to be sure of the agreed-upon story — the one Sarah was giving him.

"We came upon Liz's fleet when the Kroggs ambushed it," Ursla muttered to herself. "Saved them... helped them settle Earth... Kroggs' enemy... we're helping other side..."

The footsteps came closer, and Ursla took a last deep breath in the chair she'd had moved here from her pinnace. At least she wasn't being forced to sit on the floor...

The door opened and Sarah came through, walking next to a crimson-adorned man who was inclining his head towards her as he listened. He didn't notice Ursla sitting before him — he was too enthralled with Sarah's words.

"...and when the fleet helped us drive off the Krogg attack, they brought us to Earth where they helped us in our landing efforts, Lord Chancellor. They were a race that evolved on Earth after the great plague, no doubt placed there by the Gods to help us when our Quest came about," Sarah didn't stop talking as the doors closed behind Pat and Graham. Argyle continued to listen intently.

"And they made that big shuttle out there? And those strange ships in high orbit?"

The Second Chancellor didn't give Ursla the same threatening sense the High Chancellor had... though somehow he hadn't yet realized she was even present.

"They did, Lord Chancellor. They call themselves the Earthers, and I'd like to present to you their fleet's senior officer," Sarah raised her arm in a gentle sweep towards Ursla.

Argyle looked up and froze. Ursla had gotten used to the shock by now. She stood slowly, ending in a high crouch, and bowed slightly to the human, "Lord Second Chancellor, I am Admiral Andra Ursla of the Earther Navy. It is an honor to meet you, sir."

The room was still for a moment, Graham and Pat exchanging nervous glances behind the Second Chancellor's back. Sarah bit her lip again, recalling Liz's description of Bingham's first meeting with Setter Caine. Ursla tried not to look threatening, remembering the very same event.

Argyle smiled and rushed across the lounge with a hand extended upwards, "No, no! The honor must be mine! You and your people helped us fulfill the Holy Quest! You too must be of the Gods — they gave you the strength to help us against the Kroggs!"

As Argyle came before Ursla she gently took his hand, and the Naval officers near the door sighed in relief. Sarah tried consciously to slow her heart rate — her story had worked.

Ursla was surprised as hell, "It was all rather complicated, Lord Chancellor. I rather feared that the Kroggs might have misrepresented the Earthers as your enemy."

The Second Chancellor offered a thoughtful frown and slowly took his seat, seemingly forgetting Sarah, Pat and Graham as he nodded to the bear, "Thankfully, the Kroggs did not speak of you. I have seen the sensor scans sent by ArcGeneral Manchester to the Chancellery, and their presence in this space is much more than they ever admitted. Of late their emissaries have been silent; they have seemed consumed with their own matters. With the Quest launched, I had no reason to attempt to investigate, but now I realize."

Ursla cocked an eyebrow — realize? Realize *what*... "I fear I do not follow the wisdom of your words, Lord Chancellor."

Argyle offered a kind smile, "Fear not for your worthiness, Admiral... forgive me, but that is your title? And *Andra Ursla* is your name?"

Fortunately, Ursla had already done her best to force any reactions of surprise off her face, because Argyle's concern about her *name* bordered on unbelievable. So she simply nodded.

"Good good," Argyle nodded happily. "As I was saying, we of the Chancellery have been concerned about the Kroggs. With the departure of our Quest Fleet they'd promised to secure this system against Larosian incursion, but shortly after the Lord High Chancellor's departure, they stopped regular contact. We were ordered to restrain all our shipping to and from the asteroid belt, and to remain away from their ground installations. They did not tell us of their large fleet, and I can only believe now that they meant to betray our Quest all along."

"But why would they do *that*?" Graham blurted out the question before thinking to stop himself — but Argyle didn't take offense, or hear it with the same overtones that Ursla, Sarah and Pat did. Graham rightly thought it was a rather large jump from breaking off communications to betrayal...

Argyle looked over his shoulder to the junior Manchester with a paternal nod, "I know, faithful ArcBrigadier, it is shocking. I cannot say why, though I must admit that I have always felt the Kroggs to be sinister. They helped us so far as we needed to fulfill the Gods' mission; perhaps it was the will of the Gods that they now fall out of our friendship. Indeed, from what ArcGeneral Manchester told me briefly as we walked, it was the Krogg attack on our Quest Fleet that drew your aid."

He finished that statement by turning curiously back to Ursla, and she forced her mind to take up the threads of the fiction, "We should not misrepresent ourselves, Lord Chancellor. We aided the Genesis Fleet in the face of treachery, and now Lord High Chancellor Bingham and millions of Crusaders are settled on Earth. I was pledged to return with my fleet, in order to aid ArcGeneral Manchester in a liberation of Genesis from its oppressors."

Remarkably, Ursla realized, she had managed not to lie with that little explanation.

And then Argyle's eyes met hers, thought seeming to fill the Second Chancellor's face. Ursla's mind froze — had he seen through it? What had she said wrong...

"You are truly modest and wise, Admiral Andra. I can tell simply by your manner of talking... I can feel your faith and loyalty, while I could never feel such sentiments from the Krogg emissaries. I imagine Chancellor Bingham sent messages to this effect, but I feel I should say at once that I believe you too are a loyal agent of the Gods, and I am pleased to be in your company."

Oh. Okay. Yeah that was actually really good.

Ursla smiled, again avoiding bared teeth, "I'm an officer of the Earther Navy, Lord Chancellor, and I hope a humble friend of humanity. As are all Earthers."

Argyle bowed his head in brief acknowledgement of her words, "And you bring excellent news. The fulfillment of the Quest, I should like to hear the glorious stories! But first, I understand, is the pressing matter — the Krogg force in our system, and the Larosian Fleet to come..."

Ursla blinked. Sarah, Pat and Graham froze.

A friendly smile crossed Argyle's face again, "When the Kroggs broke regular contact with us, we thought it in the Gods' interest to find out why. Our Crusader agents have been using listening posts to intercept what Krogg signals we can."

"And there is word of a Larosian Fleet?" Ursla couldn't contain her sudden eagerness — if he was telling the truth, their gamble had proven correct...

"There is. We could intercept very little of their communications without being detected. And we have only a very rudimentary understanding of the Krogg language, mostly based on Naval terms because of the nature of our past partnership. But certainly, there is word of an approaching Larosian Fleet, larger than any before it, and what we *interpret* to be concern that it be more than a match for our defenses. We do not have the entire story, Admiral Andra — we did not realize the size of the Krogg presence in Genesis space — but the Larosians are coming."

Ursla looked quickly up to Sarah, whose eyebrows bobbed with interest.

"The pieces fall into place now," Argyle's face sobered into one of revelation. "The Quest brought us your help in our hour of need, Admiral Andra. These aliens converge on us, and it is now both our peoples, spawned of Earth, who may stand together."

It was exactly what Ursla needed to hear... if not quite in the terms she'd prefer.

Oh well, she wasn't about to look a gift horse in the mouth.

They began to speak of Earth, and Earthers, and of Genesis and the Church.

And the Larosians were coming...

CHAPTER 17

"He bought the whole bloody thing! Hook, line and dynamite!"

Graham's cheerful outburst gained a curious stare from Ursla, "Isn't that 'hook, line and sinker'? Dynamiting fish would ruin them..."

Pat grinned, "Try fishing in our oceans, Andra, and you'll want to have a good 74 in orbit to help you. Big fish, lots of teeth... bad attitude."

Sarah frowned at Pat and then looked to Ursla, "Getting back *on topic*, I believe it's safe to say that Chancellor Argyle was actually *useful*. Rather surprising, I think."

Nods were exchanged between the four officers, and Ursla leaned back in her transplanted chair with a thin smile, "We know the Larosians are coming. Takes a load off my mind... we'll just need to decide what to do."

Graham frowned, "I heard him say that, though I'm still not fully up to speed on what you expected when you cruised in. Having not seen those 3,000 ships until you showed them to me and whatnot."

"I still can't believe you didn't pick them up, Graham — really man, there were *thousands*..." Pat grinned at Graham and the junior Manchester scowled back.

"Well your lovely new Earther-built sensors might have helped. What are the chances of me getting some of those for my stations in the near future?"

Ursla cocked an eyebrow, "I'll look into it when I get back to *Agamemnon*. Shouldn't be too complicated."

Sarah held up her hand as a thought crossed her mind, "I know that whole matter is important, but I'm not sure we're done with the Church just yet."

Pat frowned, "But we've just had Argyle–"

Shaking her head, Sarah looked to Graham, "If Ben Argyle is as popular with his comrades as he was when we left, I'm willing to bet the Chancellery isn't going to believe him just like that."

The junior Manchester scratched his forehead absently, "Yes, I suppose so. Chancellor Pious is always disagreeing with him, from what I hear."

Sarah sighed and leaned back in her own chair, "And to make things worse, at some point we'll need to tell the truth... and Gods only know what we do then."

Pat nodded, "I'd ask them... the Gods that is... but that'd be very confusing to my personal lack of theology. I think we deal with that in time... maybe we could let some of our defanged Churchers from Earth help us."

Graham chuckled at the remark, and Sarah offered a single slow nod in acknowledgement, "Alright... so back to the Kroggs and Larosians then..."

She paused in thought and looked up at Ursla, "We should brief the other flags, Andra."

Ursla nodded, "Indeed, lots to discuss." Turning to Graham she laced her fingers and rested her hands in her lap, "Want to come along?"

A smile crossed Graham's face, "If it gets me new sensors, I'll carry you there."

"Deal," Ursla smiled, and Graham paled.

Pat and Sarah laughed.

An hour later, aboard *Agamemnon*, the heads of both the Genesis and Earther Fleets sat in their customary meeting space, joined by the new face of Graham Manchester. The ArcBrig was still overcoming his surprise at the Earthers' technology — and personality and size and everything else — when he boarded the ship. Fortunately, the Earther Admirals present were good enough to introduce him to the basics of Earther Naval practice as they waited to begin. Sarah talked with Pat, further exhausted by her day. The meeting with Argyle had gone extremely well, but it had been draining.

Ursla arrived after some delay, having checked on her fleet's status and redeployed several of her squadrons out from behind the Genesis ships. As she entered the lounge, the Admirals and ArcGenerals found their places around the table, Graham sitting with his sister and Pat.

Ursla quickly took her own chair, "Well, we've secured Genesis, and believe it or not, I received some *good* news from the Lord Second Chancellor. Turns out we were right, the Larosians are coming. At this point let's all pat ourselves on the back."

The assembled Admirals and ArcGenerals chuckled. Varnon Broadpaw took it upon himself to actually pat himself on the back, and Jax Furgus frowned at him, "I don't think she meant it literally."

Varnon shrugged and grinned, "Well, I still feel more satisfied and self-actualized for it."

More laughter crossed the table, and everyone settled back in their seats, contemplating what this assurance of the Larosian involvement would mean.

Pat, with a thoughtful frown, was the first to lean forward, "Well I hate to ask the obvious questions, seeing as I'm still the most junior and I keep getting asked back for reasons unknown to me, but what does that do for us? I mean, we've got a pretty good idea now that the Kroggs can't afford to come after us if we don't push them to, but what do we do when the Larosians get here?"

There were some thoughtful sighs, then Varnon Broadpaw spoke, "Well, you're right about our move — we should wait for the Larosians to arrive before we act. I suppose step one is to keep our eyes on that rift."

"So we *are* going to gamble that the Kroggs don't come after us in the meantime?" Bill Masters' voice was skeptical, but the Earthers around him seemed to nod simultaneously.

"They might try, but not in strength. They can't risk splitting their force before the Larosians come through. So far all we've done is beat them when they weren't expecting us and when we had a numerical advantage — they don't know how potent we really are. I can't see them chancing an encounter with us when they know the firepower the Larosians can hit them with," Ursla's explanation was enough to convince the ArcLieutenant-General.

"Unless they have a specific ETA for the Larosians," Pat murmured, "and they have time for the both of us."

"Feeling optimistic then, Pat?" Furgus asked with his usual irreverent humor. "I think we can afford to take the chance. And even if they all come in, guns ablaze, is it possible we could stop them with the support of the orbital defenses?"

Graham cleared his throat conspicuously, and all eyes turned to him. As he reddened slightly, Talone prodded him, "Graham?"

He reddened more, not used to the familiarity of the Earther system.

"No protocol or determined time to speak, Graham," Pat whispered. "Go ahead."

Sitting up as best he could, the junior Manchester spoke, "Well, um, sirs…" Pat poked him for the formality. "Well, the thing is the *Genesis* stations and our ground batteries can give reasonable fire support, but without some sort of enhancement, we can't hope to slow the Kroggs — we didn't even see them out there, all *3,000* of them. And I don't think any Genesis officers who've watched their SDs clean up after a battle with the Larosians will disagree when I say we're no match for them one-to-one. We need to upgrade or the Kroggs will brush us aside."

Ursla frowned, "Sarah, what do you think of that? I know there was some uncertainty about enhancements."

The elder Manchester slowly began to nod, her eyes cast thoughtfully at the table, "Graham's quite right about his stations being outclassed. I'm still not sure how the tune ups you gave us in Sol space will handle Krogg ships… but then I'm also not sure what else you can give us now that we're out here — without jeopardizing our ability to move immediately, and with the manufacturing base we've got on hand."

"And," Pat leaned forward, "just to play devil's advocate, without annoying our ArcColonels. As I understand it, James Stanton is very unhappy back at Earth because upgrades took his ship out of the line."

It was an interesting dilemma, on a number of levels. Ursla had talked to Savanna Felix about these issues before leaving Earth, but the presumption then had been that there was no reason to significantly re-engineer the Genesis Fleet — all it was expected to face was a small Krogg force. For all the internal strife the improvements were causing, the combat edge wasn't thought necessary.

So it was jury-rigging time... Ursla frowned and looked to Broadpaw, "Varnon, we've got a number of repair ships attached to the fleet, right?"

The Earther second-in-command nodded thoughtfully.

"Do you think your manufacturing plants could adapt new tech to their ships? Sensors... shields... weapons..." Ursla looked to Graham and paused in thought. "When we left Earth, several damaged Genesis ships were being upgraded, and the one that was complete was changed a bit too radically to rejoin the fleet. We could try to turn out regular retrofits to upgrade sensors and armor, maybe even laser output. Shouldn't be too tough to come up with some improvements... and perhaps improvement *kits* that your engineers could install themselves."

The humans at the table traded glances, and Graham slowly nodded, "I can put our industry under martial control... start running whatever you need me to. We've got high productivity."

"I could sell 'do-it-yourself' upgrades to my ships, I think," Pat thought aloud. "As long as everybody gets the same, and our engineers hitch the kits up themselves. And besides, who'll complain at a time like this — I mean, 3,000 Kroggs..."

Sarah simply offered a nod in agreement, "Whatever edge we can get. And I imagine everyone will be a little more inclined to cooperate with the enhancements now that we've all had the chance to see Second Fleet operate against the Kroggs."

Ursla allowed herself a smile, and she shared it with the other proud Earthers at the table — they had done well against the Kroggs, even considering their overwhelming numerical superiority. But Ursla veiled her pride quickly, turning back to matters at hand, "Splendid. Varnon, can you get that organized?"

The wolf nodded with a smile, then looked to Graham, "Meet after the briefing so you can orient me on your manufacturing?"

The ArcBrig nodded slowly... he was nervous but eager at the same time. This table of high-ranking, battle-hardened Earther veterans certainly seemed to be respecting his opinion... it was odd to ask for something from seniors and to actually *get* it. Somehow he imagined such accommodation was part of standard Earther operating procedure.

"So we wait and start non-invasive upgrades, ready to move at a moment's notice if the Larosians appear," Sarah said softly. "The only other question I have is do we send for reinforcements?"

Ursla had been toying with the same question. After eight months of steady construction, the Earthers had replenished a large portion of their lost fleet, but they were still 400 ships short of the their old strength. More Genesis ships were being recommissioned every day, but the availability of human crews was actually on the decline. Still, if Caine brought all he had, they could double the size of the fleet in Genesis, with 1,400 of the ships being Earther.

It was probably the best way to handle the situation.

"We'll send soon, I think, Sarah. First we should make sure that everything remains secure out here — if we send a sloop it'll take a month for anything to return, and if we're not certain of our position before we do…"

"The rest of the fleet could fly into a Krogg ambush and find a large debris field where we should be. Agreed," Sarah's tone was as grim as the meaning of her words.

The room was silent in similar contemplation.

"Alright. Varnon, Graham, get working on the upgrade situation. Everyone else, get your commands ready for Krogg probing." She turned to Furgus, "We'll probably put some scouts around the rift, and I'll need them well protected — your 64s, Jax."

The lion Admiral nodded in reply.

"Excellent," Ursla's tone was brighter than it had been. "Let's get to it!"

CHAPTER 18

Vice Admiral Savanna Felix hadn't served aboard a ship in half a century. Then he'd been a ship administrator aboard *Dunkirk*, a Third Rate 72-gun ship of the line. And that really wasn't the same as commanding a Battle Squadron including seven 74s from the flag deck of an 80. No, the two didn't compare at all.

The fact that he hadn't really wanted to leave his much-loved desk and stack of papers under the care of a new Admiral to go riding through space was irrelevant. Caine, Felar, and the rest of the Admiralty had taken a single look at his war-games tactics and decided he needed a chance to repeat his feat in the field. Because the particular problem they had in mind shouldn't be too much of a challenge for a squadron of 74s, it was decided that he should go.

Maybe if I blow it they'll send me back to the desk...

But as much as Felix appreciated his administrative job, that option wasn't tempting to him at all. He wasn't a line officer in his own mind, but he still had a duty to perform, a commitment to fulfill. He'd deal with this Coalition properly, and let things evolve from there.

The message buoy sent by ArcColonel Stanton's *Archangel Sword* had reached Earth two days before, warning both human and Earther citizens about the pirates, and ArcGeneral Hastings had been determined to annihilate the threat. Caine had talked her out of taking every recommissioned Genesis ship out of Sol for a hunt, but only by promising to send Earther ships to deal with the renegade humans.

They'd be brought back to Earth where they would be subject to punishment under the Genesis code of justice. It would be an interesting series of trials — Earthers never had any need of a civil or military criminal justice system, since their sense of self-control was so highly developed.

Certain humans had indicated to Felix a number of times that it was impossible for a society to live both without laws and crime, but it seemed natural to him — and to all Earthers. As such, the Earther Consulate had decided to hand over all legal proceedings to Liz Hastings, with the intent of watching and learning.

Felix agreed with the Consulate. This Coalition was promising violence against other humans and Earthers, and that was unacceptable. So for all his reluctance, he'd do his job and see these Coalition ships defeated and brought home for... *trial*.

Tonnant led the same squadron of 74s that had joined it during the war-games, though at present Felix had five of the seven Third Rates waiting in energy drive — only *Dragon* and *Hero* had returned to normal matter with *Tonnant* at Renegade's Belt. The other 74s would be ready when he called for them, but he knew that a whole squadron would likely intimidate the Coalition force, scattering it and making it much more difficult — though certainly not impossible — to capture.

As he'd hoped, the Coalition ships appeared on *Tonnant's* sensors: three Battlecruisers, two Heavy Cruisers, a Light Cruiser and four Destroyers. They angled towards the three line of battle ships, apparently not intimidated by the Earthers' substantial advantage in size.

Felix's eyes narrowed — they came straight on, arrogantly forming a vanguard for action and opening their tubes. They were still a few minutes out, but they obviously wanted to demonstrate their hostile intent.

For a second Felix thought to call for the rest of his squadron, but the Coalition ships could still scatter. He needed to keep them together and then lasso them with his other 74s once they could be properly surrounded.

"I don't think we'll need eight ships of the line for this," he said aloud. "Order the rest of the squadron to stand by to surround them. Send to *Dragon* and *Hero* to clear for action. Beat to quarters!"

As *Tonnant* and its two consorts were already under alert, the order to go to battle stations was not a surprise. The ships responded with cool Earther efficiency, their weapons and shields flaring into life while their other systems went to sleep to provide maximum offensive capability.

The Coalition ships barreled in, as if completely unaware of what they were about to meet. It appeared as though they intended to swarm, to try to outmaneuver the trio of Earther ships and use numbers and massed pinprick strikes to win.

They were obviously feeling confident today — as far as Felix understood it, the handiness of Earther ships of the line was legendary among the ranks of the Genesis Fleet. Well, either these Coalition humans thought they were better than the Earthers, or they just didn't believe in legends.

How unfortunate for them.

The human ships plotted their firing solutions as *Tonnant* and the pair of 74s closed, their forward-facing tubes already bearing on the Earther vessels. Felix chose to run down on the squadron, despite the disadvantage he would accept by having only his bow chasers in action. While they could shower him with full salvoes of missiles from this vector, his ships could reply with only a few forward-mounted weapons — perhaps fifteen guns between them.

As missile range was reached, the first volleys began to belch from the human cruisers. The missiles cycled quickly and then a second volley was in space. The rate of fire and coordination of these volleys was far superior to what the Earthers had seen from the Church months before, but that didn't surprise Felix. These were real Naval officers, albeit piratical ones.

As the missiles closed, *Tonnant's* chase guns fired a salvo of canister to meet them, and *Dragon* and *Hero* added to the energy cloud as it hurtled forward. The wave of canister was by itself not enough, but it blunted the first wave of missiles and gave the carronade crews less to shoot at. Still, missiles slashed home.

Tonnant's shields blazed as the warheads detonated against them. They were tuned to absorb the explosive energy, but the hailstorm still degraded them slowly... *very* slowly... The two forces continued to close.

The Coalition ships ceased missile fire abruptly, no doubt conserving a limited supply of warheads, and as the pressure slackened the Earthers seized a few empty seconds to act. *Tonnant* turned hard to port, its starboard guns coming to bear on the renegade ships. *Dragon* went 'up' over the 80-gun flagship, rolling its own starboard broadside 'down' to face the Coalition ships as they cruised beneath, and *Hero* mirrored its division mate's action from below, aiming 'up' at the renegades.

The humans were caught unawares, and *Tonnant's* 34-gun broadside thundered, joined quickly by both consorts' 30-gun volleys. The Battlecruisers, running in front of their squadron, were caught by the better part of a broadside each, their armor buckling under the intense fire. They were cast aside, disabled and out of action. The rest of the vanguard tried to scatter, but the Earther ships had rolled, bringing fresh broadsides around and sending new tides of energy into space.

One Heavy Cruiser and the Light Cruiser were knocked out of action in the volley, as were three of the Destroyers. The last Heavy Cruiser made a run for it, the last Destroyer rushing into its wake.

But the unfortunate pair ran straight into the 74s *Atlas* and *Donegal*, then emerging from energy drive at Felix's order. The Heavy Cruiser refused to stop, slipping between the Third Rates and accelerating quickly into flux, but the Destroyer came to a quick halt, striking its colors — or in human terms, deactivating its transponder.

Aboard *Tonnant*, Felix let his eyebrows climb — not too bad for a roundup operation. All but one Coalition ship had been captured, though he was determined not to let that one get away...

"Orders to the squadron: each take a prize in tow with grav tractors and make for Earth. *Hero* is to stay with us — we'll begin a search for the remaining ship."

Watching in the main battle tank as his squadron took hold of the Coalition ships, a strange sensation gripped the back of Felix's mind. He'd *enjoyed* that.

Maybe even as much as he enjoyed paperwork.

It had been a well-coordinated action that had fulfilled its goals without loss... well, maybe he had a future in this line of work after all...

No, best not to jump the gun with a conclusion like that, "Alright, Captain, let's get moving. Mark that ship's last course and make speed to overtake."

"Aye sir, Cruising Master, make speed 2,400 pls..."

Felix sat back in his chair, and *Tonnant,* in company with *Hero*, leapt into energy drive.

CHAPTER 19

It had been four days, and there'd been nothing. Nothing at all.

Ursla watched the green orb of Genesis spin slowly in the blackness of the system and wondered about the Kroggs and their seeming patience. Though Ursla hadn't expected a major move from the alien fleet, she'd counted on a little reconnaissance coming her way, especially after the damage they'd done to the Krogg ground installations. She'd be awfully curious about the Earther Fleet if *she* were a Krogg. But these aliens weren't acting as Ursla would — in their unsettling and completely foreign way, they were giving the Allied Fleet time to consolidate over Genesis.

Just as well too; bigger problems were beginning to emerge on the planet, and unsurprisingly, the *Church* was responsible.

As predicted, about half the Chancellors' Council — or as it was generally known, the Chancellery — was still quite wary of the Earther presence above Genesis. Suspicion seemed to be running deep in their ranks, as they'd just dealt with the supposed treachery of the Kroggs, and they had no Church representative from Earth to corroborate the Allied explanation of events.

Argyle was working hard, using *Flame's* sensor logs to solidify a strong case against the Kroggs, but despite his belief in the faithfulness of the Earthers, he could not allay the fears of the Chancellery. As such, the untrusting Council had cautiously blocked the more ambitious Allied plans. Because of the strong Krogg force in-system, Earther upgrades to the Genesis Fleet and orbitals would be fully supported, and the Genesis Navy would be free to coordinate with the Earthers. The Earthers, however, would not be permitted to deploy any forces to Genesis itself, and no Earther guests could be received planetside without the presence of a strong Crusader guard — in case of subterfuge.

Meanwhile, the 900 Genesis ships Sarah had brought into orbit were flooding the comm nets with personal calls, informing families of their well-being, delivering messages for friends and notifications of those who'd died. The crews had been informed of the cover story, and there was little doubt in Ursla's mind that it would hold well enough. The Navy had been shielding itself against the Church with lies and half-truths for centuries, after all — secrecy was a way of life.

And yet Ursla truly hated 'cover stories'. She wanted the populace to be free of the ridiculous notions the United Nations had planted in their society centuries before, but without the right messenger, there'd be no way to bring the Church on side. They needed a figure the population already trusted to take command of the Chancellery — someone who epitomized the pre-Quest Church, and who understood where it would have to go now that the Quest was complete. Only that sort of leader could ease the Genesis transition from prophecy to reality.

And despite numerous attempts to find alternative choices, her answer always came back to one man.

With a frown darkening her expression, Ursla keyed the Fleetcomm and sent a signal to Sarah.

Pope Joseph Barron's crew had been stood down for almost two days now. There was little for the Superdreadnought to do with a friendly planet under its bow and no activity from the Kroggs. Sarah had taken the first two days of the orbital stasis to catch up with Graham, but now his responsibilities were eliminating his personal time. So instead of catching up with family, she was visiting with Pat — an activity she found just as … no, *more* enjoyable.

They sat and talked in one corner of *Barron's* main leisure lounge, tuning out the crew that milled around them while they caught up on conversations they'd been denied over the two weeks of their voyage from Earth. Neither Sarah nor Pat realized the crew was giving them a particularly wide berth, letting them have their quiet corner in what was usually a bustling recreation center. Had Sarah noticed, she'd have written it off as respect for senior officers, but it was more than that. Whenever the ArcGeneral and ArcBrigadier laughed happily, knowing glances would be exchanged between the veteran spacers and officers around them. Literally, it seemed, Pat and Sarah were the only two not getting it.

And everybody else knew *exactly* what *it* was.

"So I've been reading the history behind the Earther Navy," Pat said as Sarah sat facing him and listening intently. "They based their system on the old Royal Navy of Britain — not the one we can read about in the pre-Exodus texts, mind you, but one that predated that. It was dominant in its day, not the Union States Navy. Won almost every action it fought, even when it was totally outgunned."

Sarah smiled, resting her chin on her palm, "Sounds familiar."

Pat grinned, "Aye, struck me that way too. Though from what the texts say the old Britons weren't nearly as… *agreeable* as our Earther friends — they flogged people and hung sailors for bad behavior. Glad the Earthers didn't adopt *that*, eh!"

Sarah nodded quietly and kept her gaze on Pat, but before she could reply someone touched her shoulder, "Sorry to interrupt, ma'am. Admiral Ursla needs you on the comm."

In the bustling room, Sarah hadn't even been aware of the ArcLieutenant waiting to deliver the message, nor had Pat. She scolded herself mentally, turned to the young officer and nodded, "Very well. I'll take it in the comm booth."

She looked towards the busy booth in the opposite corner of the activity room and stood, "You don't go anywhere, Patrick. I must grill you on more Earth history."

The pair matched smiles before Sarah strode across the room. She stepped to the front of the line, apologizing to a rating, "Fleet business, spacer. Shouldn't be a moment."

The leathery woman nodded with a grin, "Aye, not going to beat up the fleet commander for my spot in line, ma'am. Beatings stop after ArcMajor."

Sarah snorted a laugh and slipped into the booth as the officer in it wrapped up his conversation. She slid the door shut behind him and settled onto the stool before the monitor, keying in her code and activating the live message in her buffer.

Ursla flickered onto the screen, "Sorry to interrupt you Sarah, but I'm beginning to put together the packet for our sloop when we send it back, and I have to run something by you."

Sarah shrugged, her good mood overcoming misgivings about the lost time with Pat, "Fire away, Andra. Be warned, I'm in a marvelous mood!"

Ursla smiled, "Pat's there?"

Sarah blinked as Ursla chuckled, opened her mouth to say something and then closed it.

How did she know that?

"Anyway, the question is about the Council. We need to force it into line but I know only one person on our side who has enough clout to do that... and he's back home."

It took less then a second for Sarah to recognize the implication, "Bingham? You want him to come *here*?"

Ursla sighed and shrugged, sobering now as Sarah's mood darkened, "We need him to run Genesis. If he's really changed then he can do it — he might be our only hope with the Chancellery..."

"But it's *Harvey Bingham*, Andra! The very same Harvey Bingham who threatened to wipe out the Earther race!" Sarah's voice was cold, and her words were coming out a bit more loudly than she'd intended. She took a breath to calm herself — the booths weren't soundproof, and she didn't want to alienate her friend.

Ursla nodded slowly, "He did that at one point, but the change he's gone through is rather dramatic..."

"Andra, evil like his can't be changed!"

Ursla stopped at the outburst, fully understanding her friend's personal feeling on the subject, and trying to lighten the stress that had brought it about, "Alright, let's leave it up to Liz and Setter. Together they can decide his suitability."

At least that took the pressure off both of them — Sarah had no desire to reintegrate that man into Genesis society, no matter how much he claimed he'd changed. But to be fair, she had never met him in person; perhaps there were aspects of his character that had not been revealed in his duties leading up to the Quest.

That would be for those now closest to him to decide.

Sarah sighed and nodded, "Very well."

Silence followed for a few seconds as the dark atmosphere lingered.

Sarah heaved a sigh and tried to compose herself, "Any movement from the Kroggs?"

The question was more reserved, and Ursla appreciated the lowering of tension, "None at all. Their patience is rather frustrating in some ways, I must admit. But for the best, all the same."

Sarah shrugged, "Just so, we should probably take it as good news. Anyway, I'll be off."

Ursla nodded and cut the connection.

Another sigh of frustration escaped Sarah's lungs, and she leaned back on the stool, stretching her neck from side to side in a vain effort to relax. Collecting herself, she slid the door open and re-entered the leisure lounge.

She returned to her table to find Pat looking slightly distraught, "So what was that about?"

Sarah collapsed onto her chair, "Andra wants to bring Bingham out to control the council. We've decided to suggest it to Caine and Liz and let them decide."

Pat cocked his head slightly, "Well, Bingham might be the only one able to put Chancellor Pious in his place... our only shot at getting control, Gods help us..." He let the words fall away as he eyed Sarah's troubled face.

"Anyhow, we were talking about His Britannic King's Navy..."

Sarah slowly began to perk up as Pat talked, letting her chin sit in her palm as she listened. At least *this* was relaxing...

The alert klaxons aboard *Joseph Barron* sounded a few moments later.

CHAPTER 20

"They're definitely moving, ma'am. A heavy force... looks like 300 ships. Coming straight in at about half light speed. They'll be in range in about half an hour."

Ursla nodded to her Sensor Chief and turned back to *Agamemnon's* bridge. They'd handled 100-odd Kroggs already, but that force had been haphazard and unprepared. These Kroggs wouldn't be so easy to turn.

She could run out fast and try to use the Second Fleet to protect Genesis, but somehow she doubted Sarah would care for that. And if the Second Fleet was wrecked in a battle outside Genesis orbit, the planet would be left in bad circumstances — the Genesis Navy was tough but it still lacked the technology to handle Kroggs.

"Get me a line to ArcGeneral Manchester and order the fleet to clear for action."

"Signal already coming in, ma'am," the Signal Officer's prompt reply demanded no response, as Sarah appeared in the bridge's main battle tank.

"Spoke too soon about the Kroggs' patience. They probably want to see if we won the first round by fluke," Ursla's greeting wasn't bright.

Sarah nodded silently, "Should we go meet them?"

"Pardon my cutting in..." Graham appeared in the holo next to his sister, "but I heard you say 'go out'. I should think it would be best for you to stay under my tubes. No disrespect Ursla, but if you want to keep your force intact then why not use us?"

"You probably won't be able to get a good firing solution on any of them — you don't have upgraded tactical nets yet," Ursla noted quietly.

"Patch yours in. We can target through your sensors and deliver coordinated volleys. Kroggs might be tough, but our tubes are loaded with ship-killers designed to knock off Larosians. I think we can handle a few hundred between us," Graham's face showed confidence that was either foolish or... well, they *were* his stations, he should know what they were capable of.

Sarah looked to Ursla with a cocked eyebrow, and the Admiral nodded, "Alright. Let's show them that Genesis is not to be toyed with."

Nods crossed space over the three-way line and then the human officers disappeared from the holo tank.

"All ships into bombard positions, form lines between *Genesis One, Three* and *Four*. Run out guns when in position. Central fire control," Ursla's orders crossed space in a flurry and squadrons of ships slid apart in a sudden, chaotic-seeming ballet.

Meanwhile, Sarah deployed her larger fleet in three 300-ship clusters around the massive *Genesis* stations, her ships' tubes opening and loading, their AIs and gunners lining their sights up along the Kroggs' flight path. Graham patched his battle computers into the Earther network — a trick the Navies had labored over during their eight-month rebuilding period in Earth space — and had each *Genesis* orbital load its 400 tubes with the massive ship-killer missiles.

Too big to be carried even by Colonizers, the ship-killers made the six *Genesis* stations threatening to say the very least, though there had always been a bitter belief in Naval circles that the Kroggs would never give humans a weapon that could be used decisively against them.

Well, the Kroggs *had* provided sensors that couldn't lock onto any of their own ships — perhaps they had thought that limitation insurance enough against Genesis treachery. The missiles still might work fine against those incoming Krogg ships, now that the Earthers had provided better targeting gear. So the only way anyone would find out how far the Krogg crippling of Genesis ships went would be to see whether the big shiny trillium bicobalt warheads mounted on the missiles in the tubes lived up to the sales pitch. It'd be poetic justice if they were as effective against Kroggs as those aliens had promised they'd be against Larosians.

"Twenty-six minutes and closing," *Agamemnon's* Sensor Chief reported. "They're crawling in at sub-light, ma'am."

Ursla steepled her fingers and waited.

Captain-Commodore Novash of the Honorable Larosian Star Navy sat in his chair with what humans would call 'steepled fingers'. His silvery-gray bridge was darkened, his Warcruiser *Shanavorus* running under a cloak of stealth to remain undetected by any Krogg ships in the area. His squadron was spread out in a halo around *Shanavorus*, mimicking the stealth routine.

Novash's squadron was one of a half-ten squadrons of Warcruisers running reconnaissance for the Fourth Fleet-of-War of the Star Navy, a force of 2,000 of the Larosians' greatest ships. The Fleet was currently seeking the fleeing Krogg armada — the last of the Krogg forces known to be in this quadrant of the Larosian home galaxy. Fleet intelligence had offered no indication of how large an armada remained, but it was clear that the force which had once numbered 14,000 ships was now scarcely more than a few thousand. Eliminating it would be a point of pride for the Empire, and it would be a crucial step in the eradication of the Krogg threat. So, the Navy had been divided into ten Fleets-of-War, each numbering 2,000 ships, and had been sent to all corners of the quadrant to search for the fleeing armada. As yet no trace of the enemy had been found, but there would be no escape for the Kroggs, given time.

The Fourth Fleet-of-War, one of the most highly regarded units in the Navy, had been assigned to an area which had been the site of fierce fighting during the last campaign, and which was laden with anomalous obstacles to reconnaissance. Foremost among these difficult anomalies was a hyperspace corridor, leading to a system that had yet to be charted by a Larosian survey. Over the past two centuries, numerous scouting squadrons of Warcruisers had traversed the corridor, finding a crude, territorial, and still unidentified alien race on the other side. Communication attempts with these aliens had failed, and given the climate of war with the Kroggs, the Larosian Navy had taken little interest in the isolated planet. So long as the Kroggs stayed out, it had not been deemed a threat by the squadrons that had returned — and though a number had been destroyed outright on the other side, there had never been any indication that the Kroggs were involved. Because of the war there had been no resources to spend investigating these aliens further.

The last squadron had been through eight cycles before. Since that time, Kroggs had overrun the corridor, and there seemed a chance that at least some of the retreating ships might attempt to flee to the unknown space. Given the voracity of the territorial aliens occupying the planet on the other side, the survival of a small Krogg unit there seemed unlikely. Still, no Larosian could take the chance of having a Krogg force spring out on this flank, now far to the rear of the front lines. The Fourth Fleet-of-War would investigate.

Sir, Shandrakor *has located the hyperspace corridor in its grid.* The report came to Novash telepathically from his watch commander.

Very well. Order the squadron to converge on Shandrakor. *Send a signal to Fleet Command advising them that we are in position and proceeding with the mission. If we do not report back soon, it should be assumed that we have encountered superior Krogg forces.*

Novash's squadron assembled near the rim of the corridor as the message was sent. The Captain-Commodore reflected silently on the possibility that this was some sort of Krogg trap — that the Kroggs had overwhelmed the local aliens on the other side and were now lying in wait.

Regardless of the 'mights', Novash's duty was to investigate the corridor. So that was precisely what he would do.

Ships remain in stealth and stand by to go to battle configuration, Novash thought to his watch commander. *Enter the corridor.*

"Whoa!"

Graham looked up from his console, "What did we say about reporting yourself properly, Mister? Gods, man!"

"Sir!" the Scanner Technician repeated quickly. "They all just turned tail!"

Graham frowned from his command chair, "They *what?*"

"Signal from ArcGeneral Manchester, sir... and Admiral Ursla," the Communications Officer piped up, and Graham spun to his screen.

"Three-way it, please."

Sarah and Ursla appeared on Graham's monitor, faces matching his own confusion. "Any thoughts?" Ursla asked first.

"Intimidated?" Graham knew that wasn't the answer as soon as he suggested it.

Sarah gave him a big sister look and shrugged, "A probe to test our readiness — see how quickly we can deploy when they approach?"

Ursla opened her mouth to reply when something called her attention away from her fellow commanders. She said something they weren't able to hear, frowned, and turned back, "My sloops are reading a change in the rift. Best guess is something's coming through."

"Aha! About bleeding time they showed up!" Graham smiled eagerly. "How many then, a few thousand?"

Ursla was off screen again, only her shoulder visible to Sarah and Graham over the link. She turned back to her monitor, "Not so lucky, Graham. Twenty-five."

The younger Manchester's smile vanished and he looked between the two women, "A scout then. Running point for a fleet."

"And about to be crushed decisively, no doubt," Sarah said dryly.

Ursla paused at the words, a plan forming behind her eyes as the humans watched.

"Not necessarily," she said after a few seconds. "The Kroggs still don't know all that much about us. I might... Sarah, Graham, stay here and get ready to receive a Krogg attack. We'll be bringing some company back with us, I'm willing to bet."

Before Sarah could open her mouth to protest, Ursla disappeared.

There was a pause as the two Manchesters tried to determine what exactly the bear had in mind, but Graham was first to shake the confusion.

"Up to us then, big sister," he said in a huff, and cut his own link.

What the bloody Gods is that beast up to?

CHAPTER 21

Ten Battle Squadrons of Earther warships simultaneously vanished into energy drive. Two squadrons were composed entirely of First Rates, two were made up of Second Rates, and the last six were filled out by the workhorse 64s and 74s. With their fields expanding to 250 percent for stealth purposes, these ships surged outward towards the anomaly, their engines pushing them up to 300 pls.

Ursla was more than a little tense as she sat on *Agamemnon's* bridge. The 150-gun First Rate was leading the battle group from its foremost line abreast, so she was making no secret of her commitment to this venture. She meant to get in close with the Kroggs, and try a maneuver not unlike one she'd used against Church ships during the Naval mutiny eight months before. Except this situation was a lot more complicated than anything she'd dealt with aboard *Cerberus*, and this mission might prove particularly tricky...

Damned near impossible is more like it.

Ursla ground her jaw and shut down her internal dialogue. Cynicism really wasn't what she needed right now...

The Larosians had better appreciate this.

Novash watched the dimensional readings with some interest. Larosians and Kroggs utilized different levels of subspace to move faster than light — specifically, they used hyperpoints to allow travel through layers of subspace with different laws of physics and relativity. Standard hyperpoints took Larosians to subspace layers that were listed as 'mid-range' on the Tashtar Subspace scale, but the layer used by the hyperspace corridor he was examining now was 'lower' than any others that had been discovered, and it could allow a ship to travel much farther and faster than the average hyperspace layer.

The fact that his squadron had now been traversing the corridor for more than five minutes indicated that its exit point must be extremely far from Larosian space. Records from past expeditions had certainly suggested that this alien star system resided in a faraway galaxy. Far, far away...

It seemed unlikely that the Kroggs would have bothered to maintain a base so far beyond their known territory, but then perhaps this corridor led to *new* Krogg bases... or *old* Krogg possessions — the space which had given birth to them. Despite warring with them for 400 years, the Larosians still had no information regarding the location of the Krogg homeworld, or their earliest years of development.

Novash suspected this mission would turn up nothing to alleviate that lack of information, but prudence remained important.

All ships, full battle configuration upon exit. Ready at your stations.

The Kroggs were clearly quite committed to their blockade, but then nothing Ursla had seen them do in the past days would have suggested otherwise. Now, with the strange readings coming from the rift, the alien ships had begun to reposition themselves, probably in order to gain the best firing positions possible.

The Earther force slipped into their ranks unnoticed, hidden by the broad configuration of their energy drive fields, while the whole Krogg Fleet was paying attention to the threat they knew. Twenty-five Larosian signatures were clearly nearing the end of the corridor now, and Krogg spines began growing expectantly from the skins of their ships. Ursla detailed her three squadrons of 74s and her own *Agamemnon* to go directly to the opening of the rift and to stand by to drop from energy drive. The rest of the force took up positions randomly throughout the front ranks of the Krogg blockade, prepared to offer a distraction for *Agamemnon* while the First Rate led this complicated little grab operation.

Ursla sat and watched silently, "Pull fields into 150 percent and stand by."

Novash watched as his detectors located the end of the causeway. Hyperspace corridors impressed the Captain-Commodore — his squadron had just traveled six galaxies in a relatively short time. Under normal power, a Larosian ship would take centuries to make the same journey.

Duty, however, summoned Novash's mind from matters of navigation and intergalactic travel. Kroggs could be awaiting his squadron in this new galaxy, unlikely though that might seem, but Novash was confident he could deal with most average-sized Krogg forces. His twenty-five Warcruiser squadron was a formidable unit, with enough combined firepower to inflict a great deal of damage on an equivalent force, and with sufficient speed to outrun most larger enemies. He would form his ships as soon as he exited the corridor, and from there he would have a multitude of options for combat...

Of course, the entire issue could be — and probably *was* — moot. This was likely still home only to a militant, defensive, and essentially harmless alien race, with no interest in welcoming outside species into their space. If that was the case, Novash would simply escape after inflicting as little damage as possible, and alert the fleet to ignore this place.

As Novash thought more about it, he concluded it was highly unlikely that the Kroggs had a presence so far away from their campaign frontier.

Ready to exit. All ships standing by for battle configuration. The watch commander's telepathic voice was smooth.

Very good.

"Countdown to Larosian arrival, please," Ursla's words were calm, though she admitted to herself a certain tension.

The ships of her rescue unit were sharing the anxiety — this was to be a different sort of action than their first skirmishes with the Kroggs. Outnumbered by an order of magnitude and attempting to make rapid contact with an alien race that didn't even know the Earthers existed... this was a gamble, but to fulfill their commitment to their human allies, the Earthers knew they had to take the risk.

"Eleven... ten... nine... eight..."

The Earther squadrons that were scattered throughout space to create a diversion within the Krogg Fleet would emerge and attack at 'five'. That would hopefully give them just enough time to draw the Kroggs' attention from the mouth of the rift, and in turn allow the Larosians to survive — at least long enough for Ursla to get to them.

Agamemnon and its fellow rescue ships of the line sat at the exit point for the corridor, their broadsides loaded with canister to beat back Krogg missiles as effectively as possible. They'd drop from energy drive just as the Larosians appeared in normal space, and if all went as planned, they'd be back in energy drive within seconds. If not...

Ursla ground her jaw and refused to contemplate *that* possibility. Her people would do their job well — there was nothing else she could expect of them.

"Seven... six... five..."

The forty-seven ships of the line detailed to distract the Kroggs erupted into matter, their guns sliding from their ports in the same instant. Surrounding many of the Kroggs in groups of two and three, the ships simultaneously fired all their broadsides and chasers, stealing attention from the rift. The Kroggs took a second to react, too slow to catch their new opposition with returned fire. Spines and neuro-pulses lashed out randomly, seeking targets that had already begun to move at high speed. A few lucky shots struck home, forcing fizzling shields to repel them, but then the Earthers danced and waited for their guns to recharge. Their efforts to draw Krogg attention away from the mouth of the rift had worked well.

"Four... three... two..."

Exiting now... the watch commander reported in his smooth mental voice, and the standard layer of space retook the Larosian Warcruiser Squadron.

Novash's first thoughts, and those of his crews, focused on establishing battle formation and initiating combat protocols. Then their sensors began to see past the distortions emitted by the end of the corridor.

And what a sight they revealed.

Every alarm on the *Shanavorus* and its fellows blared instantly — the largest concentration of Krogg ships seen since the Son of Praaxus had turned back the Queen months before awaited his squadron. Some 3,000 vessels...

Captain-Commodore! Startled telepathic reports reverberated through the squadron.

I see them. Begin targeting, open fire as soon as possible. Honorable deaths to us all this day... Novash accompanied his orders with the traditional war oath of the Larosian Empire. Retreat was not an option — spines would already be incoming, and there was no time to outrun the massive volleys.

So they would die with honor.

Novash telepathically tapped his Sensor Officer's mind, viewing the scans of the Krogg Fleet himself. The massive force was configured to blockade the corridor, and behind it was an asteroid belt... a belt that was curiously scattering *Shanavorus'* sensor pulses. He could not see anything shrouded by the giant floating rocks, and his mind could not telepathically sense past them.

This was an ambush site. A perfectly developed ambush site, with a place of retreat that could not be penetrated by Larosian scans. The Kroggs had set a masterful trap...

All of these realizations took less than three human seconds — Novash was a veteran of over a century of war, and his disciplined mind was well accustomed to quickly analyzing situations.

But just as he came to understand the circumstances of his own destruction, he began to see the tides of energy fire hurtling through space — at the *Kroggs*, not him... Unknown ships were weaving through the front ranks of the Krogg blockade.

And then great swirling balls of energy started to move towards his ships...

"What are they doing?" Ursla hadn't meant to say it out loud but she had, and Tigar glanced across at her with a shrug.

The Larosian ships that had emerged from the rift were about the size of Fifth Rates, but now as they saw their enemy they seemed to be expanding in physical size — like animals puffing up to make themselves appear larger before an enemy. Their hulls bulged outwards, revealing weapons and shields, and putting more hull and buffer space between potential damage and critical systems.

It was an interesting method of preparing for combat.

Of course, it wouldn't be very interesting if Ursla sat there and watched the Kroggs blow it to bits.

"Execute."

• • •

At first Novash was unsure of the approaching energy balls — there was one for each of his vessels, and he supposed for a second they might be some sort of ship-killing weapons. Then they began to decelerate, disobeying the Tashtar laws of physics that said energy could not be *maneuvered*.

The squadron of energy balls was spreading out, each of its members coming alongside one of his Warcruisers.

And then suddenly, the swirling masses of energy erupted — into *ships*.

One was right alongside *Shanavorus*, and it was a spectacle unlike anything Novash had ever seen. The energy output was the most impressive feature — and then before the full grandeur of the spectacle could register, this unknown vessel unleashed what he presumed was a volley of energy fire.

Shanavorus was seized by what he guessed must be some sort of energy tractor, and the large unknown vessel drew the Warcruiser close to its hull. There was a distortion in the sensor feed reaching Novash's brain, and suddenly he and his ships were hurtling through the Krogg Fleet at faster-than-light speed... with internal readings suggesting they *too* had been converted to balls of energy.

Novash did not understand what was happening, but he was far too sensible to protest.

"*Leviathan* moderately damaged, *Canberra* as well. All ships are forming and returning at full speed to Genesis. The Larosians didn't get a scratch!" Tigar read aloud the quick report on his console, and the bridge replied with a quiet atmosphere of triumph.

Ursla smiled and looked at the report herself. No Kroggs had been destroyed, only a handful had been winged — literally, they'd lost a wing-appendage or two to Earther shot. Two of her 64s had been damaged, but after exactly nine seconds of action that wasn't too bad at all.

"Exiting energy drive."

And that meant they were back at Genesis already — the two minute flight from the rift had almost been too quick to believe. They were nearing orbit when the strike force reintegrated and appeared as normal matter. The 74s towing Larosian cruisers released their tractors and returned to their previous bombardment positions, guns running out again, awaiting the inevitable Krogg reprisal.

"Signal the Larosians, broadband. Ask for a direct relay with their CO. Try it in standard English for now — let's hope they've got some way of translating it," Ursla let Tigar move his ship back into position without further comment.

"And if they can't?" the Captain asked now.

Ursla looked to him with eyebrows up, "I suppose we start drawing pictures."

Tigar looked from Ursla to the Signal Officer, who shrugged. The energy transmitters spun up, and *Agamemnon* began broadcasting.

• • •

Signal on a broadband energy-oscillation frequency. Coming from the largest ship in their fleet. Standard human English. The watch commander was barely able to hide his surprise.

Novash wondered about the language — humans were a race in his own galaxy, a primitive but determined species who had yet to fully master the nuances of star travel. Of course, one of their number had been the heir to Praaxus and the Larosian savior, but as a race they remained limited.

Quickly, Novash's mind reached out to the ships in orbit, hoping to touch human mental signatures, but there was telepathic silence from all the nearby vessels. Some he could peer into and find darkness, others, perhaps constructed of minerals from the asteroid field, simply scattered his telepathic probe. Even the planet was too far below for him to get a sense of its occupants — most Larosians had the mental strength only to communicate point-to-point with cooperative minds, not broadly scan planets from such high orbit.

So he did not know what he was about to see — could it indeed be human? There was only one way to find out.

On the… 'audio-visual' interface.

Clearing his throat, Novash prepared to use his vocal cords in the unlikely event he needed them. He hadn't been required to in months, but it was a skill that — thanks to the Son of Praaxus — no modern Larosian forgot.

Ursla watched in mild surprise as the signal was immediately received and a link activated. The Larosians must have somehow learned English — a feat she would have to ask them about… later.

"Buffer's taking their signal and processing… I'll just need a moment to convert the feed for the holo tank…"

Nodding, Ursla lifted herself from her chair and paced quickly to the side of the bridge's main holographic battle plot. Moments prior it had been absorbed by a map of the system and the disposition of ships within, but as the Signal Officer began tapping the Larosian signal, a blank communications window formed in one flank, waiting as the buffer processed the transmission.

A beep sounded from the sensor console, and Ursla's eyes twitched from the communications section of the tank to the system map… just as a large wave of Krogg ships separated from the fleet.

"Four hundred Krogg ships incoming ma'am, and more look like they're getting ready to follow," the Sensor Chief's voice still hinted at pride in their daring rescue.

Ursla was about to reply, but the buffer finished its work first, and a Larosian, the first ever to be seen by or to see an Earther, appeared in the holo tank. She shifted her eyes to the gray creature, and it tilted its head at her.

• • •

Novash pondered the appearance of the great beast as it was projected through the interface into his mind. It seemed a cross between a giant savage and a civilized being — another of the Krogg's enemies... who knew of humanity?

"Commander of the Larosian force, you are among friends. I'm Admiral Andra Ursla of the Earther Navy... and I'm afraid all I can say is that I'll explain later. The Kroggs are giving chase in force. If you could form your ships around one of the unescorted orbital stations, we'll handle them."

Novash tried to think of an appropriate greeting, but his practical side denied him.

Understood. Thank you for your assistance, Admiral.

Ursla continued to look blankly through the telepathic screen at him... had he misspoken? The Admiral then looked away and bobbed her head to someone off screen, "Commander of the squadron, do you understand?"

He had replied... did the telepathic darkness he saw aboard their ships mean they could not even receive his thoughts when they were broadcast openly? It was a startling possibility — unlike anything the Larosians had seen in centuries of interstellar empire building... but it was unimportant just now. The vision of 400 approaching Krogg vessels instead forced Novash to *speak*.

"Apologies, Admiral. A communication error. Your instructions are understood. Thank you for your aid."

Ursla offered a nod, the corners of her mouth curling upward, "Very good. We'll be in touch."

The transmission cut, and Captain-Commodore Novash set his ships in motion.

"Can't bloody believe it, Sarah, but she did it!" Graham didn't bother to hide his excitement. "And company *is* on the way."

Sarah smiled at her brother over the link. Somehow, the Earthers had beat the odds yet again, and now it came to missiles under the orders of the Manchester family to complete the victory. With a slightly longer range and a faster firing rate, the missiles of the *Genesis* stations would be in action longer than the Earther guns, so the humans would draw blood for themselves in this encounter.

"Coming to range, ma'am. The Admiral has given fire command to you."

Sarah let a smile form on her face, "Graham, if you would. Your birds fly the farthest, after all."

Her brother grinned, turned away from the monitor, and gave the order.

Novash watched with silent approval as a tide of missiles — some large enough to shatter his own ships — swept from the orbiting fleets and stations of the planet. These warheads met the charging Kroggs head-on, and predictably, the Kroggs tried to plow through them. But volley after volley was shed at long range, and then as the Kroggs drew slightly closer, a geyser of energy erupted from orbit, smashing the front echelons aside with a force unlike anything Novash recalled seeing come from space vessels.

Having lost a half-hundred of their number, the Kroggs had the sense to turn away. Twenty-five Warcruisers were not worth 400 blockading vessels — the Kroggs would now try to determine a way to take these newcomers out of their element before engaging in battle again.

But who were these unknowns?

Novash was looking forward to finding out.

CHAPTER 22

Ursla wasn't entirely sure why she was so nervous. Within the past year she'd made so many first contacts it should have been second nature to her by now. Well, that was exaggerating. She'd been the first Earther to contact the humans, and she was one of the first of her species to meet a Krogg over a broadside. Dealing with the Larosians, however, was a distinctly different situation.

Novash seemed agreeable enough over the comm link, but the humans had no direct experience with this species — they'd always been forced to blow them up, and had never managed anything even close to a conversation. The officers of the Genesis Fleet did have high opinions of Larosian conduct in action, however, based on battle observations that demonstrated the aliens were not unnecessarily brutal and often endeavored to leave disabled Genesis ships intact.

The humans had not been permitted to show any quarter, and on the rare occasions that saw Krogg involvement, there had certainly been absolute annihilation. Probably in order to conceal their presence, the Kroggs had not always engaged Larosian forces when they entered Genesis space, but on the rare occasions when they did, it was only after the Genesis Fleet had been used up against superior Larosian firepower. That might have been a bitter Naval misinterpretation of strategy, but it seemed plausible to Ursla.

In any case, she had virtually no reference point from which to plan for this face-to-face encounter with the Larosian. The only real factor to her benefit was that they had at least begun their contact on good terms. After all, the Earthers *had* just saved the entire Larosian Squadron from certain destruction, giving good account of themselves in the process. Less than twenty seconds of action to get the Larosians out, then a massive bombardment destroying almost sixty more Krogg ships as they tried to pursue. Yes, certainly a good record on the day.

So credentials had been established, now questions would be answered. There would, of course, be a long and complicated explanation of the Genesis-Krogg-Earther dynamic, which would doubtless drag on for quite a while. The Larosians needed to understand that the Genesis humans, their longtime foes in this space, weren't actually hostile.

And then... or perhaps *before* all of that... Ursla would ask why they were communicating in *English*. Ursla didn't fancy herself a linguist, but so far her alien contacts were proving a bit of a letdown in that regard — there was no mystique of building communication across the language barriers. *Everybody* spoke *English*. It was as though a great force in the universe had gotten too lazy to come up with alternatives.

In any case, Ursla stood in a landing bay with Sarah beside her. Drawn up smartly behind them was *Agamemnon's* full marine complement plus a human detachment shipped over from *Joseph Barron*. Wouldn't be long now; Tigar had called down from the bridge, reporting the approach of the Captain-Commodore's vessel. The space doors slowly began to open, and Ursla waited and watched as the Larosian shuttlecraft approached the atmospheric shield.

Sharing the Warcruiser's light gray, mechanical appearance, the shuttle was far smaller than a standard pinnace. It appeared to be better suited to carrying a single passenger, perhaps two. That was certainly an unfamiliar concept, and she would have to ask about it *after* she got the rest of her answers. The list was already pretty long...

Glancing briefly at Sarah, Ursla took a deep breath.

Should be used to this by now. We really should start decorating these bays more. I suppose you don't notice how bare they are until you spend as much time as I do just standing around in them, waiting for aliens. Maybe wild flowers and a nice mural... Yep, that was the old sanity snapping — such inappropriate timing...

Ursla smiled, then took a deep breath and composed herself. Time to be official.

Novash was impressed. The fleet orbiting the system's planet was relatively small, especially considering the size of the Krogg force in the system, but it seemed formidable nonetheless. And he could hardly ignore the debt he owed these unknowns for the rescue of his Warcruisers.

As he'd cruised towards the flagship of the unknown fleet, he'd noticed the apparent lack of Carrier-type spacecraft in its echelons. The hatches on the sides of all the vessels appeared to be the same — some sort of gun hatches. And none appeared to contain oversized flight decks.

Now, upon entering the bay of the capital ship, his observations were further corroborated. Only large transport craft resided in the cavernous space, some with multiple turrets but none apparently developed for the starfighter role. Whoever these beings were, they did not use fighters, and that was perhaps a disadvantage... Or, based on what he'd already seen of their work, these creatures might have no need of such ships. Whatever the case, he would find out more when he landed.

Landing lights flashed across the bay floor, directing Novash to a landing slot near an assembly of the beings, drawn up in ordered ranks, likely an honor guard. There were probably 200 standing at attention. Interesting.

Guiding his ship to the given slot, he keyed it into ground configuration and descended towards the deck.

Floating easily over the deck, the shuttlecraft suddenly began to change.

Ursla hadn't expected anything unusual from the little craft, but its engines drew in on themselves while pieces of its fuselage expanded and seemed to grow. Legs extended towards the deck while short arms mounting what appeared to be beam weapons slid from the sides.

From a dart-shaped shuttle, a hunched, robotic biped emerged, descending into its slot. The unexpected conversion drew surprise from all present, and the marines from both services quickly trained their weapons on the strange bipedal machine.

When it came to rest, the transformed vessel stood five meters tall, its weapons looking ominously powerful — probably capable of cracking a pinnace. Fortunately, the beam cannons sagged powerless from the craft's arms as its systems deactivated.

Ursla raised her hand and waved the marines to stand down, and the Earthers returned to their parade-ground pose. So apparently it was some sort of variable-mode craft, perhaps designed to add flexibility to its ground-strike capacity. Well, Ursla was fond of pulsars and hover vehicles herself... but she'd still have to add this odd shuttle to her list of things to ask about.

From the underside of the remaining fuselage, a platform began to lower on what appeared to be a grav cushion. Similar cushions raised gun crews to their fire-control positions on Earther ships, but the Earther technology didn't require actual platforms.

The disk lowered smoothly, and on it stood the Larosian she'd spoken to, wearing what appeared to be a suit of shimmering white-silver *armor*. He was humanoid — with only *two* arms, thankfully — and stood perhaps two meters tall. His body clearly wasn't covered in an exoskeleton like that of a Krogg, nor did his head carry a single eye (and in turn a Krogg's look of cyclops-like menace). There were instead two surprisingly knowing silver eyes separated by a low, smooth nose. His mouth was a thin lipless line that looked rather unsuitable for speaking.

As the circular platform touched down on the deck, the Larosian stepped off, walking with purposeful grace towards Ursla and Sarah. Observing cautiously, Ursla reached out with her instincts in an attempt to gain an insight into the commander. Obviously his presence felt 'alien,' that was to be expected. However, the menace she felt when she saw holos of Kroggs was missing. This was a being sure of himself, sure of his skill... but not one determined to prove his supremacy over others. Earther-like, but without a seeming reliance on instinct. Logic and consciousness without intuition...

But Ursla shook off her conclusions — they were drawn all too quickly. As the Larosian closed to a distance of a half dozen meters, he slowed to a stop and seemed to stare into Sarah. Surprised at the attention, she stared back, feeling a slight bit nervous as the strange eyes examined her.

Novash could not believe it — specifically, he could not believe he had not realized it sooner. There were *humans* on this ship! He'd been unable to detect human telepathic impressions on the planet, or in the ships built of that anomalous material from the asteroid belt, or aboard the ships like this one. Now his mind stretched out and examined the mental energy patterns of those before him — the female leader and her many marines...

They were human, to be sure. Of the race of the Son — were *they* the hostile species of this space? How could the Son not have known, how could he have failed to detect their minds? And, perhaps as important, who were these larger, fur-bearing creatures, whose minds he could not detect at all?

Novash centered his psyche quickly; there were many questions, so perhaps he should best address himself to the more familiar race first. Determined to hide his surprise, he met Sarah's eyes with his own.

You're human, he thought to her, and she cocked an eyebrow in matching surprise.

"Yes, I am."

Ursla, about to say something appropriately official, heard Sarah's remark distantly. It didn't really register for a second... then it did, and she looked quickly to her side, "What did you say?"

Sarah looked up at her companion, "I said I am. Hardly a thing to dispute — I am human after all."

Ursla frowned, "He didn't say anything."

Novash looked from the human to the alien with pause.

Sarah frowned back and then turned to the Larosian, "But I heard..."

There was silence as the three contemplated possible explanations, and Novash realized his mistake first. Over the comm, the alien had been unable to hear his projected thought, and even face-to-face he could not detect its mind. Perhaps its brain chemistry was altogether *too* alien to allow an interface — there could always be a first time. After centuries of interstellar travel, stretching across thousands of solar systems, Larosians had never come across *any* advanced species with which they could not interface in some way — even on the most basic levels. Humans were some of the most open creatures, but even the *Faz'r-Haz'teya-Srta'm* had been able to convey basic feeling and imagery through admittedly painful thought transmissions.

But, Novash reminded himself, this was a different galaxy — even if it did hold humans and Kroggs.

Novash bobbed his head to Ursla, "The question was sent telepathically. What form of life are you?" The Larosian's verbal question came in a resonant voice that didn't quite seem properly timed to the movements of his mouth.

Ursla looked from Sarah back to the gray being, her eyebrow arching slightly.

"I'm an Earther. Was your question meant to be heard by others than Sarah?" Ursla's reply was both interested and slightly cautious.

Earthers had studied telepathy long ago, but it had been determined their genetic disposition would never facilitate it in the traditional sense. Their instinct was more than telepathy in many ways, and less in others. Studies of the subject had ended in the preceding century, and telepathy had since been ignored while other matters of science were addressed.

But humans *could* be affected? It hadn't occurred to Ursla before, but while Earther minds might be impregnable, human minds appeared not to be. Could they be influenced? Could Krogg Telepaths read their minds...? And how did this Larosian recognize Sarah's species?

Lots of questions. I'll have to start writing all these down... I hope he really can't read what I'm thinking right now. If I had someone reading everything I thought I'd be condemned to the asylum!

"The message was sent openly; it should have reached both of you... but you seem to be separate. Unlinked." Novash studied the Earther. Though he could not connect with its mind directly, it had obviously acted to protect his squadron. His natural inclination was to accept that it was friendly until circumstances demonstrated the opposite.

Admittedly, his lowest senses did make him feel calm around the creature, though no Larosian ever listened to such base feelings — those were all the Kroggs relied on. Indeed, whenever a Krogg Telepath met a strong Larosian mind in combat, the battle was born out as a competition of discipline against feral passion. Krogg minds were clever but emotional — leaving them capable of great deviousness and ridiculous senselessness, depending on circumstances. And in this star system, deviousness seemed to be their way.

But how, and *why*? And were the humans somehow involved? Novash needed to understand the situation, but perhaps he should not rush to take it from the human's mind outright — these Earthers seemed to be the superior beings in this galaxy, he should give them the opportunity to deliver information themselves. At the very least, he could confirm from the human brain that this alien — *Ursla* — was most skilled and benevolent.

Ursla and the Larosian studied each other for a long string of seconds. Sarah watched as well, wondering at how easily telepathy had been used on her. What else could Larosians do?

Finally Ursla shook herself into motion, "We will have to discuss our situation, sir. As I mentioned, I'm Admiral Andra Ursla, of the Second Fleet of the Earther Navy. This is ArcGeneral Sarah Manchester, of the Genesis Fleet. Welcome to the Genesis solar system."

Novash set aside his pondering for the time being — these creatures seemed to believe in formalities not entirely unlike those of his own Navy, and whatever the outcome, courtesy called for him to respect their traditions. He would gather his answers soon enough.

"I am Captain-Commodore Novash, commander of the Eleventh Squadron-of-Reconnoiter of the Fourth Fleet-of-War of the Honorable Larosian Star Navy. I agree, Admiral, we must discuss these circumstances."

Uneasy, the trio left the flight deck.

CHAPTER 23

Novash sat silently, feelings of uncertainty churning within him. The Earther ship was impressive — it was visibly superior to Larosian ships in some ways, markedly inferior in others; but on balance he could consider it an equal. He'd observed three separate families of species on his walk to the meeting room, apparently all living together in a civilized fashion. Not to mention the humans — their presence continued to appeal to his curiosity.

As he settled himself in a chair at the Earther briefing table, he watched Ursla take her own seat, and Manchester hers. The inability to read the Earther — or any Earther he'd passed — was disconcerting, but the feeling of comfort that seemed to pervade *Agamemnon* was putting him at ease.

This was a feeling he consciously refused to *trust*; it would be entirely un-Larosian to simply obey the base instincts. Wisdom and self-discipline were the traits of a good warrior — traits that had built the Larosian Empire, and preserved it.

"We have a long story, and I haven't been able to figure out a way to condense it for you, so we should get started," Ursla's tone was even, drawing Novash's gaze. She was still trying to decide how the fact that humans were vulnerable to telepathic influence had been missed before the beginning of this mission — short-sightedness on the part of the Allies, unfortunately.

Novash's head tilted and his silver eyes tracked from Ursla to Sarah, "Very well. Might I begin with you, ArcGeneral Manchester?"

Sarah cocked an eyebrow and glanced quickly to Ursla. For her part, the Admiral shrugged, "As good a place as any. Sarah, you want to get us started?"

With a nod, Sarah looked back to Novash, and their eyes met. She made to speak, and then her mind tingled. Her eyes widened just a little, and her mouth slowly dropped open.

Novash promptly accepted what he'd interpreted to be an invitation to read Manchester, and quickly he found few differences between her own mental predispositions and those of the humans he'd encountered in Larosian space. He also was able to absorb the entire briefing she'd prepared for him in bare seconds without a word being uttered. Such were the benefits of the decades of xeno-telepathic communications training given to all Larosian officers — he was able to quickly find the appropriate information in the ArcGeneral's mind.

Now he saw, and began to understand... The destruction of *Earth* society, the *Genesis* Colony, the Krogg *intervention*, the *engagement* of past Larosian scouting squadrons under the eyes of the Kroggs, the *Quest...* the *Earthers...* it all reached Novash's mind.

The situation was quite unique in this galaxy — two races seemed to have survived the wrath of Krogg expansion... and the Kroggs had been here *all along*. In force... using the humans of Genesis to disguise their presence, and hiding in those asteroids. But their exploitation of the humans had embittered this Genesis Navy... and the Earthers were now fulfilling a pledge to support human independence, no matter the cost.

Which meant that, for reasons of honor Novash found fully understandable, the Earthers were willing to help the Larosians destroy the Krogg menace once and for all. Moreover, it seemed quite likely that they were capable of playing a decisive role...

As she waited for Sarah to open the discussion, Ursla looked across the table at Novash, trying to sense something of his character and understand what her instincts were telling her about him. It was like trying to read a book in a lightning storm — she felt as though she got brief flashes of insight punctuated by loud periods of darkness. From what she *could* tell, he seemed agreeable enough, but the overall impression was still 'alien'.

Go figure. Didn't see that one coming...

"I am... up to speed, thank you Admiral," he said kindly, borrowing the colloquial expression from Sarah's mind. "The ArcGeneral's briefing was quite thorough."

Sarah's mind stopped tingling and she blinked. After a second she realized what must have happened, and as her eyes widened she glanced at Ursla in shock. The Admiral's gaze matched her friend's and then Ursla turned her eyes to the Larosian, "You just *took* it from her mind?"

Novash sat back, his face blank with confusion, "Is that not what you intended? You couldn't have meant to *tell* me all of that... or did you?"

Ursla's face was deadpan, and having gained Sarah's knowledge of the bear, Novash realized this was a lack of expression and was likely concealing shock, or maybe even anger.

"Oh I must apologize!" his tone lowered with embarrassment. "It is customary in the Larosian service to exchange reports in such ways, and I was so curious about this situation I drew careless conclusions as to your practices here."

Sarah leaned forward, still slightly bemused, "You just went in and reviewed the information in my *mind*?"

"Only the thoughts you had associated with this meeting, I assure you. It was not my intention to invade your privacy, only to increase efficiency. I must apologize again, ArcGeneral, it's our way when dealing with humans, and indeed most species. We never probe deeply. I did not think clearly, I should have realized that it would not be something you were accustomed to," Novash's alien tone provided a surprising amount of comfort, and Sarah slowly frowned.

"Yes, I suppose I can understand that. It's... quite alright. At least we won't be talking for hours," though still in shock, her mind was clearing.

Novash offered a slow bow-like nod, "Indeed, your meeting with Second Chancellor Argyle seemed most arduous."

Sarah blinked at the comment, but stopped any urge to question how he knew of the meeting. Though disconcerted, Ursla forced herself to reserve judgment on the Larosian's mind-reading escapade until she could put it in better context. Novash was quite right — this telepathy might present a privacy issue in the near future, but for now it was simplifying things.

The Admiral took the reins of the discussion, "You mentioned humans, Commodore. How do you know of humans... could you briefly explain to us your history?"

Novash tilted his head and nodded slowly. Probing his memory he began, "The Kroggs arrived in our galaxy several centuries ago. At the time we Larosians were a less-developed people, living in what you might equate with a... *feudal* system. Ours was a loosely-tied but ancient Empire, and there were several others around. These Empires resisted the Kroggs, but failed to unite against the invasions. Planets were overrun within the space of... what you would call months. Indeed, all of our neighboring Empires fell before we could consolidate or come to their aid. But our great Emperor, the Honorable Praaxus, rallied our exalted houses, centralized our Empire, and drove back the first Krogg invasion. We have been at war since."

Novash paused thoughtfully, trying unsuccessfully to gauge Ursla's reaction, then pressed on.

"Over the past five centuries we have been forcing the Kroggs back, annexing what worlds are left in their wake to be regenerated, protecting any species willing to accept our aid. The remnant territories of our neighboring Empires now exist within our Imperial borders, but the Kroggs left no survivors in their wake. It has been a protracted conflict, and it is absorbing its third generation of Larosian warriors even now. Many times momentum has shifted between our two sides, but recently we were able to deliver another decisive blow to the Krogg armada, and have been driving them back for the better part of a... *year*. My fleet's task was to track the force that is in this space, and to eliminate it as a threat to the Empire. The duty of my squadron was to scout this system for a Krogg presence."

Ursla looked towards Sarah and then back, "And the humans? Details, Commodore. I must ask you for details."

With another bow-like nod, Novash continued, "There is a colony of humans in our galaxy. We have had limited contact with them, but from what I understand they believe themselves to be native to their colony world. Owing to the war, we have not had time to closely investigate their history, though I can say with a certainty that their technology does not approach Genesis' level."

"And the name of their colony?" Sarah asked quietly, her expression one of fascination.

"Terra — given the history of Earth, a predictable enough name."

Ursla's eyebrows arched, and she leaned back in her chair, "We only ever knew about the Genesis Colony, but we have relatively few records from outside the UN about space programs. I've heard it suggested that there may have been a second space colony initiative — a private one, even — but we've never had any indication as to whether it was true or not. Come to think of it, though, I imagine it would have been a secret even then... to avoid being overrun by people wanting to escape. That could explain this 'Terra' of yours..."

"But how in Gods' names did they get out of the galaxy?" Sarah shook her head with a frown. "Nothing we have *today* could do it, let alone back then."

Novash again tilted his head, "No doubt through a subspace corridor much like the one in this system."

"Subspace... so *that's* what it is," Ursla's mind shifted just briefly from the meeting. "An anomaly that translates matter to a lower band of the spatial continuum?"

With mild surprise Novash nodded, "Indeed. We have some experience with such corridors, though no others in our past experience have connected to populated regions of space. Perhaps the Terra colony ship inadvertently passed through one."

Ursla was nodding now, her intellect temporarily overriding more practical concerns, "We toyed with the idea of a subspace-bandwidth drive about 400 years back, before we had energy drive. Turned out that the technology for matter conversion we had to use to enter the lower bandwidths of subspace made for safer travel in real space than in the lower bands. Energy drive."

Sarah listened quietly, nodding, "Our scientists called it hyper. The Kroggs have it but they never shared it. We developed flux instead."

Novash nodded, "It is generally referred to as hyper travel, yes. One need not use it to travel a corridor, though. The breaks in subspace already exist in a corridor, so it is unnecessary to artificially pass through the layers. One simply enters a corridor as though it were a subspace tunnel."

Now Sarah was starting to get lost, but Ursla nodded, "Makes sense. What relative speed can you make in hyper? In terms of light speed?"

"A well-tuned warship can travel at as much as 2,500 percent the speed of light."

Sarah caught that remark, "Comparable to our own speed, surprisingly enough."

Ursla was about to ask whether hyper-limits actually existed when she realized scientific curiosity came a distant second to the more pressing matter — Kroggs.

"We can indulge our scientific curiosities more later," Ursla voiced her thoughts. "Now there's the issue of the Krogg Fleet and what you have coming through the corridor, Commodore."

The Captain-Commodore paused in thought, regaining his focus as well, "My squadron was scouting ahead of the Fourth Fleet-of-War. We were searching for this Krogg Fleet, but frankly did not expect to find it here. Though we were aware of the presence of an unknown belligerent force in this space, the Kroggs never revealed themselves to any of the scouts or envoys that survived travel to this system."

Sarah's eyebrows arched, "You knew we were here?"

Novash attempted to shake his head, "We knew an unknown alien force was here, but it seems that the ore you have used to build your ships' hulls, and the asteroids you mine it from, have an ability to scatter our telepathic probes. We did not know humans were in this place, nor Kroggs — much as you did not know of our vector of approach. It seems the Krogg penchant for cleverness has manifested itself well in Genesis."

Ursla restrained a sigh, and Sarah frowned, "Care to elaborate on that?"

"Before entering the corridor I sent to Admiral-of-the-Fleet Narosh. If my squadron does not contact him within a day, he will bring the Fourth to this place, through the corridor. And with such a blockade at the mouth of the corridor, he will be eliminated. Given the state of the blockade, there is no way to send a ship through to warn him — ships must deactivate defensive systems to travel a corridor. So we are left with a dilemma."

Ursla had already guessed much of what the Captain-Commodore reported, but his addition of details somehow made the situation seem more dire.

"Relative timeline?" Sarah asked quietly, considering the possibilities.

Novash again began to convert his relative time to the Genesis 357-day annual calendar, then spoke, "I believe the relative time would be twenty-two days. Usually our Fleet might follow in a shorter time, but we were scouting a large section of the frontier, and so consolidation and travel time will be much greater than usual. The Fourth is made up of 2,000 ships of war, some of the most elite within our Empire. We were referred to as Warriors of Praaxus' Son before he met his end."

Sarah cocked an eyebrow, "Praaxus' Sun... a star system?"

Novash shook his head with what might have been a smile, "The last of twelve of the children of the soul of our great Emperor. The son was human, in fact."

Sarah let both eyebrows go up and her mouth fall open. She looked to Ursla who cocked her own eyebrow and shrugged. Humans carrying soul-heirs of aliens... sounded like stuff out of epic fiction. Would probably explain a lot about the Larosian situation, but it wasn't really something they could afford to focus much on right now anyway — the story could be told another time.

"Lots of things to discuss later, I should think," Sarah was wondering what Pat would say about the Larosian claim. "I would so love to know exactly what you are talking about. But in the meantime, we have a bit of a problem."

Novash tilted his head. A Larosian form of expression, no doubt.

Ursla picked up the tactical discussion again, "I don't doubt the skill of your ships, Commodore, but just to review the basics, they'll be vulnerable as soon as they exit the corridor?"

Novash nodded, "Yes. We cannot activate battle configuration while in a corridor — the strain on the hull would disintegrate the ship. It will take our vessels a few seconds to be ready for action, but the Kroggs' formation indicates their intention is to bombard our ships on exit. At best, the fleet would take heavy casualties, though I imagine the Kroggs will be able to destroy the entire Fourth if properly coordinated."

Ursla nodded slowly — the Kroggs had chosen ideal positions for this blockade. After four centuries of war, they clearly knew how to do battle with the Larosians.

Sarah ground her jaw thoughtfully, "Well, we can draw fire again, but the Kroggs will know better than to pay heed to us with your fleet coming through. We don't have nearly enough firepower to pose a serious threat, especially given that they consider my Genesis Fleet so very inferior."

Ursla nodded, keying on the system map holo. It glowed to life in the center of the table, drawing an interested gaze from the Larosian. The glowing three-dimensional projection looked much like a literal representation of what his mind's eye saw when Larosian sensors reported to him. It was an impressive piece of technology, and it displayed the grim situation in every detail.

"Rescuing us may have proved unwise," the Larosian observed quietly. "I appreciate the act very much, but it could have tipped your hand too soon."

Part of Ursla agreed — the raw strategic part, anyway. But she had no regrets about her actions to this point, and there were still ways to find victory in this situation. Genesis wouldn't be safe if the Kroggs remained in-system. So they'd have to help the Larosians remove them... and that would require all the clout the Earther Navy could muster.

Ursla looked through the holo tank at Novash, "It was the right thing to do, Commodore. Sarah, I think we send for the reinforcements. Everything that can fly."

The ArcGeneral didn't need any convincing, "No argument." She turned to Novash, "We can have another fleet of 1,500 ships here in a month. A thousand of them Earther."

Novash bow-nodded, containing his surprise that the fleet was not larger, then tipped his head, "Four weeks? Twenty-eight days?"

Sarah heaved a sigh, then looked to her friend, "We'll have to hope our courier can get there fast and that Setter and Liz can whip the fleet into order quickly."

Ursla nodded, "It's our only shot. And we have to hope the Kroggs don't come after us in the meantime... Novash, you said your fleet was *unusually* far behind?"

The Captain-Commodore offered another bow- nod.

"Then we hope the Kroggs have to sit and wait on station," Sarah said softly, her eyes shifting from the blockade fleet to its bases and back. "Or we're all rather... *dead*."

Everyone was silent, but Ursla was already plotting in her head. A sloop was going to have to get home quickly... and she had one in mind.

The request for help would reach Earth in time — it had to.

CHAPTER 24

"We get to have all the fun, don't we?"

Fox Magnus looked up at Lang Sandpelt as the Midshipman approached his chair. The Fox grinned in reply and gestured to his screen, "Orders say we need to have the fleet here in three weeks or the Kroggs will have us over a barrel."

But, Fox decided, the Midshipman had a point. Lately *Flame* had been well-used by the commanding Admirals — it almost seemed like someone up there liked the little sloop... Courier work could often be mundane, but the requirements of this particular job would doubtless make for an interesting trip.

They'd have to move *fast*. Really, *really* fast.

Chronos Claw eagerly narrowed his eyes, "The fleet can push and make the trip here in twelve days, leaving us nine to get there. My engines mightn't enjoy that..."

His concerned voice trailed off absently.

Fox nodded, "Not much we can do about it. We have to redline everything — past redline if we can. We can refit it all when we get home."

"Will we be pursued?"

Fox cocked an eyebrow at the question. The thought had crossed his mind, but he wasn't so much concerned about what the Kroggs did behind him, so long as they never caught up to him. No one knew how fast Krogg ships could really go, and since there'd be no way to expand *Flame*'s drive field when the sloop was moving at 2,500 pls, the aliens might indeed attempt to track him down...

Yes, well, that was always a possibility, but he couldn't afford to dwell on it.

"The Kroggs mightn't want us to get help, so I imagine they'll contest our departure. Beyond that, I'm sure we can outrun them."

Chronos chuckled, "You hope!"

Well, yes, that's about the size of it...

Fox smiled, nodded shortly and turned back to his console, "We leave immediately. Chronos, better get to your engines. We'll need top speed, and we'll need it to last."

"Aye," the cougar left the bridge, and *Flame* began to power its drives.

...

Sarah watched as the 236th Squadron of the line began to form a vanguard around diminutive little *Flame*. The sloop would be traveling at 300 pls on its way out of the Genesis system and would accelerate to as high as 2,500 pls as it exited. If the Kroggs sought to engage, the 74s of the 236th would intervene on their smaller comrade's behalf.

Like all Earther plans, it was theoretical. But then, Earthers had an aptitude for making practical theory. Sarah wasn't sure how they managed it, but since their skill always seemed to pull bad situations from the proverbial fire, she wasn't about to complain.

Her battle plot on *Joseph Barron* showed the Earther ships accelerating away from Genesis at a steady clip, and it also showed the reaction of the Krogg Fleet. She bit her lip as the feared aliens moved to intercept the fast-moving sloop and its consorts, and hoped that a lone squadron of 74s would be enough to protect *Flame*.

"Sensors picking up a group of Krogg ships moving to intercept, sir. Looks like they're traveling on the lower subspace bands. They're making good speed."

Fox's ear twitched and he watched the battle group skitter towards him. The Kroggs weren't pulling any punches. A dozen Superdreadnoughts, another half-dozen Dreadnoughts, and dozens of Destroyers.

"Commodore Kandam on the line sir," the Signal Officer called, and Fox nodded.

The panda Commodore of the 236th appeared in the plot, "You ready to run, Fox?"

Magnus gave a devilish grin, "We'll move like the wind, Commodore. Don't worry."

Kandam smiled, "Very well. We'll stop as many of them as we can."

Fox keyed the intercom as the panda disappeared, "Chronos, we're going to full speed right now." He looked back up to the Cruising Master, "Mister Gunth, don't run us into anything, if you please."

Flame suddenly surged ahead of its compatriots, its speed climbing to a steady 2,477 pls. The 74s turned aside, dropping from energy drive and running out their guns. *Namur* was Kandam's flag, and now it led the column of eight ships towards the enemy.

Exiting hyper, the Kroggs went to meet them.

Outnumbered two-to-one in capital ships, Kandam knew better than to submit to a long pounding match, and instead began to wear his squadron up and over the attackers. The 74s scattered as they came over their foes, ready to inflict their own damage on the Kroggs.

Flame sped outward, passing the edge of the system at a brilliant speed. For a moment it seemed to go unnoticed, but then five of the Krogg Dreadnoughts and a dozen Destroyers slipped back into the subspace hyper bands and gave chase at 2,480 pls.

With a clear head start, Fox knew better than to worry. If the humans' intelligence was correct, Krogg ships were very much like old domesticated horses — they could only go so far, so fast, before they were 'blown' and had to be nursed back to the stables and fed.

And if the humans were wrong... well, *Flame* was still fast, and he would cross that bridge if he came to it. As the sensors ran out of reach and Genesis disappeared in his wake, Magnus leaned back in his chair and watched stars fly by on the plot.

It was going to be a long flight.

Kandam had commanded a squadron of frigates against the Church Fleet eight months earlier, and Ursla, watching the 236th in her plot, could see the familiar frigate tactics in his methods as he engaged the Kroggs. The ships moved endlessly, taking damage but not in highly concentrated amounts. They dodged and weaved, sending 32-gun broadsides into Krogg ships until *Flame* left their sensors, and then they retreated at a good speed to the safety of Genesis orbital space.

The Kroggs hadn't been fully diverted, but hopefully the head start Fox had gotten was enough.

What remained of the Krogg Squadron split, the capital ships retreating to their fleet, the Destroyers turning and giving chase to the sloop. Ursla ground her jaw and wished *Flame* the best of luck.

"We're at 2,516 pls, now, Fox. I think I can give you 2,550 in a while — it'll just take a bit of time to build up to it," Lieutenant Claw's report drew a relaxed nod from Fox.

They were away cleanly, and though there were still days of hard travel ahead of them, he could already see two of the Dreadnoughts and a handful of the Destroyers drifting off the back of the Krogg pursuit pack. They wouldn't catch this Earther sloop... which was just as well because if it came to a stand-up fight, *Flame* wouldn't have a chance.

"Engines running smooth, Chronos?" Fox's voice reflected a reassuring level of confidence.

"Aye, Fox, they are."

Fox smiled to himself, proud of his ship and his crew, "Very good."

Flame raced through space.

CHAPTER 25

In the middle of nowhere, *Archangel Sword* and *Grendelsbane City* came to a stop. Well, not *quite* in the middle of nowhere, but next to an uncharted asteroid belt in the middle of nowhere. Almost the same, but considering James Stanton's pleasant mood he was happy to point out useless holes in colloquialisms, even if they were just in his own head.

It hadn't been so long ago that he'd been troubled and keen on making his own war against the Kroggs. Now he was enthusiastically ready to embark on a project to build a new human colony. This asteroid belt, not too far off the beaten path, might contain a suitable location, but that would be for the scientists to decide.

And admittedly, he'd prefer a nice planet to an asteroid...

In any case, while they scoured the sensors to look for a colony site, he'd busy himself elsewhere. At dinner, for instance, with his fellow ArcColonel.

Audrey DeBrooke watched *Sword* grow in her pinnace window as the small craft crossed the narrow gap between the two ships. She enjoyed the excellent meals provided by James Stanton's steward, and she boarded *Sword* almost every day to partake of them. James was always glad to have her aboard, and Audrey had long ago admitted to herself that she wasn't just boarding the Battlecruiser to eat its ArcColonel's food.

Of course, rumors were already circulating between the two ships, and she was fine with that. She and James were bringing the crews of their respective ships closer together by letting them gossip with each other.

We're engaging in these rendezvous for the good of our crews. Yes, that's it.

Ahem.

Apparently, they were the new Sarah and Pat for these two crews — except, Audrey realized with a smile, she and James were perfectly aware of what was going on. And soon they would be doing their part by sharing a romantic dinner while scientists aboard both ships continued their search for a place to settle down.

"Any sign of them?"

Savanna Felix felt some frustration. *Tonnant* and *Hero* had been searching for days, but the Coalition Heavy Cruiser was being positively elusive. They'd followed its base course quite a ways and had then split to cover more space, but the galaxy was simply too big sometimes.

With a sardonic smile, Felix made a mental note to complain to Caine about that.

"No sign, sir."

Hardly surprised, Felix heaved a sigh and examined his star charts, his Flag Captain arriving at his side. He turned, "Any ideas?"

The wolf twitched her ears thoughtfully, eyes tracing along the base course they'd been following. They had already crossed over the direct route to Genesis, and now *Tonnant* was exploring the space bordering it on the far side while *Hero* was in a system bearing towards Earth. They'd rendezvous near a star further out in deep space and go from there — but not for seventy-two hours.

So, with three days to kill, where should *Tonnant* go next?

"You know, sir, one Heavy Cruiser might not be worth all this effort," the Flag Captain said gently.

Felix twitched his whiskers and looked at her, "I'd rather not tell that to the Destroyer that runs across it."

The Captain nodded silently, looking back at the map. The two thought a moment more and then the Captain's finger pierced the projection and indicated a sphere.

"I'd recommend this one, sir. It's behind us a ways, but it looks like it's got potential as a guerrilla base."

"Very well, inform *Hero* and get us under weigh, if you please."

The capture of the Coalition Squadron didn't surprise any of the humans in Earth space — even the ones who wanted to break away. There were some lines that renegade humans couldn't cross without using up Earther goodwill, and as Felix had proven, even an Earther *desk Admiral* was capable of annihilating a powerful unaligned force.

When she watched the squadron being towed into Earth's orbiting docks, Liz Hastings wanted to smile, but somehow she couldn't. The capture certainly pleased her, but the breakaway itself distressed her still. The situation was stabilizing, granted, but she couldn't help but wonder whether she could have gotten it under control sooner.

Now, as the report from Admiral Felix was transmitted from *Dragon*, Hastings stood with Caine aboard one of the orbiting stations. The message found the First Lord immediately, and he and Liz viewed it quickly.

"One Heavy Cruiser escaped," he recited, "and there are only two ships out there looking for it."

Hastings cocked an eyebrow, "They may have been traitors, but I'm willing to bet whatever ship that is still knows the stealth drills. Two ships will have a hell of a time finding it."

Caine nodded slowly, "I can spare a frigate squadron to go help them out. The 111th is available."

Sending out Ursla's old squadron would make quite a statement about Earther intolerance for renegade violence. The squadron was considered the best frigate formation in the First Fleet, and indeed, the best in the whole Navy. Considering the accomplishments of both its past and present commanders, neither claim was unreasonable.

"Send them," Hastings said quietly, and Caine nodded.

Keying up a star map he found the rendezvous point at which Felix's message said *Tonnant* would be making contact with *Hero*. The frigates could be there to meet him if they left immediately...

Commodore Dran Nightclaw, once Flag Captain of *ENS Cerberus*, now commanded the entire 111th Flying Squadron. The promotion had come when Ursla had left to command the Second Fleet, and in her absence, he'd maintained the force's elite skill, gaining them an unparalleled reputation within the Navy.

But he — and the crews of the 111th — believed it was possible to do even better.

Personally, Nightclaw was pleased with the assignment — his force was certainly the best cruiser formation in the Allied Fleet, bar none, and the mission for which the 111th had been selected would be ideal for his Fifth Rates.

Nightclaw sat back in the command chair that Ursla had once filled... well, not the same chair, as hers would have been far too large, but one of the same model and in the same place on the bridge. *Cerberus* led the eight frigates towards the rendezvous with *Tonnant* and *Hero*, in a system listed on Earther charts as NV 214X.

Audrey DeBrooke was sitting with Stanton when the intercom chirped. They'd been swapping stories from their academy days over a plate of tasty hydroponics foods.

Stanton keyed his intercom with a quick frown at his dinner date, "I'm here. What?"

"Survey crew here, skipper. We can't find anything worth staying here for, aside from the dismal view."

Stanton rolled his eyes jokingly, drawing a chuckle from his fellow ArcColonel, "Well then, any recommendations for our next stop?"

There was an audible pause on the intercom, and Stanton tapped his foot as the surveyors tried to figure out an answer. Finally, the science officer spoke up, "Ahh... one the Earthers call NV 214X. Has a few planets and an asteroid belt. It's about two days from here sir."

Raising his eyebrows and opening his hands towards DeBrooke, he got an accepting shrug and nod in reply.

"Fine. We'll let the engineers overhaul the drives for... say eighteen hours, then we'll get going," Stanton said into the comm.

"Very good sir."

The line closed and Stanton turned back to DeBrooke, "Sounds like a nice enough place to look. So, what were you saying, Audrey?"

CHAPTER 26

"You're sure?"

Fox Magnus didn't even attempt to hide his apprehension. *Flame* was just under three days from Earth space, and despite its blistering speed over the first six days of its run, the sloop was still being pursued.

Krogg ships, it seemed, were true thoroughbreds... at least these ones were. Four Dreadnoughts and nine Destroyers were trailing the Earther courier, spread out in an uncertain trail behind it as they traveled in their hyper bands.

For the first six days Fox's confidence had held firm, but now the sloop had begun to tremble slightly as it passed through space. Its field slipped outwards and drew back in with horrible uncertainty as the generators which had successfully let it extend the drive field to hide in Genesis struggled under the strain.

The news was bad.

"No way around it, Fox," Chronos Claw said solemnly. "We'll disintegrate if the force fields go, and the generator is starting to fail."

Magnus ground his jaw and looked between his two officers, "So what do we do?"

Claw frowned, "I can fix the generator, but it'll take at least ten minutes, maybe twelve."

Fox cocked an eyebrow and Sandpelt turned to his senior Lieutenant, "Well then what's the trouble?"

"We'd have to stop. Go out of energy drive. Restart the generator and replace its coils with our spares."

Fox let out a breath he hadn't realized he was holding. His hand absently scratched the back of his head as he looked from his officers to his console and checked how far back the Kroggs were. All the pursuers could reach him easily if *Flame* stopped. Even the ships that had dropped to the back of the chase group could catch up. There would be absolutely no contest between that kind of fleet and the lone Earther sloop.

But if they didn't stop they'd disintegrate. Guaranteed death versus likely death — an uncomfortable choice.

"Is there a system nearby where we can hide? A nebula or asteroid belt?" Fox asked his bridge crew and the Master frowned over his charts.

After some scrutiny, the veteran Earther nodded, "NV 233X. Nice class 42 nebula — they'd never be able to find us, skipper."

Fox's tension eased marginally, "ETA?"

"Twelve minutes, sir."

Fox leaned back in his chair and smiled in relief, "Watch the engines, Chronos. Lang, get your guns ready... just in case."

The two officers were nodding and preparing to leave when *Flame* bucked.

As if tossed by a celestial wave, the decks of the little ship rolled obliquely forty-five degrees much too quickly for the grav systems to compensate. The engines began to drone loudly and painfully, the deck vibrating steadily now.

Claw climbed to his feet and sprinted from the bridge on the shuddering deck, and Sandpelt went after him, having trouble staying upright as *Flame* pitched again.

"What's going on?" Fox demanded, clinging to his chair.

"Generators are giving, sir!" the Master reported in a roar. "She's getting set to fly apart!"

Fox bared his teeth, "Hold on, just a few more minutes..."

"I can't skipper, fluctuations are too intense... the safety protocols are kicking in... she's going to exit on her own!"

"Range to 233X?"

"Too far, sir! We'll come out somewhere else..."

Flame bucked again, and the ship emerged into open space.

NV 214X had its redeeming qualities, Stanton had to admit. It was almost Sol-like in its makeup, though one of its two habitable worlds was somewhat rough — predators bigger than Kodiak bears, plagues of super-viruses, volcanoes that spewed fluorine, and many other equally *fun* features.

Still, one could build a large dome and make do. Or perhaps they should just put it into the 'maybe' file for later reference. It seemed exceedingly unlikely any ambitious colonists would pick it up if the two cruisers left it in their wake and kept shopping around. And besides, *Archangel Sword* and *Grendelsbane City* were only orbiting the fourth planet — they'd already blacklisted the third, but there was still an asteroid belt to look at in this system.

And if that didn't work out, they'd go somewhere else. There was no sense of haste in this survey — the crews had all the time they needed to find just the right base. All things considered, the mood on both ships was relaxed, nothing of consequence having happened since the Coalition engagement. There was no reason to rock that boat with a pointless timetable — and besides Stanton had to admit he was enjoying the lack of tension. He'd been on edge for so long...

"Ah... sir?"

Stanton blinked himself out of his musings and turned to his Sensor Chief, "Chief?"

"Something coming in fast... 25 cee... from Genesis sir, under energy drive.

Its signal is unstable, looks like it's having serious trouble."

Stanton frowned, "On the main screen. Link it to *Grendelsbane* as well, please."

The sensor plot appeared on the main monitor, showing the small Earther signal hurtling inwards.

"I see it, James. What do we do?" DeBrooke appeared in a corner window of the feed.

Stanton watched for another second, "Doesn't look like it's stopping."

The ship — a sloop — suddenly exited energy drive. The translation was uncharacteristically sloppy, at first surprising Stanton. Then he realized its field generator must have failed, and he was filled with a feeling of mild awe. Under flux, if the generators gave out the ship would probably be shredded and the crew would *certainly* be splattered by the gee forces.

DeBrooke looked through the screen at him quizzically. He swallowed and tilted his head as he watched the sloop come under normal drives, "I say we offer humanitarian aid — goodwill toward Earthers. We've got parts to repair Earther drives in our holds, we can fix it up, send it home, and make sure we get ourselves a good reputation."

"Right... works for me. Just don't get mistaken for the Coalition..." DeBrooke looked away from the screen just as an exclamation came from behind Stanton.

"Gods sir, huge hyper footprint coming in... Kroggs, sir! Four... five Dreadnoughts and about a dozen Destroyers!"

Stanton froze. Was that sloop all that was left of the fleet? Unlikely, the Earthers would never have let that many of their ships die senselessly, let alone the Genesis Fleet. A courier then? With news? It had to be.

So what should *he* do?

DeBrooke's eyes were clouded with shock as she looked back, "That changes things just a little. Now what do you say?"

Stanton swallowed, mind racing. The Earthers... what was peace with them worth? What was killing Kroggs worth... if they could...?

Stanton closed his eyes for a moment, thought wistfully of romance and relaxation, then summoned his tactical mind, "Like I said, we help."

Fox Magnus was thrown from his chair when the sloop translated, but considering what could have happened to his little *Flame*, he felt lucky.

"Normal space, NV 214X. Open planetary system!" the Master reported gruffly, and Fox cringed. Nowhere to hide.

"Head for the asteroids — get us every bit of speed you can!" he ordered quickly, then keyed his intercom. "Time, Chronos?"

There was a hiss on the line, "They blew, Fox. I have to rebuild at least some... a half hour. Maybe forty-five minutes."

Fox's fist hit the arm of his chair in an uncharacteristic sign of frustration, "Work fast, Chronos, we're in a bit of trouble."

The cougar snorted a laugh over the intercom, "I had figured that out, Fox. We'll do our best."

"Full speed, sir. Only sixty percent of standard. Our power grid is partially shorted out, so I can't run all systems," the Master's tone was cool.

"Deactivate long range sensor suite. Use the power for our tactical systems," Fox said quickly, then switched the comm link to the gun deck. "Lang, guns?"

"We've got power, Fox. The crews are manning them and I can run them out at your order. But you know how little damage we can do..."

As Sandpelt let the words drop off, Fox swallowed uncomfortably, "Aye. Do your best, Lang. We need all you can deliver."

Before the Midshipman could respond the Sensor Officer interrupted, "Here they come, sir, the first wave. Four Dreadnoughts and nine Destroyers... second wave is coming in too. Another Dreadnought and three more Destroyers."

Fox nodded in dark reply, "How soon until they can bring us to action?"

There was a short pause, "The Destroyers will be in range in three minutes, the Dreadnoughts four more after that. Looks like they're establishing some sort of squadron formation."

Not enough time, Fox decided silently. Not nearly enough.

"The sloop mustn't be able to see us," Stanton said to himself in low tones. "It's cruising in at an oblique angle." He frowned, then added more loudly: "Intercept course, full speed. Battle stations!"

Archangel Sword and *Grendelsbane City* thundered silently towards the small vessel.

"In range in forty seconds."

"All of the Destroyers?" Fox's tone was grim.

"Only seven, sir."

Oh *well then*... Fox knew his guns might take three or four, but even if they did, what was left of *Flame* could never handle the last eight. And that didn't consider the Dreadnoughts lumbering down from behind.

"Time to asteroid belt?"

It would offer slim protection, but better slim than none.

"Ninety seconds sir."

Fox ground his jaw and scowled. They might make it there...

"Range in twenty."

"Ready starboard broadside. Stern chaser will engage first, then our starboard, then we'll roll and give them port."

Giving the instructions helped Fox concentrate as *Flame* limped on, guns in their ports to allow the best velocity in its wounded state.

"Ten seconds... nine... eight... seven... six..."

"Run out the guns."

Time seemed to freeze as the sloop's eighteen guns slid out of their ports. So few...

"Missile separation!"

Fox cringed slightly, "How many?"

"Eighty, sir! Some of them enhanced!"

That was it then, they'd be overwhelmed... except that made *no* sense, because Kroggs fired spines...

Fox frowned... "*What?*"

"A Heavy Cruiser and a hybrid Battlecruiser entering scopes! They're moving to intercept the Destroyers!"

Fox suddenly sat bolt upright — two ships might be enough to slow down the Destroyers...

"Hard to starboard! Fire as you bear!"

"Fire as we bear, aye!"

Stanton grinned as his ships hurtled down on the Destroyers. The Kroggs hadn't paid attention to *Grendelsbane* or *Sword* until the first salvo had hit space at terminal velocity, and it wasn't until the second volley launched that the Destroyers reacted. They'd underestimated the capabilities of the human ships, as Kroggs always seemed to.

Sword's missiles had enhanced tracking systems, though at such close range the tracking qualities of the warheads hardly mattered.

Missiles slashed viciously into the neatly packed Destroyers, the Krogg point defense neuro-pulses lancing back at them. A dozen made contact with three Destroyers, immobilizing one in a shriek of pain. The rest turned in anger, their comrade's injury forcing them to ignore their immediate objective and to confront the new threat.

Seven guns barked, and energy shot raced from the Earther sloop. The little ship rolled, and the first diminutive broadside was quickly followed by a second. Guns such as these could hardly match the titanic force of the cannons found on a 74, but they'd all been aimed at a single Destroyer. That distracted ship didn't take note of the broadsides in time to maneuver out of their way, and as they surged in they caught its flank and gouged it badly.

Winged, it spun chaotically through space.

Sword and *Grendelsbane* now closed fast, getting inside the spine envelope before any could be spat in reply. Their energy weapons began to lance out, wounding ships as they passed. Neuro-pulses crackled at the human vessels, focusing mainly on the larger Battlecruiser. *Sword*'s shields absorbed the punishment with minor strain, while slightly behind it, *Grendelsbane*'s armor survived with only a few scrapes to its outer shell.

As the carronades on *Sword* forced another Destroyer to break off, pieces of it floating away in bloody gore, the rest backed away, not intimidated so much as infuriated. They reversed course, spitting spines as they went, and rejoined the other Destroyers lagging behind.

They'd come back in a minute, reinforced and ready.

"Form with the sloop, let's get into the belt!"

Fox breathed a sigh of relief as the Destroyers fell back. They'd make it to the belt, at least, "Signal Officer, my compliments to the ArcColonel of the lead ship. Offer my thanks."

"Aye sir."

The bridge was unquestionably calmer than it had been a moment ago, despite the gathering threat in *Flame's* wake.

"Time to belt?" Fox kept his voice as stable as possible.

"Entering... now. Destroyers reforming... sir, they're coming up with the Dreadnoughts now."

Fox swallowed, keying the intercom, "Chronos?"

"Identified the damage, Fox. I can rig up something... I just need ten minutes."

Commander Fox Magnus leaned back in his chair, took a calming breath, and replied, "Well maybe if I ask the Kroggs nicely..."

CHAPTER 27

"They say they need ten minutes to get their drives online, sir."

Stanton didn't offer a visible response. The Dreadnoughts would be in range in two... perhaps even less than that. The belt might delay them, but there was no way he could slow down a squadron like that in open space — not even *Sword* could go toe-to-toe with five Krogg Dreadnoughts, let alone their screening Destroyers.

No, they had to stay with the sloop, maximize their combined fire, make a desperate stand...

But the fact was they wouldn't survive.

"Sir, signal coming in, live this time. It's the sloop."

Stanton sat up straighter, "Put it on."

A red fox appeared on the monitor, looking as weary as any Earther Stanton had ever seen.

"ArcColonel, I'm Commander Fox Magnus, *ENS Flame*."

Stanton nodded, "Got your previous message, I'm James Stanton. We're going to have a hell of a time buying ten minutes, Commander."

Magnus nodded briefly, "We can't, I know. Sir, I don't know what you're doing out here but your two ships have the best chance of getting these dispatches back to Earth. We'll copy them into your databases, then we'll do whatever we can to slow the Kroggs down."

Stanton hesitated at the Earther's words, "No."

Fox's brow arched slightly, and Stanton took a deep breath. He'd have to explain himself... "Commander, we aren't exactly members of the Navy any longer. We're renegades — I don't think having us carry dispatches would be... *appropriate*."

Fox's eyes filled with understanding. These humans had chosen not to remain with the Allies, so he had no right to ask them to fight or die — as far as Fox was concerned, those duties should only go to volunteers. Even asking them to carry dispatches was a stretch; these human ships had no reason to assist...

He took another deep breath, "Then I must thank you again for your help, sir. But you have even less reason to stand with us. Go — don't die on our account. Even if you don't take the dispatches, just get *out* of here, before it's too late..."

It was as typically noble as any Earther statement James Stanton had ever heard, and it carried no undertone of bitterness. This Commander did not expect *Sword* and *Grendelsbane* to stay — he didn't want to coerce them into helping, and even though it would mean his death, Magnus was keen on seeing the unaligned humans escape.

Stanton couldn't abandon someone like that offhand.

"We may be unaligned, but we're friendly ships, Commander. And we'd never outrun Krogg Destroyers — enhanced or not. No, we stay. If we keep moving deeper into the belt we might be able to buy the time you need."

Fox paused, examining the man who had just volunteered to die with him.

"Very well, sir, they'll be in range in..." Magnus glanced down, "forty seconds."

Stanton nodded, and after meeting the Earther's eyes again, he closed the link.

Part of him felt proud about this act of selflessness, but part still wanted to make a run for it. He obeyed the first instinct: the renegades would stay.

Tonnant returned to a material state on the outskirts of the system's asteroid belt. The Second Rate's sensors hummed to life as Felix watched for *Hero*, but the 74's marker didn't come up.

Another ship's did.

Felix frowned as his sensors detected the situation further along the ring of the asteroid belt. A sloop — *Flame* — and two unaligned human ships were in close proximity, dodging asteroids. At first Felix thought the humans were attacking the sloop, but then he realized that something even more sinister was occurring.

"*Kroggs*..." his Flag Captain whispered at the sight of the markers popping up. "A heavy squadron..."

She was right, and Felix lifted himself from his chair and went to the main battle plot. What were Kroggs doing so close to Earth...

Ah, they were chasing a courier... that had fallen in with two independent human ships...? Well, there was one way to get an answer.

"Mark a course to rendezvous with *Flame* — go into energy drive. Set for 200 pls around the asteroids!" Felix's order was obeyed immediately, despite the danger of rocketing around asteroids at such a speed.

"Beat to quarters! Clear for action!"

"Entering range!"

Fox clutched the arms of his chair. His guns, virtually useless against Dreadnoughts, were being reserved solely to shoot down incoming spines. The Kroggs couldn't fire huge salvos of projectiles in the belt — too many rocks floated about, blocking their straight-line trajectories. Human missiles, on the other hand, could maneuver around obstacles and still find their targets.

"*Sword* is firing. *Grendelsbane* is firing."

The human missiles lashed out angrily, maneuvering as best they could around the asteroids that separated them from their targets. The ragged volley quickly exited the debris field, only to be blasted from the cosmos by the Dreadnoughts' point defenses.

A second salvo, a third. The missiles didn't even distract the heavy Krogg force — it swept them aside as if they were dust.

Stanton's hopes of buying time were being handily smashed.

The Krogg Destroyers, formed in a pyramid-shaped wedge, began to push into the belt, their pulses clearing a path for the Dreadnoughts behind them. Missiles raced out to meet them, but only a few struck, causing no damage to the well-armored, beastly ships.

That was it. Magnus was certain now — once the Kroggs got close enough for the human missiles to have a chance of doing damage, counter-fire from the spines and pulses would overwhelm his sloop and his renegade compatriots.

Hopes were again dashed.

"Activate comm link," Fox said quietly. At least he could still try to convince the humans to save themselves.

Fox opened his mouth to speak, but the channel was overridden as soon as it connected, "*Tonnant* to *Flame*, Admiral Felix here coming down from directly above. See your situation. Hold on just a moment and I'll be in it."

Magnus blinked. He had to be dreaming. Yes, it was a dream. An 80-gun ship of the line wouldn't be out here, and certainly wouldn't be commanded by Admiral *Felix*. For a strange moment he was disappointed in his imagination for creating such a farfetched rescue scenario.

Then a massive broadside filled the battle plot.

Felix knew a lone Second Rate couldn't tip the balance here, but it looked as though *Flame* was trying to buy time to get its drives back online. The fact that the humans were helping was all that had kept the ship alive so far — proof in Felix's mind that these so-called defections, when carried out by honest crew, were acceptable.

Tonnant's fury was being focused on the Destroyers, ignoring for now the supporting rank of alien capital ships. Coming from above, it was totally unexpected by the determined Krogg ships.

Three Destroyers were hit, one evaporating and two others taking heavy damage. Surprised again, the Destroyers turned and retreated, only seven remaining. *Tonnant* slipped slowly down into the field, coming alongside *Archangel Sword*.

Flame signaled immediately, Fox's face appearing in the main battle tank, "Commander Magnus here, sir. Carrying dispatches from Admiral Ursla."

Felix nodded, "Seem to have brought some rather unfriendly stragglers with you. Engine trouble?"

Fox nodded, "Aye sir. Very time-sensitive call for reinforcements in the dispatches. We had to redline the drives."

Felix knew it wasn't the time to ask about the situation at Genesis, but his curiosity stabbed at him nonetheless. He beat it back mentally, "We're to rendezvous with *Hero* here. It should be in the system soon. How long do you need?"

Fox looked off screen, "Eight minutes, sir."

Felix glanced to his battle plot, "They're coming in all at once. I think we scared them — they're probably wondering if we have ships hidden all over the place out here... but they'll still be in range in less than two minutes. I don't think we can handle that many Dreadnoughts alone... even if *Hero* was here..." He looked up, "But we'll do our best."

"You could take the dispatches sir — get them back to Earth," Fox's suggestion drew a blank stare from Felix, and the Commander frowned. "Sir?"

It was an idea, but an *unacceptable* one, "No, Commander. These Kroggs ran you down — we wouldn't have a hope of keeping away from them. *Tonnant* will stay with you. *Hero* should be here soon... we might be able to convince them to back off long enough to get your drives back online. Then you'll take your own dispatches, alright?"

Fox paused briefly, then nodded, "Thank you, sir."

The screen within the battle plot vanished, and Felix cast a glance at his Flag Captain. She took a deep breath.

"Signal from *Archangel Sword*, sir."

"In the plot, please," Felix turned back to the display.

ArcColonel James Stanton appeared; Felix had been acquainted with him when *Sword* had been rebuilt, and he offered him a genuine smile, "You leave us to go play knight in shining armor, James?"

Despite himself, Stanton smiled. He'd liked Admiral Felix quite a lot, though he hadn't known the cat commanded ships, "Something like that, sir. My fellow ArcColonel calls it swashbuckling. Strange seeing you on a ship, though, Admiral. Have help coming?"

Felix's expression sobered, "A 74."

Stanton sighed, looked off screen and then back, "Well, this'll get bloody then."

More cautious this time, the Krogg ships edged towards the belt. They were in a tight formation, Destroyers deployed around the Dreadnoughts in a protective shell. Fox watched with little more optimism than he'd had before *Tonnant* had arrived — even a Second Rate couldn't win this action.

"Time, Chronos?"

"Six minutes."

The Lieutenant and his engineers were working like demons and Magnus knew it. Time was simply against them. Time and Kroggs, a bitter brew.

"Sir..." the Sensor Officer paused, pouring over the telemetry that *Tonnant* was providing. "Incoming..."

Fox almost winced, but then he realized he should have the statement clarified, "Incoming *what?*"

Commodore Dran Nightclaw had encountered *Hero* when the 111th passed one of the systems the Third Rate was checking. He'd considered splitting the squadron to search for the Coalition cruiser, but elected to wait until he'd spoken with the Admiral. As such, the eight Fifth Rates had been augmented by one 74 and they now entered NV 214X at a steady pace, sliding from energy drive only a minute from the Kroggs.

A minute *behind* the Kroggs.

Though stunned by the appearance of the much-dreaded aliens, Nightclaw had immediately grasped the situation. The Kroggs were lumbering right for *Tonnant* and *Flame*, and based on the clouds of bloody gore floating through space, it appeared that the aliens meant to settle a score.

It took only seconds for the 111th to turn and run down on them at 95 pls, and the frigates' high speed was far better than that of the Dreadnoughts. In line ahead, with *Hero* taking the ninth slot, the Earthers swept in.

The maneuver was even more graceful than the Earther norm. Nightclaw entered range and ran out *Cerberus'* guns simultaneously, then wore the veteran frigate around to starboard, loosing its port broadside at the rear of the Krogg formation. *Cerberus* then rolled, its starboard guns pulsing.

As the first frigate crossed the Kroggs' course, the next in file turned, and continuing in a perfect, bending line, each ship emptied broadsides into the rear of the squadron. Then the line ahead began a great zig-zag, with Nightclaw's ship gracefully in the lead.

As *Cerberus* crossed the Kroggs' wake, the panther turned his frigate to run briefly parallel to it, then as *Hero* fired the last broadside of the first volley, the 111th's flagship completed the 'zag', recrossing the Kroggs' course and emptying both broadsides again. The ships of the squadron followed in a fluid line, and energy began to roll in sheets towards the Krogg rear. The maneuver looked much like a serpent curling back and forth across the alien wake, and this third surprise proved decisive.

The broadsides, steady and accurate, slammed into the unguarded rears of all five Dreadnoughts. Two died outright, two more were critically crippled and dropped from formation to slowly expire. The last tried to turn, spines coming to its skin in a bid to reply.

Tonnant moved faster.

At the arrival of the unexpected reinforcement, Felix had ordered the

Second Rate back up over the belt to give its guns better line. The 80's first broadside crashed into the Dreadnought as the Krogg vessel turned, the second following almost immediately after.

Sword and *Grendelsbane* erupted from the belt as the Dreadnought crumpled, pouncing on stunned Destroyers. The remaining Krogg ships were torn between retaliation and escape, but the latter option appeared ultimately more appealing. Two more fell to the human ships as they turned, the last five managing to escape the humans' missile range.

But Nightclaw's squadron rammed into the Destroyers before their hyper drives could carry them into the subspace dimensions. The Fifth Rates overwhelmed the Krogg ships, and the last five pursuers vanished into clouds of gore.

Aboard *Flame*, Fox Magnus was torn between relief and disbelief. The fates, it seemed, had conspired to save his sloop. He'd definitely be sending someone a gift basket. A large one. With flowers. And a card.

The intercom chirped, "We've got it Fox! Go!"

Magnus didn't hear the words at first, then he blinked into realization. With an ironic smile, he hit the intercom key, "Thanks Chronos. Turns out we… ahem… don't need to leave so soon. Admiral Felix and the 111th showed up to bail us out."

There was a stunned silence, and an atmosphere of disbelief spread through the ship. In the engine room Lieutenant Claw rubbed his aching brow with the palm of his furry paw and slumped against the reactor he'd been working on.

After all that, they were saved by the storied 111th Flying Squadron? Led, no less, by an administrative branch desk Admiral?

The universe was fickle.

CHAPTER 28

Felix read the message again, sent from Ursla to the Admiralty. 'Reinforcements with all possible speed... Twenty-one days from this dispatch's signing.' Looking at the date, Felix marveled at the progress *Flame* had made on the trip. At best speed, the Earther First and Third Fleets would need twelve days to reach Genesis, which meant the sloop had to make Earthfall in nine.

Six days after it'd left, it was just under three days out.

The message had to keep going, to lose as little time as possible. The Second Fleet and the Genesis Fleet depended on it.

"Send these dispatches to *Hero* and instruct Captain Arbear that it is *imperative* they reach Earth in less than seventy-two hours. Order her to depart immediately. *Tonnant* and the 111ᵗʰ will proceed directly to Genesis to support Ursla."

The 74 would be able to travel just as fast — if not slightly faster — than any of Nightclaw's frigates or the wounded *Flame*. As *Hero* turned swiftly and entered energy drive, Felix sat back in his chair.

His little battle group would hardly turn the tide against the Kroggs, but he felt it his duty to head for the action immediately, nonetheless... even if he could only tell Ursla that the message was heading for the right place and that help, hopefully, was at hand.

Before he could order his ships to Genesis, though, he had to meet with certain officers.

The summons from Admiral Felix to attend him and the Earther Captains in a briefing had come as an unmitigated shock to both Stanton and DeBrooke. What could the Earthers want with them?

If Stanton hadn't known better he would have thought they were going to be incarcerated. That might be the attitude taken by the Genesis Navy, but these were Earthers, which usually meant a more considerate approach... What would they do?

Wondering about these questions as his pinnace set down on *Tonnant*'s deck, he took a steadying breath. He moved from his seat to the main hatch, then waited for the ramp to descend and stepped nervously down it. The ship's Second Lieutenant offered a crisp salute at the bottom, then the pair waited as DeBrooke's pinnace landed beside the craft from *Sword* and watched her descend its ramp. Without speaking, the two human renegades proceeded through the large Second Rate, finding their way to Felix's briefing with the help of the Lieutenant sent to escort them.

Audrey's heart rate was elevated, though she tried to mentally control it. She'd left Earth space a month before James, and she had no personal history with Savanna Felix, the Admiral who'd taken command here. Generally speaking, she trusted the benevolence of Earthers, but she hadn't dealt with any since leaving Sol. James wouldn't let them single one ship out for punishment, she knew that... but would there be *punishment* at all?

For his part, James didn't know whether the Earthers would think him in the right or in the wrong... whether the Earthers had yet encountered the Coalition... whether his warning had gotten back to Sol...

But neither ArcColonel could escape the feeling that, for better or worse, this was going to prove a decisive day in the course of their lives.

The Lieutenant stopped before a door and gestured the pair of humans towards it. Exchanging anxious glances, they stepped into the room, immediately sensing the positive mood. The eight Captains of the 111th were present, as was their Commodore, Ursla's protégé Nightclaw. Felix and his Flag Captain were in conversation with that black panther.

"Sir, ma'am."

A short — slightly shorter even than James — fox approached them with a smile and an extended hand, "Fox Magnus. I must offer my thanks again for your intervention."

Shaking both ArcColonels' hands firmly, the fox drew back. Taken slightly by surprise, Stanton smiled and reddened slightly, "Well... it seemed the right thing to do."

"Nevertheless, you risked yourselves and your ships and for that I'm indebted to you," Fox's words were sincere.

DeBrooke and Stanton cast a glance at each other, then Felix spoke from across the room to call the meeting to order. The Captains found their chairs, as did the ArcColonels. Felix sat at one head, Nightclaw the other, and the humans sat alongside the elite Captains of the Earther First Fleet and the Commander they'd saved.

"Well, first, it's good to have the fighting 111th here! I seem to have lost my other squadron under a pile on my desk," Felix's good-natured jest caused the Earthers at the table to chuckle, and Audrey and James smiled.

"Well, they found their way home," one of the Captains said with a grin, "and well done, sir. On your entire cruise!"

"Won't just be pushing papers anymore, I'll wager," another put in, and Felix smiled and nodded in acceptance of the praise.

"Now, good Captains, you may or may not be aware of the exact situation in Genesis, but we have a resident expert in the form of Commander Magnus.

Could you fill us in, Fox?"

Having expected the request, Fox had taken a holo map of the Genesis system with him from *Flame,* and he now brought it up on the table holo projector. The great star system was projected in light blue, the Second Fleet in red, the Genesis Fleet in green, and the Kroggs in black.

The room uneasily took in the sight of so many Krogg ships.

"We got into Genesis without being picked up on the approach, and this is what we found when we blew through their pickets. Needless to say we were surprised, but based on what we've pieced together, the Kroggs are using Genesis as an ambush site during a fighting retreat. There'll be a Larosian Fleet coming through that anomaly, hoping to destroy this armada, but it will only number 2,000 to the Kroggs' 3,000. Admiral Ursla was able to rescue the Larosian scouting squadron when it came through, and it's been made official: we're taking their side in this fight. Given the odds, we want to gather everything we have and hit them just as the Larosian Fleet translates — that way we can strike them from two sides at once."

Felix nodded slowly, "Ursla has sent for everything we have left in Earth space, so as soon as *Hero* reaches Sol you can bet the First and what we have from the Third will be mobilized. We also have another 400 Genesis ships, possibly more if they're commissioned on the fly. For now I intend to take us directly to Ursla's side. We may not make a grand fleet, but I think it'd do her good to have the 111ᵗʰ in Genesis."

There were nods of approval from around the table — all the commanding officers of the 111ᵗʰ's ships had served under Ursla at one time or another, and they respected her greatly.

"Excellent, we can get under weigh as soon as *Flame*'s drives can be fully repaired. Commander?"

Magnus cocked his eyebrows at the Admiral, "We're back at full, sir, thanks to the spare parts donated by ArcCol... ahem, *Mister* Stanton."

Curious eyes turned to the human male, and he reddened slightly, "*Archangel Sword* is a hybrid. We carry parts for both energy and flux generators."

There were nods of understanding around the table, and one Captain spoke up, "You also did a marvelous job on those Destroyers, Mister Stanton. Well done, sir. And to you, Miss DeBrooke."

James and Audrey both found their breath catching. After seeing what was going on, they hardly wanted to be the subject of attention at this table. Was Felix going to ask them to rejoin the fleet... to help at Genesis? The Genesis Fleet would never accept them back, and there was no way they could keep up with the Earthers. Or would they be as forgiving as Fox Magnus and simply offer thanks?

The Admiral's next comment just added to their confusion, "The message you sent back to Earth said the Coalition Fleet had one Superdreadnought, but we only came across a wrecked hulk of one. Who gets the credit for that victory?"

Stanton swallowed, "*Archangel Sword* sir..."

There were smiles from the frigate Captains around the table, one speaking up, "No question that you know your business, sir!"

Stanton was convinced he was bright red, but he nodded in thanks all the same. DeBrooke shot him an approving glance and he replied with a familiar-seeming smile. A number of the Earthers at the table noticed the undercurrent, and Felix cocked an eyebrow.

"Well, we are left with a question, Mister Stanton. What would you and Miss DeBrooke like to do next?"

That question was probably the best one that could have been posed under the circumstances — as far as either human could tell, it didn't directly imply that *Sword* and *Grendelsbane* would be expected to return to Naval service. The ex-ArcColonels looked at each other for a moment, considering all the plans they'd made. This 'goodwill' path they'd embarked on had been dangerous... but perhaps it might prove beneficial in future... and meeting each others' eyes, they acknowledged the possibility.

Stanton turned to Felix, "Seems that Genesis could use every ship it can get right now."

DeBrooke picked up the thought before there could be reply, "We're not too busy out here as it is, and I think both our crews got a taste for the Kroggs today."

Felix twitched his ear thoughtfully, "Do you want to rejoin the Navy?"

Audrey and James exchanged another quick glance, and the latter shook his head quickly, "We've left the service of the Genesis Navy. As independent ships and crews, we'd like to offer our assistance to our Earther friends."

"All *two* of your ships?"

Felix's comment wasn't biting, just amused. Stanton looked down a bit and shrugged, and DeBrooke offered a single nod, "What we have for now, anyway."

Felix studied the faces of the two renegade ArcColonels, and felt a pang of sympathy for them. They'd never be welcomed back in their own service — they'd be pariahs among human officers who knew they'd deserted the fleet. But clearly both DeBrooke and Stanton stood on the right side of the rising conflict. Savanna Felix felt obliged to give them what they wanted... but how could he? It would be too awkward to commission the two ships into the Earther Navy — that would undermine the independence of its Genesis counterpart. If only he could let them fly Earther colors...

Felix blinked.

"I cannot accept your offer, Audrey, James. Sorry. We all know better than to think of two ships as a distinct power capable of independently joining in the

Earther-Genesis Alliance."

The humans were still. They hadn't expected such a plain rejection, even if their request was destined to be denied. The Captains at the table stared curiously at Felix — he would never be so undiplomatic...

"Instead, I am going to write letters of marquee for both of you."

Stanton frowned at the cat and then at DeBrooke, his questioning eyes making Felix realize he had no idea what the Earther term, based in history a millennium old, meant. The Captains at the table were smiling at the obscure reference, but the humans sat stupefied.

"I'm going to commission both your ships as *Earther privateers*," Felix continued, hiding a smile.

The two humans shot confused glances at each other, then quickly scanned the smiling Earther faces that surrounded them.

"You'll be completely independent of us, but our ports and those of our allies will service your ships and you'll be treated as members of the Earther Navy," the Admiral finished his brief explanation and leaned back, enjoying the humans' reactions.

Stanton was stunned — such an arrangement would be unheard of in the Genesis Fleet, but apparently the Earthers had a little more flexibility in their commissioning system. Felix continued, "You'll have my signed letters that make you official, and you can attach your ships to our forces as you please."

"And this will last how long?" DeBrooke's voice was a little uncertain.

Felix shrugged, "As long as you don't attack us or our allies it'll be permanent. Unless, of course, you don't want the letters anymore, in which case you can cancel them at will. You two will be added to the Post Captain list at Admiralty House, and your ships will be put in the Admiralty's database. You'll have the right to ask for our support if you need it, but we can't order you to do anything — you can do whatever you like."

The Earthers at the table grinned at the two human *Post Captains*, who smiled back dumbfounded.

As the two humans left the briefing room, DeBrooke stopped Stanton in the hall and turned to their escort, "A moment please, Lieutenant?"

The Earther smiled, "Certainly, Captain."

As he drifted down the hall ahead of them, Captain Stanton looked at Captain DeBrooke and smiled.

"I think I can live with this."

CHAPTER 29

Harvey Bingham whistled a brisk tune as he walked through the halls of Admiralty House. He had no idea why he'd been summoned by the First Lord, but he was in a good mood and found he wasn't too worried about the circumstances.

In his past weeks of public life, he'd begun to feel far better about himself, and he'd found himself surprisingly welcome in the company of Earther Naval officers. Genesis personnel were still obviously suspicious of him, but the Earthers seemed to recognize that he was trying to make amends — and for the right reasons. So far he'd made up for *some* of the damage he'd caused Earth in the past, but he intended to do much more.

Caine seemed to be growing genuinely comfortable in his company, perhaps even following his wife's path to friendship with the High Chancellor. Hastings seemed to be on a roughly congruent path, if a few light years behind and moving much more slowly. To Bingham, these meager advances constituted triumphs, and he was determined to improve his position even more as time went on.

And the best way to make amends was to keep helping the Navies maintain order, so the request from Caine that the High Chancellor attend an urgent meeting at Admiralty House seemed to herald another promising opportunity.

Turning the last corner to Caine's office, Bingham tugged his new Church uniform into place. He was pleased with the lighter garment — which lacked the traditionally overbearing feature of a cape — and found that its muted maroon flaps and its lack of accoutrements made it far more palatable to the Navy personnel. If Bingham had his way, the entire Church of Genesis would eventually accept the more subtle garb.

Opening Caine's door, Bingham stepped into the First Lord's office only to halt abruptly. The entire Admiralty was in the room, as were a number of fleet officers, and Hastings and what remained of her staff. And they weren't at the meeting tables, they were clumped in groups, seemingly dealing with a dozen different troubles.

Eyes turned to Bingham as he entered, and his instinct was to shrink before the gazes of so many military personnel. Instead he went straight to Caine, who stood by a holo projection with a group of his fellow Admiralty Lords.

"Kella reports the First will be ready to weigh anchor in another forty minutes, sir. Since Varnon's gone we've folded the ships of the Third into the First's command structure, and they'll all be ready to weigh within forty-five minutes."

Caine nodded at the report from the Third Lord, "Have somebody tell Lab Forepaw that I'll be joining him in *Orion* in one half hour."

A half hour, Caine thought sadly, was just enough time to get up there. He wouldn't be able to see Elandra or Phealan before he left.

Bingham was suddenly next to him, "Setter, I'm sorry I'm late. What's going on?"

Caine turned to the High Chancellor with a troubled expression, "Esther Arbear brought *Hero* in forty minutes ago with a message sent by courier from Andra. The Kroggs have 3,000 ships in Genesis. Apparently there's a major Larosian force on its way to the system, and Kroggs are waiting to ambush them. Andra's going to use the Second Fleet to distract the Kroggs, but unless we get there in time, it's a good bet she'll get wiped out."

Bingham's eyes widened at the report, but his mind seized him before shock could take over. The Kroggs had managed to bring 3,000 ships to Genesis. That was in itself a terrifying thought, and one which made his hopes of regaining the planet from alien influence seem slim... But what good was a civilian in this situation... he put the question to words as directly as he could, "Very well. What can I do?"

Caine was already moving to answer his question, "The Chancellors' Council has decided not to accept Earther interaction on Genesis without your personal endorsement. We need you to convince them, and then the planet, of... well, our good relationship."

So, rather abruptly, the ultimate test of Harvey Bingham's ability to redeem himself was upon him.

No pressure.

Panic tugged naggingly at the fringes of the High Chancellor's mind, but Caine's hand suddenly came to rest on the human's shoulder, "I know you can do this, Harvey. And Liz agrees."

It had been a long time since Harvey Bingham had taken a complete leadership role in human affairs... and back in the old days he'd been a different man. But he had no choice — much was depending on his ability to secure Genesis' loyalty. And since the structure of Genesis society was in great part a product of his rule, he was obliged to take on this challenge.

And most importantly, the two fleet leaders, once his foes, believed he could do it.

Bingham found himself nodding slowly, "How long do I have before we leave?"

Caine lifted his hand from the Chancellor's shoulder with a satisfied nod, "I'll need you back here in about half an hour, I should think. We leave immediately — every minute could count. If you'd like, I can take you aboard *Orion*."

Bingham nodded quickly, "Whatever you think is best. I'll be back presently then."

Without further words he turned and left at a brisk pace. His London apartment held enough of his belongings for this journey, and it was only five minutes away.

Watching him go, Caine turned towards the side of his office now occupied by human officers, "Liz?"

The ArcGeneral looked up from her pads, coming over to him as her staff continued to talk, "We can get 504 ships into space. I can launch with the Third."

Caine nodded, "Good. Where will you be flying your flag?"

Hastings frowned a second, returning to her own flock of aides. She took a pad from the desk they hovered over, "I'll be aboard *Pope Frederick Craig*. You're in *Orion*?"

Caine nodded and the two got back to their work.

Elandra Caine was at her clinic in Australia when her husband was finally able to reach her. She'd been working on new gene treatments for humans — treatments that could potentially extend their lives to about 220 years using the Earthers' natural long-life DNA as a template. She was making a great deal of headway, and safely predicted she'd have a working six-step retroactive treatment ready for widespread application within two years.

The promise of an achievement such as this was invigorating.

She was tracing various chromosome patterns on a volunteer's DNA strand when the intercom chirped, "Elandra, your husband is on the line."

Elandra frowned, looking at the chronometer on the wall. It was an odd time of day for him to call — they usually had lunch together, so it wasn't often he commed in the middle of the morning.

Either lunch was cancelled or something important was happening. Or both...

Leaving her kiosk she found a comm screen nearby. As she punched in her code, the live message in her network came up, and her husband appeared. His expression was grim.

"What is it?" Elandra asked immediately, knowing all too well that the expression on Caine's face did not promise good things.

"The Kroggs have 3,000 ships at Genesis. Andra needs us — *all* of us — as soon as possible."

Elandra wasn't much of a military wolf, but she knew from talks with Setter and Andra that the Kroggs had the potential of becoming a significant threat. Ursla had a fleet of 600 Earther and 900 human ships with her — nothing even *close* to 3,000 warships… so she would need all the help she could get.

"When do you leave?" she asked solemnly.

Caine looked down for a second, "I'm heading up to *Orion* in ten minutes. I'm sorry, El, I've got no time…" he wanted to say more, but she understood. He had to sacrifice time with his family now, or one third of the Navy might die. "Tell Phealan for me, please."

It was a sad request, and Elandra nodded silently. The two said nothing for a moment, and then someone called the First Lord's attention off screen. He turned back to his wife with a pained expression, "I have to go."

"Good luck, Setter. Love you."

"You too. Be safe, El."

The link cut, and Elandra stared blankly at the screen for many minutes.

Pope Frederick Craig hung in space before Hastings. She'd never set foot on the ship, but it was the one selected by her staff to be the most suitable for her flag. Its recrewing efforts had produced one of the best ship's companies in the Sol system, and the repairs had been complete for some time. Of the 500 Genesis ships the Earther Fleet was hauling with them, *Craig* was probably the best she could have asked for.

Hastings ran over the situation in her mind again. She was rushing 300-odd ships out of repair slips and shipyards to add their missiles to the 200 ships that were already on duty. Half the ships she was commissioning were still full of scars and had only partially active subsystems. All they had were their core systems and main power, skeleton crews of men and women who'd never worked together, and Naval guts.

And, of course, 1,000-odd Earther ships backing them up.

Hastings heaved a deep breath and remembered the feeling of being a leg short. She was going back to war.

Aboard his pinnace, Caine turned his thoughts away from his family and watched *Orion* grow in the window. The First Rate was by far the biggest ship of the line in the Navy, vastly exceeding the 100-gun requirements of the class. Its cannon were massive, and they numbered 175, divided into two broadsides of seventy-five guns, with fifteen bow and ten stern chasers.

Orion had been his ship through the entire conflict with the Church, and now the veteran First Rate would fly his pennant again. The rest of the First Fleet was made up of similarly experienced ships, some of its 600-vessel complement transferred in from the wrecked squadrons of the Third Fleet to fill the ranks. The Third was still incomplete, being filled more slowly with fresh ships from the yards. Crews for those newly-constructed vessels generally came from survivors of lost ships, so there was no questioning their experience in naval action… though many of the new hulls had only put to space a couple of weeks before and were still being shaken down.

But Caine still had to take them — *all* of them — to face 3,000 Kroggs.

There was no choice. The Third Fleet was only at two-thirds strength, having 395 ships in space, but combined with the First and Hastings' Provisional Fleet, they would double Ursla's strength.

His strength, once he arrived.

The pinnace slid into *Orion's* familiar bay and set down evenly. It was the last small craft destined to board the massive line of battle ship, so the First Rate immediately weighed grav anchors and fired up its drives, producing a good maneuvering speed. With a certain majesty, the ship's Cruising Master guided it out of orbit to join the assembling squadrons of the Allied Fleet.

Caine quickly descended from the pinnace, greeted Captain Labrador Forepaw at the ramp's bottom and shook his old friend's hand, "Sorry we couldn't give you more warning, Lab."

The canine smiled at Caine, "It's always good to have you aboard, even at short notice."

With an appreciative smile Caine nodded toward the door, and the pair made for the bridge.

Minutes later, 1,500 ships of war boosted hard for Genesis.

CHAPTER 30

Sarah was tired.

But that wasn't the worst part. Tired she could handle — six hours of sleep or less a night, constant planning, briefings, strategy seminars, and so on, took its toll. But that was to be expected. Something else was nagging at her, something she couldn't figure out.

Admittedly, she'd had a case of tunnel vision lately, with her focus entirely on the job of getting her fleet drilled, upgraded and ready to face the Kroggs. That preparation forbade her much time to contemplate broader matters, and that had to be the problem. Something she couldn't quite grasp was tugging at the back of her mind. *Dammit.*

Flame should have, by now, reached Earth, and if all was going well the reinforcements had begun their voyage to Genesis. Only ten days remained before Novash's predicted arrival of the Fourth Fleet.

Graham was busy with his duty — the Genesis ships in-system were being upgraded with new tracking systems as soon as the modules came out of the factories. Various squadrons and battle groups were practicing in near-Genesis space to ready themselves for action while others stood in line at the dockyards for their parts upgrades...

Everything seemed to be in order, yet Sarah still felt like she was forgetting something. She'd chatted briefly with Ursla about it, but the Admiral had her own concerns — the Earther Fleet was the Allied vanguard here, after all. And with Graham and Pat busy, they didn't really have time to talk with her either. Which meant she was left entirely to her own devices to figure this out.

So Sarah resigned herself to reading in her cabin. She'd managed to dig up some of the battle reports from old actions against the Larosian squadrons, back from the early days of ArcGeneral Turcott and his Great Silver Fleet. Depending on your perspective, it was depressing reading — the Larosians annihilated ninety percent of Turcott's fleet only a century ago; they were powerful new allies. But the Kroggs were just as strong... and there was something important about the Kroggs she was still forgetting. *Dammit again!*

Dropping her book onto the floor next to her couch, Sarah sat up and stared at the wall across from her. An almost sickly feeling was clutching her mind — it was as though she couldn't think clearly. Too much time and focus was being directed at her fleet, and it was keeping her from seeing the bigger picture. She needed to do something to break her single-mindedness.

Sparring could work... yes, go beat up a marine or two...

No, that would make her focus *more*. She needed to let go of her immediate concerns, if only for a few hours. Let her mind float.

And her inability to just force her mind to do that on its own allowed her to consider the most drastic of options. Yes, why not? This might be the only way... go somewhere she'd rarely been and do something she'd never done before.

Sarah grabbed her tunic off the back of her chair and tugged it on, buttoning it as she left her quarters.

Pacing through *Joseph Barron*, she found the entire Superdreadnought alive with activity. Systems were being upgraded, drills run... she almost felt guilty for leaving it on a matter like this. But she was getting desperate and had to break the clutch of uncertainty that was casting a shadow over her thoughts.

Even if this brilliant idea of hers was seeming like an increasingly bad one as she walked.

Sarah Manchester, commander of the Genesis Fleet, found her way to her Superdreadnought's flight deck.

Harbinger Bishop slid evenly back into formation with the fleet, followed in a flowing line by thirty-five other Battlecruisers. Pat grinned at the maneuver — it was positively Earther-like in its comfortable precision. The Battlecruisers, all of the same class and all angling through space at the same velocity, made for a stunning display.

Of course, the two squadrons of Sixth Rates dancing a deadly ballet out to port were just as awe inspiring, but Pat tried not to think about them. Such perfect maneuvers came as much from instinct as practice for Earthers, but for human crews executing perfect maneuvers was a result of hard training. So with pride he edged his squadron in towards its set position on the outer layer of the human fleet, bringing his ships to an even stop in three vertically-stacked lines of twelve. Each line then divided into four rows of three and his thirty-six Battlecruisers formed a three-deep, four-wide, three-tall wall of ships.

"Well done, all of you!" he said cheerfully. He turned to his ArcColonel Forbes. "I'd like my pinnace cleared for departure. I'll be heading to the flagship."

Forbes smiled, "The crew's already waiting for you. Your pinnace has priority on the deck."

Pat cocked an eyebrow, "And why would they be waiting for me?"

Forbes shrugged, "Habit."

Pat decided not to press further. He *had* been on *Barron* quite a lot lately, perhaps the crew was just in tune with his duties. He strode confidently from his bridge.

• • •

Admiral Varnon Broadpaw laughed heartily, and Graham couldn't help but smile. The Admiral had a certain affinity for jokes, and despite the uninspiring subject matter, their discussions about the Genesis manufacturing situation always ended in laughter. Graham more than appreciated the Earther's light-heartedness in these serious circumstances — it made him feel as though he'd known the Earthers longer than just a dozen days. With the Earther wolf's help, the 900 ships of the Genesis Fleet were getting their upgrade kits at a remarkable pace, and Graham was honestly beginning to like their chances in the coming fight.

Well, more than he *had*, anyway.

In his office aboard *Genesis One*, he and the Admiral were now going over the final figures. They could have every Genesis ship supplied with new sensors at least two days before the Larosians arrived. The Genesis capital ships would have upgrades to their missile trackers by then as well, so the fleet would have a heavier punch.

With that timetable finally worked out, the meeting reached its conclusion.

"Well, a pleasure as always Graham," Broadpaw came to his feet, and as was the case with many Earthers, he paid little heed to their difference in ranks. As far as he was concerned, the ArcBrigadier was a friend and Graham wasn't inclined to disagree.

"All mine, I assure you Varnon," Graham grinned, and the Earther laughed again.

"Right. I'm sure..." he paused and looked at the figures on Graham's monitor. "I don't think we'll need to meet for a while now. You should go spend more time with your sister. Haven't seen her for months, after all."

Graham tipped his head to the side and wore a thoughtful look, "I suppose she won't mind little brother nipping at her heels."

Broadpaw grinned again, "Good, good. A couple of days then."

The Admiral bowed out with a smile and walked off through the now-familiar corridors of *Genesis One*.

Sarah's pinnace slid past an Earther craft on the way into *Genesis One's* bay. She watched it go by absently. Her mind wasn't loosening at all, though to be fair she'd only been off her ship for ten minutes. If this was to work, she needed to release her concerns... come at things from a fresh perspective.

Once upon a time, that would have simply required a good night's sleep. But lately sleep was merely a matter of physical maintenance — Sarah couldn't count on it to refresh her mind. She needed something completely foreign to put things into perspective.

So this, in theory, made plenty of sense.

What have I forgotten?

That question continued to follow her down the ramp and into the station's extensive network of corridors. Her closed mind persisted in refusing to answer, and so she cursed her brain again. Absently wandering through the corridors, she at last found herself on the station's boardwalk — the commercial deck of *Genesis One,* installed in the orbital to help the Navy get a cut of the station crews' regular paycheck.

And she was looking for a bar.

Yes, a *bar.* As much as she didn't quite believe it herself, she was heading to the notorious *Bloody Pulsar,* the terribly-named haunt of all officers in the fleet looking to forget their troubles. It was the best-known bar in space, and despite being kept as clinically clean as any Genesis Naval food court, it had its share of entertaining stories.

Sarah had been in the bar twice. The first time she'd been an ArcEnsign and she'd only managed to stumble back to her ship with the help of one ArcMajor Hastings. The second time she'd visited the *Pulsar* she'd elected against drinking. She couldn't stand the complete lack of discipline in her mind when she drank... but today she was desperate to heave her mind out of a rut. This might be the only — admittedly drastic — way to do that.

As she arrived in the depressingly bright and metallic establishment, Sarah's mind was already shuffling away from the potential issues she could cause by just being there. It was right on the corner of the boardwalk, with windows for all to see... well that was alright, she'd be discreet, and take her drink in stages. There was only one group of off-duty spacers in the corner, nothing to worry about. She could settle down and just concentrate on loosening the mental knots that were restraining her thought. Going to the bar, Sarah sat stiffly on a stool, turning her back to the spacers.

"What'll it be, miss?" the bartender barely drew Sarah's notice.

She blinked in reply after a moment and looked up at the man, "Umm... I shall have... a Vortex."

The 'Vortex' was a blend of a lot of alcohol and a lot of other kinds of alcohol — that was the extent of Sarah's knowledge about it... and about alcohol in general. Liz had introduced her to this drink long ago, and it was rather potent, but Sarah wasn't thinking too hard on the subject of beverages. She was already turning back to the fact that she had forgotten something, and that she was hell bent on figuring out exactly what.

Sipping the bitter liquid unconsciously, Sarah tried to let her mind float — to encompass the problem. She smiled to herself as the room slowly began to drift before her eyes.

"Sir, a signal coming in for you. Pinnace off *Harbinger Bishop*. ArcBrigadier Conroy."

Graham was just clearing his desk when his aide called him over the intercom. Somewhat surprised, Graham seated himself and keyed his desk monitor on, "Patrick Conroy, what mischief are you up to?"

Patrick smiled, "Coming to claim your soul, Graham, damnation is summoning you. Or, if you're not partial to that, I might want to talk to your sister. Where is she?"

Graham leaned back in his chair with a smile, "Now Pat, you know I don't keep her on a radio collar. Why don't you try her *ship*?"

Pat's grin faded, "They told me she'd shoved off in her pinnace to *Genesis One*."

Graham paused and frowned, "She's not here... I'm sure she'd have told me if she was coming aboard."

The Irishman's brow creased slightly, "That girl... I swear... meet me in the bay, Graham."

"It must have something to do with the Kroggs," Sarah decided in a low tone. The bartender was keeping a discreet distance from the woman with ArcGeneral's pips. Of course he knew who she was, but he didn't *recognize* her. Bartenders on fleet orbitals had a condition that made recognizing people a problem sometimes.

"Alrighty then, Sarah my girl, now you just need to figure out *what* it has to do with the Kroggs!" Sarah had never been in the habit of talking to herself. She must be getting sucked into the *vortex*!

That inner joke made her smile as she leaned over the bar and rested her chin in the palm of her hand. Her other hand drummed out the beat of a marching tune on the counter without mimicking too much of the rhythm. She stopped tapping occasionally to sip the Vortex, only to discover the damnable thing was empty!

Pushing the glass towards the bartender, she wondered if she'd forgotten something about the Kroggs' heads.

"She came aboard and went towards the boardwalk," Graham said to Pat as the Irishman trotted down the ramp. "I've got a couple of good people out looking right now."

"Oh, well the walk's not all that big anyway. And we can eliminate some spots on it right now. You'd never catch that girl in a bar, or in that shop with all those religious trinkets..."

Graham cocked an eyebrow, "Glad you're sure of that. You've got her number, I'm sure."

"She's drunk after so much as sipping *anything* with alcohol. And come on, Graham, *Church stuff*? Give her credit."

Graham snorted a laugh, "You certainly do. I didn't know she knew alcohol existed!"

Pat shrugged, "We talk."

Graham smiled, "Aha. *Talk*, eh?"

A 'buddy-buddy' elbow jabbed Pat in the side, and Pat frowned at the junior Manchester, who was grinning.

"What do you mean, Graham?" Pat brushed past him and started walking.

He caught up in a few jogged meters, "Come on Pat, I know you've got your eye on her. I'm actually all for it, you can look out for her while I'm stuck here. From what she tells me, you did on Earth."

Pat was trying not to listen — he had other things to worry about. And Graham was making no sense with his half-coy remarks... "You're daft, man. I can find her on my own! I'm in no mood for bloody foolery anyway!"

Pat never used such dated words as 'foolery' unless somebody hit a nerve.

"I'm daft?" Graham's knowing grin began to fade — surely Pat wasn't denying what everyone in the fleet already knew...

Pat was too busy walking and trying not to process Graham's words to give the younger man an answer.

But then those words started to sink in... and his mind started putting different situations together. Spending tons of time together, talking about everything, chasing each other through *Genesis One*... *Oh damn.*

The Irishman slowed to a gradual stop in the middle of the corridor. No, it wasn't at all possible...

Let's have another look... friends... that whole Antarctica incident... plenty of time together... Oh dear Gods. Oh bloody dear Gods.

Graham stopped ahead of the frozen Irishman, "Pat?"

Pat blinked.

"Pat, I didn't mean to intrude... I thought you were used to it. I mean everyone talks about it..."

Pat blinked again, "Everyone *who*?"

Graham's eyes widened and he realized that Pat really didn't know. He shrugged, "*Everyone* everyone. Earthers, ours, the marines... hell, one fellow said they should put the two of you on a recruiting poster. 'Romance in the Navy'!"

Pat's eyes widened, but he took a calming breath against the mild anger summoned by that poster suggestion, then started walking slowly, "Romance? Gods man, I'd never even thought it."

Graham opened his mouth to make a sharp reply and then shut it when he saw Pat's expression. Half confused, half angry, half understanding... well, at three halves, it reflected the Irishman's sudden bout of inner turmoil.

Oh dear *Gods*.

"So the Kroggs are black, which means they probably like dark-colored things," Sarah was more than a little pleased with her deduction. Part of her said she was tipsy and completely off her rocker, but she happily used expletives to silence it.

She was half was through her second Vortex.

Yes, as she mused it the phrase came out 'half *was*' instead of 'half way' through the drink.

Her occasional mutterings went as unnoticed as possible by the bartender, who waited at the other end of the bar for more customers. Rush hour would be soon, lots of people off duty. Meanwhile, the spacers in the corner seemed to be working up courage enough to get social.

As far as the gruff ratings could tell, the lady at the bar was just a tad over-indulged and no one could possibly see her rank pips from behind. It was an oddity within the Genesis Navy — from behind, no one could easily tell commissioned officer from rating.

Fatal flaws, these things.

Sarah softly tapped out the rhythm to the marching tune and pondered what else Kroggs would like because of shade. Hmmm... space. Space was *dark*!

"Ahem, miss. Are you looking for anything... companionship, maybe?"

It was a spacer first class, over thirty and clearly with indiscreet intentions. His mates snickered behind him at the table, and the bartender looked up, observed the situation, shook his head and looked down.

Sarah heard the question in her dreamy state and turned to face the spacers, "Well, spacer, I must say I'm *bloody* tempted, but I should think not."

The man's rough smile vanished into a look of shock. One, two, three, four, *five* stars on her collar. Not a plain-fronted tunic. She was a full ArcGeneral... *Manchester*, now that he looked more closely... and he'd just asked her...

His mates nearly died in their chairs.

"Oh, don't feel bad man, I'm just on official business, you see! But if you leave your name..."

"Uhh... ma'am... pardon... I have... duty..."

The spacer fled to his mates and then the shocked non-coms promptly ushered themselves from the bar.

"Hmm, suppose they had somewhere else to be," she remarked to herself with a satisfied smile. "Kroggs must like dark places. Harder to see them..."

Pat was more determined to find Sarah now, though he wasn't entirely sure why. Was it what Graham had said? He saw a cluster of ratings quick-stepping for the corridor and got in their way. The one leading didn't even notice the officers — he was too busy yelling at his comrades.

"How could you miss who she was? You idiots! Fleet commander and you let me go—"

He walked right into Pat, and though the Irishman would only have been of average height if he was an Earther, the spacer had to look up at him. And recognize him. And recognize who he was and remember what the word was about him and the fleet commander. And have the color drain promptly from his face.

"Uhh... sorry sir... I wasn't looking where I was going."

"We noticed that, spacer."

Pat hadn't spoken, so the spacer risked a glance to his right at the other man. And blanched a bit more. Not only was he the ArcBrig commander of the station, he was the fleet commander's brother... And the spacer prayed to the Gods to get him out of this so he could mend his ways.

"Name, spacer?"

Pat's voice left no way out.

"Keats, sir."

"You were saying?"

"Ahem... ah, ArcGeneral Manchester is in the *Bloody Pulsar*, sir."

"And?"

"Ah... I spoke to her sir."

'Spoke' like a bloody Krogg. Pat imagined himself spinning the man over his head and pitching him down the boardwalk, but decided against it. There'd be an awful lot of paperwork involved, and some innocent spacer would have to mop up the mess.

"Go about your business, Keats. Quickly."

"Sir. Aye aye, sir."

In terror for his very life, he scuttled away, followed hastily by his mates.

"That was bloody fun," Graham grinned.

"What the bugger is Sarah doing in a *bar*?"

"Dark... like underground. Aha! Kroggs must like to live *under the ground*! Like in their base out in the asteroids."

Someone cleared his throat behind Sarah, so she sipped her Vortex and turned with a sweet smile, "Decided to leave your name, spacer?"

The expression on Pat's face was beyond description. He suddenly regretted not pummeling Keats to a bloody stump. Oh well, he could always kill the man later.

"Patrick, Graham. Oh my word. Trying to figure out what I've forgotten, see."

"We should get you back to *Barron*," Pat said softly.

"How many has she had, barkeep?" Graham turned to the bartender.

"That's her second, sir."

Graham groaned as he looked at the glass and recognized its toxic content, "She's drinking *Vortexes*. She must want to put herself into a coma..."

Pat tried to help the ailing ArcGeneral to her feet, attempting to forget what Graham had told him as he slipped an arm around her waist and lifted.

Sarah squealed happily, "Patrick!"

The bartender closely observed the alloy of the bar's wall.

Sarah got her feet under herself but was wobbly at best, "Patrick, I think I might be a bit tipsy. Best get me home!"

Pat held Sarah upright and started to turn her towards the door. Her legs slipped out and she fell into him. Not expecting the shift, she toppled both of them, just as Graham turned to help.

Sarah, landing on top of the Irishman, looked down at him with a sudden thought in her mind, "Pat! I know what it is!"

"Come on, Sarah, you've had a little too much to drink..."

On her own, she sat up and slid over the deck to sit against the bar. Her hand absently rubbed her head, "Gods Pat! I know that! No... we forgot the base! The Krogg base in the field! If it's armed..."

Pat blinked. His mind was partially filled with Graham's words about Sarah, and about the fact that he was beginning to see Sarah in a different light... but the other half of his brain kicked him.

The *base*. The Kroggs had a fleet base there... Gods, she was right.

He sat up and shot a glance at Graham. The junior Manchester nodded, "I'll call Ursla as soon as I get back to my office. You get her home."

Sarah was starting to come to her senses a little, and she suddenly reddened, "Oh dear. I'm drunk and I'm sitting on the bloody floor. Of the *Bloody Pulsar*. Pat... what am I doing?"

Pat picked himself up and then gently hauled Sarah to her feet, "Discovering a critical flaw in our strategy, Sarah."

Wrapping an arm around Pat to stay standing, she rubbed her head groggily, "I hope I don't have to do this every time I need to remember something..."

The two shuffled towards the door and left Graham with the bartender.

"Call a hauler for her," the junior Manchester ordered as he watched them.

"Already did, sir," the bartender said. "Between my odd bouts of blindness, that is. I should see a doctor about that... can't even identify customers sometimes."

Graham smiled at the barkeep, "Good man."

He left to call Ursla.

CHAPTER 31

Sarah felt awful. Something large seemed to be trying to beat its way out of her head. Everything was spinning, she felt nauseous, and her eyes hurt... She vaguely remembered being sucked into a vortex... No, *drinking* a *Vortex*.

Oh Gods, what had she done?

Opening her eyes she discovered the room was mercifully dark. She'd been at the bar... what had she been *thinking*? Had some spacer made a pass at her? She hoped not. Her hand rubbed her eyes ruefully as she tried to push the pain away.

She sat up unsteadily in bed, noting that part of her discomfort came from the fact that she was still wearing her uniform — the tunic was gone but it seemed that someone had done all they could to get her into bed quickly.

It had to be Pat. She could remember falling on him...

Or was that a dream?

"Easy, Sarah, lie back down. You drank a bit too much," it was Pat's voice, though she couldn't see him.

The lights came up then, slowly so as to cause her as little difficulty as possible. She winced and looked down all the same, trying to shade her face with her hand. A weight pressed the bed down next to her and she turned to see Pat sitting on the edge offering a bottle of water and two pills.

"Detoxers, take them."

Sarah obeyed sluggishly, swallowing a great deal of water to try and clear the grogginess in her head.

"Alright, Pat... what happened?"

The Irishman gave one of his trademarked smiles and Sarah shuffled back to sit closer to him. As she pressed into his side, Pat shot to his feet so quickly Sarah fell backwards onto the bed. She frowned at him as he stood with hands thrust in his pockets, rocking back and forth on his feet.

"What's wrong, Pat? I didn't catch something did I?"

"Hey? Oh, no. No, just... stretching... To answer your question, Sarah my dear, you found a variable we hadn't paid heed to."

"What, liquor's effect on flag officers?"

Pat chuckled a little uneasily, "Not that, Sarah. Besides, you may be unaware of it but a large number of our commanders enjoy the drink now and then. Anyway, you remembered the Krogg base."

Sarah blinked and nodded, the memory of her babbling coming back to her, "We have to tell Ursla. Get a sloop out that way to check it."

"Graham told her about twelve hours ago. *Speedy* left six hours ago on the run. I was on *Genesis One* two hours ago and they still didn't have anything certain," Pat said, leaning against the wall.

"Well, I should be seeing the preliminary information then," Sarah started to sit up but was halted.

"Nope. Ursla said she could handle it. You should rest."

"You better not have told her. You *didn't* tell her, did you?" Sarah sat bolt upright.

"Of course I did!" Pat's tone was all too serious. "You've got a touch of a fever — probably brought on by exhaustion — and you'll be down for a while."

Sarah heaved a sigh of relief, then slowly swung her legs out of bed. She examined herself — she looked like a hurricane had tossed her around. Trousers were wrinkled, shirt bonded to her like some sort of second skin, hair projecting at all angles. She laughed to herself at the state — no doubt the way that spacer would have liked to have found her. He'd probably dropped dead of a heart attack by now.

Pat seemed to be carefully avoiding looking at her, something odd for her best friend. He'd never been awkward around her, no matter what was going on. Now, he seemed to be examining the bareness of her walls.

"Problem Pat?"

His eyes whipped around to meet hers and he shook his head. "No... not at all. Walls just a tad bare..." he bit his lip, "... could do to be covered up..." he kicked himself deftly in the shin. "You know, nothing's wrong."

Sarah eyed him curiously, running a hand through her hair. It was longer than she normally wore it — the circumstances didn't allow much time for getting to the barber. Refocusing on getting herself back into fighting trim, she levered herself onto her feet and wobbled involuntarily towards Pat as she did. She started to tip, but Pat grabbed her quickly and steadied her.

"Thank you," she said, voice still a bit shaky.

"Aye..." Pat made it his business not to watch her.

"I think I'll have a shower. Might put me back to rights. Give me a hand getting over there?"

At this point Pat knew better than to so much as think about it. He had never felt so awkward in his life... *Damn you Graham!*

Time to exercise the better part of valor.

"Actually, Sarah, I have to... umm... go..." he helped her back to the bed and sat her down, avoiding looking at her as much as he could without falling over for his lack of visual recon. He backed away unsteadily, "Pills will have your balance back in a minute. Just relax... I'll see you later..."

Before Sarah could object he turned and fled, taking deep breaths to compose himself all the way back to his pinnace.

In her quarters, Sarah struggled to the bathroom and examined herself, looking earnestly for a second head. She certainly looked positively disreputable in her present state, but Pat had seen her through scrapes before. What was he playing at?

Trying to ignore the question, Sarah slipped out of her grimy uniform and into a nice hot shower, finally waking up and feeling refreshed.

CHAPTER 32

Ursla silently watched the telemetry coming in from the sloop *Speedy*. Beside her, Captain Tigar ground his jaw, wondering how they'd managed to overlook the Krogg installation in the system. It was perhaps an understandable omission, Ursla consoled herself. After seeing 3,000 ships, conventional Earther wisdom suggested that fixed positions buried deep in an asteroid field were relatively insignificant. They couldn't *move*, after all, and they'd spent their history in Genesis space staying out of sight.

But it had been an oversight to ignore them. These were Krogg installations — there was no telling what capabilities they had. The fact that Ursla had failed to recognize that potential threat was mitigated only by the fact that she was now looking at them before the coming battle. She didn't even want to think of what could have happened had her fleet been somehow caught between those stations and the Krogg Fleet, unlikely though that outcome might have been.

Good thing Sarah had thought of it. Humans seemed to have odd moments of brilliance when under the influence of fermented grain...

Fever, right. Pat said to say 'fever'.

Ursla had seen through the fever excuse as soon as Pat had presented it to her, and she'd quickly managed to exact the truth from the Irishman. It neither shocked her nor changed her opinion of Sarah; she was actually rather amused. And most importantly, she was busy watching the telemetry being sent to *Agamemnon*.

The Krogg installation was *massive*, making it clear that the Kroggs had made use of more than just the corridor in the Genesis system. First, they'd connected dozens of large asteroids together into one sizable mass with the help of the flesh of their strange organisms. Then, it looked as though they'd grown what could best be described as a giant ball of organic matter over and between the floating rocks, creating some sort of living — hopefully not sentient — feeding station. The fleet was *grazing* off it.

It hadn't occurred to Ursla that Krogg ships might need to feed, but the fact was imminently clear now. The asteroid belt in the Genesis system offered enough food for the Krogg Fleet to live on quite happily. They probably didn't need regular meals, but if they were well fed they'd doubtless prove even more formidable than usual.

The ball, however, worried Ursla less than the conglomeration. Based on the scans she was seeing, that massive structure had multiple weapon mounts and, based on its size, could put out enough fire to hold off the entire Second Fleet. If any of her force got stuck between the base and the Krogg armada, there'd be no surviving.

So the two Krogg strong points would have to be handled separately.

The base was on the far side of the fleet, to the corridor's right flank. If it could be surprised from the side open to space and bombarded...

The doors on *Agamemnon*'s bridge parted and Novash entered slowly. Ursla had requested he view the telemetry they gathered as his experienced analysis of what they found would be far better than Earther guesses. The Captain-Commodore had been happy to oblige — despite their biological differences, the Larosians and the Earthers seemed to share a common fundamental approach to their Naval services, and the two groups were getting along remarkably well.

Novash had been continually impressed by Earther methodology and the blend of military doctrines they relied on to make war. Ursla had been impressed by the way the Larosians conducted themselves in general, especially in their honest and straightforward manner. So succinct were her verbal communications with Novash that he was finding his lack of telepathic connection irrelevant to his dealings with her, and Ursla had stopped worrying about any Larosian misuse of telepathy now that she'd come to better understand the Captain-Commodore.

Apparently, the 'feudal' system Novash had mentioned was similar to that of ancient Japan's shogunate — one based on absolute codes of honor. The Larosians were even prone to the use of swords, weapons the Earthers had never even considered developing. Ursla couldn't help but question their usefulness against the Kroggs, but knew the Larosian confidence in them was based on experience.

In any case, the issue at hand demanded a better analysis than the one she was able to give, so Captain-Commodore Novash had boarded *Agamemnon* in his fighter — the small craft he'd startled the Earthers with on his first visit — to assist.

The military concept of the 'fighter craft', as Ursla recalled, was something of a white elephant in the Earther Navy. She'd read about them in Earth history, but recent Naval doctrine held the development of fighters impractical because of the massive distances the small craft would have to traverse in space and their inevitably limited firepower. The Larosian philosophy was clearly different — they had Carriers full of the small vessels.

"As you requested, Admiral, I have arrived," Novash stepped evenly across the bridge to Ursla's side.

Millisecond-long glances at the alien were stolen by Earthers on the bridge crew, but Novash did not notice them.

"Our sloop is taking these readings right now. It's undetectable by the

Kroggs with its field spread," Ursla explained, and Novash nodded. Energy drive was theoretically quite impossible by Larosian standards, but its development by the Earthers demonstrated the contrary reality. Though Larosian scientists likely had the means to create so-called energy drive fields, none had thought they could truly violate Tashtar's laws of physics...

Novash's musings halted abruptly. Ursla had centered her holo map over the section which held the Krogg base, and had she been able to read Novash's expression she would have recognized his shock.

Though the Captain-Commodore was a battle-hardened line officer, he'd only seen such a Krogg complex once before. It had been when he was with the Fourth at the Kroggs' capital planet in his home galaxy, when the Son of Praaxus had led the Larosians against the Krogg Queen.

The complex they were looking at was a Queen's Hive.

Novash's mind raced. The Larosians had always assumed there was only *one* Queen, and when the Son destroyed her months earlier the Krogg war effort had appeared to collapse. Without the Queen, it had been expected that the Kroggs would be easily annihilated — the universe could be cleansed of the xenocidal scourge, once and for all. Yet here was another Hive... another Queen? It would explain the clever trap set in this system...

"What is it?" Ursla's instincts finally picked up on Novash's tension and he looked up at her.

"A Queen's Hive."

Ursla froze, but only for a second, "I read in the reports you gave us that you and the Fourth eliminated the Krogg Queen. And that there was only one."

Novash stared at the Hive and tilted his head unevenly, "We thought there was only one, Admiral. But it seems the Kroggs planned for every contingency, including the loss of their Queen."

Ursla looked at the alien ball of rock and flesh and remained silent.

"What does having a Queen alive mean, Captain-Commodore?" Tigar asked quietly, and the Larosian looked across at him.

"We believe the Queen to be responsible for the organization and genetic evolution of the Krogg race. We believe her control comes through incredibly powerful telepathy, and the Son proved that in his last hours — it was in a duel of minds that he destroyed both her and the surrounding star system. We believe she is more powerful than the average Larosian by a multiple approaching 17,000."

Tigar forcibly kept his mouth from falling open as he glanced up at Ursla, who met his eyes with an 'oh *great*' expression.

"With that telepathic-blocking mineral in the asteroid field, we could not sense her when we arrived, nor could our scouts of the past... making this system an excellent secret position..." Novash paused in thought, his mind slowly refocusing after the shock. Then, looking quickly to his Earther companions, he persisted, "If the Queen... *a* Queen... is here, the Kroggs can rebuild and fight again... perhaps indefinitely."

Ursla ground her jaw. This was a slightly larger complication that she'd expected from the base... but better they knew now, before the battle.

"So if that Queen survives, the Kroggs can still win."

"They can indeed," Novash's voice seemed slightly off its usual pitch.

Ursla frowned deeply and opened her mouth, but Tigar spoke before she could, "Then we'll have to destroy her, won't we?"

Novash sat uneasily across the desk from Ursla in the latter's quarters. The room was more thoroughly decorated than he personally liked — featuring a few holos of ships, family and friends — but he imagined that it was relatively spartan by Earther standards.

"Can we destroy that thing?"

Ursla's question was straightforward and Novash was pleased that it was so direct. He had been pondering the same problem continuously over the past twenty minutes. It could be done...

"The last Hive we engaged cost the Son of Praaxus his life, and it caused a great deal of damage to the Larosian Star Navy. However, it was established in a system fortified far more intensely than Genesis. I believe this Queen's destruction is possible, but the demolition would require a team to plant a large antimatter charge in the Hive's core where she resides. The exterior is likely far too resilient to quickly give way to bombardment, and the firepower the station mounts would make any attempt to do so fatal."

"A fast squadron of frigates might be able to make it in under their guns and drop a team, but how easily could they get to the core? And sorry, I'm no telepathic specialist, but couldn't she just use her mind to crush anybody who gets in?" Ursla eyed Novash curiously, and the Larosian's eyes seemed to narrow thoughtfully.

"Perhaps she could, but I have just suggested that question to Captain Torallis of my Stealth Guard. He is a stronger telepath than I, and he is trained in telepathic war. Given our lack of any telepathic indication of the Queen's existence, he believes the minerals of the belt are restraining her power: she obviously can communicate with her ships, but by now she would have killed us if she could. Torallis believes we have a chance to take advantage of this weakness, and I agree that we must try."

Ursla managed to stop herself from saying '*Better him than me,*' then her own eyes narrowed, "Regular old explosives then?"

Novash offered a long bow-nod, "All corridors in such a facility ultimately lead to the core. The team would need only enter the chamber and detonate... or ideally set a weapon on a timer and escape, though that likely will not be possible given the expected resistance."

Ursla scratched her chin thoughtfully, "Our marines fared pretty well on Genesis, but what they had to attack were small posts in open country. I have a feeling we wouldn't be so lucky in a complex. For one, we couldn't unload everyone we've got into such a small space."

"My ships have a unit of fifty Stealth Guardsmen trained specifically for such missions. They should undertake the attack alone."

Ursla frowned, "Only fifty in your squadron? Two per ship?"

Novash nodded shortly, "The telepathic abilities of a Stealth Guardsman must be cultivated over an extended period and are extremely rare."

"Ah," Ursla replied smoothly. "Well, I must insist our marines support you. They will prove most able, of that I'm certain. Even if your warriors need a diversion, we should be able to accommodate."

Novash sat silently and pondered. The Stealth Guard made a point of operating alone, however under these circumstances a compromise might indeed be necessary. But could these Earthers live up to the standards of Captain Torallis... they'd have to. Ursla was quite correct — no fifty Larosians could hope to pierce a Queen's Hive alone.

The Captain-Commodore nodded again, this time more slowly, "I will order my Captain of the Guard to join you here to plan the assault."

Ursla smiled and nodded in reply, "I'll call General Grieve."

CHAPTER 33

ENS Tonnant approached the Genesis system in the company of a small battle group. The 80-gun ship of the line had with it the 111th Flying Squadron, the sloop *Flame*, and the two privateers *Archangel Sword* and *Grendelsbane City*. Admiral Felix was proud of his command, and he looked forward to presenting it to Ursla.

Flame and *Cerberus* led the force, and as the ships dropped from energy drive just within the system limits they cruised slightly ahead, checking the approach vector for Krogg intrusions. None were detected.

Felix wasn't willing to risk his squadron's discovery when it was still alone, so he ordered his Earther ships into energy drive with fields drawn out to 250 percent. *Sword* and *Grendelsbane* entered flux, fully detectable by the Kroggs, but by no means a unique or significant target in a system full of human ships.

Together, the mixed battle group slipped in-system at an even velocity.

"Reinforcements?" Ursla frowned at Admiral Broadpaw over the comm. "Far too early."

Broadpaw shrugged, "They're definitely in energy drive — only ten ships though, by the looks of it... and a Battlecruiser and a Heavy Cruiser."

Flame must have run across a few ships in open space as it had made its way back. One extra squadron certainly wasn't decisive, but the arrival of some fresh ships — *any* fresh ships — was comforting.

"Alright, how long until they make it to us?"

Broadpaw glanced away, "About five minutes."

"I'll take *Agamemnon* out and meet them," Ursla was already turning to Tigar who nodded as the link cut. The First Rate's drives spun up and the ship slid from the formation of battleships it had occupied since last reaching Genesis.

"Coming into transponder range, ma'am. Ships of the white, all of them."

Little surprise there — each of the Earther fleets had its own individual transponder code color, simplifying unit identification on the battle plot and helping things stay well organized during action. The First Fleet's transponders were white, the Second Fleet's red, and the Third Fleet's blue. Unassigned Allied ships registered gray on sensor displays, and Liz and Sarah had given the Genesis ships a green transponder code.

Ursla left her chair and strode to the battle plot, keying a holo overview of the ships up over the table. The white icons glowed on their inbound course, and *Agamemnon's* red icon moved to meet them. The transponders displayed the name, class and assignment of each ship next to it, and Ursla felt a grin forming.

Tigar, arriving next to her, was briefly confused, "Good news?"

Ursla smiled back, "The 111th has arrived. With *Tonnant* and *Flame*."

A matching smile — one of understanding more than anything else — formed on her Flag Captain's face. The 111th had sentimental value to Ursla, and it was known to be one of the best frigate units ever assembled.

"*Flame* must have come across this squadron and sent another messenger back to Earth," Tigar said after a moment. "Strange, I thought Genesis ships were green."

Ursla cocked an eyebrow and looked back at the two fluxing ships, both *white*, not green or even gray. She selected them and used the keypad to zoom in and query orders. The question lanced across space from *Agamemnon* to the AIs of *Sword* and *Grendelsbane*, and the letters of marquee, duly drafted and signed by Felix, were sent in reply.

During the split second that the computers were querying each other, Ursla recognized the name of the Heavy Cruiser... "*Grendelsbane City* left under its own orders over a month ago, didn't it?"

Tigar frowned and nodded just as the holo projected each ship's status into a window facing Ursla.

By the Earth, they were indeed a detached force... a *completely independent* force, that was operating with the 111th and *Tonnant*...

"Privateers," Ursla said with a twinge of surprise. "Letters signed by *Savanna Felix*."

Tigar's eyebrows were up, "Must be quite a story behind that..." he paused. "How will the Genesis crews react, I wonder?"

Deciding that he was close enough to Genesis, Felix drew the fields of his ships back in to 100 percent and exited energy drive, the two privateers decelerating from low flux.

The 111th formed a line abreast for cruising, with *Flame* out ahead and *Tonnant* slightly behind. *Sword* and *Grendelsbane* held a position off their starboard flank.

As the force edged inwards, *Agamemnon* loomed large before them, out-massing all of the vessels — even *Tonnant* — by quite a margin. A signal raced from *Tonnant* to *Agamemnon* as the latter turned and formed with the incoming ships.

Ursla re-took her seat as an Earther glowed into existence in the main battle tank, "Good day to you, Andra. I trust all's well!"

By the Earth... that was *Savanna Felix!*

That realization took a long second to process properly — a desk Admiral commanding an 80, commissioning privateers... there certainly did have to be quite a story behind this.

"Savanna! By the Earth, Caine finally drafted you into a ship!" Ursla grinned and the cat smiled in reply.

"He did, and he sent these miserly frigates along to you. Terrible outfit, this 111th Flying Squadron!" Felix shook his head in mock disappointment and next to him in the plot, Commodore Nightclaw appeared.

"Dran," Ursla offered a warm smile to her former Flag Captain.

"I think this Admiral has gone somewhat mad with the power of 80 guns beneath his feet, Andra," the panther smiled and delivered the comment with his rare, understated humor.

Ursla nodded happily, "Really... Well, which of you would like to fill me in? Actually, when we reach the fleet both of you should come aboard, as should Commander Magnus..." Ursla paused briefly. "And our two *privateer* Captains as well."

Felix smiled, "Noticed the letters, then. Yes, we should talk all this through. I'll board *Agamemnon* as soon as *Tonnant* anchors."

As Ursla had hoped, her old friend Nightclaw came aboard early in order to catch up with his former commander. Ursla was waiting in *Agamemnon's* conference room when he arrived, and she smiled broadly as he came in.

Though Dran Nightclaw's stealthy panther nature sometimes seemed to leave him devoid of visible signs of happiness, he made an exception and smiled as Ursla gestured him to a chair.

"I hadn't expected to see you for another nine days, Dran, but I'm very, *very* glad to have you here! What's been going on?"

The panther had been awaiting the question, and he smoothly dove into an explanation of the Coalition, *Tonnant's* dispatch and resulting success, and the 111th's call to hunt the last Heavy Cruiser.

Ursla listened closely to Nightclaw, relying on her long-developed understanding of his tone and manner to absorb all his impressions of the run from Sol to Earth. She'd be amply prepared for this meeting...

By the time Felix, Magnus, and the two human Captains arrived, Ursla was reasonably caught up on Sol current events.

She was quite pleased with all she'd heard.

CHAPTER 34

Sarah was completely shocked when word of the privateers reached her. She'd recovered from her bout of 'creative thinking' by the time Felix arrived in the system, but she was having a tough time understanding what exactly had happened.

After receiving the news, she'd instantly called Pat, and he'd advised a meeting with the two human ArcColonels... well, *Captains*... in order to determine what was motivating them. She'd known there had been desertions before she left, but to have lost *Sword* and then to have found two deserting ships flying Earther colors...

So she sent a formal letter to Captain Stanton and Captain DeBrooke asking them to join her for a meeting aboard *Joseph Barron*. Stanton's formal reply had expressed a willingness to meet aboard *Archangel Sword*, and after again discussing it with Pat, she decided that would indeed be the most practical option. She could see how a human *Captain* could be unnerved aboard a Genesis battleship with a crew of 2,500.

Now, Pat's pinnace was coming to rest on the deck of *Joseph Barron*, ready to pick up Sarah and bring them both to the meeting. Sarah tugged at the collar of her tunic as the small craft settled onto the deck and its ramp lowered. As the walkway touched the deck she started to climb it, passing through the hissing clouds of coolant as they vented.

Entering the cutter near the nose, she waved to the pilot who nodded and closed the hatch, bringing the craft back up into the air almost immediately. Sarah wandered into the back cabin of the small vessel, remembering her own from her days aboard *Warlock Prophet*. Pat was sitting quietly reading something on a pad as Sarah entered the passenger compartment. He looked up with a smile and a bit of relief that she was back in her usual fine professional form.

After the conversation with Graham, Pat had tactfully checked around and confirmed everything Sarah's junior sibling had said. And now he felt damned awkward whenever he saw her. It was positively immature, he knew, but after such a long time being oblivious to their chemistry he couldn't do much to avoid it.

As Sarah settled into the seat next to him, Pat shifted uneasily, trying to keep his arm from rubbing hers.

"What are you reading?" Sarah leaned towards the pad and Pat swallowed.

"Files on *Grendelsbane City*. I didn't know all that much about the ship, other than the fact that it was at the belt with us."

Sarah nodded and 'hmmmed' and leaned closer to read the pad. The last millimeter did it, and her shoulder touched his.

"Here, I've been through it enough by now, I'm sure," he handed — well *threw* — the pad at Sarah.

She caught it evenly and looked across at him, "Pat?"

The Irishman tried to look anything but nervous, "Sarah?"

Sarah opened her mouth to speak and frowned, laying the pad on her lap, "Have I done something to embarrass you?"

Pat reddened noticeably and scratched his temple. He wasn't being all that subtle, he supposed, "No... not really... well not in any way I might've thought possible..."

Sarah cocked an eyebrow, "Meaning?"

Oh well, he could always blame Graham.

"Well, we... Graham and I... were coming to get you from the *Pulsar* two nights ago..." he paused to breathe.

Sarah prodded him on, "Yes?"

Pat swallowed and tried to get the words out, "Well, you see, Graham thought that I was unduly interested in you. And he also told me that the entire Alliance Fleet thinks we're unduly interested in each other. And they want to put us on recruiting posters. To show romance. Romance in the fleet..." Sarah's playful, prodding expression had frozen in place, and Pat elected not to say anymore.

Not what she'd been expecting. Graham said this?

"He... he must be pulling your leg. Graham loves to pull a prank now and then."

Pat shook his head slowly, "I checked around. He wasn't kidding."

Sarah looked as if she'd just... well, not much else could have elicited such bewilderment from the ArcGeneral. No, it couldn't be. Of course not, undue interest would mean spending time together, talking, and...

Oh right, just about everything they were doing. Great.

But surely it was a misunderstanding... or not so much... oh.

"Well... well it's positively... umm... silly, eh Pat?" she said finally, and the Irishman nodded fervently, unsure why he was agreeing.

"I know, bloody bunch of lunatics, no question there."

"Right, quite right!" Sarah felt like she should be squeaking. "Well, we should be ready to meet Stanton... I'll read this..." she hefted the pad.

For the rest of the flight they cowered on opposite corners of their seats.

By the time Pat's cutter made its entry in the landing bay of *Archangel Sword*, Sarah had sorted out enough of the chaos filling her brain to feel confident she would seem credible to Stanton. Pat had as well, though neither told each other that in so many words. Sarah avoided looking at the Irishman and he avoided looking at her, and they managed to share only a few highly awkward and accidental glances.

As soon as they descended the ramp to *Sword's* deck they transformed into professional Naval officers, ready to deal with whatever the privateers brought them.

Sword's marines were drawn up smartly in the landing bay, an ArcMajor at their head. The Naval officer offered a crisp salute and came to attention, "Commander Davis, ma'am, sir."

Sarah and Pat returned the salute, both eyeing the rank bars on the man's collar. An ArcMajor usually had three diamond-shaped pips, but instead the Commander had three slim Earther silver bars.

"If you'll come with me," the Commander gestured to the door and then led them through the decks of *Sword*.

Originally built in the same class as *Harbinger Bishop* and *Warlock Prophet*, the decks were familiar to Sarah and Pat, despite some add-ons that made the vessel a hybrid. Sarah looked around carefully as she walked, noting that the ship was seemingly maintained in excellent condition by its renegade crew. Any of those individuals who passed by the ArcGeneral and ArcBrigadier eyed the officers nervously, and Sarah felt rather like a bad omen.

Coming to the briefing room, the Commander stood aside at the door as Sarah and Pat went in. Stanton and DeBrooke were standing courteously behind the briefing table as the senior officers entered.

"Captain Stanton, Captain DeBrooke. Good day to you," Sarah nodded to each of them formally, and they stiffened.

Pat almost wanted to frown at Sarah, but owing to his minor terror at the sight or her, he elected to lighten the atmosphere under his own initiative. It wouldn't do to make enemies of these independents — especially not now that they were half Earther... or whatever.

"Love what you've done with the place, James. Carronades now, is it?" the ArcBrig's tone was friendly and devoid of sarcasm.

For their part, Audrey and James released tense breaths, the latter offering a thin smile.

Sarah wanted to cast a withering glance at her compatriot, but quickly understood his strategy... and it was uncommonly better than hers, actually.

"I can't say I had a lot to do with it, but I'm not going to complain. How are you Pat?"

The Irishman grinned and stepped in front of Sarah, extending a hand, which Stanton took, "Not too bad." He looked then to DeBrooke, "Can't say I've had the pleasure, Captain."

DeBrooke avoided narrowing her eyes at him, instead offering a genuinely kind smile and her hand, "Audrey DeBrooke."

Pat nodded to her with a matching smile, then took her hand, "Forgive Sarah, she's a bit under the weather."

Sarah reddened but accepted the excuse, "Stress is a bit heavy, just now."

Appearing human could at least put these *Captains* at ease... and disguise other discomforts she was suffering.

Stanton gestured to the table and the two pairs of officers took seats facing each other in the rather small briefing room.

"Well then," Pat got comfortable in his chair, "I take it you decided to leave, James?"

Stanton nodded, "My crew and I didn't feel too kindly about being left out of the fight, especially with *Sword* being taken apart and rebuilt without our consent. ArcGeneral Hastings and I had a number of discussions about the predicament, but she wasn't willing to budge. The Earthers were kind enough to let us go, though Hoshi Chen tried to blow us out of space."

Sarah frowned at the reference to the officer — Chen had been one of her most loyal compatriots not long ago, though she'd managed to lose track of the ArcMajor.

"She always did have a bit of a temper..." Sarah said somberly. "I take it you didn't have to fight her?"

Stanton shook his head, "A good Earther Captain in a 74 bailed me out. Then we went to Renegade's Belt and ran into a squadron of ill-wishers..."

"Aha, the Coalition. Andra filled us in on that," Pat said with a grin. "My third-hand info says you knocked out their SD."

A proud smile crossed Stanton's face and he nodded, "That's where Audrey and I crossed paths."

DeBrooke was sitting with a quiet smile, not nearly as familiar with these officers as her fellow Captain, who had served in their squadron. While she appreciated Pat's relaxed conversation, she wasn't about to engage herself without having a better feel for the Genesis officers' opinions and agendas.

"Right," Sarah remarked softly, directing the comment to Audrey despite the latter's silence. "I read that you played cat and mouse with them for a couple of weeks."

DeBrooke offered a confident if hesitant nod in reply, "We lost long-range flux capabilities when they ambushed us, so we started running in and out of nebulas."

Sarah nodded, hoping her positive opinion of what she'd read and heard was obvious from her expression. She did admire how these two fought their ships... but she also wanted to understand why such capable officers hadn't remained in the fold. These two didn't seem disagreeable — if she hadn't know better, she'd have thought she was still speaking to ArcColonels in her fleet... yet they had been driven away.

"And then you saved *Flame*," Pat interrupted Sarah's thoughts in an effort to move the conversation along.

Stanton continued to lead the replies, still much more comfortable with his old comrades. "We were scouting for places to set up a camp and Commander Magnus dropped right into our laps. We just helped him out until the Admiral arrived."

The brand of understatement was one that amused Pat, and he grinned, "Helped, did you? As I understand it, it wasn't so much 'helped' as it was 'saved from destruction'. No false modesty, eh, we know what you did."

Stanton smiled again, "We just did our best. And we were lucky. So Admiral Felix gave us those letters of marquee and we offered to accompany him."

Sarah pursed her lips and nodded, "Very good. So what do you plan to do now, Captain? It's your choice, after all."

The comment was much less relaxed than Pat's words had been, and the pair of Captains hesitated slightly as they mentally combed it for signs of prejudice.

Pat offered a conciliatory smile, "I think the main question is will we benefit from your help when we hit the Kroggs?"

Sarah avoided glancing at her companion, but both Captain's eyes passed to him, much more at ease with his attitude.

They shared a quick glance, then Stanton answered, "Think we came all this way to watch? We'll be with you when you attack the Kroggs. Though we'll probably weigh with *Tonnant*."

Sarah nodded slowly, "You know, if you wanted to cruise with Pat I'm sure his Battlecruisers wouldn't mind the help."

Pat looked at Sarah and cocked his eyebrow, "I would so mind. I should send them to look after you — then you'd have someone to keep you out of trouble who you couldn't order off!"

Stanton chuckled, "I think we'll stay out of that disagreement entirely, actually."

"Bah!" Pat grinned.

"Well, I can't say for certain where we'll fight, but we'll fight," Stanton finished. "Let us know if you need us somewhere and we'll do our best."

Sarah nodded again, "Very well then. I must say it's... *good* to have you both here. I really do appreciate it. Best of luck to you."

She rose slowly, Pat rising with her. Stanton and DeBrooke matched the movement, and the former smiled, "Now, if you'll excuse us, we have a dinner to attend."

Sarah didn't hear the comment as she was already leaving, but Pat turned, "With who?"

Stanton smiled again glancing back at DeBrooke, whose eyebrows twitched knowingly.

"You know what that's all about yet, Pat?" Stanton gave Pat a hinting look and the Irishman paled.

"Not a bloody clue what you mean..." he stammered a bit awkwardly, then turned and fled.

Standing in the briefing room, Stanton laughed and DeBrooke frowned at him, "I missed something."

"Seems Sarah and Pat are still oblivious to each other. Some things never change."

CHAPTER 35

General Andros Grieve had been briefed by Ursla about the target for his next mission, and he couldn't say he had been too pleased with what she was asking him to do — working with foreign troops, in a heavily fortified and garrisoned installation, in extremely close quarters...

But it had to be done, and Grieve was growing accustomed to getting things done.

When he'd been introduced to the Larosian Captain of the Stealth Guard the day before, he'd been unsettled by how *alien* the fellow was, but he had at least overcome that feeling... as the Captain had overcome his own uncertainty about the General. Now, they sat in a conference room on *Agamemnon* and started to discuss details.

Torallis was a Stealth Guardsman, one of the elite of the Larosian Guard, and his appearance differed noticeably from Novash's. Bulkier and showing a better-defined musculature, his armor was heavier and to his back was strapped a sword. He had considerable telepathic ability, and he was very agile in his movements. Standing about two meters tall, he was a couple of heads shorter than Grieve, but felt supremely confident in his own abilities, and did not find the General's size at all intimidating.

"So," Grieve was keying notes into the holo projector that glowed on the desk, "we enter here..." a red dot began to flash on the surface of the three-dimensional model "...and your warriors go for the core. My marines and I hold the Kroggs off at the entrance until you get back. And, as you mentioned, if the Queen manages to kill you all, your dead man switch starts the bomb timer and I get the warning to get out."

The path planned for the Stealth Warriors was highlighted in silver, and the marine position was marked in blue.

"Indeed," Torallis' silver eyes scanned the display with approval.

"Right, that's out of the way. Now, whose ship do we use? Our dropships can carry a hundred each, but they don't have any cutting gear to crack the hull."

"We will supply a strike craft. It is equipped with focal-point lasers and it should be capable of opening the hull at close range."

Grieve cocked an eyebrow, "Sounds *complicated*... I won't ask."

Torallis mimicked a smile at the Earther — the General was an agreeable character, despite the oddness of his species. Working with him would produce a genuine friendship, Torallis was fairly certain of that.

"How many marines do you have room for?"

Thoughtfully tilting his head, Torallis adjusted the standard complement of such a craft to fit Earthers of Grieve's size, "Approximately fifty."

Grieve nodded, "Very good..."

Well, the situation as it stood qualified perhaps only as 'good' — after his experience on Genesis, Grieve knew holding Kroggs in close quarters wouldn't be particularly easy.

"We'll have to keep the Kroggs back by hand unless we can choke them up in the corridors — our guns have only moderate effect on them."

Torallis nodded slowly in understanding, "We faced that difficulty as well. Our best means of defeating Kroggs is with these."

In a swift movement the Larosian's sword was in one hand, held high above the table. Torallis went on, "Our swords are enhanced to allow them to cope with Krogg carapaces. Energy fields are used to force the atoms on the cutting edges of our blades into a state of controlled overactivity. When they come into contact with matter, their state of rapid motion at the atomic level allows them to destabilize its molecular structure. With proper technique, they can be used to cut anything."

The General frowned at the weapon, and eyed what appeared to be a razor-sharp blade from a distance. So that thing, when activated, would theoretically have a blade only a single atom wide — and that blade would be *moving*...

"An atomic chain saw," Grieve vocalized his appreciation for the weapon. "Is it on now?"

Torallis shook his head, "No, it is only an alloy sword now. It requires me to push a button to activate the... *chain saw* aspect."

Grieve smiled at what he took to be a minor joke, "Weapons like that would be useful to our marines... could you supply us with some?"

Torallis sheathed his blade, "I am afraid these swords require much training to use safely, and only Stealth Warriors carry them. We carry no surplus."

With a cocked eyebrow, the General leaned back in his chair, "Training isn't a problem. But you don't have any more?"

Pausing to recall his human gestures, Torallis shook his head, "Each warrior is responsible for his own weapon. We do not mass produce such swords, as common Larosians could not use them. Regular soldiers are given weapons that fire ultra-dense particles, but those are by no means as effective as our blades."

Grieve nodded silently. The sword seemed to be a very decisive weapon... if he could arm fifty of his best marines with such blades they could be trained on them in days... and they *had* days until the Fourth Fleet-of-War was due.

"Can you give me the specifications for the technology? My engineers could develop something to give my marines."

Torallis thought about the suggestion momentarily, his doubts about the agility of large and presumably unwieldy Earthers such as Grieve beginning to surface, "The technology of sword forging is not known to all Larosians, General — only members of the Stealth Guard are taught the techniques, only we produce the blades. Given the circumstances I believe I can disregard that tradition, though only under one condition: I must be certain of the martial skill of your warriors. Clearly, these are dangerous weapons."

Grieve leaned back in his chair, concealing his slightly wounded professional pride. In most cases an energy bayonet was just as dangerous... but this wasn't 'most cases'. And it was Torallis' right to ask to see the Earthers in action — and to demonstrate Larosian skill in return — since they'd be going to war together.

So with a short sigh Grieve nodded, "Very well, you can test yourself against me."

Agamemnon's gym was constantly occupied by off-duty crew, but when the Larosian entered it with Grieve the Earthers carefully made way. Matches were ended quickly and silently, jests stopped, and all eyes trained on the pair of commanders.

"We will spar hand-to-hand," Torallis said, "as you have no experience with a sword as yet."

Grieve agreed readily, and had to admit he was somewhat eager to test the mettle of this alien. As they came to a sparring mat at the center of the great chamber, the Earthers filled the space around them to watch. None of them had been witness to Sarah Manchester's famous match with Sergeant Major Lupus aboard *Cerberus*, but they'd heard stories, and now perhaps a second occasion worthy of story was playing out.

Grieve shed his tunic and pulled off his boots. Seeking to remove unfair advantages, Torallis removed his outer armor and laid his sword and helmet carefully atop it just beyond the ring. The Earthers were fascinated by the Larosian equipment, but did not think to venture near it. The Larosian's heavy boots were laid next to the armor, and in bare gray feet — each one with two digits — he entered the sparing circle, quickly dropping into an alien combat position. Grieve stood opposite him and entered his own fighting stance.

Grieve had no intention of attacking first — Torallis was an unknown to him, so he wanted to sit back and observe, find the weak spots. Torallis was of a similar mind, though in this instance the simplest codes of the Stealth Guard governed him. One edict taught to every trainee was 'he who first flinches is likeliest to lose, for he is less confident'.

So the two stood facing each other, completely unmoving, muscles holding them in rigid forms.

Word of the match spread quickly through *Agamemnon*, and interested parties from across the ship began to gather in the gym, discovering two motionless warriors patiently awaiting the other's move. When Ursla heard what was going on, she went immediately from her quarters to the gym, and found the same tableau when she arrived. Grieve was observing the Larosian — Ursla was well aware of that tactic, and she could only assume that Torallis was doing the same.

After twenty minutes, neither had moved.

Grieve watched coolly for movement in the silver eyes of the alien, but the disciplined warrior gave none. Torallis stared back, waiting for a similar sign in his opponent, but Grieve did not oblige either. They waited ten minutes more.

The crowd was substantial by that time, Earthers focusing on each of the sparring pair, looking for weaknesses to be exploited. But neither seemed to have any.

And then finally, Grieve decided time was too precious to allow the stalemate any longer. It would put him at a disadvantage, but he had to get this done.

At first Torallis didn't realize his opponent had moved because Grieve's eyes seemed to remain focused on the same point; however, the bear was sliding across the floor with even speed and supreme agility. As he neared Torallis, the Larosian moved to deflect the blow that came a second later — then the Guard Captain sent a strike in reply.

Grieve sensed the blow before it came, and his arm was in its path when it was thrown — a preemption Torallis had not thought a non-telepathic Earther could manage. Krogg instinct often allowed certain preventive movement, but Kroggs were also partially telepathic. Grieve was not.

Grieve's blows started to come in earnest, and Torallis used well-honed reflexes to deflect, though the Larosian found that his own strikes were completely ineffective. Grieve pressed closer, his leg lancing out to trip the smaller Larosian, but Torallis slid off to the side and broke contact.

Grieve let the alien go, not wishing to over commit and lose balance. He drew himself into another stance and circled the alien. Torallis took the initiative this time, coming forward with near-blinding speed and delivering several blows... only to be deflected by Grieve, who forced the Captain back with a combination of sheer power and precise control.

Torallis again retreated, his mind tackling the problem of the Earther, while Grieve was directed by his instincts. He retained the impetus as the Larosian backed off, and while Torallis steadied himself, Grieve's arms and a leg attacked in separate areas. The Larosian evaded deftly but overbalanced, and a fast leg from Grieve swept around, knocking his legs out from beneath him.

Torallis hit the mat with a thud, leapt back up to his feet, and accepted two more blows before he fell a second time. As far as he was concerned, the match was over. Grieve agreed.

Helping the Larosian to his feet, Grieve shook his hand, "Well fought, Captain."

The Larosian appreciated the honor in that statement, "And you, General. I will have to work on my hand techniques, though I am uncertain of what use they might be against Krogg blades."

Grieve paused and smiled in thought. He turned to a cougar at the side of the ring, "Grab a shield for me, would you?"

The cougar went to the small cache of weapons — kept on the deck in case of a need, however unlikely, to repel boarders — and drew a shield belt. She quickly returned as Grieve finished dressing and Torallis secured his armor.

Strapping the belt to his waist, Grieve faced Torallis, "Your sword, Captain. Activate it and attack me."

Torallis tilted his head, "That would not be wise."

Grieve's eyebrows climbed, "Trust me, Captain. I've lost limbs twice before... and I'm not eager to lose another."

Torallis did as requested, and in a fluid motion he was in a battle position with his sword encompassed by a barely visible glow. Grieve entered a simple stance and the crowd watched carefully. A black bear moved to the gym controls and activated the shield around the sparring ring — one like the military models used on the Antarctic Plain, designed to isolate a sparring zone in case of flying weapons or target practice.

Torallis waited a moment but presumed Grieve knew what was coming. With a motion far more familiar than the hand battle of before, the Larosian swept forward in an unglamorous but highly effective surge, ending a meter from Grieve.

The sword came around in an ark and crashed downward, but Grieve's shielded arm deflected the direct blow. With a sizzle from the protective energy field, he took hold of the blade in one hand and carefully wrenched the entire sword to one side, tearing it from the grip of a *very* surprised Torallis.

As far as the Larosian could have known, the General's maneuver should have cost him his entire arm... but this Earther 'shield' clearly changed the dynamics of the situation.

Torallis stood in shock, watching as Grieve keyed the deactivation button on the sword and handed it back to him.

"We use these," the bear said plainly, and deactivated his shield.

That sort of field had never been achieved by Larosian technology, so a long time ago they'd chosen a different sort. Slinging his sword, Torallis reached to his left forearm and keyed his armband.

A swirling disk of silver energy hummed into existence, about half a meter in diameter.

"Our version is somewhat less... adaptive."

There was *almost* a collective 'oooooh' followed by an 'ahhhhh' from the assembled Earthers, but they had the sense to remain silent despite their interest in the shield.

"It is entirely impenetrable, but as you can see, it offers limited coverage," Torallis drew his sword again, activating it with a smooth motion. The assembled Earthers watched as he carefully flung his weapon into the air. It came down blade first, aiming directly for the Captain's head...

In a swift move, the Larosian shield came up, and the atom-sharp blade glanced off the energy disk and was cast sideways towards the sparring ring's perimeter shield. Both fighters moved to catch it, but with his height advantage, Grieve snatched it from the air and deactivated it again.

"We've all got our own ways of coping, it seems. Yours is quite effective, I'd wager."

Torallis offered a nod as he deactivated his shield, then caught his sword as the General tossed it back to him, "It is indeed."

There was a slight pause as everyone in the gym processed the situation, then Grieve offered his counterpart a smile, "So, Captain. Think we can handle ourselves?"

The Larosian drew himself up and bowed, "Certainly. The sword plans will be sent over promptly."

A quickly-concealed ripple of excitement ran through the gym crowd. Standing back and still observing the sparring ring, Ursla wondered whether she'd ever handle a *sword*.

CHAPTER 36

Agamemnon's main briefing room glowed cyan with the light of the large three-dimensional star map that hovered over the central table. Thousands of icons marked the positions of the Allied and Krogg vessels, and the once-incomplete section that held the Krogg station was at last filled.

Now they had to come up with a strategy to use against the Hive.

"The flank is guarded only by Destroyers... my Warcruisers are best suited to it," Novash spoke with some authority, and as his silver eyes swept over the holo he pushed his open hand into the projection to indicate the Hive.

Ursla shook her head, "You'd be cut to ribbons on your own. There must be a hundred Destroyers there, not to mention the base defenses themselves..."

"Defenses designed to engage large capital ships, Admiral. My Warcruisers would likely be able to out-maneuver the attacks."

"Not under fire from the Destroyers as well," Ursla said firmly, her determination quieting the Larosian. "I'm not going to bog down your cruisers, Novash. But I will give you a frigate squadron in support."

Tradition and honor demanded Novash attack the Hive on his own... but prudence seemed to conflict openly with those tenets in this case. He had seen firsthand the Earther warships in action and had been very impressed by their agility and power. A squadron of *frigates* might well complement his Warcruisers... and the Admiral was being firm. This was an addition he could allow.

"A frigate squadron..." Novash nodded to Ursla, verbalizing his concession. "Very well."

"Good."

Ursla turned her chair to look down the table at two of the Earthers watching in silence, "Savanna, Dran."

The two, sitting next to each other, leaned forward into the glow of the tank and looked from Ursla to Novash. All eyes at the table turned briefly and curiously to Ursla, and the Kodiak delivered her orders to the Captain-Commodore.

"Novash, I'm going to give you the 111th, the best we have. Commodore Nightclaw commands, and they've already successfully engaged Kroggs of superior force. Savanna, I want *Tonnant* with them."

Admiral Felix nodded, as did Nightclaw. Ursla had already spoken briefly to both about the role she was contemplating for them, and they'd been eager to make the attempt on the Hive. Their ships, detached as they were from the Second Fleet, could carry out this duty without compromising her order of battle.

"Who will have command?" Novash asked cautiously.

"You will command your ships, of course; Admiral Felix will have the 111th and *Tonnant*. You can coordinate on the landing."

Novash nodded slowly, having read the files provided to him about the exemplary actions of both Earther commanders against the Krogg chase pack.

"Savanna, I think your privateers might best serve by accompanying *Tonnant*," Sarah suggested thoughtfully, leaning into the light for the first time during the briefing. "It'll be a good place for cruisers, and I fear all of mine will be committed to fleet work and screening."

Felix nodded, "I'll discuss it with Stanton and DeBrooke."

Ursla nodded and the two officers leaned back. They'd covered most of the plan already... and they'd only been at this an hour and a half. Sarah was quite satisfied with the smooth progress of the preparations to date, though she found that her head was aching. Pain of this sort was becoming slightly more familiar to her lately — even before her escapade at the *Pulsar*, she'd found herself much more fatigued than she was used to. It was undoubtedly a product of cumulative stress, and it would probably subside once she had another chance to rest and recover. Things had just been so intense lately... they were bound to improve after the Kroggs were dealt with. And with that reassuring thought in mind, she refocused herself.

Sarah's role in the operation was clear — her ships and the Second would move directly against the Krogg rear. There would be no fancy maneuvering, it would be the kind of stand-up slugging match she preferred. The frigates and cruisers would stay out of it as much as possible at first, and be ready when the Destroyers and the Motherships' corvettes came to engage. With luck, none of those small ships would make it through the net of escorts, and thus the capital ships would be free to trade blows with the Krogg behemoths.

The attack would be launched as soon as the sloops watching around the corridor detected the first Larosian ships entering the other side, and with luck the two forces would hit the Kroggs simultaneously. If not, the Larosians would pay dearly as they attempted to exit the corridor... or the Allied Fleet would pay in the rear.

"That settle everything?"

Sarah turned to Ursla and nodded. Novash inclined his head with approval, and the rest of the assembled officers offered their own signs of agreement. The meeting broke. With four days until the action was likely to start, they had plenty of time to communicate attack plans and prepare squadrons. They all stood and left, including Sarah, who scolded her mind for its willingness to wander and stuffed whatever fatigue she could gather up into a tight mental box. She really was looking forward to some downtime — they'd just have to rout the Kroggs first.

Wandering through the bowels of *Agamemnon* at an easy pace, Sarah headed for the flight deck.

Thoughts of Pat were resurfacing to prod her in the stomach. Graham's little 'admission' had complicated things. Sarah could understand why Pat had felt awkward around her... especially after the whole *Pulsar* episode. She could even see how all the time they'd innocently spent together could be misconstrued.

Pat was, after all, a very eligible bachelor by any reasonable standards a female serving in the fleet could set. Looks, brains, humor, and a good character, Sarah was well aware of the Irishman's virtues — just as she was aware of Ursla's, or Caine's. To be sure, there could be romantic overtones in those observations, but surely that wasn't the nature of their relationship...

Everyone else had to be wrong.

Everyone in the entire fleet. Because I'm right... there's nothing...

The plausibility of this delusion had already begun to fade, but now it was plummeting.

"Good Gods, I'm in... *love*... with Pat...?" she chewed out the revelation under her breath, scowling at herself as she did.

This wasn't at all like the movies — why hadn't violins played early on to warn her? Damned reality...

Indeed, reality. She had to contend with the fact that she wasn't *in* a movie. She'd be wearing impossibly tight clothes and sporting overly long hair if she was. No, this was Gods' honest, down-to-Genesis reality. And that meant the universe wouldn't make everything easy and rosy if — *if* — she and Pat tried to explore a deeper relationship.

There were plenty of issues to mull over... only after she'd sorted out quite a few of them would she even consider letting herself get deeper into this whole affair.

She'd have to be detached, think about this strategically... and avoid getting drunk at *all* costs.

Sarah continued to wander.

Neither Pat nor Graham drank alcohol on a regular basis, but they were currently in the *Pulsar* aboard *Genesis One* because the Irishman felt obliged to seek guidance from the Englishman. Pat had already been through the drill cycle of the fleet, so his ships had nothing to do but remain on orbital station while they waited to attack.

That being the case, he had plenty of time to reflect on his predicament.

And who better to brood with than Sarah's brother, the man who'd hit him over the head with the proverbial Shovel of Zeus. Well, that's what it felt like, though the Irishman half wished Graham had literally just hit him with a spade... it might have been a lot simpler.

Graham, for his part, was humoring his future brother-in-law. Not that he'd dare call Patrick Conroy that. The junior Manchester was positively amazed by the oblivious bubble his sister and this man had managed to create for themselves; he was also distressed by the fact that they were having such a hard time coming to terms with reality.

And what did they have to hide from? They were in love, and they were perfect for each other. It wasn't as though there was a lot of suffering attached — if Graham had the same chance at love he'd throw himself in fully.

"So, what do I do?"

The question came out of nowhere, and Graham looked up and shrugged in answer, "About Sarah? You go find her and leave me alone until you want to build a garage."

Pat chuckled, "Advice from the wise guy. Brilliant."

"Well?"

Graham let the question hang and Pat sighed, "Nah. She's busy."

With a groan, Graham took another deep gulp of his drink and let his chin rest in his hand.

CHAPTER 37

After four days of hard training, the marines were in good order and beyond formidable in their skill. Fifty had been armed with atom-swords manufactured hastily in *Agamemnon's* machine shops and had been trained in their use by their counterparts from the Stealth Guard. The Larosians had professed several times that the Earthers were excellent pupils, and the marines took pride in the compliments. But it was true: Earthers had a natural way with blades, probably an offshoot of their inherent ability with martial skills.

When Ursla had stopped by the training gym, she had picked up one of the weapons. Examining it, she found it looked surprisingly Japanese in its design, though it lacked any of the character of a blade that had been carefully crafted. After all, it had been rattled together in the course of a day. Better models would come when time and resources allowed actual development of proper fighting swords — for now the crude version would suffice.

Nonetheless, the fast turnaround on even rudimentary working models of such alien technology spoke glowingly about Earther ingenuity. Ship engineers had tackled the project with enthusiasm, managing to turn out the weapons in record time. And fifty Earther marines were now trained in the sword and ready to rise to the challenge of Krogg combat. Moreover, most of the Genesis Fleet had enhanced itself with Earther technology, and the Fourth Larosian Fleet-of-War had to be close to the other end of the corridor. The time for action was at hand.

The time for action is almost *at hand, actually...* Ursla corrected her overeager musings.

And it was the *almost* that was agitating her — she'd waited in suspense for days, knowing that Novash's estimate of the Fourth Fleet's arrival time was the best marker she had, but that it could be completely wrong if unforeseen circumstances had changed the fleet's speed. She'd drilled her squadrons, gone over deployment strategies again and again, and hoped pensively that Caine would somehow reach Genesis early.

Now, with the Larosians expected to arrive in a little more than twelve hours, the officers of the Allied Fleet were scheduled to meet one last time. Admirals, ArcGenerals, Commodores, and a Captain-Commodore boarded *Agamemnon*, and their usual briefing room was quickly filled. The assembled flag officers spoke quietly to each other about various preparations and ideas, waiting for their leading Admiral to arrive. Taken together, their moods weren't pessimistic, though they did register as somber.

Ursla only realized she was late for the gathering as she made her way down the corridor to the room. After she'd finished inspecting the new swords, she'd spent a much-needed hour working out anxious tension with some bear marines in *Agamemnon's* main gym, so at least her mind was focused. Coming to the room's door, she took a single centering breath, then entered. Nods came from Varnon Broadpaw, Dran Nightclaw, Sarah and Pat, and most of the other officers as she stepped in. She offered a reasonably confident smile in return as she found her seat and called the room to order. The assembled officers quickly took their places, all eyes turning to her.

"So, less than twelve hours now, by our estimate. Captain-Commodore?"

Novash nodded slowly, "I expect the Fourth Fleet to translate today."

Ursla nodded, "Well, if they turn out to be a little late I don't think we'll hold it against them. How's the upgrade situation looking, Varnon?"

"All the Superdreadnoughts, Dreadnoughts, and Battlecruisers, and most of the Heavy Cruisers have been supplied with their kits," Broadpaw reported. "We just finished building the gear to work on the rest of the fleet, but we're having some distribution trouble. Most of the Light Cruisers and Destroyers have been on constant maneuvers since yesterday, and we don't want to call them off their war-games without good cause. I've got pinnaces out delivering to whatever ships they can catch, but I think most of those ships will have to make do with what they have."

"Frankly," ArcLieutenant-General Bill Masters added quickly, "I wouldn't want to install the kit now anyway. Even assuming these crews got everything hooked together before the Larosians arrive, there'd be no time to practice on it or to make sure a wire somewhere isn't crossed. Those ships are better off as they are, I think."

A few nods were exchanged around the table, then Felix leaned forward, "Well our privateers have been brought up to code, and they've been on maneuvers with the 111th and *Tonnant* and *Flame*. They'll be ready and able to cruise with us when we deploy."

That comment drew dark looks from a couple of humans, but Pat's glare stopped any commentary before rash remarks could be made. Ursla chose to ignore the silent tension.

"Good then, our fleets are set and standing by," she said, garnering nods. "What about the Hive strike, Andros, Torallis?"

The two infantry officers nodded, Grieve in his usual, heavy manner, Torallis with his nominally slow half-bow. The Earther General spoke for them both, "Our Larosian strike craft has been loaded aboard *Tonnant*. We're all set — it'll just be up to Savanna, Dran, and Novash to get us there."

Nightclaw cocked an eyebrow and looked to the General, "And we will."

Novash and Felix added their own nods of confirmation, and Ursla matched the gesture, "Very good."

The words hung in the air as Ursla looked down the long table. Everyone met her gaze with a mixture of grim confidence and veiled apprehension. This was going to be quite unlike the Battle of the Pluto Orbital Plane, and for Grieve, nothing like the Battle of the Antarctic Plain. They were going into action against an alien race, in defense of another alien race, in this unfamiliar star system.

As they'd promised Liz and Sarah, the Earthers would help defend Genesis, even though that now meant joining an intergalactic war.

"Well, I suppose there isn't a great deal more to say," Ursla's tone was low. "We have to hope that our reinforcements are going to make it in time for the action, but we can't wait for them. As soon as the Larosian Fleet enters the rift we have to attack, or both our forces will be annihilated. And I can't pretend to know how we'll do. I have a feeling Second Fleet is going to get roughed up pretty badly, as will the Genesis Fleet. Still, we must persevere."

Broadpaw, Furgus, Talone, Nightclaw and Felix all seemed to catch Ursla's eye at once, and in their collective gaze she saw confidence.

"I do believe we'll succeed, and our suffering will not be in vain. We're defending Genesis today, and the lives of honorable Larosians. The Earthers at this table and in this fleet are here to uphold the pledge of support we made to our human friends. The humans here are protecting their homes, and making amends for a history of being manipulated. And the Larosians... well, I don't mean to speak for you Novash, but this is more your moment than ours. This is your war, and we're ready to stand with you."

Novash offered a bow-nod, "We are glad of your help, Admiral."

A very thin smile formed on Ursla's face, "And we're glad to give it. I think it's safe to say we're all rather alien to each other, but we go to war united. I'm sure a wiser person would say something historic about that, but I think the best thing to say is this: let's get the job done. Whatever that costs us."

No one at the table spoke. The room seemed to fill with quiet determination as everyone made their own peace with the action to come. Almost nine months before, humans and Earthers had battled the Church, but somehow this was different. The Church had embarked upon its Quest for the betterment of its own race, even if the course it had taken was misguided. And humans and Earthers shared a birth world — they were not so alien to each other.

But today would be distinctive; the Kroggs were a vicious enemy who gave no quarter and expected none. Blood would be spilled in great quantities, and it seemed likely that the side willing to give more and to suffer the greatest pain would be the one to succeed.

These Allies would fight the Kroggs and either win or *die*. There wasn't a third option.

"Alright, to your commands," Ursla said the words with a certain finality, wondering if this was how Caine had felt nine months before. She endeavored to end positively, "Good luck to you all. May fate smile on us today."

Everyone came to their feet soberly, then slowly moved away from the table, meeting each other to shake hands and pat backs in final farewells. Ursla shook each commander's hand and watched her flag officers file out, until only she, Sarah and Pat remained.

She eased herself back into her chair, "A grim business."

Pat stood with folded arms and nodded, "Aye, that it is."

Ursla ground her jaw uncomfortably at the Irishman's confirmation.

"We'll be bloodied by the end of this," Sarah said quietly, sitting on the edge of the table a meter from Ursla. "I think we might just win, though."

The Admiral smiled sadly and got to her feet, extending her grand hand down at Sarah who took it as best she could, "Best of luck, Sarah."

"And to you," Sarah nodded somberly to her friend and counterpart.

Then Ursla turned to Pat, and took the hand he offered, "Take care, Pat."

"Don't bump your head on the ceiling when it gets rough," he smiled.

Ursla grinned, "I've never gotten such practical advice..." her voice trailed off, and she glanced between Pat and Sarah. "Hmm... I'll leave you two, then. Good luck."

With a last nod to Sarah, she left the pair, hopefully to sort out their relationship before the bloody business began. Ursla wouldn't mind going into this battle with at least *some* pleasant news.

Pat stood awkwardly near the door, and Sarah glanced at him, trying to decide if there was something she should say.

But Pat spoke first, "My cruisers will be out ahead of you, so I can't look out for you today, Sarah. Don't try to knock off a Mothership alone, alright?"

Sarah chuckled softly, "Right. I'll try."

Pat turned to the door and made to leave, but Sarah, feeling forced by the moment, spoke quietly, "What do you think, Pat? Are we just good friends?"

The Irishman froze at the question and swallowed, feeling altogether too melodramatic, "No, Sarah, I don't think so."

He stood with his back to her for a few more seconds, then went out the door when she remained silent.

Stepping heavily down the corridor, Pat realized that if the universe played the whole situation out the way the novelists often did, either he or Sarah would end up maimed or dead, and there'd be no chance to finish the conversation.

He ground his jaw and silently threatened the universe — if it had any concept of what was good for it, it'd keep its miserable fingers out of their lives. Damned thing!

CHAPTER 38

First Lord Setter Caine sat silently in his cabin. Stacks of books and data pads had taken over his desk, and his eyes ached from reading them all. He'd gone over everything he needed to and had committed all the pertinent information to memory.

In fourteen hours he'd need to be ready to use it.

Orion was hurtling smoothly through space under energy drive, at the head of a fleet of some 1,500 ships from both Earther and human Naval services. Racing to battle.

Genesis was going to test Ursla, and the Earthers and humans with her, and if she was defeated by the Kroggs it would leave this combined fleet following *Orion* in poor circumstances upon arrival. Even if Ursla held her own, and the Larosians made a successful translation, Caine's command would still be required to join the battle.

He had no real concept of who they were facing — beyond the files, and beyond Ursla's speculation and Felix's quick encounter. The battle at Pluto had been tough, and the Earthers had fared well there, but an action against Church ships wasn't a great test of mettle. Nothing that could give Caine any certainty of his ships' abilities against these new aliens.

There was no common frame of reference, no sure way to know how the Kroggs would behave. In trying to understand the humans, Caine had enjoyed a number of advantages — the human histories from Earth and a common birth-world not least among them.

No such advantages existed here. The First Fleet, Third Fleet, and Genesis Provisional Fleet were racing through space to join a fight for which they were essentially unprepared. And now that Caine had read and reread everything available that held even a scrap of information about the Kroggs, he was even more uncertain about their fate.

Orion and its fellows, he knew, cruised to meet a purely alien foe...

The door chimed.

At first Caine didn't process the sound, but his mind lurched back into activity as his eyes shifted from the mess on his desk, "Yes, come."

The hatch opened, and silhouetted in the light of the doorway was a balding human, "Sorry, Setter, was this a bad time?"

Caine blinked twice and forced himself up out of his chair, "Not at all, come in Harvey."

His mind was slowly catching up with his words as he gestured the human into his cabin. Less than a year ago he wouldn't have dreamed of letting the man back aboard *Orion*, but of late Harvey Bingham had risen greatly in Caine's estimation. The man was genuinely concerned with righting the wrongs of the past, and he seemed quite capable of doing so.

Thoughts at last began traveling at normal speed in Caine's head, and he waved Bingham to a chair, "Why don't you sit, Harvey. What can I do for you?"

Harvey Bingham wasn't sure there was anything Caine could really *do* for him. He'd spent the entire trip reading up on his Chancellery, and all the information Sarah Manchester had forwarded from Second Chancellor Argyle. The task of pacifying — then perhaps even *uniting* — Genesis was daunting, and doubt was inevitably seeping into the High Chancellor's mind.

He'd done a damned good job splitting the planet apart decades before, following in the footsteps of Chancellors before him...

Caine took a seat opposite Bingham, and watched as the human kneaded his hands anxiously, "I'm not really sure why I wanted to stop by."

Well that's a good start.

"I've been doing a lot of reading about Genesis... and I suppose I needed to just *talk* to someone about it."

Caine cocked an eyebrow, "Not that I mind chatting with you, but mightn't you want to be getting some sleep? We'll be in Genesis space this afternoon."

Bingham frowned, "Sleep?"

With a wry smile, Caine pointed at the chronometer ticking in one of the holo tanks on his desk, "It's 03:00 hours. Three o'clock in the morning."

Harvey looked at the clock, thought for a moment, then released a short laugh, "That's why I was yawning so much..." He paused and looked from the chronometer to the piles on Caine's desk and then back to the First Lord, "...do Earthers yawn?"

Caine's smile broadened, "Not in front of guests. So I guess sleep hasn't been on your mind either?"

With a matching smile, Bingham shook his head, "I've got a lot to think on, Setter. Starting tomorrow... well, later today I suppose, I'm going to be responsible for rebuilding my world. And I'm not the man I was."

It was surprisingly easy for Caine to sympathize. Bingham had gone through a great deal in the past months, and even now the human was trying to master the particulars of his identity. Circumstance wouldn't allow him the time to dwell on the past or present, or indeed to spend a great deal of time planning for the future. He was getting tossed right back into the deep end, and the fate of billions of humans rested on his shoulders.

Somehow, Caine believed this man would not falter under the burden. Bingham had overcome so much on Earth alone, and *earned* the respect that had let Caine welcome him aboard *Orion*, and even into this cabin right now. He'd emerged as a leader, reformed and clearly genuine. Caine's instincts no longer burned around this man; instead he found him to be a sensible peer.

"You'll be fine," Caine's voice was kind. "As much as I didn't care for your disposition when we met, I must admit that you successfully *led* your people to Earth. Now I think you can lead Genesis in a new direction altogether."

Harvey met Caine's eyes briefly, his smile fading slowly, "I mean not to turn back into that man, Setter. But I don't know that I can do this job without some of his power."

Caine shook his head and held up a hand, "Your power has been proven. Your determination was my bane nine months ago, but today it's my asset. You've done a most incredible thing, Harvey. You've *truly* changed. You understand all that's happened and you want to make it right today. The fact that you've come this far tells me that you won't be stopped now, and that you won't be going back to the old ways. And you've earned *my* trust. After that, getting back your Chancellery will be easy for you."

For a moment Harvey was silent. He considered the First Lord's words, and in them he found some solace. Of course he still wasn't certain, but perhaps Caine's confidence would help temper some of the sharper fears. If this wolf, the great leader of the Earther people, could believe in him, he must be at least competent.

It was a small comfort, but it was a comfort. He'd just have to make sure he didn't disappoint this expectation when he arrived in Genesis later today... or whenever he managed to get back to his throne. That would be the final test.

For now he should stop taking up Caine's time. The wolf undoubtedly had much to do to prepare for the engagement — Caine would consider the possibilities, and be ready to think on his feet, and the Kroggs would have no chance against this Earther-Genesis armada.

The First Lord was a great leader; he wouldn't let this fleet down.

"Thank you, Setter," Bingham said quietly, and then he glanced up with a fresh smile. "But I should let you get back to your reading. I don't want to burden you with any worries with all the work you have ahead of you."

As the High Chancellor stood, Caine came to his feet in surprise, "Actually I finished my reading about three hours ago. I was just thinking, I suppose... I've got some concerns of my own ..."

Bingham smiled, "I appreciate the attempt, Setter, but I think I know better than that. I'll be fine, don't worry. No need to try to commiserate. The only thing I *am* certain about is that I'll be getting to Genesis tonight, and that the Kroggs will be long gone when I arrive."

Caine opened his mouth to speak, but Bingham had already turned and started walking to the door, "Thanks for the support, Setter. You have no idea how much it means for me to have your confidence."

The High Chancellor turned as he reached the hatch, and Caine watched, surprised at the seeming haste of his departure. It took him a few seconds to find words, "Well... umm... I'm not sure what to say, Harvey. But we all make do, I think. There's no point worrying about it now, I suppose. We're going in, we'll either succeed or fail... and somehow I expect you'll succeed."

Again, the two leaders' eyes met, and in his once-rival's eyes Caine saw admiration. Then, with a last nod, Bingham opened the hatch, "Fourteen hours then."

"Indeed."

As Bingham stepped out into the corridor, Caine remained standing in his cabin, somewhat surprised at his own state of mind.

He'd just told the *High Chancellor* of Genesis not to worry, that he believed in him and that everything would work out for the human planet.

And in order for Harvey Bingham to fulfill that prophecy, the combined fleet would have to defeat the Kroggs. Bingham deserved a chance... and Caine was determined that the human would get one.

With that resolution in mind, First Lord Setter Caine sat down on his couch and smiled.

A few minutes later he went to bed and slept.

CHAPTER 39

Admiral-of-a-Fleet Narosh sat on his flagship's bridge musing silently. The Admiral was a veteran commander, having fought the Krogg Queen alongside the Son of Praaxus. The Son had left him in command of the Warriors of the Fourth, and they followed him with a loyalty beyond the normal duty of a warrior, not only because he had been personally chosen by the Son for this leadership role, but because he had long since proven himself worthy of the honor.

He found himself thinking almost longingly for the glorious days, only months in the past, when the Son had led the Fourth to war and himself to a noble end. It seemed so long ago... But Narosh disliked nostalgia, and he resisted empty wishes for the glory of the past. It was his duty to bring honor to the actions of present, and the future.

Perhaps most importantly, it was his duty to defeat the Kroggs — to pay tribute to the Son's sacrifice with their destruction.

And that was his goal this day. After the message from Captain-Commodore Novash weeks ago, there had been no further contact with the scouting squadron. Novash's prolonged silence seemed indicative of enemy action. He would have reported immediately had he found nothing on the other side, so it seemed likely that this hyperspace corridor led to the missing Krogg armada, and the Warriors of Praaxus' Son would soon confront it.

It had occurred to Narosh, on the bridge of his Warcruiser *Lycrotar*, that the corridor could offer a means of ambush for the armada and that the Fourth could indeed be cruising into a Krogg trap. Regardless, Narosh remained supremely confident. Ambush or no, the remnants of the defeated Krogg hordes would die by the Larosians' power. After the loss of their Queen, the invaders simply could not have recovered to pose a true threat to the Son's champions.

The Fourth *would* win this fight. For the Son.

All ships report being in position, Admiral Narosh, the report came from Narosh's chief of staff in the standard telepathic wavelengths.

Very well. First squadrons enter rift. Standard deployment, Warcruisers and Battleships lead, Destroyers and Carriers second echelons.

The Warriors of Praaxus' Son entered the corridor.

Ursla was more agitated than she wanted to admit to herself.

The tension that had built up over the past weeks was now flowing freely through *Agamemnon's* crew. The whole fleet was similarly suffering, as were Genesis and its orbitals.

The very void of space itself seems to be trembling with—

Ursla halted her internal monologue — it was decidedly melodramatic...

"Ma'am! Signal from *Alacrity*, vessels entering the rift. They're Larosian."

Alacrity was a Fifth Rate sitting above the corridor with a stretched energy drive field. It would see the Larosians first... then *Speedy*...

"*Speedy* confirms. *Flame* confirms."

Magnus had demanded that he help picket the corridor, and it was his sloop that gave the third and final confirmation of the incoming Larosians. So Ursla, at last, was obliged to move. And that immediately took the edge off her stress — her instincts and her mind ticked into battle mode, and she began to deliver orders with her accustomed precision.

"Very well, all ships beat to quarters! Clear for action!"

Earther crews had supposedly been stood down while they waited for the Larosian Fleet's arrival, but anxious energy had driven most personnel to relax next to their duty stations. The last ship was cleared for action twenty seconds after the order was broadcast.

Sitting aboard *Joseph Barron*, Sarah received the very same report. Her mind had been dwelling more on Pat than duty, despite the numerous mental scoldings she'd delivered to herself. The knowledge that the Larosians were on the way, however, brought her out of her moody reflections and into full readiness.

"All ships to battle stations!"

The human fleet was at action stations within thirty seconds.

"Begin deployment," Ursla's order was cool, and it surged through the Second Fleet in the blink of an eye. "Cruisers forward."

The generic term 'cruiser' was liberally being applied to frigates, sloops, and Destroyers, as well as the ships actually classed as Heavy, Light, and Battlecruisers within the Allied Fleet.

"Battle echelons. Second to form line abreast."

Within moments, the mass of Allied ships hurtled into motion, their drives flaring. Cruisers moved out ahead in individual squadron and battle group formations, all with the duty of corvette suppression. The smaller ships appeared to be a cloud of disorganized wasps, but the appearance was deceiving — intentionally.

The Kroggs wouldn't know what was going on.

The battleships in the wake of the cruisers formed lines abreast. Ships lined up side-by-side, one above or below another. In seconds, a wall of warships appeared in space and began to increase speed.

The cruisers accelerated into flux and energy drive, making 400 pls towards the rear of the Krogg forces, and the battleships followed.

Narosh led the first squadron through the corridor. It was tradition for the flagship to lead the fleet into action, and that was the reason Larosian Admirals commanded from Warcruisers and not Battleships. Larger vessels were more dangerous but less maneuverable, so the Kroggs tended to engage them first, giving agile vessels like *Lycrotar* an advantage, even when first into battle. A mere Warcruiser among other such Warcruisers as well as a horde of much larger Battleships, the flagship would not draw fire immediately.

The fleet was pouring into its side of the corridor as *Lycrotar* entered the final stretch. Narosh watched the orderly but swift entry with pride. The elite Warriors would never appear sloppy.

All ships enter battle configuration as you emerge from the corridor. Narosh's telepathic order permeated outward from *Lycrotar* and was received by his leading squadrons. Fifty Battleships and 100 Warcruisers prepared to go to battle stations.

The cruisers came out of energy and flux drive first, their weapons ready as they did. The Earther frigates and sloops led the way as they required no deceleration. Their guns ran out smoothly as their hulls reconstituted, and they did not slow with the approach of the Krogg ships to the rear.

Broadsides lashed out and crashed into unsuspecting Dreadnoughts and Superdreadnoughts, while carronades carved anything in range. These first shots served to do little more than annoy, but then that was precisely their goal.

Accelerating into the armada of Krogg ships, coordinated packs of frigates and sloops evaded the lumbering and careless shots of Krogg capital ships and ignored and shrugged off the shots of the speedier Destroyers.

The human Light, Heavy and Battlecruisers came next, missiles venting against whatever targets might be found. The tubes cycled quickly — more quickly than Earther guns recharged. Even before some of the first volleys found targets, a second salvo entered space, and then the human escort ships scattered as their Earther counterparts had, leaving open space behind the Krogg Fleet.

Angry, the Kroggs made to engage. Their Dreadnoughts and Superdreadnoughts were far too slow to attack the swift and deadly cruiser groups, but the multitude of small Krogg Destroyers could and did join action.

In their own hastily-formed packs, the Destroyers began to break screening formation to chase the harassing ships. The Krogg capital ships began to maneuver as well, leaving their tightly-knit, point-defense formations to avoid the stinging wasps.

When the wall of Allied battleships appeared behind them, they had no way to protect themselves.

First, Second, Third, and Fourth Rate ships of the line accompanied by Superdreadnoughts and Dreadnoughts held their tight wall formation despite different rates of deceleration. They exited their FTL drives to find a disorganized Krogg rearguard formation, and they took full advantage of the turmoil.

The human ships didn't have to wait — their tubes began to belch salvos immediately, the enhanced heavy missiles screaming down on the Krogg capital ships without much opposition from point defense batteries. Krogg Dreadnoughts and Superdreadnoughts flared in space, screaming in agony as the fireballs consumed them.

As this happened, the Earther capital ships made hard and simultaneous turns to port, their starboard guns running out within a split second of each other. As momentum carried the massive Earther vessels along, gunners took seconds to lay their gunsights on targets, and then the collective starboard broadside of the Second Fleet capital ships hurtled outward in a deadly crest of energy.

Missiles erupted into space again from the human ships, and the Earther ships rolled and sent a second massed broadside into the Krogg rear. The thunderous volley was unimaginable in its power, and the Kroggs met it without protection. Ships screamed, gore filled space, and at least 100 Krogg vessels completely disappeared, with dozens more being quickly wounded.

For the moment, an air of triumph filled the Allied Fleet. A few seconds stretched out as the chaos cleared, and the utter destruction wrought by the salvos proved to all — and particularly the previously-besieged humans — that the Kroggs were not invincible.

Just damned hard to beat.

As the gore floated away, a second echelon of Krogg ships drifted past the corpses of the first. The Earther guns were recharging, the tubes on the Genesis ships cycling.

Three hundred Krogg Dreadnoughts and Superdreadnoughts entered the open space beyond the dead and dying, and spines began rising through the newcomers' skins. For a second, space seemed to hold its breath, as if it was watching this new contest with interest...

Then all plunged into true destruction.

The Kroggs were more than just *angry* at their opening losses, and they had more than enough ships to gain revenge. The 300 that had already reached the rear began this quest, and savagely launched themselves forward, their triple volleys of spines spitting into space ahead of them.

Ranges closed with a vicious speed, and the two capital ship forces slammed into each other.

Lycrotar began to expand as it exited the corridor, its hull entering battle configuration. Narosh became aware of the Krogg armada in the same instant the Fourth's leading Battleships, following close behind their flagship, came under fire.

The bombardment was truly withering, spines crossing through space with such ferocity that survival seemed impossible. The unfortunate battlewagons drew almost all the onslaught, and of their fifty, only a ten-and-four reached battle configuration intact.

As antimatter guns began to spit their harsh replies at the Krogg Fleet, Narosh counted his foe... The Fourth was *outnumbered*. And ambushed.

The Warriors of Praaxus' Son did not stand a chance. They would die defeated... but they would still fight with honor!

Admiral Narosh! This is Captain-Commodore Novash! Stand by!

The signal came out of what seemed to be a cloud of oblivion, but Narosh recognized the telepathic voice of his junior. Somehow the Captain-Commodore had survived *this*...

And then a data stream of all that had happened to the scouting squadron filled Narosh's brain. Much of the information took him off guard, being formatted in a manner entirely unfamiliar to the Admiral-of-a-Fleet — he took seconds to understand it all, but as it processed he acknowledged quickly.

There were allies fighting to reach his forces from the rear of the Krogg armada. He had to establish a foothold while those newcomers distracted part of the overwhelming Krogg force.

As more Battleships lumbered from the corridor, the experienced Larosian ships began to coordinate fire, and with faint but appreciated hope, the Fourth Fleet-of-War began to make its mark on the Krogg armada.

Dreadnoughts of both sides evaporated into oblivion with an ease that was sickening. Fourth Rates suffered the same fate, many of the 64s vanishing under the withering salvos of spines.

The Allied Fleet's wall shattered into a cloud of squadrons, all of them bent on angry reprisal. Broadsides and missile salvos tore outward in reply to the Krogg assault, and the ships charged down the wakes of their weapons as the battle descended into a melee.

Earther ships, ever bonded by the instincts of their Captains, seemed to fight together, 80- and 84-gun ships pairing off with vulnerable 64s, Third Rate 74s joining each other, First Rates clustering amongst themselves. As in a Napoleonic skirmish line, ships fought in pairs — one covered the other as its guns recharged, then the ships switched roles.

In the chaos of the battle, these fighting duos survived rather well, though they still absorbed significant punishment.

Meanwhile, the human ships suffered. They lacked the natural skill of the Earthers, and though they fought viciously, the Kroggs' attention seemed to be drawn to their more familiar and vulnerable hulls. Superdreadnoughts beat off spine attacks with angry missile salvos, some clustering together, others lashing back alone. Spines ripped Genesis hulls to pieces, neuro-pulses ravaged ship systems, and many human vessels spiraled away without power. But still, missiles at close range were devastating, and while the humans bled so did the Kroggs.

The division of 300 Krogg ships that the Allies had attacked had been outnumbered by the 600 Allied battleships to begin with. As the fight reached two minutes in length, the Krogg force evaporated under the combined guns and missiles of the Earther-human force... but only a scant 400 Allied ships remained.

The small victory brought a sigh of relief to the Battle Squadrons of both the Earther Second and Genesis Fleets. They had survived.

Then, with somewhat appropriate timing, another wave of Krogg ships, this one numbering 500, cruised from the rear of the formation, passed through the coagulated gore, and opened fire.

CHAPTER 40

While the fleets hammered at each other near the rift, *Tonnant* and its party appeared suddenly near the Krogg Hive. The alien Destroyers in the vicinity were too numerous to count. But they were also disorganized... and *distracted*... perhaps hoping to be called to action against the enemies now assaulting the blockade's rear.

As Felix watched the Kroggs' disorder he tipped his head, "Be careful what you wish for."

His Flag Captain acknowledged his quiet comment with a cocked eyebrow before running out *Tonnant's* guns. *Shanavorus* and the twenty-four other Warcruisers attached to him, as well as the 111th Flying Squadron and the privateers, came to battle readiness as the 80-gun ship of the line hammered out its first broadside.

The tide of energy knocked a dozen Krogg Destroyers away, leaving them in various states of destruction. Lethal volleys from the guns of the 111th broke apart a dozen more as the Earther Fifth Rates closed range, and then the Larosian Squadron chased the wake of the Earther shot, closing fast with vicious antimatter guns and spreading destruction among the enemy flotillas.

Without much resistance, the defending Destroyer force crumpled, and so fierce was the fighting around the rift that no notice was apparently taken and no reinforcements sent. Felix took this as a good omen — Ursla was causing so much trouble that the Kroggs couldn't even protect their Queen.

Unlikely though that might seem.

The Warcruisers turned away from the bloody debris field and picked up speed, the 111th traveling with them. *Tonnant* paused as if sizing up the massive battle that now fully encompassed the Second, then as the privateers tucked under the 80's flanks, Felix ordered the Second Rate to follow in the frigates' wake — to the Hive.

Aboard *Archangel Sword*, Stanton's heart was racing. They were actually going to engage a *Krogg installation* — a fortified fleet base and Queen's Hive. Though now a veteran combat officer, the Captain couldn't help but be pleased with the prospect of action against the aliens. *Sword* was playing a role in this fight — something that Liz Hastings would not have let the ship do only weeks before. He might well die in the coming hours, but the Kroggs would get a little of their arrogant brutality back first.

And if everything went according to plan, a bit of regicide too.

So the Battlecruiser hybrid and its consort would be written into the history books as privateers who contributed to the fall of a Krogg Queen. Stanton had absolute confidence in Felix — he *knew* this would work out. In the meantime, he had a ship to command.

While the proud Larosian and Earther cruiser squadrons marked course towards the unsightly alien clump of asteroids, Stanton ordered *Sword* to watch *Tonnant*, and *Grendelsbane City* remained alongside the Second Rate as well. The 80 could potentially be vulnerable to a force of fast-moving, light Krogg ships — it was better that the privateers stayed behind, to add their fire and maneuverability to an encounter with any enemy formations.

Just like the one that appeared suddenly on *Sword's* main screen.

Apparently the attack on the flotillas hadn't gone *entirely* unnoticed, and now a dozen Krogg Destroyers hurtled from shelter in the asteroid belt far above and to the rear of Felix's Allied force. They simultaneously popped up on *Tonnant's* scopes and those of the 111th, though such a light force warranted no attention from the latter unit.

The Fifth Rates were too far away to defend Felix's flagship, and their duties compelled them to probe the Hive — there was no support detailed to *Tonnant*, save for the privateer duo…

"Move to engage!" Stanton barked the order more loudly than he needed to, and *Sword* accelerated up and away from *Tonnant*, *Grendelsbane* quickly coming up alongside its partner.

As the two privateers rushed out to meet the Destroyers, *Tonnant* wore around quickly, dumping one broadside and then the other into space. Energy shot tore through the void, passing the independent human cruisers, and slamming wholesale into the Krogg Destroyers. Three of the Krogg ships spun away, spraying blood and losing internal organs in their weightless tumble. The nine other ships closed quickly with the privateers, seeing them as easier prey while *Tonnant* began to climb to engage the Destroyers with carronades.

As *Sword* emptied its tubes, the hybrid Battlecruiser's carronades sawed off one of the Destroyer's wings, drawing a horrible shriek from the creature. The missiles blasted another of the Krogg ships completely apart, and the remaining seven scattered to avoid further punishment. Recognizing the weaker ship of the duo, they quickly refocused their attention on *Grendelsbane City*.

Far off the port quarter, *Grendelsbane* bucked as spines slashed into its armor. The smaller cruiser's lasers had far less effect on the passing Destroyers, and at such close quarters the ship's front-mounted tubes were proving a liability — not even the Heavy Cruiser was handy enough at helm to bring them to bear on the speeding Krogg Destroyers.

Sword turned to take pressure off its compatriot, but as it did volleys of spines tore through its shields and sprayed acid into its drives. The ship's human-designed thrust nozzles disintegrated, and as the hybrid ship suddenly lost its main steering gear, it was thrown into a wild spin.

Tonnant, still coming up, was too far off to use carronades in the privateers' defense, and as *Sword* spun before the Earther ship's guns it became clear that a broadside would be unsafe — shot could easily hit the flailing Battlecruiser.

Grendelsbane's aft section was torn open by a neuro-pulse, spines exploiting the breach before the Heavy Cruiser could roll to hide it. The main generators were knocked offline and the privateer suddenly collapsed into a drift.

"Cover her, dammit!" Stanton roared as his ship struggled to gain trajectory control, not entirely sure whether the 'her' he referred to was *Grendelsbane* or its captain.

"No control, skipper! Going to backups..."

Sword came to a sudden halt and lunged again at the Destroyers. Carronades swept up another one, and *Tonnant* drew two more under its guns, but four still prowled around the wounded Heavy Cruiser, circling like vultures over a wounded animal. Seeing *Grendelsbane's* complete lack of activity, they began to close range, preparing to–

A broadside slashed by them suddenly, diminutive but effective. Light energy shot cracked one Destroyer's carapace and sent it into a spiral, and the other three turned to find the shooter.

Flame fell on the Destroyers at almost-light speed, its remaining broadside emptying into another Destroyer as it passed at point-blank range. The sloop's small carronades prodded one more, drawing its attention while the last one spat spines down its wake. As the last Krogg attempted to make chase, it was abruptly swallowed in the beam of one of *Tonnant's* carronades.

Sword fell furiously on the last Destroyer, its carronades pounding the Krogg vessel apart in a measure of revenge. As that foe shattered, space seemed to fall silent — though despite the haunting telepathic cries of the Krogg ships, it had been silent the entire time.

Aboard *Sword*, Stanton realized he was breathing hard and that his teeth were bared, so he consciously settled himself against his adrenaline. *Grendelsbane* had been spared... hopefully without casualties on its bridge.

"Signal from *Tonnant*, Captain. Admiral Felix says we should attend to *Grendelsbane City*. He'll rejoin the attack force."

Stanton swallowed and steadied himself, "My compliments to Admiral Felix... we'll do exactly that."

Tonnant slowly turned and accelerated away from the debris field, entering energy drive to make up for time lost to the cruiser squadrons that were surging through space toward the Hive.

"Signal coming in from *Flame*. Commander Magnus is requesting live communication."

Stanton blinked, "Put him up."

Fox was smiling when he appeared on the main screen, "Captain Stanton."

James smiled weakly in reply, "Gods bless you, Commander Magnus."

"It's Fox to you, Captain. And it seemed fair enough that we help you — nice to know we could be of some assistance."

Stanton's smile broadened — the young commander was fast becoming James' favorite Earther, and given his positive history with the species, that really was saying something.

"Can you stick around, Fox? We might need some extra cover while *Grendelsbane* gets back into a movable state."

"Damned right we will!" the screen split and Audrey appeared, a notable sigh of relief coming from *Sword's* Captain.

"We're detached duty," Fox bobbed his head to both of them. "We'll stay, for whatever good eighteen guns can do. Get repairing, though — this seems to be a dangerous piece of real estate just now."

Shanavorus slowed just beyond the Hive's weapons range... and found it unguarded. The conglomeration of skin and rock mounted plenty of weapons of its own, but experience in dealing with Krogg complexes told Captain-Commodore Novash that such weapons hardly ever succeeded in engaging Warcruisers and other quick vessels of a similar type.

Signal Cerberus *and inform Commodore Nightclaw that it is best to engage at full speed. We can outmaneuver the weapons on the Hive.*

The notice was translated from the thoughts of the Larosians to the language of the Earthers in a brief second, and as the ships of Novash's squadron broke formation to attack, the 111th ran out its guns and moved to join them.

The Krogg Queen was under siege.

CHAPTER 41

Pat watched the capital ships sling hell at each other and was suddenly very glad he was in the cruiser line of work. His little ships were suffering at the hands of well-formed Dreadnought and Destroyer squadrons, but they certainly didn't have to cope with the apocalyptic gunfight the Allied battleships were enduring.

So Pat was as safe as anyone could be in the maelstrom.

But Sarah wasn't.

He forced himself to breathe despite that, checking again to see *Pope Joseph Barron's* live transponder code in the midst of the fray. The Superdreadnought had two others with it, and it seemed to be faring well enough. *Agamemnon* was fine too, fighting in a pair with the 125-gun *Algenon*. That was quite a formidable coupling.

Pat forced his eyes away from the action — he had more pressing matters at hand. His screen showed how much of his cruiser group remained, and though there were more survivors than he might have expected to this point, the losses still made him shudder. Of his thirty-six, thirty-one remained.

"Sir, Mothership coming into range. Looks like it's heading for the battleships."

Pat quickly called up his sensor display, finding the lumbering eyeball-ship in his scope. If he got all 900 Allied cruisers together he might be able to slow that thing down, but without real capital ships there was no chance of stopping it.

No, the massive vessel would survive its approach to the action... but Pat's cruisers *could* stop the corvettes it meant to launch against the Allied Fleet.

"How many squadrons see it?" Pat demanded evenly, turning to the Sensor Chief.

"About forty separate groups have it locked, sir. Including us."

That was half the cruiser force, hopefully enough to wreak havoc on the 700 corvettes in the Krogg behemoth's launch racks. A Mothership could literally put a small fleet into space, and if this one could deploy against the Allied battleships...

That was what Pat was out here to stop, so there was no point concerning himself with the possibilities — the corvettes would never reach their targets.

As the great eyelid on top of the Mothership slowly began to open, a deadly halo formed around the huge vessel. The first corvettes began to eject seconds later, the smaller-than-Destroyer ships rippling from their hangars with unfolding wings and feral, telepathic war cries. Though familiar with the humans, they had yet to see action against the new aliens... But they were sure of their ability to smash these newcomers as easily as they could smash so many other things.

What they weren't counting on was an unwelcome interruption as they launched.

Allied sloop and Destroyer groups got in amongst the speeding little warships, their diminutive volleys proving effective against the small Krogg craft. From beyond the stream of corvettes, Earther broadsides came smoothly to bear, their guns running out loaded with canister. Clouds of energy appeared in space, slamming into corvettes seconds after firing, and knocking dozens at a time off their course.

Missiles came next — the tubes of the human cruisers sent hundreds into the writhing corvettes as they tried to break away from their tormentors. Pat's battlecruisers each put salvoes of sixty missiles into space, and Earther tracking systems made the enhanced weapons fly fast and true.

The space above the giant eye blossomed with energy, explosions, short-lived flames and immense amounts of gore.

The 500 Kroggs that had charged the remnants of the Allied capital ship group hit a wall of vessels now hardened against them.

Instead of being weakened and demoralized by the first losses, Ursla's ships had learned from their action, and from *Agamemnon's* bridge she watched her ships counter the Kroggs' animalistic fury with both instinct and logic. The human ships were surviving as well, their enhanced missiles tearing at the Kroggs.

Ursla's confidence began to build, though she cautioned herself against it. There were a *lot* of Kroggs in the space around them, and the Fourth Fleet-of-War remained cut off.

"They're receding again, ma'am."

Ursla watched *Agamemnon's* battle plot as the Kroggs dropped back, then observed as Krogg reinforcements from the armada folded themselves into ranks with the survivors of the last attack. The battle plot estimated that the new group numbered approximately 300, and as the black icons representing that force moved back toward the Allied ships, Ursla frowned at the alien strategy. Most of the Kroggs were still focusing on the Larosians... which meant in order to preserve the Fourth Fleet-of-War, she'd have to get farther in.

Her battleships numbered 380 — almost half of them gone in fifteen minutes of melee, but still enough left...

"Ships advance! Don't give them time to form up."

•••

The last squadrons of the Fourth Fleet-of-War had made it through the corridor, and while almost 400 ships had been lost while emerging into the small region of space now occupied by the Larosians, the Warriors of Praaxus' Son were determined never to surrender.

Carriers, Battleships and Warcruisers began to launch their fighters, the Kroggs' corvettes racing out to meet them in the same old style. The Fourth could put 5,500 fighters into space by the time the casualties were accounted for, while the Krogg corvettes were available in smaller numbers — too many of them had been drawn away by the newcomers' forces to the rear.

Satisfied that the Warriors of the Son were sufficiently organized, Narosh ordered his squadron to sally outward.

Ursla's capital ship force hurtled into disorganized Krogg ranks. The loose force of Krogg Dreadnoughts and Superdreadnoughts that had been sent to check her progress only minutes before had been reduced to 300, and as those alien vessels were trying to shake themselves back into an ordered combat unit, Allied vessels infiltrated their ranks.

Agamemnon headed the attack, and it was savage and quick. The unprepared Kroggs were thrown into chaos as broadsides and missiles began to slam home from extremely close range. The poorly-established formation came apart as Krogg capital vessels threw themselves out of the way of incoming fire, and the Allies drove through before they could collect themselves to mount a counter attack.

"All ships drive for the corridor — don't stop until we're between the Fourth and the Kroggs!" Ursla's order was hurried, and as it was signaled to *Agamemnon*'s consorts, the force redoubled its efforts.

The Larosians would have close support soon enough.

Pat's cruisers slashed into another flight of corvettes, missiles and broadsides from the Allied light forces breaking apart the formidable squadrons of the Krogg ships. Motherships — left without anything to eject into action — retreated in their cumbersome way, and the cruisers let them go. Without corvettes they were virtually toothless.

As the battleships began to make progress in their drive towards the Fourth, individual cruiser squadrons slipped into protective formations around them. Pat frowned at his plot as Fifth Rates and Battlecruisers began beating back uncoordinated Krogg strikes, shielding the battered capital ships from the brunt of the Krogg wrath.

The recombination of cruisers and capital ships took its toll on the alien opponents — the Krogg Fleet seemed to give way before the Allied column as it pressed inward towards the Larosians.

Pat eyed his squadron status wearily as more capital ships drove past it. Cruisers were evaporating now — their ability to outmaneuver incoming strikes did them little good when they were purposefully shielding slower-moving battleships. His battle group was down to twenty-two... twenty-one. His Battlecruisers, the Genesis Navy's best, were bleeding badly, but they were giving as good as they got.

The Allied Fleet pushed inward.

Narosh's mind flared angrily as the Fourth's attempts to force itself out of this defensive pocket were tossed back. The Kroggs knew this enemy far better than they knew the strange aliens behind them, and they were able to easily shrug off the Larosian strikes. More Motherships were coming from the rear now that the unknown hostiles were making towards the corridor, and corvettes soon matched fighters in number.

Perhaps 2,000 of the Krogg armada remained, but only 1,100 of the Fourth was still in fighting condition. The chances of survival seemed to dwindle — if they could not break out, they would be utterly crushed.

Lycrotar shuddered as spines impacted its shield, then its antimatter guns smashed a Krogg Destroyer in quick reply to the strike. Krogg vessels were closing in greater concentration, and the Warriors of Praaxus' Son were finding their numbers insufficient to hold the onslaught back...

The situation was worsening.

Ursla held the arms of her chair tightly. *Agamemnon*'s deck was steady as a rock, but her heart was pounding in a predator's instinctive reaction to combat, and she still felt as though her veins might burst from the strain.

Agamemnon's bow chasers wiped away a Destroyer and the First Rate emptied its port broadside into a marauding Superdreadnought. Down to just a little more than half strength now, the fleet clawed its way forward. Eight hundred ships of all classes, fighting hard to reach and reinforce the Larosians... and they were making progress.

The rear of the Kroggs' innermost containment sphere appeared before the Allied guns with some suddenness, but the fighting was too ferocious to allow any of the Allies to take pride in that minor victory.

Missiles erupted from tubes, broadsides came to bear, and the ships pouring fire into Narosh's command had a new adversary... for a few seconds.

The combined fire of the Allied ships blew a massive breach in the Krogg formation, and they moved to exploit it with haste. They dove into the defensive pocket, their fire supporting that of the remaining thousand Larosian ships. Fighters wove tight paths around them, drawing the attention of the corvettes that prowled throughout the area. Allied sloops and Destroyers broke ranks to support the Larosian fighter craft, and within seconds the two fleets merged in the space before the corridor.

Only then did the reality of what Ursla had just done occur to her. An Earther tactical adage succinctly stated: "There's a fine line between 'divide and conquer' and 'being surrounded'."

And in her single-minded drive to reach the Larosians' side, she'd led the Allied Fleet right across it.

Fresh Krogg ships — ones not yet engaged in the horrible fighting — suddenly swept into the breach left in the Second Fleet's wake. More Krogg ships also moved to bolster the containment lines that surrounded the pocket.

They'd played right into the Kroggs' hands.

They were trapped.

CHAPTER 42

Tonnant sat idly just beyond the range of the Hive's spine batteries, and aboard the 80-gun ship of the line, Savanna Felix wondered at the base's lack of mobile defenses. The lighter ships attached to the landing force were flying in close, outmaneuvering the rapid-fire spine batteries that were numerous on the installation's outer crust. Frigates and Warcruisers were systematically taking out those batteries, and the base seemed unable to bring anything to bear against them. Why hadn't the Kroggs sent a force of Destroyers or Dreadnoughts to stop this sort of assault against such an important installation?

Hopefully this is a gift horse. No looking in the mouth for me... let's hope Andros gets this simple a job on the inside.

"Getting the all clear from Commodore Nightclaw, sir."

Felix tuned back into the universe at his Signal Officer's report.

"Helm, move us into drop range."

The Second Rate ship of the line slid into the space around the Hive, an untouched 111th forming around it.

"How's the battle going?" Felix ask in low tones, and his Flag Captain shook her head.

"The fleet's being penned in."

Felix shot a look at the wolf who in turn pointed to the battle plot. Felix ground his jaw anxiously. There was nothing his little force could actually do in a battle of titanic proportions like that — his cruisers, even if most of them were Larosian, would be virtually useless in such a cloud of destruction...

But that didn't mean he shouldn't *try*...

"We're in drop range."

Felix blinked and looked up, "Drop."

In *Tonnant's* main bay, Grieve sat aboard the uncomfortable alien strike craft and felt it lurch into motion. The landing ship accelerated away from the Second Rate with impressive speed, though the ride was far rougher than any Earther dropship would have offered. The General cast glances at his marines around him — the fifty who had trained on swords over the past several days. They were mostly veterans of the attacks on Genesis, and he knew they would handle this mission with skill and professionalism.

The Stealth Guardsmen were essentially unknown to him, but he trusted

Torallis and was confident these veteran warriors from centuries of war against the Kroggs would acquit themselves admirably. He would rely on their experience today.

As the craft descended towards the strange mass of flesh and rock called the Hive, the comm link in Grieve's ear chimed.

"Andros, Ursla's in trouble, we're going to try and help. I'm sending to *Flame* to pick you up on your way out."

The words did not inspire confidence — if the battle outside was going badly, this mission might prove to be one-way. Andros Grieve wasn't really partial to that sort of assignment...

I don't expect anyone is. But we're going in anyway, so enough worrying.

Grieve frowned at his musing and dismissed it, "Good luck Savanna."

"To both of us."

In his magnified-picture window, Grieve could see the gray hull of *Tonnant* turn and speed away, the frigates of the 111th and the Warcruisers of Novash's squadron following. It was disconcerting to watch, especially since he was hurtling towards a major Krogg installation.

"Well," he glanced at Sergeant Major Lupus, who sat silently across from him, "this better go well."

The wolf was one of the few non-bears Grieve had brought along due to his storied martial skill, and now he cocked an eyebrow, "Is that an order?"

The General smiled and shrugged — they were about to find out.

"Our engines are back up... we can do about .80 cee," Audrey's voice betrayed her relief, and James offered a smile over the comm.

"We'll get moving then."

Guarding *Grendelsbane* during the Heavy Cruiser's recovery had been tense — though not for reasons Stanton might have suspected. He was watching the Allied Fleet get pinned, leaving the Hive assault force isolated and the privateers in a precarious 'no man's land' on the fringes of the fight. Hopefully they'd go unnoticed...

"Skipper, looks like Admiral Felix and the assault force are making for the fleet," the Sensor Chief reported suddenly, and James turned to his battle plot.

"Things are looking pretty bad... we better get back to Genesis quickly," James looked back at Audrey. "I wish we could do something, but we're in no shape for a fight."

She nodded in reply, but before they could say more *Tonnant* and its consorts sprinted past, sending a quick signal to *Flame* as they went. A few moments later, the comm chirped again, Fox's face appearing as the screen split.

"I've gotta run. They need me to pull Grieve out when he's finished. You two get back to Genesis."

James heaved a sigh, "Bad as it looks?"

Fox nodded somberly, "I don't think the Admiral would leave General Grieve if it wasn't."

James nodded silently, then examined the fox's face, "Thanks again, Fox. For everything."

With a certain dapper smile, Fox nodded, "It was an honor to fight with both of you."

The link cut, and *Flame* turned and accelerated away.

The strike craft shuddered as the gravity of the Hive slowly enveloped it. The ship came down fast and hard, the surface of the alien complex rushing up to meet it. At an altitude of what couldn't have been more that five meters, the ship halted in midair and two focal point lasers lanced out from its belly.

Each laser consisted of four emitters focusing on a single point, and the combined energy breached the outer armor of the complex. As the ship descended gradually to the surface, the lasers continued to work, and just as the strike craft landed they finished their job. A circular hole opened in the surface of the Hive — one exactly matching the lock on the belly of the Larosian vehicle.

Grieve's marines rose to their feet, hefting their rifles and securing their swords at their sides. Grieve led them from their cabin into the boarding chamber of the craft, where opposite him Torallis' Stealth Guards brought themselves to order.

No words were exchanged — this event had already been planned and rehearsed several times. The hatch was keyed open and the first Stealth Guardsman dropped through.

Tonnant slowed as its accompanying mixed squadron neared the Krogg armada. Felix knew the same old 'run in and shoot' trick wouldn't work against numbers so vastly superior, so he'd have to recall those dreaded war-games of his. He'd defeated superior odds on that day, but those odds hadn't been *this* bad.

"Send to Novash, tell him to fight his ships however he can. The 111th is to join us. We'll begin executing *non-standard* maneuvers..."

The explanation didn't take long. Felix's plan was simple enough to be carried out on short notice and quick enough to keep his force alive.

He hoped.

Tonnant and the 111th entered energy drive and sped inwards.

There had been a few Kroggs in the corridor beneath the ship, but the Stealth Warriors had dispatched them easily. Their entire force dropped quickly down the chute, and then with an uneasy glance at his troops, Grieve hit his shield and followed.

The Earther marines dropped into a dark tunnel with several cross connections. It took Grieve's eyes a few seconds to adjust to the blackness, but the efficiency of his natural Earther night vision paid off.

Sweeping the corridor with his rifle, the General moved into a defensive position at the corner of one of the nearby intersections. Torallis was impressed by the smoothness of the bear's movements, and even more so by the speed and ease of the rest of the Earther deployment. Within a minute, fifty Earther bears and wolves crouched in the corridor, rifles leveled, all possible angles covered.

With a nod, Grieve sent the Captain of the Stealth Guard and his troops on their way to the Queen's chamber.

In the midst of a number of Krogg Dreadnoughts, all intently bombarding the pocket which Ursla and Narosh were desperately trying to hold, *Tonnant* and the 111th exited from energy drive. Guns ran out the second matter reconstituted, and broadsides and carronades scarred the alien vessels bitterly.

The Kroggs began to swing their weapons to bear on the little squadron but it disappeared back into energy drive. One Krogg Dreadnought lay dead.

Felix sat back in his chair and swallowed, looking at the battle plot. That left only a thousand or so more to destroy. Sure, he could do that…

He watched on his plot as Novash's ships dove into a cloud of Krogg Destroyers near the armada's exterior, their antimatter guns blowing great holes in the little vessels. One Warcruiser took several volleys of spines and exploded viciously, the rest rammed their shots home, closing with the small ships to use their focal point lasers to devastating effect. Thirty Destroyers were left dead when the Larosians fell back in the face of an equal number of Dreadnoughts.

His small squadron could harass, Felix decided, but there was little good that could come of it. Ursla was pinned in, and without more firepower the would-be desk Admiral was incapable of assisting her…

If only…

The battle plot beeped to alert the bridge of the arrival of new ships.

…Caine and the First could arrive. I can almost hear the plot beeping now…

Because it actually is beeping, you fool.

Felix smiled, remembering something he'd read as a cub.

"Here comes the cavalry," he said softly.

CHAPTER 43

"Looks like we're just in time."

Orion still led the combined fleet, and aboard the 175-gun ship of the line, Setter Caine sat with narrowed eyes as he nodded to Lab Forepaw, "We are indeed."

After all the worries and doubts, his mind at last settled on a singular vision. His eyes fixed on the situation as revealed in the main battle plot, and he came to his feet, lacing his hands behind his back.

"Orders to all ships, beat to quarters. Disengage energy drive in... thirty-four seconds. We'll fight in battle group order. My compliments to Admiral Felar, she is to take command of the Third. I'll handle the First."

The commands reached the fleet almost as soon Caine gave them, and the First Lord tilted his head just a little. He watched as the Krogg Fleet, now some 1,800 ships, squeezed a defensive pocket at the mouth the hyperspace corridor. *Agamemnon's* transponder pennant was in the center of that collapsing position, along with *Joseph Barron* and *Algenon*. The Allied Fleet had fought its way in on a gamble, and now the gamble would pay off.

Tied to their bombardment positions, the Krogg ships were about to get a very unpleasant surprise.

Caine felt his mind slip into its old combat rhythm, and a familiar and only marginally uncomfortable calm settled over *Orion's* bridge. Forepaw stepped up beside the First Lord, looking to the Cruising Master, "Bring us out of energy drive. All ahead 96 pls."

"Fleet translating, sir."

Caine nodded in reply to the report, and fresh but veteran Earther ships of the line and frigates emerged into regular space on the Krogg flank. The aliens were committed to their blockade, and the combined fleet was determined to rout them.

"We're on our way, Andra," he said quietly, then added more loudly to the Signal Officer, "General broadcast: 'The Earther Navy rallies to Genesis' side. Good luck to all Allied ships; we shall carry this day.'"

The First and Third Fleets of the Earther Navy cruised to war.

Liz watched her screens as the situation was fleshed out with Earther telemetry. As Caine gave his orders to the First and Third Earther Fleets, she turned to her Comm Officer and delivered similar commands to the Provisional Fleet, "Orders: maintain fleet formation, decelerate and form battle division in twenty-eight seconds."

As she turned back to her panels, she noted *Joseph Barron's* transponder, still broadcasting the Superdreadnought's existence through the din of battle and death. Sarah was there, with Ursla at her side, fighting hard for the sake of the Larosians, and ultimately, her fellow humans.

This was the sort of day Liz Hastings had envisioned for the free Genesis Fleet. For decades she had groomed her force and dreamed of a time when she could take her ships into battle without Crusaders aboard. Thoughts of dissenters fell away now; Liz was leading her ships to what would be a defining moment. The Kroggs would be made to pay, and Genesis would play a key role...

"General broadcast from *Orion*, ma'am."

Caine's voice interrupted on the speakers, "The Earther Navy rallies to Genesis' side. Good luck to all Allied ships; we shall carry this day."

A smile crossed Liz's face, and the Genesis Provisional Fleet began its deceleration behind the Earther Navy.

"Send this in the open, Comm. 'The Kroggs won't know what hit them.'"

There were a few sharp laughs on the bridge, and Liz led her fleet towards the fray.

Agamemnon bucked as another volley slammed into its shields. The First Rate's defenses were on the verge of being overwhelmed, as were those of most of the ships in the pocket. It had been a gallant attempt, but as the last of the Larosian ships emerged into the melee it seemed painfully clear they weren't going to pull it off, and all avenues of retreat were blocked.

Getting out through the corridor meant enduring Krogg wrath while ships stood down from battle stations, deactivated external energy systems like shields, turned their backs and entered the rift. Not an option at present. It was all the carronades could do to deflect *some* of the incoming spines — without shields the fleet would be turned into a spectacular fireworks display.

The Second could withdraw under energy drive, but the Genesis Fleet had no such option. And Ursla wasn't about to abandon them. No, it would be a fight to the death.

A bloody one.

Ursla's mind struggled to find an appropriate quip to take the edge off that cold fate. But there really couldn't be one. They'd just have to die well.

Agamemnon's broadside roared again.

Joseph Barron was amazingly untouched. The Superdreadnought was fortunate in its position — near the center of the pocket, where Allied point defense was at its thickest. It was, however, running low on missiles...

Sarah gritted her teeth as another of the 100-missile volleys she launched was incinerated far from its target. They couldn't keep up the fire much longer, and the Kroggs seemed to sense this as they were already pressing in. She looked to her battle plot, saw *Harbinger Bishop* maneuver in the distance, felt a pang of fear, then turned to her Comm Chief.

"Get me Ursla!"

The bear appeared on screen seconds later, her face as grim as Sarah's.

"Get out of here, Andra. You can't do anything more. Protect Genesis."

The Admiral cocked an eyebrow and shook her head, "We won't abandon you, Sarah. We couldn't protect the planet on our own anyway. That'll be up to Setter when he gets here... if only he'd gotten here a little sooner..."

Sarah was about to protest when the sensors chirped. Her head whipped around to the plot as the screen filled with white, blue and green markers.

Caine let Forepaw fight *Orion*, while as First Lord, he focused his attention on the First Fleet. *Finally* his confidence had surfaced, and he knew they'd do well today.

The First Fleet was a magnificent sight as it crossed space. Its 600 ships were arranged in seventy-five lines abreast, and as the formation surged ahead, the silver hulls, so fresh from the yards, glowed. In the silence of space the lines of vessels seemed to weave a beautiful tapestry. Caine could see it both in the plot and in his mind's eye. It was a splendid visage... and yet one bent on destruction.

At first the Kroggs seem to ignore the newcomers, but as the great formation crossed space they were forced to take notice, and some of their rear echelons turned to face the approaching battle fleets. The seething mass of black vessels began to branch back towards *Orion*, with a seemingly disorganized horde of Krogg ships repositioning themselves to meet the new threat.

Having demonstrated its austere elegance during the advance, the First would now prove its ferocity.

"Fleet to energy drive. Let's take a page from Savanna's book."

Felix watched the approach of the combined fleet with more elation and relief than he had ever experienced before. Caine had the First drawn up in broad lines abreast, and he was cruising to the rear of the Krogg Fleet. He meant to openly challenge the aliens, and Felix had no doubt of who would triumph.

Then the First reentered energy drive.

For a second Felix was surprised, but it took only that long for the 600 ships of the Earther Navy's leading formation to reach the Krogg rearguard, and in scattered squadrons the ships of the line and frigates returned to their material state — *within* the Krogg formation. Keeping squadron order, experienced

Earther Captains avoided collision with their foe, and thus without accident, the momentum of battle shifted.

The Kroggs who had turned to confront the newly-arrived enemy were suddenly facing the wrong direction, and broadsides from the First lashed out to take advantage of their predicament. Caine wielded the fleet like a pistol, and in an elegant dance the squadrons of the First tore through nearly 200 unprepared Krogg ships.

The Third hit next. Felix saw Kella Felar's flag flying from *Endymion* at the head of that reconstituted force, and she led the attack with her usual sharpness. The Krogg rearguard was caught between two Earther Fleets, and as the broadsides began to crash home, the first alien ships took flight.

At first only a few vessels fled, but as hundreds more were incinerated by the withering fire from these two Earther formations, Krogg capital ships began to sprint from the action by the dozen. Liz Hastings' force now entered missile range off the Third's left flank, and salvos of thousands of missiles ripped through space to add to the confusion. More Kroggs began to take flight, and the noose around the corridor loosened.

The First Fleet hammered harder, as did the Third, and as the two great Earther forces sliced their way through the Krogg armada, Felix saw something he honestly hadn't expected to see. Piecemeal Krogg retreats escalated. More and more of the armada began to drain away from its blockade position, and a steady stream of the alien ships broke away from their combat stations.

Caine had turned the tide.

Standing on *Orion's* bridge, hands still laced behind his back, Caine watched the plot with silent satisfaction. Forepaw was still giving fast, incisive orders that put the First Rate's 75-gun broadsides to good use against the fleeing Krogg ships...

But the Kroggs *were* fleeing. Harvey Bingham would have his chance to unite Genesis, and Ursla would fight another day.

As though in tune with Caine's thoughts, *Orion's* First Lieutenant, standing at his post behind the Sensor Officer, turned to the First Lord, "That's it sir, they're *all* running!"

Caine took a breath and smiled, and as he did there was a rousing cheer from the bridge crew. The cheer turned into a roar, and even as *Orion* fought on, every ship in the Earther Navy was flooded with a brief swell of pride.

The day had been carried; the battle was won.

CHAPTER 44

In a dark tunnel in the Krogg Hive, Grieve held down his trigger and *kept* it down. The heavy blasts from his rifle joined a dozen others, bringing down Krogg after Krogg in the base's broad corridors.

Behind him other marines did the same, trying desperately to slow the tide of enemy soldiers that sought to break their grip on the docked strike craft. Slowing the tide they were — stopping it they certainly were not.

As one Krogg fell, another would step over the body, but hopes that the large number of alien corpses would block the corridors and form barriers were dashed when the floor actually began to *absorb* the fallen. Aside from the tactical loss of cover, it was a very disturbing process to watch, and his marines were becoming wary of remaining in any one place for too long lest the floor attempt to swallow them as well.

Grieve swung himself back around the corner, hefting his rifle out of his way as he keyed his comm link, "Torallis?"

Far down one of the corridors, Torallis and his Stealth Warriors crept silently and invisibly. Thus far the Queen had not detected them, meaning the theory that this strange mineral caused telepathic interference must be true. With their presence thus secure from telepathic detection, Torallis' party let numerous soldiers pass by so as to remain undetected. Even concealed from Krogg minds, they had to conserve their advantage for the inevitable battle with the Queen's Guard — the toughest warrior Kroggs known to the Larosians.

Torallis ordered his force to halt and they complied as he telepathically answered his comm link. *Yes?*

The thoughts were processed into a signal pulse which came out on Grieve's side as a voice.

"How long?"

The words were projected through the comm and directly into Torallis' mind — no voice was actually heard to give away their position.

The Captain looked down the hall thoughtfully. *We will reach the chamber in five minutes. When we arrive the pressure on your position will be relieved.*

"Roger. Out." Grieve heard a commotion coming up the corridor as he cut his conversation short. He swung quickly and poured energy down the hall, knocking down a few Kroggs with the help of the other marines, but it was quickly becoming clear that persistent Krogg pressure would break the firing line...

The first Krogg crashed into the Earther ranks like a battering ram, already dead but serving as a shield and distraction for his fellows. Grieve dropped his rifle and grabbed for his sword just as a Krogg blade swiped at his neck.

Flame sat silently in the space around the Hive. Aboard the little ship, Fox Magnus waited uneasily, watching the Larosian strike craft on the surface. The thought of fighting these Kroggs in person frightened him, and it was chilling to think that down there, Earthers were going blade-to-sword with them.

The chirping battle plot drew Fox's attention. As he turned to the sensor display his eyebrows shot up — he found himself looking at pennants from the First, Third and Provisional Allied Fleets. And the Krogg Fleet was running — Caine had come, and he'd driven the aliens off their blockade. Krogg ships were fleeing from the guns of the newly arrived Fleets... the Allies had won!

Well, that took the pressure off just a little...

Oh damn.

The Kroggs were in full retreat, and apparently for some of the alien ships that attempt to escape was taking them right to the Hive. Three squadrons of Dreadnoughts were scant minutes away, and they were angling in the direction of *Flame* and the massive station.

Hmm, I have eighteen guns. They're panicking and they've got about 1,000 times my firepower. Ha, Flame *can handle those odds. For five seconds at least!*

Fox wasn't impressed with his mind's dark humor, "Send to flag, we need support. Quickly, if they could."

Grieve's shield blocked the razor edge that would have decapitated him, but the force of the blow nearly snapped his neck anyway. Displeased, the General came to his feet with his sword in hand and it took him only split seconds to activate both it and his extra shields.

A barely visible, rather unsettling flame seemed to crawl around the blade as the 'chain saw' started the atoms in the air around it moving, and almost instantly Grieve thrust forward. The point of the Japanese-style sword had been leveled at the Krogg's chest, and the blade didn't even slow down as it passed through the soldier and withdrew.

As the body collapsed to be absorbed, Grieve watched most of his marines drop their guns and bring their swords into play. The corridors were suddenly lit by the eerie glow of displaced atoms.

"Extra shields — we don't want to get grazed!" Grieve called thoughtfully, swinging fast as a Krogg came at him.

The wolves and bears activated their additional shields and met the Kroggs head-on.

• • •

Torallis and his Stealth Warriors crept closer to the hatch, certain from the intelligence gathered on the last Hive attack that this was the core. The Son had been the last to assault a Queen's nest, and alone he had succeeded, though at the price of his life. Today Torallis would honor the legacy of the Larosian savior — this Queen would die.

Torallis sent the telepathic order for his Guardsmen to stand ready, stepped forward and drove his sword into the thick door protecting the Queen's chamber. The hatch sizzled as the atoms speeding around the blade disrupted it, and several more swords stabbed in, together carving a large portal through which the Warriors could gain entry.

To the rear, the first Krogg soldiers — finally detecting the invaders — came at the Larosians. The Guardsmen met them with their blades, and the Kroggs were pressed back swiftly, many left in several states of dismemberment on the deck.

As the hatch breach was completed, Torallis led his Guardsmen through without delay.

For the Son!

None of the Warriors had any illusions as to their chances of escaping the chamber. They expected the Queen to be protected by the Queen's Guard, Kroggs of unsurpassed ferocity and physical power. Aside from the Son, only Stealth Warriors, the elite of the service, truly had a chance against such menaces… and even in their case, it would be a battle to survive long enough to set off their charge.

So as Torallis entered the chamber he expected a surge of enemies, and a sense of imminent death.

One that certainly did *not* come.

The massive chamber, designed to hold the mother of the Krogg people, her super-powerful guards, her Warlords and her retainers, was completely empty.

It took only seconds for understanding to sink in — the attack on this complex had been easy and there had been no additional guard ships or soldiers because there was *no Queen* here. She must have left this Hive…

Torallis felt his mind freeze for an instant — the whole operation had been a waste.

Taking the antimatter charge carried by one of his Guardsmen, Torallis set the bomb down on the chamber floor and activated it, setting it for remote detonation. Although there was no Queen to destroy, many Krogg warriors would still be killed by this blast.

Some consolation, at least.

Satisfied with the device's placement, Torallis turned and led his Guards back through the portal, up the corridor to the strike craft.

• • •

Orion, *Agamemnon*, *Endymion*, *Lycaeon*, and *Algenon*, all First Rates that were far more heavily armed than most of their class, as well as *Tonnant*, the 111th, and three squadrons of 74s came out of energy drive just short of *Flame*.

The Krogg ships had picked up stragglers and now a group of several dozen Dreadnoughts and escorts were hurtling towards the Hive.

Fox Magnus allowed himself a long sigh of relief, sitting back in his chair with a slight smile. These Dreadnoughts wouldn't have an easy time if they attempted to come to the aid of their Queen — Earther flagships made for a potent force, which was undoubtedly why Caine had brought them to *Flame's* side.

"Thirty seconds out, skipper. The First Rates are running out their guns."

Nodding in reply to the report, Fox turned to the Master, "Present the starboard broadside."

With a cocked eyebrow the Cruising Master nodded, "Aye sir."

For whatever it was worth, diminutive little *Flame* would add to the–

"Skipper, the Dreadnoughts are reversing course... they're going up and over!"

Fox frowned — *what?* Were they coming at the Hive from another angle? He came out of his chair and walked to the main battle plot. The Krogg vessels had veered upwards, staying just out of range. They now accelerated over the Earther force and continued on their way at a blistering speed, entering hyper as soon as they cleared the asteroid belt.

They hadn't even fired a shot... in defense of their Queen?

Grieve was becoming increasingly adept with the blade, as were his marines. Their ability was such that they were pushing the Kroggs involuntarily down the halls, taking ground from the aliens without fatalities of their own.

The swords made the difference. Krogg blades were able to deflect the atom chain saws, but only if they struck the flat sides of the sword — any contact with the blades or the points and Krogg armor offered no protection. As such, they finally became aware of the futility of attacking the Earther position. The Earthers were too strong, and in such close quarters with bottlenecked access points, the Kroggs could not take advantage of their extra arms and blades.

Grieve, the Queen is gone. It appears she has not been here for some time.

Torallis' message, vocalized through the General's comm, came as quite a surprise. He paused as the report reached his ear, "This a trap then?"

Unlikely, based on what we've encountered... or what we have not encountered. There has been no counter-check. I imagine the Kroggs were simply using this complex as a defense station for their fleet grazing field.

Grieve grunted, "Well, I suppose we should blow it anyway. How far out are you?"

About five minutes.

...

"No *Queen*?"

Ursla didn't think to conceal her surprise, and Artemis Tigar nodded, "General Grieve just informed *Flame*. The Hive's empty."

The bridge was still stirring with relief after having been pulled from the jaws of destruction only minutes before, and the report that this objective had been a mere distraction brought frowns and confusion. If it was a trap, it didn't seem to be a very good one — the Krogg Fleet was running fast and hard out of the system.

Based on what Novash had told Ursla about the last Queen his people had faced, the alien super-telepath masterminded wars and then sent her Kroggs to fight. The development of Genesis as an ambush site suggested to Ursla that the Queen who had once resided in the system was now out *there* somewhere, running Krogg combat operations from another Hive.

And Genesis would never be safe while she was alive, which meant the Allied Fleet would have to go after her...

Well, that was a lot to assume in the last minutes of the biggest fleet engagement the Earther Navy had ever seen. Concerns about the survival of the Queen could be left to another day; right now they had to extract Grieve's team and secure this solar system.

"Pass that information along to *Orion*, Artie. Just in case they didn't pick up the broadcast."

Ursla released another deep breath and slumped slightly in her chair.

One marine was bleeding, but the wound to his hand was minor. Grieve patted the bear on the back as they both climbed the chute into the strike craft. Nodding to Torallis as they returned to its passenger deck, Grieve keyed the lock shut.

"Any of yours wounded, Torallis?" the General stood up and slung his rifle.

The Captain-Elite replied evenly, "Two minor wounds; they are receiving treatment in the medical compartment."

Grieve gestured to his wounded marine, "One of mine got a cut to the hand — he got blindsided and his first shield went down before the other two went up. Can your facilities handle minor cuts?"

The Captain nodded, and Grieve turned to the bear, "Head down back; you should put that back together again..."

The marine grinned, "It's alright General, really."

Grieve leaned in close, "Now be *polite*, Borth."

With a smile and a brief nod, the marine paced down the passenger compartment to the rear bay, and found two Larosians carefully treating themselves. One looked up at him and offered a bow-nod. *You fought well, comrade.*

The marine didn't hear the thought, but got the impression he'd missed something. The Larosian, not focused enough to reproduce human speech after the ordeal, simply took the marine's hand. Silver blood mixed with red, and the two soldiers nodded to each other in appreciation of their feats.

Watching the exchange from down the hall, Grieve glanced at Torallis, "We did alright then?"

The Captain of the Guards approximated a smile, "Very well."

Get this craft off the Hive!

The strike craft lifted from the Hive's side as Ursla pondered, leaving a hole that opened part of the complex to space.

"Destruct signal being sent from the craft, ma'am."

"All ships, brace yourselves…"

Nothing happened.

Before Ursla could think, a signal came from the strike craft and Grieve appeared in the main holo tank on *Agamemnon's* bridge.

"Well?" Ursla's clipped question betrayed her anxiousness.

Grieve's face appeared slightly amused, despite his evident fatigue, "It appears our boy Torallis put the bomb on the *floor*, which we think absorbed and disarmed it."

Ursla cocked an eyebrow in a mix of surprise and disconcertion, "So we'll have to do it the hard way?"

Grieve nodded and cut the link.

Ursla turned to Tigar, "One last thing to take care of."

A moment later, the Earther force turned its broadsides on the Hive, and battered the defenseless base to smithereens.

CHAPTER 45

Ursla was exhausted, her mind aching, her mood generally unenthusiastic and bordering on despondent. The fight had taken a lot out of her — perhaps more even than her fights in Earth space — because so many lives had depended on her decisions here in Genesis, and because so many lives had been lost.

Pacing through *Orion's* corridors on her way to a debriefing, Ursla couldn't keep the casualty lists out of her mind. Of the Larosian Fourth Fleet-of-War, 900 ships remained in serviceable condition; of Sarah's Genesis Fleet, about 500 were still in fighting shape; and of the Second Fleet, only 300 of Ursla's original 600 ships had survived.

Given the odds they'd all faced at the opening of the action, the losses could be described as acceptable. But while that was a statistically accurate claim, Ursla wouldn't let herself accept it when half her ships were gone, and fully one-third of her crews *lost*. Unlike the engagement at Pluto's Orbital Plane, the fighting here had been too quick and close to allow many Earthers to reach their lifeboats at the destruction of their ships, which just added another dark element to the action.

There was a deeply tragic side to this victory, and all Ursla could think of were the thousands of Earther volunteers, loyal human spacers, and veteran Larosian warriors who were dead. Perhaps to a more experienced commander her concerns might have seemed amateur and pointless, but the tragedy and loss weighed heavily on her. She was confident she'd done right here, and saved many lives by stopping the Kroggs wholesale, but it was still a bitter price to pay.

In any case, it was done... at least for now. The Kroggs were running, though if Genesis and Earth were to be safe from potential retaliation, the Allied Fleet would likely have to go after them. Based on what Novash had told her of the strategic situation in the Larosian galaxy, their fleets were occupied clearing thousands of star systems of Krogg influence. This galaxy qualified as a sideshow — one with which the Earthers could help.

But that's a decision for another time, not now. We have to rally first. We'll be of no use to anyone without reorganizing.

Ursla's mind restored its focus as she came to the door of *Orion's* main briefing room. Stopping, she calmed herself with a deep breath, then entered the room somewhat stiffly. The only other occupant was Setter himself. The

First Lord, seeing her arrival, quickly stood and walked over to her, extending his hand with a relieved smile. The very gesture seemed to take the edge off Ursla's anxiety, and she took his hand gratefully.

"Glad to see you're well, Andra," Caine's voice was quiet and meaningful.

Ursla nodded, "Glad you showed up when you did."

An understanding smile crossed Caine's face, "We got here later than I'd have liked."

He waved to the table and the pair began to move. "Your losses... I regret not being able to mitigate them, Andra. Any word on how bad?"

As the two found chairs at the briefing room's massive table, Ursla recalled the all-too-familiar statistics in her head, "Jax Furgus' ship didn't survive. I think Varnon lost a leg. I don't know about Talone yet, or the human officers. We're having a lot of trouble with comms and wreckage... as for ships, just about fifty percent casualties for everyone."

Caine's ears twitched, "Indeed. We paid for this... paid dearly. I think we'll have many more dead Earthers after this fight than we had at Pluto's Orbital Plane... the Kroggs didn't seem inclined to give us time to get to the pods, or to leave the intact ones alone."

Ursla's gaze dropped to the table itself and she nodded slowly, "A lot of good people."

It was something that warranted reflection; the Earthers weren't at home this time and couldn't simply justify lost lives with the certain understanding they were protecting Earth's wellbeing...

"It's easy to forget why we're out here," Ursla admitted after a moment, and Caine offered a slow nod.

"When it comes to it, though, the crews we lost were the ones who remembered best our pledge. They lived it to the end, and I imagine they've saved Genesis. As have you, and the rest of the Second, Andra. You did a damned fine thing out here, and I think the Genesis Fleet will be the first to say that..."

For a second Ursla thought about that, then her mind shifted momentarily from its brooding, "How can *they* say it first when you just did?"

Caine paused, blinked, and then chuckled, "Well I'm sure they'll say it sometime in the top five then."

As if to emphasize the statement, Liz Hastings came through the briefing room door. The weary ArcGeneral instantly smiled at her dearest Earther friends, then went to Ursla and offered a pat on the huge Admiral's back, "Good to see you Andra!"

Ursla smiled and nodded in reply, "Likewise... especially considering the circumstances."

Hastings took a seat down the table next to Caine, "We should have gotten here sooner; my ships were just a bit too slow."

Caine frowned at her in reply, "Hardly the case. Your ships were as well handled as any I've seen."

"Come on, Setter, you don't need to–"

Sarah came through the door unsteadily. All eyes turned to her, and the collected senior officers immediately recognized her fatigue. They also saw some disillusionment. Her brow furrowed as she eyed the people present.

"Good day, all," her voice was soft and almost painfully detached. "Rather a slaughter, wasn't it?"

The comment was neither bitter nor aggressive — Sarah's frayed mind was just in need of sleep. She'd spent hours combing wreckage and trying to pull her fleet back together. After personally having examined so many broken hulls, debris fields, and floating corpses in space, she needed to focus on something else — *anything* else.

The Kroggs had been as vicious as their reputation, and it was only a miracle of timing that had saved the Allied Fleet from annihilation. As far as Sarah could tell in her current state of exhaustion, there weren't too many ways to put a positive spin on that... except to acknowledge she was still alive.

"If you want to put it that way," Ursla's soft reply hid her own deep discomfort, and Sarah nodded slowly.

The young ArcGeneral collapsed into a chair next to her counterpart Admiral and leaned back into the Earther cushions, trying not to think about the number of ships she'd lost *this* time.

"Well, our ships are out searching now," Caine's tone was soothing. He'd already had to conquer a number of his own demons after the death of the Crusaders in Earth space, and he well understood the discomfort of those around him. "We'll find more survivors, of that I'm sure."

Sarah looked grimly at the First Lord, and Caine resisted the urge to frown as he met her troubled eyes. The fatigue and the death was beginning to wear away at the ArcGeneral. It was sad to see one so young and able in such a position.

He hoped for her. He hoped she could get past the bloodletting.

"I hope so," she said simply, almost as though she knew his thoughts, and he offered a silent nod.

Pat absently rubbed his neck, watching the short-range sensors as *Harbinger Bishop* picked through the wreckage that had been part of his squadron. Occasionally they'd find a life pod and bring it aboard, but all too often the fields of debris were devoid of life.

What remained of his squadron was cruising with him, though only seven of his Battlecruisers were still capable of carrying out the mission. Four more were limping towards yards at the asteroid belt, and might one day see service again. For now, what remained of the force floated through blood and gore, debris and lifeless pods, hoping to find survivors. *Any* survivors.

What... do I have to say please for the universe to show some mercy? Gods, there are so many empty pods... Praise Gods, at least Sarah's not out there.

Even as *Bishop* floated through this scene of utter destruction, part of Pat was wondering about Sarah... wondering how she was coping... wondering where they'd end up when this all ended... wondering whether she had any idea of how to cope with such a bloodbath, because he certainly wasn't finding the adjustment easy...

"Active pod to starboard, skipper."

"Bring it in."

Felix hadn't been part of the clash of fleets out at Pluto's Orbital Plane, so he had no firsthand experience with the kind of slaughter left in the wake of such a battle. *Tonnant* and the 111th had come through the entire action today virtually unscathed, and now they were helping the limping survivors of the Allied Fleet make it to Genesis yards. Two of those survivors, thankfully, were the newly commissioned privateers *Archangel Sword* and *Grendelsbane City*; they'd slid slowly from the field under the protection of Earther guns.

James Stanton and Audrey DeBrooke would be treated as Earther Captains when they reached repair ports, and Felix planned to check on them to make sure all was well once *Grendelsbane* found a yard slip.

For now, though, his presence was required at the meeting on *Orion*. The big First Rate's flight bay had just swallowed his pinnace and he'd be heading to his debriefing in a minute. At some point in the future he'd have time to reflect on the fighting he'd done in the last weeks... just not now.

There was much to be learned from days like this, and as a good administrator and even better line Admiral, Savanna Felix meant to understand everything he could. Eventually.

Captain-Commodore Novash guided his fighter into the bay of the *Lycrotar* with precision befitting an officer of his rank. Admiral-of-a-Fleet Narosh waited in the bay for the junior commander, hoping for insight into the new circumstances surrounding the war. Such complex impressions could not easily be communicated between ships, even for two Larosians as experienced as Narosh and Novash. Besides, Narosh favored this young Captain-Commodore, and so following the Son's example, he enjoyed personal meetings with officers of promise under his command.

Thus, a certain muted pleasure pervaded Narosh's mind as he watched Novash descend from his fighter, cross the flight deck, and come to attention.

At ease, Captain-Commodore. You have been through quite an ordeal.

Novash relaxed with a telepathic undertone of thanks, then reported his news. *I am sorry we failed, Admiral-of-a-Fleet. Our best estimates now suggest the new*

Queen had abandoned before we even arrived here...

Narosh digested the news in silence. There was certainly another Queen, but her current location — even in intergalactic terms — remained a mystery. She could be anywhere, but she would be found. The Larosians might fight for eons to locate her, but she would pay for the millions, *billions* of deaths, and for the sacrifices demanded from Praaxus and the Son. Honor would be satisfied.

Your appraisal of the Earthers, and these humans, Captain-Commodore? Will the former join this war, and are the latter fit to follow in the Son's legacy?

Novash thought about the question for a second. *I believe both are capable, and both will fight... I can provide my thoughts on this matter to you, sir.*

Narosh digested Novash's impressions of both newly-found groups as they were offered up by the Captain-Commodore's mind, and he came to understand his comrade's respect for and silent confidence in these aliens... as well as the ineffable, *instinctive* trust in them.

Most interesting. I will look forward to speaking with them. There is much to discuss...

Narosh contemplated the new possibilities for war — they were more positive than before.

Perhaps the Fourth had found a decisive ally.

CHAPTER 46

Two days after the last ships of the Allied Fleet limped into the space around Genesis, Lord High Chancellor Harvey Bingham sat on a pinnace awaiting liftoff. The Chancellor had ridden out the battle in his quarters aboard *Orion*, and he had to admit the massive engagement had revived some less-than-pleasant memories of the Church's fight against Earthers in the open space on the Pluto Orbital Plane.

But the fleets of the new Earther-Genesis Alliance had survived, he reminded himself. They were battered and bruised, but they were certainly alive. And now he would fight his own battle to ensure their welcome in Genesis space.

The pinnace was running preflight checks as Bingham waited, and he found that under the circumstances, even the Earther seats were a little uncomfortable. He was so preoccupied that he failed to notice Liz Hastings enter the pinnace behind him.

"Good morning, High Chancellor," Hastings said with the curt politeness that had become her standard.

Bingham jumped at the unexpected greeting, looked behind him and nodded, "Good day, ArcGeneral."

He turned back and tried once more to get comfortable in his chair while Hastings took a seat behind him. For a few moments he sat silently, again contemplating his upcoming confrontation with the Chancellors' Council... until it occurred to him he had no idea why the ArcGeneral was sitting in his pinnace.

Bingham turned again, "Umm, might I ask what you're doing here?"

Hastings, who was reading through files with a frown, didn't bother to look up, "I was of the opinion that seeing the original ArcGeneral who had commanded the fleet might help your case. Make it seem less likely you'd been brainwashed by the Earthers."

Bingham paused at that, "Maybe if Shappa Bactule was here, it'd have that effect. You're more likely to face unfortunate questioning and be treated badly. I don't think you should have to endure that."

Hastings wasn't entirely sure what to think of that comment. She had actually decided to go with Bingham to make sure he didn't betray the Allies, though it wouldn't be politic to tell him that in so many words. And yet from the sound of his voice he was genuinely concerned for her well-being.

"Nothing new, High Chancellor. I've faced the Council before."

Bingham sighed heavily, then decided the ArcGeneral's presence offered him a chance to demonstrate his transformation. A definite opportunity then. Resigning himself to Hastings' company, Bingham shifted in his lumpy chair.

The Chancellors' Hall was the most elaborate building in the capital city of the Genesis Colony. Constructed of local alloys, it had a brown-green tinge despite its coat of red paint. In the center of an open square, and designed to look like the Unity National... *United Nations* buildings of Earth's twenty-first century, the great structure was a focal point for the culture of the entire planet.

As Bingham and Hastings stepped out of the Church hover car onto the long paved walk that led to its main door, a crowd of faithful citizens watched in silent awe from behind a perimeter of Crusaders. Bingham had ordered the Chancellors' Council to maintain silence about his impending arrival — he had no desire to hold a media event, given the circumstances surrounding his return — but evidently some citizens had heard of the meeting that was about to take place. It was a small group compared to ones he'd seen in past years, and it probably represented the most faithful of Genesis citizens.

Just the people Bingham would have to work the hardest to change.

Sporting his new, far less intimidating uniform, Bingham walked beside Hastings instead of taking a position ahead of her — a visible gesture of equality that drew confused and shocked murmurs from the crowd.

As the pair entered the building and paced down the central corridor, Crusaders came smartly to attention in recognition of the High Chancellor, while ignoring the Naval officer as if she wasn't even present. The icy relationship between the classes was very much alive on Genesis, Hastings decided. She'd been spoiled by the fairness of life with the Earthers.

Bingham, for his part, ignored the Crusaders completely, and marched determinedly down the hall. At the far end of the long passage lay the doors to the Council Room, where the entire Chancellery was waiting for him.

Each step seemed to make the High Chancellor's heart beat faster, and he found his confidence growing as he remembered something of his past. He *had* been a great leader, and perhaps he could still be one — a *better* one, even. The doors drew closer, and he felt his stride quicken. The boots of the ArcGeneral followed behind him, their raps against the floor quickening with his.

The Crusaders stationed by the doors at the hall's end moved to open them as he neared, and the great chamber, lit by the daylight streaming through its windows and sporting a view of the capital unparalleled anywhere else in the city, appeared. At a long table beneath that window, the Chancellors sat staring at him.

Though his mind was abruptly flooded with memories of the choices he'd made in this place, Bingham didn't slow as he neared the door. The two Crusaders stepped to a ready position as he passed, leveling their guns at Hastings.

"Present yourself, scum," one of them growled.

Without thought, Bingham turned on the Crusader, using one hand to force his rifle down and the other to clutch the man's shoulder, "Show respect man — you are addressing the *ArcGeneral* of the Genesis Navy, a great servant of the *Gods*."

The other Crusader froze immediately, then slowly lowered his weapon. Bingham released the shocked Church warrior, then looked back to Hastings with a dark scowl... which she somehow understood wasn't directed at her personally.

"ArcGeneral, please ignore these unenlightened heathen."

The Crusaders were blanching beneath their hoods, and now both backed away reluctantly, their shock translating into jerky movements.

When Bingham turned back to his assembled Chancellors, the dozen men were staring at him, mouths open and wordless.

Bingham's throne sat at the head of the table, but nearing it, he decided not to sit. As the doors closed behind him he stepped forward a few paces, then eyed his old colleagues. "*Friends*, it is truly heartwarming to again be at *home*," he offered an almost pleasant smile.

One of the older Chancellors managed to speak, his face twisted in disgust, "What is *that*?"

His old finger stabbed towards Hastings, and Bingham's smile faded, "I thought I'd just explained that, Chancellor Pious. *She* is ArcGeneral Hastings, of the Genesis Fleet, and I expect you've already been introduced to her. Much to her displeasure, I would suspect."

Hastings wasn't sure who was more shocked — herself or the Chancellors.

"But... she's... no woman... no Naval officer... here..." the incoherence of Pious' stammering actually amused Bingham.

"But what?" a twinkle came to Bingham's eye. "Oh of *course*. I know what horrible offense you're mumbling about..." he whirled on Hastings, drawing relieved sighs from the Council. For her part, the ArcGeneral stiffened. Bingham smiled and nodded curtly at her, "Would you care to sit down?" One of the High Chancellor's hands grabbed the back of his throne-chair and the other offered the seat to Hastings.

Shocked, she just stood there.

Understandable, Bingham decided. His actions were flying in the face of centuries of tradition, but he needed to rattle the Council and make an impression, else he would never be able to assert his control.

Bingham turned from Hastings to see all but one face — Second Chancellor Argyle, the most moderate — looking as if they'd seen a ghost. Or a demon.

"Brother Chancellors, whatever is wrong?"

Mouths moved in attempts to form words until one voice finally came out, again that of Pious, the most traditional Chancellor on the Council, "This is a travesty, High Chancellor! How can you bring that scum in here? How dare you make a mockery of this Council and all it stands for!"

Feeling the passion of indignation, something Bingham had mistakenly interpreted as the power of the Gods in his younger years, the Chancellor thrust himself to his feet, and a half dozen more joined him. "You may have encountered amazing things on the Holy Quest, High Chancellor, but this borders on *heresy*! I will not stand for it—"

"Will you not, indeed?" Bingham's tone sliced sharply into his subordinate. "Damn your insolence, Chancellor — you have no place telling *me* what the edicts of this Church are! I have spent the last eight months fulfilling *prophecy*. The Gods have shown *me* what we have been doing right, *and* what mistakes we have made!"

The Chancellors froze at the rage in their leader's voice. Bingham let his words sink in, watching three of the challengers descend bewildered into their seats. Argyle met his eyes with interest.

Pious spoke up again, "We would not tell you your place, High Chancellor, just hers. And it seems to some of us that you have changed… you are not the man you were when you left us."

Bingham rounded the table evenly, silencing the man with his stare.

"Surprising what the Gods do for you when you fulfill prophecy, isn't it?" again his words cut quick.

The man swallowed and sat, and Bingham began to pace around the table, staring down every Chancellor one at a time.

"We arrived at Earth, brothers, to find a great obstacle between our Quest and our victory. I will have to explain this at length, but for now it should suffice to say that the Earthers, those noble creatures you have barred from this world, met us on the Gods' behalf. They told us we were unworthy of Earth because of the *division* in our society — because we could not stand together. But now, united, our people live in harmony on Earth with the Earthers. Millions of Crusaders and, until this recent battle, countless thousands of Naval humans. And it is the paradise prophecy promised us."

Glares came from virtually all the Chancellors as the abridged story was delivered, but Bingham matched them all with a cool, paternal gaze, "I *told* Admiral Ursla to blame our strife on the Kroggs, but it was in fact the Church that nearly failed prophecy — while the Navy pledged its commitment to Earth, our Shappas and Shaspas fought the *Earthers*, the arbiters of the *Gods*. And because of their foolishness, many, including Elias Bactule, were killed. Yet the Earthers accepted us, Navy and Church, on their world. Prophecy is fulfilled, and union of society is the vehicle."

Bingham came to a stop next to Hastings, and eyes shifted from the High

Chancellor to the ArcGeneral and back. The balding human offered a thin smile, "My duty now is to remake our society, to create a paradise here, to see the will of the Gods done at last. Elizabeth Hastings is similarly bound, as are all humans. And the Earthers have come to aid us, as they proved with their deaths two days ago. This is the dawn of a new age for humanity, brothers; a new epoch of cooperation and union. As the sun rises tomorrow, I shall go to the people with my words, and none shall stand against the fulfillment of Gods' will."

Silence settled over the table with Bingham's last statement, and the Chancellors looked to each other. Some of the more moderates appeared at least to be neutral, but men like Pious and his fellows exchanged dark scowls. At last that old conservative ringleader glared up at Bingham, "You speak for the *Gods* in this matter, High Chancellor? Or the *Earthers?*"

Bingham bristled, but surprisingly Benjamin Argyle came to his feet. Probably the most moderate man to sit with the Chancellery for two generations, he felt immediately compelled to rally to his superior's side, "Lord Pious, you reproach the *Gods* with your remarks! Have not we seen it already — have not the Earthers given us the means to free ourselves of Krogg treachery? They *are* the servants of the Gods, it is plain. And that you question our greatest leader as he stands before you with our Quest *fulfilled* casts into question *your* faith. I speak here for myself: if the Gods demand that we unite our people to serve them, I shall do all I may unto death to unite this planet. All men of faith should stand with the Chancellor, and the *Gods!*"

The quiet was restored, and conservative Chancellors began to exchange quick, almost panicked glances. And then Argyle's moderate comrades came to their feet, one at a time, each reciting the words with somber tones, "I stand with the Chancellor, and with the Gods."

Only four remained in their seats, and Bingham's eyes settled on them. An enormous pride began to swell in his chest — not because he'd changed the minds of his fellows, but because the majority were willing to give this new union of peoples a *chance.* Much would have to be done to turn vision into reality and this Council was but one stage... But it was a start, an important start.

Pious came slowly to his feet after another moment, with his fellow hard conservatives standing too, "We stand for the *Gods.*"

Not willing to recognize my radical authority, then? As I expected, I will have to deal with these men in harsher terms–

Bingham's musing was halted as Liz Hastings, until now silent and wide-eyed at this rather remarkable exchange between the leaders of her nemesis institution, placed a hand on the High Chancellor's shoulder, "If I may..."

There were gasps from the Chancellors, all appalled that a *Naval woman* dared make contact with a Chancellor's person, but Bingham merely nodded, shrouding his surprise in his cool stare at Pious, "By all means."

Liz's eyes narrowed as she stepped forward, and her gaze swept from the moderate Chancellors to lock with the burning eyes of Pious, "You're a fool, and an ass. And my Naval 'scum' have long *known* that. You can't see what the High Chancellor has accomplished, can you? He has unequivocally secured the cooperation of the Navy, under the guidance of the Gods. I stand with the Chancellor because the union he brings serves to empower humanity, and makes fulfillment of the Gods' will possible. The Genesis Navy is pledged to the service of that will, as are the Crusaders on Earth. If as you say, you stand for the Gods, then you stand for the High Chancellor. If you resist his leadership, my Navy and your own Crusaders will crush you in a divine whirlwind."

Bingham barely contained his surprise at the abrupt threat, delivered with such force in this chamber. Had she gone too far — driven away the supporting moderates who had already pledged themselves?

Shocked glances were being traded, but Argyle was quick to intervene, "You see what anger disunion breeds? Holy fury is unleashed amongst *faithful* people, and we are wrong if we do not acknowledge that fact. To me it seems clear that all the humans of the Quest understand the new vision laid out for us by the Gods. I do not doubt its sanctity, and I will by no means resist it. Will any of you?"

There was silence, and Pious' wide-eyed expression revealed the rage he was trying desperately to contain. Two of his compatriots, however, slowly began shaking their heads. If the Navy had fully pledged themselves to the Church, and to the Chancellor, despite their well-established reputation for poor faith, this new vision must truly be as great as Bingham claimed.

Only Chancellors Pious and Paine stood aloof, and the room remained tense around them. Bingham's eyes shifted between the pair of conservatives — having two holdouts wasn't bad, considering the size of the change he was proposing. By sheer force of personality, he'd driven them this far; now he needed to restore some calm. This redirection could never be finished in a day.

"The Gods will forgive skepticism, I think, brothers, for there is much evidence yet to come. I thank you all who stand with me now; your faith is strong and wise. I believe, though, that soon we will *all* stand together in the service of the Gods, and this vision will reach out and grasp Genesis. Our new world will be a great utopian paradise, as Earth is. Gods' will: may it be done."

And somehow, Liz Hastings believed what Harvey Bingham was saying. Her outburst hadn't really been a bluff, and now, as the tension in the room at last seemed to ebb, only one word came to her mind.

Amen.

The Chancellors and the ArcGeneral found seats and began to speak.

CHAPTER 47

Fox Magnus was quite happy to be the first Earther to board *Genesis One* without official business. Humans in the corridors watched him with interest, many of them never having seen an Earther in person before, and he courteously nodded to each of them as they stared.

Though none of the humans could have known it, he had another reason to feel rather pleased with himself today. He was, after all, wearing an extra pip on his collar — Commander Fox Magnus had been promoted to *Post Captain* Fox Magnus, and soon he'd be given command of a 74-gun ship.

Part of him knew he'd miss the agile little *Flame*, but another part knew he was leaving it in good hands. Lieutenant Claw had been promoted to command of the sloop, so the diminutive ship's reputation would be preserved in Fox's absence.

Between the promising future for his first command, and the promise of a new ship of the line under his orders, Fox would have plenty to talk about when he met with a couple of Captains he'd recently become quite fond of.

Now that the fleet was in Genesis space, the *Bloody Pulsar* was becoming a popular site for informal meetings. It wasn't the only bar orbiting the planet — each *Genesis* station had one — but it was the most famous. No one really knew why, though most people suggested it had something to do with the name. It had also been the first to publish a welcome to all crews of the Allied Fleet, race not withstanding, and it had been bubbling over with business ever since. Mainly human crews without ships or on shore leave had passed through — Earthers not having any experience with alcoholic drinks — but that was about to change.

Fox entered the bar quietly, trying to be inconspicuous. Despite his best efforts, there wasn't a single human in the bar who *didn't* notice him — he was a giant *fox* after all. The bright red hair tended to tip people off, even if (or perhaps *especially* if) they were inebriated.

A hundred eyes fixed on Fox as he came through the door, and as they did he froze, his mind flipping a coin to choose between fight or flee…

"I'm buying him the first drink!" one spacer roared through the curious silence, and then a rumble filled the room as interested spacers swamped him, trying to shake his hand, asking him questions, offering him drinks…

Fox found himself being swept to the bar and plopped onto a stool, demands for answers and stories from the battle coming at rapid fire. He didn't disapprove of the attention.

When Felix arrived in the establishment ten minutes later, he found the enterprising Captain Magnus holding the entire bar in utter suspense with his tale of *Flame's* flight from the Kroggs. In fact, Felix appeared just in time for the new Captain to point to him and say, "That's the Admiral who got me out of it!"

Felix was duly surrounded and overwhelmed.

An hour later the two Earthers sat at a corner table having related their stories and graciously accepted the pungent beverages thrust before them. With supreme tact, they'd managed not to drink any of the foul-smelling liquids.

Felix, having recovered from his somberness of recent days, laughed heartily, enjoying the friendly atmosphere, "I wonder where they are... they said they'd meet us an hour ago."

Fox shrugged, "We were surrounded by a mob an hour ago. They probably came and left again, but I'm sure they won't abandon us."

The Earthers were referring to the two privateer Captains who had insisted that Fox and Felix share a drink with them in thanks for all they'd done. James and Audrey had made it to Genesis safely, where they'd been welcomed as damaged Allied ships, despite their lack of Genesis Navy status. The goodwill had been appreciated, though both doubted it would last long after the battle's fallout was cleared away.

Grendelsbane City would be laid up for weeks, but it had suffered only a dozen fatalities despite its troubles. Once it was back in open space, the Heavy Cruiser would join *Sword* in some other renegade misadventure, but for now its crew — and its Captain — were relatively idle. Stanton had thought it a good idea to track down the new Captain and the desk Admiral and demand they meet at the *Pulsar* — a haunt James reported to be a great old favorite.

Aside from the near-poison being served at the bar, the appraisal of the establishment seemed fair.

Felix opened his mouth to confirm Fox's remark when he spotted two humans wearing the uniforms of the Genesis Navy and the pips of the Earther service walking slowly into the bar. The other humans present were too occupied to notice the anomaly of Earther tabs on non-Earthers, so the newcomers were mercifully ignored by the crowd.

In the lead, James panned the room, finding Fox quickly. He grinned and led Audrey to the corner table.

"Looked like a mob in here when we arrived, so we decided to come back a little later."

Felix grinned, "Wise, I think."

The four officers conversed for a time, recounting tales and laughing over bad jokes. They were as comfortable with each other as old friends. James had even noticed the twitching noses and ears of the Earthers as liquor arrived, and discreetly ordered them water.

After an hour of pleasant conversation, the inevitable questions finally surfaced.

"So I really have to ask, James, Audrey, what are you two going to do now?"

The human pair shared a glance and James shrugged, "We'll probably keep looking for a place to settle down. Set up a base to keep us in business."

"Still sure you want to stay detached?" Fox's question was delivered in a pleasant tone, and it was met by adamant nods.

"Don't get us wrong, we really love being around you guys," Audrey said in answer. "But even after all this, I don't think we're ready to have the Genesis Fleet dictate our involvement from here on. We'd rather serve with Earther pennants flying... it's much simpler."

Fox leaned back in his chair and nodded, "I can understand that. Well, you've got friends in high places..." the fox's thumb stabbed at Felix, "...I think you'll be able to get whatever supplies you need."

Felix smiled and shrugged, "Send me a list, I doubt the Admiralty will mind at all. You've long since proven yourselves."

The human Captains chuckled, James picking up, "We'll see. So what are you two up to now *Captain* Magnus? You haven't told us what kind of ship you'll have!"

Fox grinned, bobbing his head, "I'm getting my very own 74. I'll be able to cause a whole lot more trouble, I think."

"I'll bet," Audrey offered him a matching smile.

"I'm to be given the Third Fleet," Felix said a bit hesitantly.

The table paused, Fox looking at his comrade, "The whole thing?"

Felix shrugged, "Yep. Kella Felar commands the First, Ursla the Second. Varnon Broadpaw was in command of the Third, but since it was being rebuilt when the Allied Fleet shipped out here he decided to come along to back up Ursla. Now he has to head home to get a new leg, and Caine's keeping the Third in action... so he has to give it to someone. And that's me, I suppose."

The three listeners chuckled at the Admiral's apparent lack of self-appreciation. Finally, James lifted his glass, "I'll drink to that!"

Audrey tapped her glass to his, and then they waited for the two Earthers to catch on and raise their own mugs. The glasses clanged together in an old ritual.

A few hours later, when the time came for the four battle-forged friends to part, they shook hands.

"If you need backup, give us a call anytime," Stanton said seriously, and both Earthers nodded in reply.

"Good luck, James, Audrey," Fox was the first to say it, and Felix nodded in solemn agreement.

"It has been an honor. Good hunting to you both."

The human pair smiled in reply, feeling rather lucky at the twist of fate that had brought them to this time and place.

"I'm pretty sure the honor was ours, gentlemen," Stanton offered his own meaningful nod.

"And good luck to both of you out there," Audrey said simply.

They exchanged final nods, and then the new friends parted ways.

CHAPTER 48

In an entirely more reputable section of Genesis space, another group of friends was about to meet to catch up. Why Graham Manchester was being included in the group, he wasn't quite sure. He felt somewhat like a fifth wheel, but Sarah had insisted he join the elite gathering, and he knew turning down the invitation would not be a good idea.

His sister was part of an exclusive, albeit unofficial 'club', and Graham did have to admit that inclusion in it seemed like a positive thing — he'd be on good terms with the greatest Earther and human leaders in the Alliance. At the very least it could be beneficial for his career; at best he'd grow to like these people.

So he'd arrived on *Orion* in his pinnace, landing only seconds after Sarah, seconds before Pat, and a minute ahead of ArcGeneral Hastings herself. He'd descended his ship's ramp to a bustling bay and had been immediately awed by the sheer size of the First Rate — *Agamemnon*, by comparison, was small.

He'd found Sarah almost by chance in the mighty landing cavern, and had waited with her, watching the incredibly efficient Earther deck crews moving about as they maintained *Orion's* dozens of pinnaces and guided small craft to slots across the deck.

Pat had tapped Graham's shoulder a moment or two into his daze, keeping the junior Manchester somewhat in touch with reality. But it actually took a sharp jab in the ribs from his sister to restore his attention and alert him to the fact that Ursla was coming down the ramp from her pinnace, and that Hastings had already arrived and was talking to her two loyal officers from the mission to Earth. Over the next few minutes he remained quiet as his group paced through the corridors, until at last they reached the First Lord's cabin. The hatch wasn't locked, so they knocked and entered to a bright welcome from Caine, who heartily shook Graham's hand. As the nervous ArcBrigadier scooped up a handful of fruit from a plate on a table nearby and then found a chair, be began looking at the pennants on Caine's wall. There were a great many, and they seemed to outline the wolf's career.

Soon everyone had found a seat. The chairs were arranged in a roughly circular pattern, and when Graham realized Caine's seat was directly facing his, he tensed for a minute... then something told him to relax.

"So he actually has a great deal of charisma, it seems. And it looks like his heart's been pushed into the right place, too," Hastings was saying. "He managed to admit that Andra and Sarah's story was a construct without taking any blame — he's positioned the Earthers as a warrior race serving the Gods, who showed us the error of our social division."

"And I left my halo in my cabin!" Ursla said with a smile, and a couple of people chuckled.

"So he's got the Chancellery in hand, then?" Pat's tone reflected some uncertainty.

Hastings half shrugged, "For now, though you know how unstable politics is. But I think I actually trust him to keep working at it. He's not behaving in any manner we'd expect from the High Chancellor. Starting tomorrow, he's planning to go public with the truth — that is, the truth where you Earthers are Archangels, I think... not officially named that way, of course."

Ursla, next to Caine, bobbed her eyebrows appreciatively, glancing at her canine friend, "I could live with that."

"I'm not changing my name to Gabriel," Caine's smile was genuine, but tinged with weariness.

For his part, the First Lord hadn't completely recovered from the strain of the long run in from Earth. Now that the Kroggs had been dealt with, at least in immediate terms, his subconscious was seemingly compelling him to rest. He was resisting — there were still far too many things to look after in Genesis space to allow him much downtime...

The room had fallen silent, many of the assembled officers suffering from fatigue similar to the First Lord's. Graham, perhaps marginally more energized than most, still felt too out of place to revive the conversation.

Despite his weariness, Caine noticed the junior Manchester was feeling awkward — though he was trying to shroud that sentiment with a pleasant posture and expression. Well that wouldn't do...

"Feeling like a fish out of water, Graham?"

The junior Manchester blinked when the First Lord addressed him, and felt himself reddening. *Time for tact, I think... if I have any left...*

Graham offered a friendly shrug, "Unless you're all desperately waiting for me to relate stories of a dull bachelorhood aboard a space station, I can't contribute."

Caine chuckled, "I'll bet you have a few stories to tell. In my experience, you don't count out the Manchesters."

Graham cocked an eyebrow, glancing at his sister, "Really? What's she been up to?"

Ursla laughed outright, "Tell us what she admitted to. We'll fill in the holes she left out."

Sarah cleared her throat loudly. With everything that was already going on in her head, she didn't need to have to start defending herself about her time in Sol... but neither Earther seemed to notice her objection and Pat simply chuckled.

"How about when Sarah picked a fight with that big fellow?" Caine asked.

"Which, the Superdreadnought or the Shappa?" Pat leaned forward in his chair with a not-so-fake frown.

Graham's eyebrows went up, "Do tell. I imagine a bit of a chewing out is in order!"

Sarah turned red.

Slowly, the atmosphere in Caine's cabin brightened, and the assembled officers, for all their fatigue, found themselves laughing and joking. It had been a long month of war, but at least there was some respite.

And so they talked on into the night.

It was hours later before the gathering broke, and Sarah felt plenty embarrassed... in a good way. There were certain things she hadn't related to Graham about the Quest — to keep him from worrying, or maybe from lecturing — but Caine and Ursla recounted them in a disarming enough way that Graham hadn't preached too much on safety.

Of course, as much as she loved her brother, something else had been nagging her throughout the entire evening. She hadn't said so much as a single serious word to Pat since before the battle, and now it seemed a conspicuous silence. After so much destruction and chaos, there seemed to be very few potentially positive subjects to occupy her mind, but Pat was one of them.

But in all honesty, she had no clue how to deal with him. As terribly cliché as it was, she, an ArcGeneral of the fleet, had absolutely no concept of how to deal with her *friend*... or whatever the burly Irishman actually was.

So she desperately needed advice from someone who had relationship experience. Normally, Liz Hastings would be her first choice when it came to guidance, but the ArcGeneral was noticeably unattached. In fact, in all the years Sarah had known her, Hastings had been a part of exactly one relationship, and it had been platonic and involved a beloved pet bronzefish.

So Hastings couldn't help.

Graham, her caring little brother, had no doubt frolicked about from time to time — such was his lifestyle — but she hardly expected *frolicking* to have provided the right sort of expertise, and she couldn't really talk to him about this anyway. He'd done more than enough by getting Pat mixed up in it.

Ursla suffered from the same problem as Hastings — romance simply didn't seem to interest the bear yet.

So that left just one individual, a happily married father who was about 150 years her senior — and who happened to be the head of the Earther Admiralty.

As Caine's room emptied, Sarah lagged behind. The tired commanders were eager to get back to their posts, check their messages, and get to bed, so she didn't have to wait long. Once the room was empty, Sarah turned to Caine with a concerned expression, "Can I trouble you for a few minutes?"

Cocking an eyebrow, Caine offered a smile, "I'm sure we troubled you enough with Graham, though I somehow doubt you're actually going to cause me any consternation..."

Sarah shook her head and nervously knit her fingers in front of her, "I need advice."

Caine frowned, waving her back into his cabin and gesturing her into a chair, "About what?"

Sarah opened her mouth but found that the words weren't coming. Caine frowned and watched her try to get started, tuning his instincts to her state of mind... Ah, it had come to this. Sarah had never been able to conceal her emotions about Pat, even when she wasn't aware of them herself.

As Sarah's mind stumbled over words and phrases, Caine recognized her strife with a sympathetic smile. While the ArcGeneral was indeed struggling with weariness much like his own, she had another distraction — a good one.

Sarah, too flustered to notice Caine's expression, kept inhaling and opening her mouth to speak, then closing it awkwardly.

Finally, Caine broke her consternation, "You've figured out your feelings for Pat, I presume."

Sarah froze.

Somehow she'd wanted to convince herself that no one else really knew about this situation — it was so trivial, especially considering the brutality they'd all just witnessed.

Caine chuckled softly, "And I'm the only married one around here."

She nodded again, feeling altogether silly.

Caine offered a calming smile, "It's probably not much different for humans."

Sarah frowned.

"*Love.*"

Caine resisted a smile when the ArcGeneral's head whipped up at the word. She blinked twice and opened her mouth belatedly, "Oh. I imagine it's pretty similar, yes..."

"Then my advice might be applicable to your situation."

Sarah paused and then nodded, leaning forward anxiously. She could use some guidance, "It really just seems so inappropriate right now — after all we've lost."

Caine leaned forward as well, looking absurdly father-like, despite the difference in species. Perhaps, Sarah thought wistfully, she'd found a surrogate father in the wolf — someone who could fill the role of the one she'd lost long ago. The thought, altogether too emotional, was immediately dismissed.

Caine opened his mouth and Sarah held her breath. The answer was coming...

"This is the most profound advice I can give," the First Lord said quietly. "And it is fully appropriate for you to follow it now. The fleet will be glad of some happy news, not distraught by it…"

Sarah frowned — sure, there was logic in that. However, justifying her problem didn't solve it, "But what do I do?"

Over a century of wisdom manifested itself in Caine's serious expression, "Talk to Pat."

With a groan, Sarah flopped back in her chair. Talk to *Pat*… that was it? What a crazy idea.

In the corridor on the way back to *Orion's* flight bay, Pat was pondering the very same 'what to do' question. He'd felt like… nothing he could think of properly represented the pure awkwardness he'd felt sitting across from Sarah at the gathering. Now he too was in a search for somebody with answers.

The most likely candidate was the guy who'd gotten him into the mess in the first place, Gods help them both…

Ursla and Hastings, catching up on the news after more than a month apart, didn't even notice as Graham was yanked from the corridor behind them. The junior Manchester didn't have time to react as Pat's big arm pulled him into an empty conference room.

"What in the bloody… Pat? What the devil are you doing?"

The Irishman heaved a sigh and leaned against the conference table, folding his arms, "I'm looking for advice, and I figure you owe me some after you got me into this whole mess."

Graham's expression transformed into a sly smile, "Aha! You're trying to figure out what to do about my sister, aren't you?"

Pat's eyes narrowed in mild frustration, "*No*, I want a recipe for biscuits — what bloody else would I bloody expect, man?"

Graham folded his arms and grinned, "You know, it goes against the grain for a man to offer advice to a friend who wants to date his sister."

"I'm sure that bothers you so much it *hurts*," Pat scowled outright.

Graham chuckled, strode to the wall thoughtfully, then turned on his heel and came pacing back, "You really amaze me. You and Sarah both, actually — you've got the emotional intelligence of *teenagers*! And I fear I'm not an expert with these things… I've left a rather rocky trail of less-than-happy ladies in my wake, so what I say mightn't be of much use…"

"Yes, I'm sure both those ladies would love to see you suffer. Perhaps they'd *pay me*. Now, is there anything constructive you can suggest?"

Graham chuckled and his smile broadened, "Maybe you should go *talk* to her."

Pat paused.

Talk to *her*. Why would he want to do that?

CHAPTER 49

Pat had missed seeing Sarah on *Orion* — when he'd finished interrogating her brother, he'd found her pinnace gone from the bay. He wasn't about to be stopped though — now that he actually knew what to do, he needed to keep his momentum. He ordered his pinnace's pilot to take him to *Joseph Barron*, and the pilot had happily obliged.

Unfortunately, Sarah had been of a similar mind. She'd known Pat was still on *Orion*, but she had no idea where to find him. Instead she decided to wait for him on *Bishop*, so her ship set down on the Battlecruiser's deck just before Pat's hit *Joseph Barron's*.

Again of a similar mind, the wayward pair chose to wait aboard those flagships for the other's arrival, and aside from deckhands no one knew where the unfortunate officers were. It was all rather cruel.

After about half an hour of waiting, Sarah started to lose her nerve. It was completely understandable — this whole situation was so foreign to her dedicated Naval life, she really didn't want to address it. Despite what Caine had said, there were many more important things she needed to deal with, and she couldn't shirk her responsibilities for some self-indulgent talk with Patrick Conroy. Her pinnace launched without her even having stepped out onto *Bishop's* deck.

Pat, on the other hand, had become more resolute as he waited. Determined not to miss Sarah, he ordered his pinnace pilot to leave him aboard *Barron* and return to *Bishop*. Pat remained on the flight deck for a few minutes, wondering whether it would be best to meet Sarah in public on the deck, or in private. The latter option seemed far more appropriate, so he went through *Barron's* corridors to Sarah's quarters. Sarah had long ago given him the key code to her lock, so he let himself in, sat on the couch and waited.

In the space around *Joseph Barron*, the two pinnaces passed without acknowledgement, and Sarah soon found herself wandering through the corridors of her ship, rocked by inner turmoil about the whole situation. She admitted to herself she'd completely lost her nerve, and she pledged that one day, before she was Caine's age, she'd address the issue.

She was thinking along the lines of 'down to the wire' for that deadline. The day before she turned 180. Yes. That would give her enough time... presuming she somehow lived to double the Genesis life-expectancy age.

The situation was far too absurd, and she knew it. She paced through the decks to her quarters, hoping that sooner or later Pat would take the initiative. Part of her dreaded that moment, another part wished it would happen immediately. Though she found it hard to admit, a *large* part of her actually wanted him to do something... she just had to ignore it. She was beginning to see this whole problem like a sparring match — patience would be the key to a positive outcome.

These thoughts were filling her head when she stepped into her cabin. Her eyes were downcast as she entered, hands already loosening her collar. She didn't even notice him.

"We need to talk."

Sarah hit the roof — literally. She seemed to launch upward in surprise, the unforgiving doorframe stopping her vertical motion with a sharp crack. Pat froze for a second as she collapsed back against the door, then rushed to his feet and to her side.

Rubbing her head woefully, Sarah tried to get up but found herself without any will. She could feign unconsciousness and get out of the whole bloody mess. But that would be counter-productive...

"Pat! What the hell...?"

The Irishman was quickly helping her to her feet, "Sorry... Gods, girl, I thought you'd be a *little* happier to see me!"

Sarah scowled at him as she rubbed her head.

"You're skulking about like a bloody bandit..." she muttered as he helped her onto the couch and ran to her little kitchen for an ice pack.

"Bandit am I?" Pat grumbled in reply, returning with an icy bag and handing it to her. "This wasn't a good idea, was it?"

Sarah held the ice to her head and glared up at him, "What, the skulking part? Very *perceptive* of you!"

"I wasn't skulking! I was sitting!" Pat frowned defensively, folding his arms over his chest.

"A fine line..." Sarah suddenly felt like laughing. This whole thing was ridiculous. Positively ridiculous. She was running about being as dense as a brick, and Pat was being as subtle as a brick through a window, so maybe there were some commonalities they could work with...

But combined with the stress of the week... no, the *month*... no, the *year*... this senseless division and emotional tumult was too much. She couldn't afford this many complications — her personal life needed to settle down, or her professional work, her *fleet*, would suffer.

She took a deep breath and looked up at Pat's scowl, smiling tiredly in reply, "Well sit down again, Patrick."

The Irishman's scowl faded only slightly, and he cocked an eyebrow, "Back to friendly conversation, are we?"

She nodded, "I hope so."

Pat sat slowly in a chair opposite Sarah, "So what have we accomplished?"

Applying the cold pack Pat had brought from the kitchen to her head, Sarah heaved a sigh, "I think we've decided we should talk."

Pat's expression softened slightly, "I can live with that. You first."

Sarah raised her eyebrows, "Me? You got us into this?"

"Ladies first."

Sarah shrugged, "What am I supposed to say?"

Pat paused in thought. "How in hell's gulags am I supposed to know?"

"Well you brought it up!"

Pat sat back thoughtfully. He hadn't a clue what to say — he'd worked it out in his head minutes before, but it all seemed to disappear now that the conversation had started.

"Well you read those romance novels, don't you? Say something fitting!"

"I haven't read one since I was fifteen!"

"That still means you've got more expertise than me!"

Sarah heaved another sigh — this discussion was sounding ridiculous. Two eligible officers in their mid-twenties, and they didn't even know how to get past the first words of a conversation like this...

"Well, if we follow the pattern, I utter something ridiculously melodramatic like 'I've always loved you' or 'I need you like the air' and then I fling myself at you like some sort of missile."

Pat stared at her for a second, "Right, let's not go that road then. If you ever say 'you need me like the air' I'll leave the room to see if you suffocate."

"Thought so," Sarah nodded with a bland expression.

The two sat in silence again, trying to think of a way to break the ice. Of course, Pat realized with a smile, there wasn't much ice to break because they were obviously of the same mind.

"Well," he related his thoughts, "this is sort of redundant, isn't it? We both know what we're talking about, so there isn't a great deal of *innuendo* to be traded about, is there?"

Sarah contemplated that, "No, I suppose not."

"Right. We've both realized we've been totally oblivious for ages and that we should fix that, haven't we?"

Sarah nodded, "I think that sums it up, then, doesn't it?"

"And we've managed to do it without a whiff of bloody *romance*," Pat frowned at the last word.

Sarah nodded, hiding a very small smile, "We did."

Pat nodded, "Good."

"Indeed."

"Right."

Pat and Sarah sat silently for another moment. Now what?

"So... now what?" Sarah felt the smile she'd been hiding creep onto her face.

With a shrug, Pat huffed a sigh, "You read the books... I think you said it was a missile thing. Is there any way that plays out in a professional manner, befitting officers of the Genesis Navy?"

Sarah looked thoughtful for a moment, then stood up slowly, "No, not a chance at all."

There wasn't a great deal of professionalism in what came next.

While the two romantic icons of the Allied Fleet made up for their past blindness, word spread through the back channels to every ship. It was an amazing feat of uncoordinated signaling which had started as a whisper from Pat's pilot to a friend of his on the flight deck. That friend had called his pal aboard *Paladin Saint*, and from there it had rippled outward.

Of course no one would actually comment publicly — that would have been both disrespectful and uncalled for. No, everyone simply got the satisfaction of knowing the great romance of the fleet had finally been realized.

They'd have to make posters... maybe someone would write a book. They might even option it for a movie...

CHAPTER 50

Caine sat silently in *Orion*'s briefing room, Ursla at his right hand, Felix at his left. Everyone was quiet as they waited, lost in thoughts of the future and the Earther Navy's potential contribution to the war against the Kroggs.

It had been decided that the Earthers would join the chase for the Krogg armada, and Hastings had expressed the will of the Genesis Navy to aid in the pursuit. There was really no alternative — were that armada to survive, its quest for revenge would endanger both Allied powers, and since the Fourth Fleet-of-War had absorbed enormous losses during battle, it would fall to the Allies to lead the chase.

They would need to confirm this assumption with the Larosians, then sort out the particulars of what the Earthers and humans assumed would be a new alliance. The Krogg threat would be neutralized, no matter the cost.

For their part the Larosians had been surprisingly unapproachable over the past days — since the battle they'd been withdrawn, repairing their damage without local help, collecting their own survivors, and generally keeping to themselves. Caine had finally received notice from Narosh that they were willing to meet, and the Larosian had insisted that it be aboard *Orion*.

It seemed the Larosians liked to keep their ships to themselves.

So Caine and his two Fleet Admirals waited for Captain Forepaw to escort the Admiral-of-a-Fleet to their conference room.

Ursla, despite being happy for Sarah and Pat, was somber. She'd had the most contact with the Larosians in her weeks here, owing to her close collaboration with Novash, and she neither appreciated nor understood the distance the alien allies were putting between themselves and the Earthers. However, she was forcing herself to ignore their diplomatic habits as she waited to see what they had in mind.

They'd just have to learn to get along.

The doors opened on the far side of the room and Admiral Narosh, Captain-Commodore Novash, and Captain-Elite Torallis entered. Behind them Lab Forepaw nodded to Caine, then backed out of the room, closing the hatch.

Narosh had finally come to a decision. Inner turmoil over the Earthers had delayed his response to the new allies, and for that he felt a pang of regret. In the end it had come to an appraisal of what the Son would have done, and examining the situation from that viewpoint, Narosh had found his inevitable course of action eminently clear.

The Larosian sat silently, and his two fellows flanked him, facing the Earther Fleet commanders.

"I appreciate you finally agreeing to meet with us, Admiral Narosh," Caine began stiffly, and Narosh offered a bow-nod.

"I apologize for the distance we have placed between ourselves and your forces. It was thoughtless and a function of habit, not an indication of our opinion of you."

Caine found that statement somewhat comforting, though he kept that reaction from changing his expression. The Larosians had not been avoiding the Earthers maliciously or suspiciously, it seemed, and they were willing to apologize in the name of diplomacy.

"After the casualties you suffered, it was completely understandable," he said graciously. "In any case, we shouldn't dwell on the past."

Narosh nodded again at the wisdom of the wolf's words, "Indeed. I have come to officially request that the Earther Navy aid us in the pursuit and ultimate destruction of the Krogg armada."

To the point.

"That had been the plan, Admiral," Caine said with a small smile.

Again Narosh nodded, not surprised by the Earther reaction after his briefings from Novash. Indeed, he had as much as expected such a response from the First Lord. Perhaps his kind would come to comprehend Earthers more fully than they had the humans they'd encountered...

"We don't have all that many ships, Admiral," Ursla said quietly, and Narosh abandoned his musings and turned his head to the bear. "I understand you have several fleets, each of which outnumbers our own."

Narosh tilted his head, "Most of those fleets you speak of will likely be employed pressing the Krogg flank from other directions. I cannot speak for the Admirals-of-the-Navy, though I would imagine they will not commit a great deal of fire power on this front, but will instead attempt to press the main frontier in our own galaxy, while your forces agitate the flank."

"We're just a flank?" Felix's eyebrow was cocked at the thought of a war carrying on in entirely different *galaxies*.

"There are many corridors in space, and more must lead to the Krogg Empire in this galaxy. In any case, with such a small fleet in this region of space, the Kroggs will no longer be able to engage you in major actions. They will likely use guerrilla tactics to slow your advance while they attempt to rebuild."

For a second the Earthers digested the statement.

"So in other words," Felix put in slowly, "this war's going to become a squadron affair. Small groups in action against each other?"

Narosh nodded again, and Ursla cast a smile at Felix, "Right up your alley, Savanna, and mine too."

The cat nodded, recalling his endeavors of the past weeks. His success had been impressive — even he had to admit that — and it had been entirely on the small scale. The Kroggs hadn't caused any of the Earthers difficulty with even numbers in small-unit actions. Perhaps this war they had agreed to would not be as bad as the battle in Genesis...

But it was rather early to make such an assumption.

"I think that could suit us quite readily, Admiral," Caine pressed on with the dialogue while Felix pondered. "We have some commanders who are quite adept at that sort of fighting."

Narosh sat in silence, contemplating that boast. To Larosians, such warfare was not only dishonorable, it was senseless, relying on instinct and the baser levels of the mind. But the Kroggs had, in the past, used the constraints of Larosian honor against Narosh's race — until the Son had freed the Navy to think and fight with more flexibility and cunning. These Earthers could do much the same, and perhaps might prove very useful to the war effort in the coming years.

"Very well," Narosh said with a tone that implied his appreciation of the offer.

It seemed an unfittingly abrupt end to such a momentous intergalactic conference, but Caine would take it. He had to admit that meeting silver eyes felt slightly awkward — he found it difficult to recognize meaning in them. But today the earnest exchanging of gazes with Admiral-of-a-Fleet Narosh was made worthwhile; the alien was a warrior unlike any other Caine had known, but like the First Lord, he was indeed a *warrior*.

It would be an honor to fight alongside these Larosians.

Coming to his feet, the First Lord nodded to Narosh, "Alright, that's settled then. Now, before you go, perhaps I could offer you a tour of *Orion*. We've seen each others' ships in action, yet you have had no time to observe our technology up close."

Narosh had not predicted an offer like this — one more disadvantage of not being able to read these Earthers' minds. Perhaps it wouldn't be a bad thing to see their largest ship — he could evaluate their capabilities of construction and organization.

"I would... *enjoy* that."

Caine smiled and led the Larosian out of the room, Felix and Torallis following. Novash seemed less motivated to move, and Ursla frowned at him as he remained in his chair. The Captain-Commodore was the closest thing she had to a friend among the Larosians, though she certainly hadn't connected with him as easily as she had Liz and Sarah. His expression was impossible to read, and his eyes didn't help facilitate understanding...

"Something wrong, Captain-Commodore?"

The Larosian offered what she guessed was a smile, "I recall you had questions about our people. Before the battle, I mean. Perhaps this would be a good time for me to provide insight, as I have seen your ships already."

Ursla's eyebrow arched, "That's very good of you... let me see now..."

She hadn't been thinking too much about Larosian society lately — their political and military inclinations had seemed more important. Though she still did have plenty of questions that she hadn't gotten to ask before the battle.

"Well, I suppose my biggest question is about the *son*... you said he was human, but you really didn't explain who he was."

The Larosian offered a brief bow-nod, his expression... thoughtful... *probably*, "I cannot say his name — that is tradition, we must not dishonor him by speaking his name again. Suffice it to say he was the first in a generation to enable us to turn the tide against the Kroggs."

Ursla frowned slightly at the Captain-Commodore's reverence, but let him continue without commenting on it.

"We Larosians depend almost exclusively on logic and consciousness to guide our actions, Admiral. We sometimes lack the... *intuition* to wage war in the Krogg manner. We fight with discipline, courage, and honor, and we are great warriors. For much of the war, structured war-making was enough — we held our territory and defeated waves of Krogg ships. But the Queen came, and she proved *cunning*. Before her arrival, Kroggs had fought like animals — they had come in packs, fought viciously, and fled before organized firepower. The Queen forced them to fight with organization *and* intuition; they did not break and flee, but were able to act almost with precognition."

Novash paused after the last words, gauging Ursla's reaction to the implication, but she nodded him on.

"We could match their ferocity for a time, but after several decades their numbers were too great, and our frontiers were pushed back. Our prospects in the war appeared grim, and yet there was hope: Praaxus' powerful conscious mind had been telepathically transplanted through time and space at his death; we believed a piece of him existed in our space. Though I was not certain of the reality of such a claim, we searched, and Captain Narosh found the Son. He was human."

Ursla nodded slowly, marveling in part at the versatility of Larosian telepathy, "And because he was human, he had the intuition to counter the Kroggs."

Novash replied with a bow-nod, "He led us well, allowing us to retain our honor and discipline and merely speeding our actions through his foresight. His leadership was decisive, and we quickly reversed our fortunes. When it came to the Queen, though, the Son was forced to sacrifice himself for our survival. The Fourth Fleet-of-War escorted him to his death on that mission, and now we are committed to the fulfillment of his legacy.

"It is our hope that you Earthers will prove the next step on our path to victory... you are a race unlike any we have encountered. Your instincts seem like those of the Kroggs, your discipline and your honor are akin to our own, and while we were somewhat uncertain as to your nature at first, we believe now that you were perhaps the Son's gift to us. Or, more precisely, that he knew of you somehow, and that because you existed he felt his presence was no longer necessary to defeat the Kroggs."

So that was it. Twice in the same week, someone was labeling the Earthers a fulfillment of some divine prophecy.

Don't let it go to your head, you'll be in robes doing Gregorian chants if you're not careful!

Ursla almost grinned at her mental quip, before realizing abruptly that her internal wit, which she hadn't been able to summon for days, had been restored.

So she did grin, and Novash tilted his head slightly, "You agree with our theory? The Son knew of you?"

With her grin broadening to a smile, Ursla shook her head, "That's really not for me to say, though I can tell you I'm certainly not a mystical deliverance of prophecy. I'll do my best in this fight — we all will. We're here because we made a promise to the humans, and now we've made a promise to you. That's how we operate, nothing divine about it at all."

Novash was very pleased by the answer, if puzzled by the Earther's smile, "I believe your perspective is flat-headed and appropriate — most appropriate, and I thank you."

Ursla's smile broadened and she cocked an eyebrow, *"Flat-headed?"*

Novash tilted his head, "Is that not right... my meaning is 'grounded', I believe."

"Ah, *level*-headed. Almost the same," Ursla's smile grew further. "Working English colloquialisms into the vocabulary?"

"Trying my best, though I am no grand linguist," Novash tilted his head the other way.

Ursla nodded slowly, "You're doing fine... well, while they're touring, why don't we get something to eat? I can help you with any language problems while I introduce you to one of my favorite things in the cosmos."

Novash leaned forward curiously, "If I am collecting your nouns and verbs correctly, you are implying you enjoy food a great deal."

Coming slowly to her feet, Ursla nodded, "Your instinct's bang on about that one. Has anyone checked you out to see if our food will agree with you?"

Standing as well, Novash shook his head slowly.

"Then it's to the med center with us first, and if that goes well, we'll go find some Earth food. In my experience, nothing aids inter-alien understanding like a plate of salmon and potatoes!"

• • •

Aboard *Joseph Barron*, Sarah woke up.

Something was different about this wake-up...

It occurred to her that she was in an awkward state of undress, and that was disturbing — she always wore her regulation pajamas to bed.

Then she realized that there was an arm around her waist... a *foreign* one.

She panicked for a moment, trying to recall what was going on...

Then she remembered.

Aha.

Sarah found herself smiling as she went back to sleep.

EPILOGUE

It took several weeks for the damage that came with the Battle of Genesis to be repaired, but by the end of that time the Allied Fleet was ready to actively pursue the Kroggs. Of course, they only had a general direction to follow, and in the vastness of space the Kroggs could be anywhere. But the fleet was confident the enemy would be found and dealt with.

Narosh's prediction that the armada would break up into smaller guerrilla squadrons was accepted by Caine and Hastings as they divided up their forces. The First Lord suggested a simple forward deployment with no units larger than battle groups crossing through space. For the most part, the search would be carried out by Flying and Battle Squadrons.

The cruisers of the Flying Squadrons would seek out the enemy and call the capital ships of the Battle Squadrons when they found them. Hopefully it would prove a Krogg-beating strategy — fast eyes and available firepower. The goal was to keep them running, and thus to make sure they couldn't turn around to raid Genesis, or Earth.

To Hastings, the situation seemed almost surreal. She had chosen to base herself on Genesis, organizing the Genesis Navy's contribution to the Allied campaign from a secure central location, while still keeping an eye on the Church.

Surprisingly enough, she was taking a liking to the post.

The mood on Genesis had already begun to change — Hastings had been right about Bingham's charisma, and the High Chancellor addressed the public daily about the new teachings of the Gods. Those who had been moderate before — men like Argyle — were coming around most quickly, and for the first time in Genesis history, the second class was seeing the hope of equal rights. It was exciting for someone who had lived under the Church's iron grip for so long, and Hastings very much looked forward to seeing how it turned out.

For Bingham's part, he felt alive. The same confidence which had helped him lead his people through the years leading up to the Quest had returned in full, but he was proud of the fact that it was backed now by noble sentiments. Caine had given him this chance, as had all the Earthers, and whether they had truly been sent by 'the Gods' he did not care to know. He addressed the people of Genesis confident that his own intentions were right, and in time he would make a united Genesis reality. Such was his goal, and his redemption.

•••

Captain Fox Magnus found himself commanding the 74-gun ship of the line *Atlas*, with Battle Squadron (BatRon) 301. His ship, together with the 74s *Vulcan, Donegal, Hero, Cumberland, Mjollnir, Bellerophon,* and *Dragon,* as well as *Tonnant,* formed the flag Battle Squadron of the Third Fleet, under the personal command of Admiral Felix.

Fox took immense pride in the assignment, and as soon as he boarded his command he began drilling his crew in the arts of sloop warfare — something he felt could be well adapted to a 74's hull.

Felix was happy to have Fox's *Atlas* — and indeed, he was very pleased with his entire command. Caine had transferred most of the original 74 squadron that had been with him since the war-games to the Third Fleet where they could fight with him, and Felix had gladly promoted them all to the title of 301st Battle Squadron. They had been the first warships he'd actually led into a fight, and having them under his orders made him feel right at home.

And as promised, his newly-promoted Flag Captain — once First Lieutenant and coincidentally the daughter of Varnon Broadpaw, the past commander of this fleet — had bolted a desk to the floor of the bridge.

It sat next to the battle plot, looking ridiculously out of place, but Felix was glad of its presence — not because he necessarily wanted to go back to Admiralty House to work though papers, but as a reminder of where he'd come from.

That and it personified the old jokes about admin branch Admirals: he was indeed flying a desk now, and he was rather happy about it.

Far and away from the fleets preparing for war, James Stanton and Audrey DeBrooke led their privateers back towards the systems they'd been searching. There was still a lone Coalition cruiser out there to be destroyed, and there was a colony to be set up as well.

Not to mention swashbuckling adventure and romance on the frontier.

ArcLieutenant-General Graham Manchester had been given administrative Naval command of the Genesis system. The promotion had surprised him but he had come to appreciate the idea of being the man in charge of the comings and goings of the fleet in-system.

And of course he had to be happy for his sister. She'd finally gotten herself out of the lonely life, something the junior Manchester was certainly going to try to do over the next few years.

Of course, he had no idea where to look for someone, but he was sure he'd figure it out somewhere along the line. He was an ArcLieutenant-General now. Rank had its privileges.

Sarah was as happy as her little brother, for reasons that were no secret to anyone. Of course, no one dared say anything about her newfound joy — they had more sense than to look down the barrel of that particular loaded gun.

To Sarah, everything just felt a little better. As much as the losses at Genesis continued to weigh on her mind, a new counterbalance was helping her keep her guilt in check. There was a long war ahead, but as long as Pat was on her side the long-term prospects looked a little brighter.

As for the war, she would have a major part to play. Hastings had broken the Genesis Fleet into squadrons very similar to those organized by the Earther Navy, and it had become Sarah's dubious duty to try to coordinate them all.

Pat, meanwhile, refilled the ranks of his Battlecruiser force and it took on the title of the 444th Cruiser Squadron. He didn't hunt for promotion — he wanted to stay in cruisers, especially after what he'd seen in the battle. The tradeoff, of course, was the inevitable parting with Sarah. That wasn't particularly easy, but the two kept their goodbyes simple.

It had occurred to Pat that before the battle he had threatened the universe into staying out of their business. It became habitual now — every night before bed the Irishman would faithfully threaten the universe into behaving. And, so far at least, it seemed to be working.

Novash was made Admiral-of-a-Division for his exemplary actions with the Earthers. Narosh sent word to the Larosian command of all that had taken place and recommended they gather the remaining search fleets to probe the outer systems for other corridors to Krogg territory.

Over time, the Admiral-of-a-Fleet was softening towards the strange Earthers, though he could not pretend to understand them. They were logical and yet they relied on intuition... in that manner they acted like the Son. Perhaps he had sent them...

And Ursla had entered what she described to herself as her *thoughtful* phase.

Much as had been the case just before she and the Second Fleet had left Earth for Genesis, she found herself contemplating the state of the universe. The Earthers were joining a war effort that was over half as old as their race, and a great deal was riding on the actions of alien enemies, and alien allies. It wasn't exactly what she'd expected to get herself and her Navy into when she'd come out here.

Well, you did. Whether or meant to or not...

These thoughts were preoccupying Ursla as she stood on *Orion's* main observation deck, waiting for Caine's arrival. When last she'd been this reflective, it had been her oldest, best friend who'd helped her make sense of it. And as much as Ursla felt she'd come to grips with the chaos in the past month, she still craved Setter Caine's perspective on things.

"Last time we did this we were aboard *Agamemnon*, weren't we?"

Lost in her thoughts, Ursla hadn't even heard Caine come in. She turned towards the door with a smile and a shrug, "Figured I'd save you the trip."

Caine met his friend's smile and bobbed his head in reply, "Good of you. So what's up this time? You sounded thoughtful, which is always dangerous."

Ursla chuckled, and as Caine arrived next to her, the pair turned to look out the windows, spending a quiet moment watching the echelons of Earther ships surge into energy drive and hurtle out of the system.

The Earthers were stretching out into the unknown...

"How'd we get ourselves into this, Setter?"

Caine cocked an eyebrow at the question.

"Technically, *you* got us into this my friend. I think you're the one who promised Sarah we'd come out here in the first place, and you picked our side in this war..."

Ursla frowned, "Well..."

With a chuckle, Caine looked up at her, "Of course, I ordered you to do all of it, so I suppose it's actually *my* fault... not that I'd ever tell you that. Oh wait... I just did."

The mood, at least, was less somber than it might have been, and Ursla took a deep breath as she smiled, "Yes, that's how we got here then... but aren't you concerned at all? I mean, we jumped right in here, turned on the Kroggs, sided immediately with the Larosians, and went to war..."

Caine nodded slowly, scratching his chin, "Yes, we could be in for a lot of grief, but I believe we're doing the right thing. Aside from abiding by our word, this *feels* right. And even though I don't completely understand the Larosians, I *trust* them."

"You too, then?" Ursla nodded as she replied. "They're like us in some ways, and so very different in others."

Again Caine offered a thoughtful nod, "We share with them a similar mindset and strong determination, but they're not too good with the instincts and the humor."

"I can see why you get along with them then," Ursla's jibe drew a snort from Caine, but he neglected to counterattack.

"My *point* is, I can understand them enough to trust them. Aliens or not."

Ursla sobered and cocked her eyebrow, "But you can see something familiar in the Kroggs too, can't you? Their reliance on instinct..."

Caine's ear twitched and he nodded slowly, "Though I've never met one face to face, I'd guess you're right about that."

The thought didn't appeal to Ursla — to see even an aspect of herself in such an enemy was disconcerting. These weren't humans; these were *aliens*. And to have a war between two races, each side demonstrating some of the Earthers' best qualities, was unsettling.

"So we have things in common with our friends and we have things in common with our enemies," Ursla said with some finality.

It was true, and Caine knew it. They would be facing a race that epitomized their instinctive strength, while standing next to one that depended on rationality.

"Well, we'll just have to find our place, I suppose. We do our jobs, fulfill our obligations, and protect our homes. And if we see aspects of ourselves in both the creatures we fight and in the creatures we stand with, I don't think we should take it as a metaphorical judgment on our own character. I'm not fighting the Kroggs because I don't trust instinct, or because I place my rationality above everything else. The Kroggs are a threat; the Larosians deserve our help. If we tried to get deep and philosophical about this it wouldn't make sense or be at all useful. This war isn't going to turn me, or any of us, into Kroggs or Larosians. We're always going to be Earthers."

Ursla blinked a few times and nodded silently as Caine took a breath.

"Anyway," he went on, "that said, I don't think it's bad to see something of ourselves in these aliens. They're not like us… they are *alien*, after all. And we're alien to them. Partially alike and partially different. I expect that's one of the immutable laws of the universe, so we'll just have to deal with it. The bottom line is that we set our own standards for our own lives. We judge ourselves by Earther standards, and we don't expect anyone else — Larosians, Kroggs or humans — to fit our mold."

And then a smile crossed Caine's face, "…and being that it's so relative, I think I have a name for it."

With a thoughtful frown, Ursla looked down, and Caine shrugged, "I'm a stickler for consistency."

Ursla smiled as her mind followed the hint to its natural answer, "It's…"

Caine nodded and looked back out to space with a smile.

"The alien equation."

APPENDIX A: CHARACTERS

The following brief blurbs provide some insight into the major characters of *The Alien Equation*. Wondering why certain individuals were included and others weren't? You'll just have to check Appendix A in *The Human Equation* for clues… or maybe wait to see who plays a key role in *The Renegade Equation*…

Argyle, Benjamin – Lord Second Chancellor
The most moderate man to sit in the Genesis Chancellery in two generations, Benjamin Argyle was left in control of the colony's government when Bingham personally took command of the Quest. He's not thought to be a very independent sort of character, and often the political rumors suggest that the conservative Chancellors — mainly Pious and Paine — control his actions. Although he inherited his seat, Argyle should not be overlooked as a leader in his own right — just a leader in circumstances that displease him.

Bingham, Harvey – Lord High Chancellor
Harvey Bingham isn't the same man who left Genesis in hopes of fulfilling prophecy. To the shock of Hastings and almost all the Earthers and humans, his mental collapse after the Church's defeat in Sol was thorough, and he's now focused on reforming himself. His ultimate aim is to make restitution to all those he's harmed, though that seems a tall order, especially to him. The Earther Consulate is willing to give him the benefit of the doubt, and envision him returning to the public scene as a progressive leader. Whether he succeeds in this endeavor will be up to him.

Broadpaw, Varnon – Admiral
A wolf who fancies himself one of the funniest Earthers in the fleet, Varnon Broadpaw had served as the commanding officer of the Third Fleet up to the Battle of the Pluto Orbital Plane. With the decimation of that formation both in action and through reorganization to fill the battered ranks of the First and Second Fleets, he was left without a major force to command. As such, he decided to join Ursla as second in command of the Second Fleet, and he departed for Genesis aboard the 125-gun *Algenon*.

Caine, Setter – First Lord of the Admiralty
Setter Caine remains the most crucial Earther in the Genesis-Earth Alliance, and not just because of the combat skills he honed in the battles for Sol. More than just a capable flag officer, this wolf's wisdom and experience are crucial to maintaining the delicate balance between the Earther and Genesis Navies — only his tact and his leadership skills seem to be able to keep the humans from coming to blows over how to deal with their new position alongside the Earthers. Still flying his colors from the mighty 175-gun First Rate *Orion*, Caine is both a formidable warrior and a great leader.

Claw, Chronos – Lieutenant
This cat is Fox Magnus' First Lieutenant in *Flame*, and he doubles as the sloop's chief engineer. Always innovative and willing to experiment, he allows his skipper the confidence to attempt daring feats in the diminutive 18-gun ship. Rumor has it that he's come up with a rather *innovative* idea of combining energy and hyper drives to create some sort of *super* drive... the Earther science community is watching with interest (and with fingers in ears as they wait for the inevitable explosion).

Conroy, Patrick – ArcBrigadier
The Genesis Navy's best cruiser man, Pat was sent out ahead of the main Allied Fleet at the beginning of their voyage to Genesis. He's Irish, he's fierce, he's funny, and he still doesn't realize he's quite in love with Sarah Manchester — even though everybody else certainly does. His predicament might seem a bit amusing to casual observers, but if you said that to this burly Irishman's face, you'd likely not enjoy the ensuing conversation.

DeBrooke, Audrey – ArcColonel
Audrey DeBrooke commanded *Grendelsbane City* through the battles in Sol. Her first distinction was actually being saved by Ursla during the defection, when both *Grendelsbane* and *Darymanis City* were cornered by Church ships. Now she and her cruiser have elected to reject Liz Hastings' leadership. Not eager to have Fleet Command attempt to replace the Kroggs with the noble Earthers, she and *Grendelsbane* deserted a month before the Allied Fleet left for Genesis.

Felar, Kella – Admiral
Still in command of the First Fleet, Kella Felar remains one of the Earther Navy's steadiest line Admirals. A relatively young cat with a house on the sometimes hurricane-prone island of Trinidad, she has remained in Sol with the majority of the Earther Navy, returning the fleet to an adjusted state of normality with renewed war-games and training cruises.

Felix, Savanna – Vice Admiral

A formidable administrator, Savanna Felix long held command of the Earther Navy's Antarctic Base, only being evicted from his post by the threat of the major Crusader landing force that ultimately occupied the installation. During the eight months of reconstruction, he served as a liaison between the two fleets, but thereafter a new 'opportunity' arose. Caine had always believed this tiger had great potential as a combat line officer, and when war-games proved that skill, he was given *ENS Tonnant*, 80 guns, and a squadron to lead in irregular operations out of Sol.

Forepaw, Labrador – Captain

Skipper of the venerable 175-gun ship *Orion*, and by extension, Caine's Flag Captain, Lab Forepaw is one of the most trusted officers in the Fleet. Repeatedly rejecting promotion, this canine has remained with his ship in order to keep it in its best fighting trim, just in case circumstances should demand future combat service. He is one of Caine's best friends, and his leadership skills have seen him marked as a First Lord of the future.

Furgus, Jax – Vice Admiral

One of most respected officers in the Earther Navy, Jax Furgus enjoys serving in and commanding the 64-gun Fourth Rates that are so often overlooked by fleet planners. While the bigger 74s are generally accepted to be sturdier, Jax remains firm in his attachment to whatever 64 he's in. This attachment naturally led the lion to a quick turnover in commands after his gallant participation at Pluto's Orbital Plane; he moved his flag twice during the battle, and had two 64s shot out from under him. He still likes serving in them for some reason.

Grieve, Andros – General

Still the supreme commander of Earther ground forces, Andros Grieve joined the operation to Genesis expecting that infantry action against Crusaders, Kroggs, or both would be required. This bear remains his usual grizzled self, his bloody experiences at Antarctica having made him wiser without dampening his commitment to the service.

Hastings, Elizabeth – ArcGeneral

Remaining on Earth, Liz Hastings has come to lead the Naval component of the Genesis population on the planet, while she still works to reconstruct her decimated fleet. The tensions tearing at the seams of the Naval tapestry continue to dog her, though, and with renegades and debates over Earther relations becoming increasingly heated, she's seeing the prospects of a human utopian society in Sol slip through her fingers. Only with the help of Caine and Bingham will she have a chance of correcting that problem.

Hodge, Gillian – Commandant
As one of the few Genesis Naval Marine Corps' senior officers to survive the slaughter at Antarctic Base, Gillian Hodge was awarded command of the Genesis Navy's ground forces for the return trip to their home colony. Formerly marine commander aboard Pat Conroy's *Harbinger Bishop*, she has a wealth of combat experience, and a good working relationship with General Grieve.

Lupus, Beckett – Sergeant Major
This elite wolf is one of the Earther Marine Corps' most seasoned non-coms. Commanding an excellent squad of recon wolves, Beckett Lupus had extensive experience in action at Antarctica, both participating in the latter stages of the main battle and then working with Sarah Manchester to clear Crusaders out of the complex. The Corps' best hand-to-hand fighter, Lupus was asked to join the expedition to Genesis because of his martial expertise.

Magnus, Fox – Commander
The dapper young Fox Magnus is one of those intrepid officers in the tradition of old Earth's Lord Cochrane. Dashingly red-coated, he's prone to feats of unbelievable daring — a term many humans might exchange for 'suicidal stupidity' if they didn't know better — and has a distinct way of getting results. Though he and his diminutive 18-gun sloop *Flame* saw relatively little action in the battles for Sol, their services will prove very useful in Genesis.

Manchester, Graham – ArcBrigadier
The younger of the Manchester siblings, Graham Manchester remained in Genesis during the Quest. Despite sometimes giving impressions to the contrary, he is a highly capable and versatile officer, and earned his command of the *Genesis* Orbital Battle Stations through hard work and clear skill. With the Genesis Fleet gone, he became not only the ranking line officer in the system, but the leading Naval influence in space increasingly dominated by Kroggs. He is well liked by Genesis crews, and respected by his seniors; Graham looks to follow in his sister's footsteps to the top of the Navy.

Manchester, Sarah – ArcGeneral
Having taken the reins of the Genesis Fleet after its reconstruction, Sarah was assigned command of that formation for its return to its home colony. The position of authority certainly wasn't unfamiliar to her after her command of the human ships in the combat in Sol, but the magnitude of her 900-ship force's mission remained daunting. Flying her flag from *Pope Joseph Barron*, she has set off to free her homeworld of its oppressors. And no, she doesn't realize she's in love with Pat either.

Nightclaw, Dran – Commodore
With Ursla's rise to command of the Second Fleet, her once-Flag Captain
Nightclaw was elevated to command the elite 111th Flying Squadron. This
panther's reputation as an Earther cruiser commander has since come to be
heralded above all others — save, perhaps, for Ursla herself. Unfortunately, his
force did not accompany the Second Fleet to Genesis, as Caine wanted to keep
the elite formation at Sol, both as a strategic reserve and a training force.

Stanton, James – ArcColonel
Once one of the commanders from Sarah Manchester's elite Battlecruiser
squadron, James found his ship in a sorry state after the Battle of the Belt.
Shortly into the repair process, Liz Hastings ordered his ship reconstructed as a
hybrid, and despite his objections, the Earthers have reluctantly rebuilt *Archangel
Sword* into a vessel that exemplifies the best of both worlds. Unfortunately, the
changes left *Sword* too powerful to rejoin the Genesis Fleet and too slow to join
the Earthers; it was left behind in Sol, and James has been forced to seriously
consider his ship's future.

Tigar, Artemis – Captain
A veteran officer, this tiger serves as Ursla's Flag Captain in *Agamemnon*. With
plenty of experience in combat, including distinguished service in the 150-gun
ship during the Battle of the Asteroid Belt, he has earned his posting as chief
Captain of the Second Fleet. A fast friend of the Admiral, he has joined the
expedition to Genesis, though he remains skeptical about what the Allied Fleet
will find upon arrival.

Ursla, Andra – Admiral
Andra Ursla is one of the Earther Navy's savviest combat officers; the epitome
of military professionalism, her internal sense of wry wit is exceeded in voracity
only by her battle instincts. As a frigate Commodore in charge of the 111th
Flying Squadron, this kodiak was the first to take the initiative in greeting the
humans at the Pluto Orbital Plane, and also the first to befriend humans — Liz
Hastings, then Sarah Manchester and Pat Conroy. With the Second Fleet under
her charge, and flying her colors from the 150-gun *Agamemnon*, she has joined
Sarah to relieve Genesis of its Church and Krogg burden.

APPENDIX B: TACTICS IN SPACE COMBAT

The Earthers have entered an interstellar war, and now the tactics that they've developed for space combat are being put to the test. Partially adapted from the history books, and partly based on simulated battle experience, these techniques will have to see Setter Caine's fleet through some severe challenges. So what are the fundamental tactics of the Earther Navy? Glad you asked...

The Earther Line of Battle
Just to get this question out of the way from the outset, I don't know whether or not Earther warship technologies could ever exist. According to the laws of physics, they really shouldn't... but then again, 700 years ago, a lot of people thought that human health was based on a balance of the four humors. Basically, I've approached the space combat in the *Equations* from a semi-historical perspective — I'll leave the purely scientific space warfare to people who are far, far smarter than me.

So with that qualifier in place, what did I base Earther ship tactics on? Well, let's turn the dial back about 200 years, and visit with a great British Admiral named Horatio Nelson. It's the classic age of fighting sail, and coincidentally, the Royal Navy of Britain is relying on rated ships of the line, frigates, sloops, and so on. The Earthers read these same history books, then decided that their energy cannon would be most useful mounted in broadsides like those of the old sailing warships. And mounting guns in broadside requires a certain set of rules of engagement.

In Nelson's day, the 'line ahead' was the standard formation of battle, and interestingly enough, Dran Nightclaw uses a line ahead at least once in *The Alien Equation* (for anybody interested, I actually borrowed his maneuvers in part from Admiral Togo at Tsushima in 1905, who turned — 'wore' in Naval terms — repeatedly across the enemy's course). Anyway, line ahead means column — all ships travel the same direction in single file, and keep their enemy on one side so that all ships in the squadron can fire without hitting each other. The tactic actually dates from centuries before Nelson, and lasted well into the twentieth century. Now the Earthers have picked it up.

The other basic battle formation is the 'line abreast' — basically, a line of ships 'shoulder to shoulder'. This formation masks broadsides, but it allows ships to advance together. The Earthers use this one a lot when they're trying to close range. When it's not a long-range gun duel, they try to get in close and deliver overwhelming levels of punishment before they can be countered. This is again an allusion to the tactics of Nelson's day — the original carronades were essentially short versions of ships' cannon, able to throw a lot of shot at close range. They became preeminent in Naval warfare from the end of the American Revolution.

So that's a quick dose of Naval history. But that certainly is not the only resource the Earthers relied on when developing their tactics. There are some major differences they must contend with in space, most importantly the third dimension. In space, the same ship can travel and fight in all three dimensions. What does this mean for an Earther ship of the line? Well, first, unlike their Royal Navy ancestors, Earther ships can roll along their axis to present fresh broadsides without changing course. That's a very helpful ability — turning flat through 180 degrees to reengage was always historically dangerous. Wall formations also come into play, though not too much. The Earthers tend to protect their tops and bottoms by rolling their broadsides, though you mightn't be surprised to see two Earther squadrons in action flying perpendicular to each other to cover multiple directions.

So the Earthers get to deal with a third dimension; they also have the means to cut across space with incredible speed. Energy drive provides a serious tactical advantage. As you see with the likes of Ursla and Felix, there's a distinct advantage to being able to close to point-blank range unexpectedly and unopposed by enemy fire. At Trafalgar, Nelson used a technique philosophically similar. His two lines ahead drove straight into the enemy fleet's port side, drawing close action, but the difference was that he was under the power of the wind: it took him hours to get into range, and for much of that time he was under fire. The Earthers are much more fortunate, and thanks to their instincts they have the ability to utilize their skills to great effect.

So a brief review: line ahead and line abreast, two centuries-old sea combat terms that the Earthers have reused, along with ship classes to provide something of a basis for their methods of space combat. Mixed in with my imaginings, the Earthers thus get a pretty effective combat system. It will be further refined as gunboats turn up on the scene, but I'll leave those until *The Renegade Equation*. Just a hint though, gunboats in the age of fighting sail weren't the sort that prowled rivers in later years — they were oversized rowboats with large cannon in the bows, designed to keep enemy ships out of harbors. In the space context, they might almost seem like a compromise between Larosian fighters and Krogg corvettes...

The Genesis Navy

Briefly, I should point out that the humans work from a completely different doctrine. What some might notice about Genesis ships is their similarity to triremes in design philosophy — triremes being oar-powered ram warships commonly associated with ancient Greece and ancient Rome. Genesis ships mount their missile tubes facing forward, and so like triremes they cruise straight into battle, and are relatively vulnerable on the flanks. It's quite a tactical predicament... so Hastings' Navy borrowed and replicated the ideas of those who had to deal with it in those bygone centuries.

First, to the history: in 1571, the Battle of Lepanto was fought between Christian and Muslim Fleets in the Mediterranean Sea. It was a massive galley engagement — a product of the Crusades, which is as much as I'll say about the politics of it — and it panned out as a line abreast action. Both sides came at each other in long rows, slammed into each other, and started ramming. Both sides then desperately tried to extend their own lines, to get around the vulnerable flank of their enemy. Now, while a ship of the line — Earther or otherwise — is weakest at its ends, a trireme and a Genesis ship are both weak on the sides.

Poor design? Consider it from a Krogg perspective, as those aliens were undoubtedly responsible, at least in part, for the design. How can you best encourage your inferior minions to charge forward against a superior enemy? Make sure their ships' strength is to the front, and that presenting any other side would be a liability. Charming masters to have, the Kroggs...

In any case, the human fleet may not be so well served by its ship designs or its tactics, but it's too late to change any of them. They'll have to make do.

We'll see how that necessity works out for them in *The Renegade Equation*. See you then!

ABOUT THE AUTHOR

Born in 1984 in St. John's, Newfoundland, Kenneth Tam holds both a Bachelor's and Master's degree in history from Wilfrid Laurier University in Waterloo, Canada. His MA thesis examined the creation and operation of the Caribou Hut, a hostel for Allied servicemen in St. John's during the Second World War.

In 2006, Kenneth received a prestigious Canada Graduate Scholarship from the Social Sciences and Humanities Council of Canada. He was also awarded a Balsillie Fellowship at the Centre for International Governance Innovation during 2006-07. In that capacity, he worked for Mr. Paul Heinbecker, Canada's former ambassador and permanent representative to the United Nations. He presently serves as a Communications Consultant for Kitchener–Waterloo's federal Member of Parliament, Peter Braid.

Since first releasing the first *Equations* novel in 2003, Tam has promoted his books across Canada, speaking with junior and high school students, delivering writing workshops, and doing book signings at bookstores and Iceberg-organized events. He frequently appears as a guest author at science fiction events across the country.

Kenneth is a partner in Iceberg Publishing, the company he and his family started in 2002. He has authored many of the company's existing titles, and is also responsible for graphic design, including the company logo, website, banners, advertisements, and other marketing materials. He acts as a primary contact with printers and suppliers, and is also key in new author development and recruitment.

He remains very lazy about writing his author bios. When they told him to make this one longer, he mostly copied and pasted it together from the Iceberg website, www.icebergpublishing.com.